THE
GOOD
NEIGHBOUR

A GRIPPING STORY OF DETERMINATION, COURAGE, LOVE AND FAMILY

ANNIE DOYLE

LITTLECROFT
PUBLISHING

For my beloved nana, Ena Todd,
who inspired kindness.

ACKNOWLEDGEMENTS

Publishing my debut novel *The Cocoa Girls* was a dream come true. The inspiration for the story, based on my nana's life and that of her grandmother, mother and aunt, came from family history research my mam asked me to do (and something Nana never wanted doing as her start in life was so sad). These remarkable women continue to inspire me and I hope the third instalment in my trilogy does credit to their incredible legacy. Writing can be a lonely business and I must thank my ever-faithful support at home for never complaining when I'm locked in the attic for days on end. So many ideas arrived and plot holes were solved when I was out walking with best dog Alfie. Sadly he had to leave us this year but I can still sense him at my feet, snoring gently as I write. Authors would be nothing without readers. To anyone who has read my novels, thank you. To anyone who has reviewed them (and liked them!), thank you. To anyone who has attended any of my talks, thank you. My family and friends; thank you for your constant support and encouragement. In particular, thanks go to: the incredible Jacky Collins, aka Dr. Noir, dear friend, editor extraordinaire, powerhouse of all things fiction, and the provider of wise words whenever I need them; my lovely, constructively critical beta readers Sue and Deb; Rob Barnes for typesetting, fantastic cover design and illustrations; Valerie Speed for my wonderful author photographs; my exercise family for badly-needed time away from the laptop; terrific independent book shops and local businesses for taking a chance on a debut author – Helen and the team at Forum Books, the bound and The Accidental Bookshop, Nicole and Stephanie at Featherbed Books, Emma at Collected, Mandy at 1b Books, Sam at Whickham Cottage Crafts, Brian Rankin at the Come View My Art Gallery, the team past and present at Whickham Cards and Gifts and Bob Stone at Write Blend. Many more people helped along the way.

To each and every one of you, thank you.

FICTIONAL CHARACTERS
IN ORDER OF APPEARANCE

Ena Leighton/Todd/Evie Brown – eponymous central character.

Elizabeth Ann Brown/Lizzie – Ivy and Mona's cousin.

Ivy Dinah Jane Leighton/Dinah Jane Brown – Ena's aunt.

Jack Todd – Ena's husband.

Theodosia Brown – Ena's grandmother, Ivy and Mona's mother (deceased).

Henry Brown – Ena's grandfather, Ivy and Mona's father (deceased).

Lady Grace Opal – opera singer and actress, Walter's wife and Ivy's friend.

Lord Walter Hampson – Ivy's friend.

Agatha Brown – Lizzie's mother and Ivy and Mona's aunt (deceased).

Mona Leighton/Henson/Margaret Brown – Ena's mother and Ivy's sister.

Herbert Joseph Primavesi (Bertie) – Ivy's first husband (deceased).

Lydia Stamp – Ivy's barrister.

John Todd – Jack's uncle.

Rachel Leaman/Love – Ena's friend.

Seymour Love – Rachel's piano teacher and father-in-law.

William Love – Seymour's son and Rachel's husband.

Peggy Willow – English dancer and actress, Mona's friend (deceased).

Marvin Marvel/Marv – American director at the Paradise Theatre.

George Scott-Smith – Ivy's second husband.

Cyril Leaman – Rachel's elder brother.

Catherine Primavesi – Bertie's mother.

Lena, Isabel and Gertrude Primavesi – Bertie's sisters.

Miss Kinghorn – Ena's teacher at South Street Infants School.

Solomon Zettler – director at the Diamond Music Hall (deceased).

Vernon Revill – ship's steward, Mona and Ivy's friend, vy's third husband.

Wilfred Henson – Vernon's friend and Mona's husband.

Jeannie – Theodosia's friend (deceased).
Mrs Swann/Madame Desperéaux – guest house owner at Springbank Lane.
Bartholomew Bundell – Ena's landlord at her flat on Bottle Bank.
Beatrice Bundell – Ena's landlady at her flat on Bottle Bank.
Dolly Turnbull – warehouse clerk at Dunston Flour Mill, Ena's friend.
Nancy Glover – Ena's friend (deceased).
Isabella Holliday (Bella) – wealthy American, Mona's friend (deceased).
Marty Turnbull – Dolly's father.
Olive Turnbull – Dolly's mother.
Tilly Tucker – American dancer and actress, Mona's friend.
Teddy Parr – Lydia's friend, nightclub owner.
Vivienne Lawson – Lydia's friend, doctor.
Daphne Bloom – Lydia's friend.
Zebedee Scott – Lydia's friend, artist.
Ned – host at Keens steakhouse.
Mabel Henson – Wilfred's sister.
Duncan – Mabel's fiancé (deceased).
Albert Revill – Vernon's brother (deceased).
Irene Revill – Vernon's mother.
Meta Leaman – Rachel's mother.
Edwin Leaman – Rachel's father.
Mr Young – manager at Dunston Flour Mill.
Giulio Cesare Primavesi – Bertie's father.
Leo Primavesi – Bertie's brother.
Donovan Leaman – Rachel's younger brother (deceased).
Charlie Tremblay – speakeasy owner, Tilly's friend.
Shirley Kindred/Sparkle – Ena and Jack's schoolfriend, music hall star.
Nellie Pilkington – dancer at the Diamond Music Hall, Mona's nemesis.

Violet and May – dancers at the Diamond and in the Leighton Girls troupe, Mona's friends.

Tommy Dawson – Fire Brigade superintendent.

Ursula Innes – Grace's theatrical director.

Kenny Earnshaw – comedy show producer at the Hippodrome.

Cockney-John – miner.

The Parker twins – miners.

The Miller sisters and the Wood sisters – dancers in the Leighton Girls troupe.

Alfie Atherton – theatre impresario.

Robert Martin (Bobby) Turnbull – Dolly's brother.

Mr and Mrs Fox – Ena and Jack's next-door neighbours in Whickham.

Corky – Madame Desperéaux's companion at Springbank Lane.

HISTORICAL CHARACTERS

Arabella Goddard – English pianist (1836–1922).

Thomas Andrews – British businessman and shipbuilder. *Titanic's* architect (1873 – 1912).

Edward Pomeroy Colley – Irish civil engineer. *Titanic* passenger (1875 – 1912).

Helen Candee – American author, journalist, interior decorator and feminist. *Titanic* passenger (1858 – 1949).

Elsie Bowerman – British lawyer, suffragette and political activist. *Titanic* passenger (1889 – 1973).

Marie Lloyd – English music hall singer, comedian and music theatre actress (1870 – 1922).

Gwen Farrar – English duettist, cellist, singer, actress and comedian (1897 – 1944).

Norah Blaney – pianist, composer, comedienne and music hall performer (1893 – 1983).

Charlotte Augusta Marsh/Charlie Marsh – militant British suffragette (1887 – 1961).

John Pierpont Morgan – American financier and investment banker, dominating Wall Street corporate finance in the Gilded Age and Progressive Era (1837 – 1913) .

Lillie Langtry – British socialite, stage actress and producer (1853 –1929).

Herbert Mundin – English character actor (1898 – 1939).

Harold Monro – English poet and co-proprietor of the Poetry Bookshop (1879 – 1932).

Alida Monro – writer, editor and co-proprietor of the Poetry Bookshop (1892 – 1969).

Robert Frost – American poet (1874 – 1963).

Flora Murray – Scottish medical pioneer, member of the WSPU, suffragette and co-founder of Endell Street Military Hospital (1869 – 1923).

Louisa Garrett Anderson – medical pioneer, member of the WSPU, suffragette, social reformer and co-founder of Endell Street Military Hospital (1873 – 1943).

Emmeline Pankhurst – British political activist and founder of the WSPU (1858 – 1928).

David Lloyd George – UK Prime Minister from 1916 – 1922.

Stanley Baldwin – UK Prime Minister from 22 May 1923 – 22 January 1924.

Ramsay MacDonald – UK Prime Minister from 22 January 1924 – 4 November 1924.

Mary Louise Cecilia "Texas" Guinan - American actress, producer, entrepreneur and speakeasy manager during Prohibition (1884 – 1933).

John English/Lang Jack – local Whickham man of enormous strength (1800 – 1860).

Edith Sitwell – British poet and critic (1887 – 1964).

Millicent Fawcett – English politician, writer and activist (1897 – 1919).

MUSIC

'It's Three O'clock In The Morning' – composed by Julián Robledo, performed by Paul Whiteman and His Orchestra (1922).

'Auld Lang Syne' – traditionally sung to bid farewell to the old year at the stroke of midnight on New Year's Eve. First recorded in a manuscript and collected by James Orchard Halliwell c. 1815.

'I'm Always Chasing Rainbows' – music by Harry Carroll, melody adapted from Frédéric Chopin's Fantaisie-Impromptu, lyrics by Joseph McCarthy (1917).

'Toot, Toot, Tootsie (Goo' Bye!)' – composed by Stephen Foster with music and lyrics by Gus Kahn, Ernie Erdman and Danny Russo (1855).

'Home Sweet Home' – lyrics by John Howard Payne, composed by Sir Henry Bishop (1823).

'Siman Tov u'Mazel Tov' – celebratory song for Jewish weddings.

'You Can't Keep A Good Girl Down' – from Jerome Kern's musical comedy Sally of the Alley, lyrics by Clifford Grey and P.G. Wodehouse (1920).

'It Ain't Gonna Rain No More' – composed by Wendell Hall, sung by Norah Blaney and Gwen Farrar (1923).

'No, No Nora' – lyrics by Gus Khan, music by Ted Fiorito and Ernie Erdman, sung by Eddie Cantor (1923).

'The Little Church Around The Corner' – from Jerome Kern's musical comedy Sally of the Alley, lyrics by Clifford Grey and P.G. Wodehouse (1920).

'Everybody Loves My Baby' – composed by Spencer Williams, lyrics by Jack Palmer (1924).

'All Things Bright and Beautiful' – Anglican hymn, words by Cecil Frances Alexander, first published in her Hymns for Little Children (1848).

'It Had To Be You' – composed by Isham Jones, lyrics by Gus Kahn (1924).

'Yes, Sir! That's My Baby!' – music by Walter Donaldson, lyrics by Gus Kahn (1925).

'I'm Sitting On Top of the World' – music by Ray Henderson, lyrics by Sam M. Lewis and Joe Young (1925).

'Daisy Bell (Bicycle Built for Two)' – composed by Harry Dacre (1892).

'I Dream Of Jeannie With The Light Brown Hair' – composed by Stephen C. Foster (1854).

PROLOGUE

Prologue

Gateshead East Cemetery, North East England
December 1931

Ena

Ena Todd rubbed her gloved hands together and pulled her coat tighter. Needles of icy snow stung her cheeks and in her head she apologised to her unborn child for coming out in the unforgiving weather. The vicar spoke and she turned towards him. His long, white surplice billowed in the vicious wind and snow fell on his bare head. 'Shall I start, Mrs Todd? Are you expecting anyone else?' He looked around and Ena followed his gaze. The grave diggers waited silently to one side and two women shivered at the graveside, local vultures who couldn't resist a burial, even in the depth of winter. Strangers to her. Had Lizzie known them? Ena didn't know. She nodded, putting the vicar out of his misery.

The vicar walk to the head of the open grave and the women stepped back as Ena approached. She saw one tilt her head towards the other and she heard a low whisper. She lifted her head and locked eyes with one of them. Ena held the stranger's gaze, defiant in the face of her contempt. Through chattering teeth the vicar began. Ena gave him her full attention, knowing they wouldn't be there long. When she learnt of Lizzie's death, she agreed to make the funeral arrangements. There was no one else. Lizzie had no other family living nearby and no friends. Ena was torn; the woman was cruel to her in life but in death Ena decided her mother's cousin should at least have a church service and a burial.

'Give us this day our daily bread.' The vicar's words were barely audible above the howling wind and Ena shook her head. Lizzie hadn't bothered with daily bread, sometimes Ena went days without food. All Lizzie cared about was her daily visit to the Globe Hotel. 'Forgive us our trespasses.' Ena joined in with the Lord's Prayer, 'as we forgive those who trespass against us'. She had forgiven Lizzie, deciding that holding fast to her anger and hatred didn't help, it only festered. Aunt Ivy told her Lizzie was given no choice in the matter of looking after Ena. The person Ena couldn't forgive was the woman who left her to live in poverty with neglectful Lizzie. The woman who ran away, to London and then to America. The woman who abandoned her four-year-old daughter without a backward glance. Her mother. Ena shook her head and fat flakes of snow dropped onto her coat. She pushed thoughts of her mother away. Her life was happy now, there was no place for those dismal memories.

'Lead us not into temptation but deliver us from evil, for thine is the kingdom, the power and the glory, for ever and ever. Amen.'

Ena stared at the coffin being lowered into the ground; would Lizzie be delivered from evil? Ena decided she would, to think otherwise was to imagine Lizzie forever trapped in misery, as she was in life. Ena nodded at the vicar and he took off towards the church to shelter from the brutal elements. She hung back, waiting for the strangers to leave. The wind carried snippets of their conversation to her. '…not much of a funeral. Where's her family?' '…they should've buried her out the back of the Globe! She spent most of her life in there!' Faint cackling reached Ena before the women disappeared round the corner. She took a last look at Lizzie's final resting place and turned into the wind. A bright light caught her eye. The churchyard was otherwise dark and the small light gleamed, a few rows away from Lizzie's burial plot. Ena looked towards the light, grimacing as she exposed her face to the bitter wind. A woman, standing in front of a gravestone. No, not standing; dancing. Ena watched the woman's skilful movements, the silver adornment on her black veiled Juliet cap sparkling with each twirl and turn. Ena stood in the driving snow, transfixed by the woman's lively, energetic dancing. She swung her arms and moved her feet, despite the wind howling around her. The Charleston. Ena left the woman to her reverie and hurried towards the gates, holding her tummy as if protecting her baby from the foul weather. Jack hadn't wanted her to come, it had been the cause of a rare disagreement between them. In the end he'd said while he didn't understand, he respected her decision. Ena turned left out of the churchyard. She walked quickly, desperate for home and Jack's arms. She lowered her head to avoid the falling snow and hurried past the smart car parked outside the church.

The woman in the passenger seat held a tattered old picture and she stared as Ena hurried past. The man in the driver's seat leant over to look at the picture. 'She's so young.' The woman's voice was barely audible. 'She was four years old.' The man looked back at the churchyard, now locked and in darkness. 'Is this the right place?' The woman nodded, 'yes, Ivy said this was where cousin Lizzie was being buried and that Ena would be here. The man narrowed his eyes and peered through the condensation on the windscreen. 'Is it her?' The woman took a deep breath before whispering. 'I haven't seen her for years but yes, I think it's my daughter.'

ACT ONE

Chapter 1

London - nine years earlier

Ivy

Ivy Leighton paced, her heels echoing in the tiled corridor. She trailed a gloved hand along the smooth wood panelling and an image of another corridor filled her mind. She stopped and stared at her shoes. The pretty orange, gold and cream floral Art Deco design blurred when she tried to block out the old picture. She shook her head but the memory persisted. When she was 19 it fell to her as the elder daughter to register her beloved mother's death. Having already lost their father; it was her responsibility to make it official. The Registrar was matter-of-fact when she objected to the wording on the death certificate.

'The 16th of June 1903, at the Union Workhouse Hospital, Theodosia Brown, female, age 41, the widow of Henry Brown, a railway fettler of Gateshead, cancer of the uterus.'

She argued the one line of information did nothing to reflect her mother's achievements. Theodosia was a dancer before she became a mother, she was a woman who insisted her daughters could achieve anything if they set their minds to it. The Registrar said the certificate was a legal document, required to state when, where and how an individual met their end. Ivy hid her frustration and signed where indicated. When she left, she summoned all her strength. She, her sister and her four-year-old niece had faced an uncertain future without Theodosia. Grace touched her arm and she was jolted back to reality. She turned to face her friend, grateful for her support. Grace and her husband Walter had been loyal to her for many years, since they met at Hampson

Hall in 1903. A lifetime ago. When her mother died, Ivy was sent there to work as a scullery maid. She'd learnt her mother was in debt to their vicious aunt, and this was Aunt Agatha's solution for Ivy to repay the debt. Her sister was meant to suffer the same fate but Mona disappeared, leaving her four-year-old daughter behind. When Grace and Walter learnt about Ivy's missing sister, he paid for her to travel to London. Grace arranged an audition for her at the West London Theatre, and an introduction to Mrs Newbold and her guest house. Despite her friends' help, Ivy failed to find her sister. She visited the sleazy music hall where Mona worked, only to find her sister had disappeared again, this time to America. Grace went with her to the Paradise Theatre on Broadway, then the trail went cold. The director there told her Mona was back in London. Grace and Walter supported her when Bertie, her first husband, died, and they remained steadfast now. Grace touched her arm again and gestured towards a wooden seat outside the barrister's office. 'Sit, please.' Ivy continued to pace, 'how can I sit when horrific things continue to happen to girls and women without consequence?' She pointed at the newspaper in Grace's hand. 'They should never have been working in such dangerous conditions. Nineteen killed dismantling explosive cartridges and none of them over the age of 15. We accepted danger during the war but not now, in peace time. Someone must be held to account for this!'

Grace put the newspaper down. 'We can't fight every battle. You have an uphill struggle of your own we need to focus on.' Ivy took a deep breath. 'Injustices continue despite the best efforts of the suffrage movement. When will things change?' Grace sighed, 'I know, and it's marvellous that since the war ended women have been able to enjoy greater freedoms and achieve financial independence, but you know it's about taking small steps. Our step today is to try and convince the barrister lurking behind that huge oak door to take your case, to help you divorce your monster of a second husband.' Ivy sat and turned to her friend. 'I'm impatient. We've waited too long and suffered too much inequality for us to stop fighting now.' Grace took her hand, 'I agree, and isn't this action an example of you continuing to fight?' She nodded. 'I suppose so.' Grace smiled, 'we both know the legislation isn't yet in place to help you but Lydia is confident it's coming and we should start preparing your case now'.

The door opened behind them. They stood and turned to face Lydia Stamp. Earlier that year, London's legal community had buzzed with talk about Lydia. She made history in becoming the first woman to be called to the English bar. Walter wasted no time in contacting her to ask if she would take Ivy's case. The barrister's sleek black hair was styled in a severe, slicked-down Eton crop and Ivy smiled took in Lydia's smart black wool trouser suit and starched white shirt. Lydia extended her hand and smiled broadly; her intense eyes sparkling. 'Ms Leighton, I'm delighted to meet you.' Ivy smiled back. 'Likewise, Ms Stamp.' Their strong, assured handshake demonstrated a shared determination to succeed, despite the obstacles ahead. Grace followed Ivy into Lydia's office and closed the door behind them. Lydia unbuttoned her jacket and asked them to sit.

Whickham, North East England

Ena

Ena Leighton stood at the corner of Fellside Road and West Street. She reached for Jack's hand and pointed. 'Look, Jack. Right at the bottom on the left-hand side. That house will have views across the fields. It's the last one in the street, there might be gardens on all sides.' Jack squeezed Ena's hand. 'You're right, Ena. Look at the trees. I think we could walk down to the Seven

Sisters.' She looked up at him. 'The Seven Sisters?' He smiled. 'It's a row of ancient oak trees. We should be able to walk through the fields from our house all the way to the trees. Then I think we can carry on, along the banks of the River Derwent to the Butterfly Bridge.' Ena gazed into the distance, 'what a beautiful name for a bridge'. Jack nodded, 'the Derwent Valley is a butterfly collector's paradise. In summer, the meadows are reported to come alive with common blue and meadow brown butterflies'.

Ena savoured Jack's words. *'Our house.'* He'd been one of the few bright sparks during her miserable childhood. Along with her friend Nancy, they made her time at South Street Infants School bearable. They shared their food with her and saw past her threadbare clothes and second-hand shoes. Without them, she doubted she would have survived Lizzie's neglect. Her mother's cousin, Lizzie proved to be an altogether unsuitable guardian. Lizzie spent more time in the Globe Hotel than at home, drinking herself into a stupor and mixing with the worst men of the area. Ena waited outside the Globe in all weathers; freezing, starving and longing to be part of a loving home. If it hadn't been for Jack, she might never have escaped. Once he had helped her get to his uncle John's house, Aunt Ivy collected her and took her to London, where she was staying at a guest house. Ena was welcomed into Mrs Newbold's home, where the kindly landlady provided accommodation for theatrical performers. For the first time in years Ena slept soundly, safe in the knowledge she had put her miserable old life behind her. Having spent years living on tenterhooks, waiting for Lizzie's next spiteful outburst, Ena revelled in the noisy house full of colourful, theatrical guests. After a few months Aunt Ivy took her to Bournemouth, where she was preparing to marry Herbert Joseph Primavesi. Known to her as Uncle Bertie, he became the only father figure she had ever known.

Ena made a dear friend in Rachel Leaman and they became inseparable. When war was declared in 1914 and Uncle Bertie signed up, she and Rachel, along with many other women and young girls, did their best for the war effort. Initially Ena joined the knitting army, having seen them in action at the community hall in Bournemouth. Hundreds of women, knitting and singing, needles clicking out the rhythm of the army recruited to make cotton slings for wounded troops. At the library, Ena had spotted a request for people to write short stories to be sent to soldiers in the trenches. She pictured her notebook and her descriptions of the walks and nature trails she took with Uncle Bertie. She busied herself writing stories until her talent for arithmetic led to a book-keeping job at the community hall.

Rachel's perfect opportunity came when a number of voluntary organisations asked people to write songs and compose music for travelling entertainment groups to perform for soldiers. This fitted with her ambition to be the next Arabella Goddard, a famous pianist with the Philharmonic Society. Rachel knew their music teacher Mr Love was too old to have signed up, and she wasted no time in talking to him about composing something on the piano.

After the war Ena used her book-keeping experience to gain a job at Reeves Solicitors in Bournemouth. The family firm was run by the Reeves brothers before the war. At her interview, Alice Reeves told Ena she took the business on following the tragic events that took her brothers' lives, and the passing of the 1919 Sex Disqualification (Removal) Act. On the same day Alice offered her a job, Ena decided to look for a place of her own to live. She had learnt there were vacancies at a block of flats on Littledown Road. Having secured a job and a flat, Ena fell into a satisfying routine. On her days off she and Rachel walked to the beach and sat in their favourite spot on the sand looking out to sea, or they packed a picnic lunch and went cycling in the

New Forest. They shared news of their days; Ena's job and life on Littledown Road and Rachel's continuing musical journey and plans for her wedding to William Love, her piano teacher's son. One Saturday, Ena stepped over the threshold at the library, pausing to inhale the familiar woody, earthy fragrance. Before she could breathe out, the friendly librarian was in front of her, propelling her to the newsroom. 'You must read this article, Ena.' Ena laughed. 'What is it?' The librarian directed her to a chair and pointed at the newspaper spread out on the table. 'It's where you're from. Gateshead.' Ena blinked hard. The headline sent her back in time. *'Gateshead football team lost in deadly Western Front battle.'*

The article provided background information about the working-class town in Gateshead, where the soldiers who died had made up the local football team. Like the communities that lost whole streets of men who signed up together, Gateshead lost its footballers. The words blurred in front of Ena's eyes as she read about the deadly fighting the poor men had faced. The article said one man survived. Ena traced the man's name with her finger. Jack Todd. Her breath came in quick bursts as she learnt the fate of Jack's friends. Something tugged at her. She stared at Jack's name in the newspaper. A connection. With him. The pull to return to Gateshead and her childhood friend was suddenly stronger than any desire to stay in Bournemouth.

Southampton docks

Mona

A warm breeze caressed the back of Mona Leighton's neck as she hurried up RMS *Homeric*'s gangplank. People chattered excitedly behind her, many taking their first voyage to America. She kept walking; she was travelling alone and had no desire to enter into conversation. At the top of the gangplank she almost walked into the two young women in front when they stopped suddenly. She studied their outfits. Other than the colour, their capes and hats were identical. Formal yet luxurious, Mona's eyes traced one, the cape a warm biscuit hue, then the other, a deep gunmetal grey. The capes curved out at the hip then tapered in, reaching to the ankle. Bands of white fur finished off the sleeves and collars of the impressive garments. The womens' snug-fitting cloche hats were adorned, on the right-hand side, with an ostrich feather. Mona pictured her friend Peggy; she was the epitome of petite elegance in her royal blue travelling suit and matching hat. On a different voyage, ten years earlier, with a tragic outcome. Mona shuddered and turned around. Eager passengers jostled for position on the crowded gangplank. It was too late to change her mind.

The young women in front of her started to move, one gesturing towards an empty spot at the rail. 'That's a good vantage point; we can wave to mother and father!' The one in front grabbed her sister's hand and they hurried away, laughing. Mona walked in the opposite direction, desperate to put distance between the womens' joyful farewell and her solitude. As she reached the staircase leading to her cabin and privacy, a little girl appeared in front of her. She stopped suddenly and stared up at Mona. Her lower lip quivered. 'I've lost my mummy.' Mona went cold. Before she could speak, a woman and man arrived. 'Florrie, what have I told you about running off?' Florrie reached for her mother's hand. The woman smiled. 'I do apologise Miss; she must have startled you.' Mona mumbled it was nothing. As the family walked away, Florrie's mother and father taking a hand each between them, she pictured her own daughter. Ena, like Florrie, lost her mummy a long time ago. But Ena, unlike Florrie, hadn't run away. Mona had abandoned her daughter.

She hurried towards her cabin. As she passed the ship's lounge the strains of an orchestra tuning up reached her. Her friendship with Peggy was cemented through their shared love of music and dancing; it took them to New York City to work for Marv Marvel, renowned director at the Paradise Theatre on Broadway, 12 years before. Mona paused to listen. She picked out a trumpet and a violin, then soft piano notes provided an introduction for one of the sweetest voices she had ever heard.

'It's three o'clock in the morning,
We've danced the whole night through.
And daylight soon will be dawning,
Just one more waltz with you.
That melody so entrancing,
Seems to be made for us two.
I could just keep on dancing forever dear with you.'

She closed her eyes and pictured another dance floor on a different ship. Not a waltz, a Military Twostep. She had danced with Thomas Andrews, RMS *Titanic's* architect. They danced and laughed and four hours later, *Titanic* sunk. Peggy didn't survive that night and to her knowledge, neither did Thomas Andrews. Her legs shook and she held onto the wall outside *Homeric's* lounge. She grabbed hold of a rail running along the corridor and used it to steady herself on the way to her cabin. Once she was safely inside, she lowered herself onto a chair and pulled her coat around her. She waited for the small electric fire to heat the room. A leaflet about *Homeric* lay on the table and she flicked through it. Another White Star Line vessel; the leaflet reassured passengers of its refit for increased safety. 'RMS *Homeric* is the largest twin-screw liner built to date.' Mona sighed; she didn't know what that meant. She continued reading. 'The vessel's double bottoms extend up the sides of the water-lines, giving them double hulls. The bulkheads are extended to make the compartments fully watertight.' Mona shook her head. It was too technical. All she wanted was someone to tell her *Homeric* wouldn't sink. That its 529 passengers travelling from

Southampton to Cherbourg and onwards to New York City, would survive.

Her cabin was a little warmer so she removed her hat and coat. She took Marv's letter out of her handbag and re-read it. At first, the thought of boarding a ship again after being on *Titanic* terrified her. She hadn't planned to return to New York. Then she considered how little she had in England. After years apart she had been reunited with her sister and daughter in London, but the disappointment she saw in Ena's eyes haunted her. When she asked Ena what she was doing with her life, it was like having a conversation with a stranger. They parted with no promise to see each other again. She was between repertory theatre jobs when Marv's letter arrived. With no one to miss her in England, she resolved to conquer her fear. She booked her passage on *Homeric* and left.

Chapter 2

Ivy

Ivy sipped the glass of water Lydia had placed on the small table in between her and Grace. When the barrister invited her to talk about George, Ivy hesitated. Her cheeks grew warm when she recalled her humiliation at discovering her husband was not who he claimed to be. 'Rest assured, Ms Leighton, I have heard many stories of horrific husbands.' Ivy gave a tight smile. 'I feel foolish. Why did I allow myself to be taken in by him?' Lydia shook her head. 'None of this is your fault. You are the victim here.' Ivy pursed her lips; she didn't want to be seen as a victim. 'Remember what Cyril said in Bournemouth.' Ivy turned to Grace; her brow furrowed. 'It was at the picnic Ena arranged for you. After…' Grace stopped and Ivy saw an apology in her eyes. She squeezed her friend's hand. 'It's all right. This may be important background.' Lydia sat back and removed her spectacles. She waited. Ivy took a deep breath.

'When I met George, I was bereaved, my first husband had died during the war.' Ivy stopped and Lydia made a note on her writing pad. The barrister looked up and gestured with her hand for Ivy to continue. 'I didn't realise it at the time of course; we'd all seen so much death and destruction during the war and I grasped at what I thought was happiness.' Lydia stopped writing, 'did you work during the war, Ms Leighton?' Ivy nodded, 'yes, I was an orderly at Endell Street Military Hospital'. Lydia leant forward, 'a fine example of women coming to the fore. Women already qualified yet unable to practice in their chosen profession. Not unlike female solicitors and barristers'. Ivy agreed, 'yes. I saw things I hope never to see again; I also witnessed effort and collaboration on a scale previously unimaginable. While I was there,…' Ivy stopped. Lydia raised her eyebrows, her pen poised above the pad. 'My first husband, Bertie, died in 1916. I took some time off work and returned to Bournemouth, where Bertie grew up.' Ivy hesitated. Her heart thumped and her ears rang but she continued. 'Not long after the war ended I became ill, and was admitted to Endell Street. I, along with many others, contracted the war's biggest killer; the Spanish flu. I was one of the lucky ones. Bertie's mother and sisters and my niece took care of me as I recuperated in Bournemouth.' Ivy lifted the glass to her lips, her hands shaking. She took a drink then readjusted her position, her back poker-straight in the plush leather chair. 'Between 1912 and 1918 I suffered three miscarriages.' Ivy heard Grace gasp and saw Lydia carefully place her pen on top of the writing pad.

'My dear, please accept my sincere condolences. You have suffered great losses.' Ivy mustered a sad smile. 'Many people suffered loss during the war. Mine was no greater and no less.' Lydia leant across the desk. 'Do you want to reconvene at another date?' 'No, thank you. I would prefer to continue.' Lydia nodded, 'very well. May I ask about your second husband?' Ivy sighed, 'I attended the Patriotic Meeting at the Royal Albert Hall with colleagues from Endell Street'. Lydia made notes as Ivy spoke. 'After the meeting we visited the cocktail lounge. He introduced himself as Squadron Leader George Scott-Smith, on leave from the Air Force. His first lie. He said I looked familiar and offered to buy me a drink. I refused, saying I was married. I still considered myself married, despite being widowed.' Lydia met her eyes, 'how did he take your refusal?' Ivy shrugged, 'he was very well-mannered. He gave me his business card and said he would welcome the opportunity to make my acquaintance properly'. Lydia gestured for Ivy to continue. 'The day after the Armistice was announced, he visited me at work. He had sought me out, now the war was over, hoping I would agree to have dinner with him.' Ivy stared at her lap and shook her head. Lydia waited. 'Take it slowly, Ms Leighton.' Ivy sipped her water before continuing. 'I should have seen him for what he was, a charlatan. But I didn't. I was desperate for a new beginning. It is the biggest regret of my life.'

Ivy took a handkerchief from her handbag. She blew her nose and dabbed at her eyes. When she looked up, Lydia was staring at her. 'You are not responsible for George Scott-Smith's behaviour; none of this is your fault.' Ivy managed to smile. She had bared her soul to this woman and Lydia showed no judgement or disapproval. 'Please, call me Ivy.' Lydia smiled. 'Ivy. I will need to ask you more detailed questions about George's behaviour during your marriage; today I want to set out your legal position.' Ivy waited. 'As you know, the law does not currently allow women to petition for divorce on the basis of their spouse's adultery alone. That privilege is reserved for cheating husbands. Adding insult to injury, until 1910, the accepted rule was no punishment was too severe if a wife committed adultery. She might lose her husband's financial support and have her home and children taken away. She could be divorced for adultery only, yet a husband's alleged adultery had to be aggravated by another matrimonial offence such as cruelty or abandonment.' Ivy found her voice. 'What barbaric inequality.'

Lydia agreed. 'The good news is it appears things are changing. The law moves very slowly, but the signs are there. Before the war and in response to extensive campaigns outside Parliament and various failed Bills, a Royal Commission examined ways of reforming our outdated Victorian divorce law. The existing law is full of inconsistencies which make it difficult, particularly for women, to end unhappy marriages. This work has gained momentum in recent years and I am hopeful for real progress before too much longer.' Ivy nodded, 'what happens next?' Lydia leant forward, 'we prepare our case. The moment the law changes in our favour, I want to pounce! I want you to make history, Ivy. I want you to be one of the first women in Great Britain to successfully petition for divorce on the same grounds as men. What do you say?' Ivy met Lydia's gaze. 'I say yes! Let's prepare to pounce!'

Ivy and Grace shook hands with Lydia and prepared to leave. When they rose from their seats, Ivy heard Lydia mutter something under her breath. 'I beg your pardon, Lydia?'

Lydia looked up; her eyes narrowed. 'I was thinking out loud about something that might help our case.' Ivy sat again. 'What?' 'Bigamy.' Ivy stared and Lydia smiled. 'Is it possible, do you think, that "Squadron Leader" George Scott-Smith has another wife somewhere? That his marriage to you might not have been legal? If so, it raises the possibility of using the crime of bigamy as a defence.' Ivy's eyes opened wide. 'Could you repeat that, please?' Lydia obliged and Ivy started to smile. Her excitement at the idea of freeing herself from George triumphed over her previous humiliation. 'I think it's possible, don't you, Grace?' Grace laughed. 'I do, Ivy.' Lydia stood and shook their hands again. 'Very well. Now we must prove it in a court of law.'

Ena

When Ena returned to Gateshead, she found Jack living with his uncle John. Their childhood friendship deepened quickly into love. Jack told her he worked at the CWS, the Cooperative Wholesale Society Flour Mill at Dunston Staithes on the banks of the River Tyne. 'What do you do there?' He looked at her and smiled. 'I'm a General Clerk.' Ena frowned, 'what does that involve?' Jack explained he was responsible for keeping records of grain in and flour out, making sure the books balanced. She told him about her book-keeping work during the war and her job with Reeves Solicitors in Bournemouth. He nodded, 'you might be able to do that kind of work here, at the flour mill. If you decide to stay'.

Ena based her decision to return to Gateshead on the strength of her feelings for Jack, and on a desire to have a family life similar to the one she enjoyed with Aunt Ivy and Uncle Bertie in Bournemouth. When Aunt Ivy took her to Bournemouth in 1912, she met Bertie's parents, his three sisters and his brother. She was also introduced to the Leamans, the Primavesis' good friends, They showed Ena what true family was. She had vague memories of a time in Gateshead before her grandmother died and her mother left. Aunt Ivy was the constant source of love in her young life, but she was sent away to work as a scullery maid at a country house in Northumberland. She tried to forget the awful years with Lizzie. Her life in Bournemouth, by contrast, was loving and secure. It was all too brief, cruelly interrupted by war and brought to an abrupt end when news of Uncle Bertie's death arrived. Her reunion with Jack reminded her how family life could be, and on the train back to Bournemouth, she had written to Aunt Ivy and to the CWS Flour Mill. She gave notice at Reeves and on her flat and Aunt Ivy travelled to Bournemouth for a farewell celebration. A few months later, she was calculating invoices for grain at the flour mill, and living in a small flat above the Lyons Tea Shop on Bottle Bank, a short walk from Jack's uncle's house. Each morning Jack met her outside the tea shop and they walked to work together.

When she and Jack heard about the new village, they went there one day after work. Their walk took them through lush green fields and past little villages. Ena had known there were better parts of Gateshead, nicer homes than the one she endured as a girl. She'd never seen them, until she reached Whickham. At the top of Carrs Bank, a magnificent beech tree stood in the field to her right. Two brown horses grazed under the tree, oblivious to her and Jack. Jack said his work colleague called Whickham 'the village on the hill'. They walked along Whickham's long Front Street and through Chase Park, where ancient oak trees held the village's secrets. Ena looked up at Whickham Parochial School's stone exterior, where a bellcote housed the school bell. She pushed away memories of the bell at her infant school. It boomed from its tower; warning pupils tardiness would not be tolerated. As a child she often struggled to get to school on time and suffered Miss Kinghorn's harsh punishments. She shook her head, no child of hers would ever go to bed hungry or arrive at school unwashed. She and Jack continued walking, passing St Mary's Church with its wide expanse of green stretching from the church gates down to Front Street.

After months of visiting Whickham, always ending at the top of West Street where new houses were being built, Jack started talking about his plans for the gardens. They allowed themselves to dream, and agreed on a name for their perfect house; Littlecroft. Ena said she could see herself sitting looking at the garden, while she read. When Jack proposed, Ena accepted without hesitation.

Mona

As she read Marv's letter, Mona pictured the Paradise. Peggy had told her about the Broadway theatre, after their chance encounter aboard RMS *Matilda* twelve years earlier. When they met, Mona was panic-stricken. She was travelling under a false name, having taken drastic steps to escape from her sadistic employer. After seven years working for Solomon Zettler at the Diamond, a rundown music hall in one of the worst parts of London, Mona was desperate. Fearing she wouldn't survive another winter in the flea-ridden excuse for a lodging house, she agreed to dance at a private member's club to earn enough money to leave. When events at Billy's Club took a horrific turn, she fled, having attacked her employer and stolen her friend Nellie's name, money and passage on RMS *Matilda*. Dismayed to learn there was a dancer on the ship who knew her true identity, she was determined to keep a low profile on the voyage. Until Peggy bumped into her and, feeling seasick, asked Mona to help her back to her cabin.

Mona surprised herself by telling Peggy her story. She didn't know if it was the comfort of Peggy's cabin, the gin, or Peggy herself. Perhaps it was the combination; her story poured out. Abandoning her daughter, her miserable life dancing half-naked for sleazy drunks at the Diamond and the incident at Billy's Club. She waited for Peggy's judgement but the petite, beautifully turned-out dancer poured them both another drink before saying, in her experience, circumstances could lead anyone to do things they never thought possible.

Now, Mona's lip trembled. Peggy would have had the cabin warmed up and drinks mixed. She took a deep breath and stood up. Her hands shook as she picked up a glass and poured a generous measure of gin. She added ice and Angostura Bitters then lifted the glass. 'To you, my dear, absent friend.' She took a sip of her drink, kicked off her shoes and lowered herself onto the plush sofa, upholstered in a striking chintz pattern. She closed her eyes and pictured Peggy on their last evening together, ten years earlier. It was Peggy's birthday, and with the help of Vernon Revill, the friendly ship's steward, Mona visited *Titanic's* gift shop to buy her friend a present. At dinner that night, with the pin brooch attached to her gown, Peggy had never looked more beautiful. A tiny pair of ballet shoes, made of pale pink crystal stones, hung from a silver diamond bow. The shoes glistened and twinkled when Peggy moved. After dinner, Peggy went to the Reception Room with Edward Colley, to listen to the ship's quintet. Mona stayed in the A La Carte Restaurant with her new acquaintances Helen Candee and Elsie Bowerman. In their cabin later, they shared stories of their evenings. Mona entertained Peggy with snippets from her conversations with Helen and

Elsie. 'Helen is an author, journalist and feminist. Elsie is a law-yer who is committed to the suffragette cause. They are women doing things for themselves, without mention of a man!' Peggy talked about Edward, the civil engineer who had caught her eye on the voyage. She had learnt that during the Klondike Gold Rush Edward opened a brokerage firm in Vancouver and made some very successful investments in mining stocks. 'He wants to take me out for dinner in Manhattan and for us to visit him in Vancouver.'

Peggy had found love on *Titanic*, and, for the first time since leaving Gateshead in 1903, Mona found a sense of purpose. It was 11.40 pm when she felt the bump, like a train pulling into a station, then *Titanic's* engines stopped. In her cabin on *Homeric*, pictures ran through her mind as the memories un-folded. Numb fingers struggling to fasten lifejackets, crowds pan-icking and pushing, screams and shouts and ice-cold water. On deck; the freezing night air, chaos, noise and the vast, dark sky. Peggy desperate to find Edward, Mona desperate to get Peggy into a lifeboat. Then Peggy's icy hand slipping out of hers and Mona staring at the back of her friend's honey-coloured fur coat as she was swallowed up by the agitated crowds. Mona opened her eyes. She stood and opened the wardrobe door. She would dress up and go to dinner, that's what Peggy would have told her to do.

Chapter 3

Ivy

When they left Lydia's office, Grace insisted on Ivy coming home with her. 'Walter will want to know how the meeting went.' Ivy agreed, it would be good to see him. Walter poured drinks as Ivy relayed details of the meeting. He stared at Ivy, his drink half-way to his mouth. 'What? Lydia asked you if George was already married?' Ivy managed to laugh. 'She did! I know it sounds ridiculous,…' Grace rubbed Ivy's arm. 'With him, anything is possible, darling.' Ivy looked at her. 'I didn't know him at all, did I?' Grace wagged her finger. 'This is not your fault. None of it. Do you hear me?' Ivy turned away. She wanted to believe Grace but she replayed her time with George repeatedly in her mind. Why hadn't she seen through his lies? Why had she allowed herself to be fooled by him?

She realised Grace was talking to her. 'I'm sorry, Grace. What was that?' Grace smiled. 'I asked if Walter told you how I met Lydia?' Ivy shook her head. 'No, he only said there was talk of her at his chambers. How do you know her?' Grace sipped her drink, 'she came backstage after a show. She was with Marie Lloyd'. Ivy gasped. 'The music hall singer? How does Lydia Stamp know Marie Lloyd?' Grace held her glass out to Walter for a re-fill. 'Well, here's the thing. You must have read about Ms Lloyd's turbulent private life? The poor woman has been subjected to some very salacious reporting.' Ivy said she'd seen stories in the newspapers and Grace sighed, 'did you read about her appearing in court to give evidence against her husbands?' Ivy nodded. A shiver ran down her spine. Marie Lloyd had been married three times and divorced twice. In court she gave testimony against two of her husbands who had physically abused her. An image pushed its way into Ivy's mind. She was curled into a ball on the bathroom floor of her flat on Garrick Street while George pounded on the door. She forced the image away and focused on Grace. 'Lydia was Marie Lloyd's solicitor. She couldn't represent her in court due to our antiquated laws, but she provided legal advice and accompanied her to court. Thankfully the law has changed and Lydia will be the best advocate you could wish for.' Grace raised her glass. 'To Lydia Stamp, Ivy's secret weapon!' Ivy clinked her glass against Grace's and sipped her drink. She would need as much help as possible to free herself from George.

Ena

As soon as she could, Ena joined Gateshead Library. Her love for reading started after Aunt Ivy insisted she should have her eyes tested, something Lizzie had neglected to do. At school, Ena had struggled to make out words and numbers; it wasn't until Aunt Ivy arranged for an eye-doctor to visit them in London, that the problem became clear. When Ena's spectacles arrived, a marvellous new world opened up for her. Her reading ability improved overnight and once they were settled in Bournemouth; Aunt Ivy took her to join the library. Ena smiled, remembering her excitement at learning she could have her own library card and borrow two books at a time, for up to two weeks. The books she borrowed were *Little Women* by Louisa May Alcott and *Opera Through the Ages*. She was soon back for more.

Gateshead's Public Library stood on Swinburne Street. Ena stopped on the opposite side of the road to view the Victorian street in all its glory. Four separate buildings on Swinburne Street and the magnificent Town Hall round the corner, made up Gateshead's municipal infrastructure. The frieze-inscribed ornamental stone above the entrance to the first of the buildings proclaimed it as the National Provincial Bank of England, established AD 1733. Ena took in the large arched windows and the row of decorative stones running horizontally along the length of the building, on either side of the ornate doorways. The classically designed buildings continued with the town's Building Society, and at the end of Swinburne Street was the Post Office with its elaborate clock tower. The building Ena was most interested in stood between the Building Society and the Post Office. She forced her gaze away from the clock tower and stared at the Public Library and Art Gallery. The three storey Baroque building, with its highly ornate, theatrical style took her breath away. She shook her head as she crossed the road. She'd lived near the library when she lived with Lizzie, but she didn't know it existed. Hers was another world where she'd struggled to survive. She stood on the step outside, savouring the anticipation of joining a new library. She pushed open the heavy door, her life was different now.

Back at her flat she placed her books on the shelves Jack's uncle had built for her. She was delighted to discover she could borrow three books at a time and she slid them onto the shelf, alphabetically by the author's surname. *The Mysterious Affair at Styles* by Agatha Christie, *The Phantom of the Opera* by Gaston Leroux and *War and Peace* by Leo Tolstoy. She straightened the books and stood back to admire the additions to her prized collection. She glanced at her bedside table where her current read, John Buchan's *The 39 Steps*, waited. The next day she woke with a word on her lips. 'Littlecroft.' She whispered it as she straightened the woollen blanket on her bed. She smoothed the blanket out until it was perfectly flat. She smiled at the multi-coloured hexagonal shapes, made with remnants of wool from the knitting army, each one knitted with love. She looked around the small flat. She wanted to marry Jack but she relished her independence here, as she had in her Bournemouth flat. She read long into the night without fear of disturbing anyone. With Lizzie, she'd existed in a small, miserable space but something in her memory told her cleanliness was important. She hadn't asked Lizzie for anything; everything led to an argument. She tried to look after what little room she had; it was something she could control, a sense of order amidst the chaos of Lizzie's life. Now, she took pride in keeping her flat clean and tidy.

She washed and dried her breakfast dishes then put them in the cupboard. She brushed her teeth and hair then applied a small amount of blood red matte lipstick and rosy rouge. In Bournemouth, she and Rachel had watched excitedly when more women started wearing makeup. Since the war ended, they saw women asserting a new public presence. It became easier for women to work and be educated; they were also demonstrating their new-found mobility through a distinctly modern appearance. Ena and Rachel revelled in the new fashions; tight-fitting garments were discarded in favour of looser, more comfortable clothes, skirts were shorter, women bobbed their hair and unashamedly wore makeup in public. They started seeing images of the women they aspired to be in advertisements and newspapers. Aunt Ivy sent Ena copies of Vogue magazine and she studied the fashions and images of women promoting sophistication, independence and individuality. A recent cover design featured a woman wearing a sky blue sleeveless dress. Ena cut the picture out of the magazine and fastened it to the inside of her wardrobe, next to a small mirror. Every time she opened her wardrobe the picture reminded her what was possible. The long, fitted dress finished with a flowing, scalloped hemline, slightly longer at the back than the front. The backless dress fastened with two pearl buttons and loops at the nape of the neck and a small zip. Ena removed her fur collar wrap coat and nodded approvingly before closing the wardrobe door. Along with her coat; three smart dresses, two pairs of good shoes, a hat, a pair of gloves and a handbag, her wardrobe was complete.

She stood at the window and saw Jack striding down Bottle Bank. She knocked on the glass and he looked up, tipped his hat and waved. She waved back then fastened her coat, picked up her handbag and locked the door to her flat before hurrying downstairs.

Mona

Before she left her cabin to go to dinner, Mona read Marv's letter again. He said he had spotted her review in the Western Morning News. She was performing with the London Travelling Company, and they took their production of Jerome Kern's musical comedy *Sally* from the New Theatre London to the Plymouth Repertory Theatre. The show gave her the opportunity to, in the reviewer's words, 'be seen to advantage as Madame Nookerova's maid'. Marv said he was keen to give the show an American feel and wanted Mona to play the lead character of Sally. 'Sure, I can think of no one better for it!' Mona smiled wryly, hearing his deep American drawl. She could think of someone better and she suspected Marv could too. She tried not to think about Peggy. Despite her misgivings about the voyage, she sent Marv a telegram accepting the job and booked her passage on *Homeric*.

A porter had delivered her trunk to her cabin and a stewardess had unpacked her belongings. She opened the wardrobe and stared at the row of fashionable garments. An image flitted past her eyes; an emaciated woman in dirty, threadbare clothes boarding a ship, pretending to be someone she wasn't. She shook her head to shift the memory. She carefully removed a silk evening gown. The crimson backless gown reached almost to her ankles at the back and the scalloped hemline was lifted at the front, creating an elegant flow. Tight on the hips and at the waist, the design emphasised her slim figure. She picked up her small beaded drawstring bag and fastened it around her right wrist before taking a last look in the mirror. The sequins on the neckline and the front of her gown shimmered in the light. She turned to the side to admire her black sequined headband, adorned with an ostrich feather and diamante clasp. Her black single strap shoes fastened with black silk ribbon bows looped through the eyelets on either side and tied in the middle. A long beaded necklace, tight around her neck and falling down her back, completed the outfit. She nodded at her reflection and left her cabin.

She walked towards the First-Class Restaurant, her head high. People acknowledged her and she responded with a slight nod. The ornate doors to the lounge came into view and she took a deep breath. She practiced the words in her head, 'a table for one please,' and 'yes, I am dining alone this evening'. A voice cut into her thoughts and she turned. She smiled, a real smile that reached her eyes. 'Vernon! What are you doing here?' Vernon Revill gestured with his hands, pointing out his steward's uniform. 'You're back?' 'Yes. It's my first voyage since…well, you know.' Mona touched his arm. 'It's brave of you to return.' Vernon smiled, 'you too. How is it so far?' She nodded. 'Alright I suppose.' Then she shook her head. 'No, it's awful; she's gone and it's terrifying, …' Vernon stepped towards her and took her shaking hands. 'We survived, Mona. We lived to tell the tale.' She sniffed and lifted her chin. 'You're right, we must concentrate on the future, not the past.'

Vernon's reply was drowned out by a shout from behind Mona. They saw a smart young man striding towards them. Vernon shook the man's hand. 'Flight Commander Wilfred Henson! Fancy seeing you here.' Mona watched the man take Vernon's hand and shake it purposefully. He greeted Vernon with a wide smile. 'What is the chance of you being on this voyage?' Vernon turned back to Mona. 'Mona, please meet my friend, Flight Commander Wilfred Henson, esteemed officer of the Royal Naval Air Service. Wilfred, this is Miss Mona Leighton, theatrical stage star.' Wilfred extended his hand in Mona's direction. 'I'm delighted to meet you, Miss Leighton, but I must correct Vernon. I'm plain Wilfred Henson bank clerk now; my service days are behind me.' Mona shook Wilfred's hand, 'and Vernon exaggerates my accomplishments, don't you, Vernon?' Mona and Wilfred smiled at their mutual friend. His eyes shone and he laughed. 'I don't think so. I think you're both remarkable. Now, are you heading in the same direction?' Mona met Wilfred's kind eyes. His handsome face betrayed no sign of the horrors of war; what did he see when he looked at her? Were the secrets and the shame she carried inside visible? He smiled. 'Would you care to join me for dinner, Miss Leighton?' She nodded, unable to think of a reason to refuse.

Back in her cabin later, Mona reflected on her meal with Wilfred. He was a gentleman and their conversation flowed easily. They ate well and the orchestra in the restaurant provided the perfect background for an enjoyable evening. She learnt he was born in Dudley in the West Midlands, where he lived with his parents and sister Mabel until war was declared. He'd followed in his father's footsteps and joined the Royal Naval Air Service, the air arm of the Royal Navy. With no arrogance, Wilfred quietly explained he, along with a small group of spirited young men who signed up together, had helped to develop ship-borne combat aircraft, anti-submarine warfare and the first aircraft carrier. She listened as Wilfred told his war story and found herself liking him for not asking her to reciprocate. Had he thought her lack of candour suspicious? She told him something of her theatrical career, omitting the sleazy music hall in London and her earlier disgrace. He hadn't probed. When she asked how he knew Vernon his face darkened. She apologised, saying it wasn't any of her business. He shook his head. 'It's all right, it's one of my bad war memories.'

In that moment Mona saw the goodness in Wilfred Henson.

His cheerful countenance and easy manner hid the horror and sadness now carried by their generation. Wilfred continued. 'Meeting Vernon helped.' Mona sipped her drink and waited. 'After the war, a chap I'd served with offered me a job as a bank clerk in London. I'd planned to go home to Dudley, but being in London proved fortuitous when I learnt my sister's fiancé had been admitted to Endell Street. That's where I met Vernon. Do you know about the hospital?' Mona gulped. Endell Street. Where her sister was an orderly and where Vernon had visited his injured brother. Stunned, she shook her head. 'It was a hospital established during the war and staffed entirely by women. The chaps all knew about it and hoped to be shipped there if we fell victim to an attack. I went to see my sister's fiancé when my mother wrote to say he'd been badly injured at Amiens. Vernon will say he was there to visit his brother, but he did so much more. One of the nurses said he was the only thing keeping some of their patients alive. He spent hours wheeling casualties around, talking to men who got no other visitors, men who couldn't reply. She described him as the bright light in an otherwise incredibly dark place for those men.'

Mona found her voice. 'And your sister's fiancé?' A dark cloud passed over Wilfred's face and he shook his head. 'He'd lost half of his face and in the days I visited him, he lost his mind. I was with him when he died.' He stared down at the remains of his Waldorf salad. Mona reached across the table and took his hand. 'I'm so sorry.' Wilfred raised his eyes to hers. 'War is a monster. It stole from so many of us. I refuse to allow it to spoil the life we survivors have left. We must live it well out of respect to those who cannot.' He took a deep breath. 'Anyway, how do you know Vernon?' 'May I take these plates away, Sir? Madam?' Mona breathed a sigh of relief. The waiter's interruption allowed her to change the subject. As she got ready for bed, she considered Wilfred's refreshing attitude, his refusal to allow the war to affect the rest of his life. Until now, her life had been one disaster after another, a series of misadventures to navigate. She shook her head; she knew her poor choices had contributed to her woes. She pushed back her shoulders. Tonight was different. With Wilfred she'd enjoyed pleasant conversation and laughter. As she closed her eyes to go to sleep, she smiled, realising that for the first time in years she felt able to trust someone. She thought Wilfred would listen to her story and might think she deserved a second chance. Her last thought before sleep claimed her was that she wanted to see Wilfred Henson again and she wanted to tell him everything.

Chapter 4

New Year's Eve, 1922

Ivy

Ivy and Walter clapped their hands and joined the rapturous standing ovation for Grace and her fellow performers. New Year's Eve was the troupe's final show of the year and as they took their encores, unable to leave the stage, Ivy made herself a promise. In 1923, she would leave no stone unturned in her mission to divorce her cruel husband. She needed to move on with her life. Walter tugged her sleeve and she turned. 'The curtain is coming down. Let's go and meet Grace backstage.' She nodded. Walter stood back, allowing her to exit the row and she thanked him. 'I think that was their best performance yet, don't you?' 'I do. What a finale!' *The Cabaret Girl* had been running at the Trafalgar Theatre for a week and the sell-out audiences meant it was set to continue into January. The musical told the story of James Paradene, who faces a dilemma: he must marry a lady approved by his trustees, but he's in love with Marilynn Morgan, a chorus girl. He suggests they pretend to be married to win approval, but things don't go to plan. The jazz-age comedy was brimming with romance, twists, and unexpected misunderstandings and Ivy had enjoyed every moment. Grace took the part of Marilynn, and Ivy thought her friend's musical numbers were note-perfect. Ivy hummed the tune to 'Dancing Time' as she and Walter walked towards the front of the theatre. They skirted the side of the stage until they reached a heavy velvet curtain. Walter held the curtain to one side and when Ivy passed him, he started singing.

'Dancing time is just when the music is playing,
When the stars are shimmying up in the sky.
Dancing time is just when your shoulders are swaying,
When your feet have simply got to fly.'

'Isn't it beautiful?' Walter nodded. 'Yes, and she sang it perfectly.' Ivy smiled. 'She's improved over the years, hasn't she?' 'I think so. Do you remember the first time you heard her sing?' Ivy laughed. 'I'll never forget it.' When Ivy had worked for Walter's parents at Hampson Hall, the highlight of the summer was the family picnic. Ivy was astounded to learn staff were allowed to attend the picnic alongside the Hampson family. The year of Ivy's first picnic, she heard Walter's father had invited someone from London to sing for them. Everyone at the picnic fell silent when Grace started singing, and her performance tonight was no less impressive. Ivy glanced at her friend, Lord Walter Hampson, a Lord in name only. There was nothing arrogant or pompous about him; Ivy had always found him to be friendly, kind and helpful. When she arrived at Hampson Hall, Walter was working at a barristers' chambers in London. He returned to the North East in 1910 to establish his own practice in Newcastle. After his father died, Walter met with his younger brother James and suggested he take over the day-to-day running of the family estate in Northumberland. The arrangement suited James, the riotous second son whom Walter had rescued from legal proceedings on numerous occasions when he was younger. Now a happily married father of five, James was content to run the estate and go hunting, shooting and fishing. Ivy knew Grace and Walter felt no loss in not having children, they said their nieces and nephews were all the family they needed. Walter preferred living in London, where he supported Grace in her increasingly successful career. He'd always wanted her to shine as brightly as possible and he hadn't practised law for some years. Ivy would always be grateful for their presence in her life; the unwavering friends who supported her no matter what.

The music and laughter from Grace's dressing room reached them and they smiled at each other. 'This promises to be a spectacular New Year's Eve celebration, Ivy!' Ivy laughed. 'You're right, Walter. Grace knows how to throw a party!' They pushed through the throng of guests in the corridor and crowding the entrance to Grace's dressing room. A tray of bubbling champagne flutes was proffered towards them and Walter took two, passing one to Ivy. She held her glass high and squeezed through the well-wishers. Hearing a call, she stood on tip-toe and returned Grace's greeting. Her friend shone; her loose fitting gown of gold chiffon with its dropped waist glittered as she talked to her guests, her beautiful smile lighting up the room. Grace excused herself from an admirer and opened her arms to them.

'My darlings, I'm so happy to see you.' Walter stood back when Grace hugged Ivy. Then Ivy made way for him. She watched their eyes when they embraced. Grace had once told her a room full of people could disappear when Walter was standing in front of her. 'Ivy! Over here!' Ivy turned in the direction of the voice and spotted Lydia's statuesque figure waving at her. She returned the wave and Lydia pushed through the crowds. 'I'm glad you're here. I have news.' Ivy raised her eyebrows. 'About George?' Lydia nodded, 'about what you can do to rid yourself of him, yes. Come and see me next week. I'll ask my secretary to call you to make an appointment. Is that all right?' Ivy moved closer to Lydia, 'can't you tell me now?' Lydia shook her head as her friends pulled her away. 'Next week, I promise.'

Ivy stared at Lydia's slim figure disappearing into the throng. Lydia's friends put their arms across each other's backs. The group, three women and two men, lowered their heads for a moment before raising their glasses in a toast. 'To our star!' Ivy raised her glass in their direction. She knew the toast was for Marie Lloyd. Sadly, their star had given her final performance in October, at the Alhambra Theatre. Three days earlier, against her doctor's advice, she appeared at the Empire Music Hall in Edmonton. Ivy shuddered when she read a review of the performance. It was a harsh critique of the former lauded queen of the music hall. Critics were quick to vilify performers if their star began to wane, and no exception was made for Marie Lloyd. The newspaper shook in Ivy's hands as her eyes took in the cruel words. '*Lloyd's performance was weak; she was unsteady on her feet and eventually fell over on stage.*' Ivy knew from friends that the brief, erratic performance had proved hilarious for the audience, who believed it was part of the act. At the Alhambra, Marie Lloyd was taken ill on stage. She returned to her dressing room where she was found crippled with pain and complaining of stomach cramps. That evening, at 52 years old, she died of heart and kidney failure. Ivy read that more than 50,000 people attended Hampstead Cemetery for her funeral.

When Ivy read the announcement of Marie Lloyd's death in *The Times*, the commentary sent her back in time, to her mother's music hall career. 'In Miss Lloyd the public loses not only a vivid personality whose range and extremely broad humour as a character actress were extraordinary, but also one of the few remaining links with the old music hall stage of the last century.' Ivy's own mother was a dancer in the music halls of Paris. Theodosia was engaged at the Folies Bergère when the director of an English dance troupe offered her a job in London. There, she and her friend Jeannie worked at the Metropolitan Music Hall until the horrific truth about their director became impossible to ignore. Threatened with life in one of his seedy brothels, Theodosia and Jeannie fled. They travelled to Newcastle upon Tyne, where Jeannie's late fiancé Fred was from. Once there, they made their way to Mrs Swann's guest house on Springbank Lane, the only address they had. Ivy had learnt of her mother's history from her diary and it told her something of

Theodosia the woman, before she became a mother. In addition to Theodosia's music hall career, Ivy learnt how her parents met and fell in love. Ivy was ten and Mona nine when their father Henry died in a tragic accident on the railway. Ivy remembered him regaling her and Mona with tales of maidens in distress and swashbuckling heroes. His stories always ended happily with his daughters calling, 'more, Papa, more!'

Theodosia struggled after Henry died. Most of their belongings were second-hand but everything was polished until it shone. Theodosia believed in dressing in the best clothes she could afford and approaching every new day with hope. She urged her daughters to fight for their rights and be ambitious, to strive for a better life and recognise their value. Ivy looked around the room. She counted the women she knew; independent women who were living as Theodosia would have wished. She raised her glass in a toast to her mother. She saw Grace and Walter walking towards her. Walter took her empty champagne flute and handed it to a passing waiter before standing to her left hand-side. Grace stood to her right and they linked arms. They joined hands and as the circle grew, a chain of people filled Grace's dressing room. The singing began and Ivy smiled.

'Should auld acquaintance be forgot,
And never brought to mind?
Should auld acquaintance be forgot,
And auld lang syne!'

Outside, the streets thronged with people, voices raised in celebration of the new year's dawn. Big Ben's deep chimes rang out, marking the arrival of 1923.

Ena

Ena reached up and pulled the chain on the gas lamp above her small writing desk. When the flame started heating the mantle, the room was slowly illuminated. She removed her coat and shoes and put them in the wardrobe. She pushed her feet into her fur-lined slippers, a Christmas present from Aunt Ivy. The blue pom poms adorning the top of the slippers jiggled when she walked. She looked out of the window. The gas street lamps cast a greenish hue upon the shop fronts opposite her flat. Eerie, flickering shadows danced in the shop windows and she pulled the curtains together to shut out the night. She poured some milk into a pan and set it to boil on the gas ring.

When she heard about the flat on Bottle Bank, she went to view it with some trepidation. It was in the same area of Gateshead where she lived with Lizzie. Some streets close to the river Tyne remained uninhabitable, and parts of Bottle Bank weren't much better. The bank was on a steep hill leading up from Pipewellgate towards the town centre, and she walked past two pubs on her way to the Lyons Tea Shop. She watched people cross the street to avoid The Hawk and the Full Moon; she held no such fear. As a girl, she spent countless hours outside the Globe Hotel, waiting for Lizzie to emerge and take her home. The unsavoury characters Lizzie rubbed shoulders with became familiar fixtures in Ena's young life, and she taught herself not to be afraid; or to pretend not to be. She carried on up the hill, passing shops and crowded tenement buildings until the aroma of tea told her she had arrived. She pushed the door open and a bell tinkled above her head.

'Good day, Miss. How can we help you?' Ena looked towards the cheerful voice and saw a man and woman standing behind the glass counter. They smiled in unison and the man pointed at a large canister on the counter. 'You look as though you'd enjoy this strong tea from India. Would you like to try a cup?' The woman reached for the canister and Ena shook her head. 'Thank you. I do like tea, but I'm here to look at the flat. My name is Ena Leighton.' The couple clapped their hands and came out from behind the counter. They took turns to shake her hand and introduce themselves. 'Mr Bartholomew Bundell, Tea Shop proprietor. Very pleased to make your acquaintance, Miss Leighton.' 'Mrs Beatrice Bundell, Tea Shop proprietor. Very pleased to make your acquaintance, Miss Leighton.' Beatrice's smile lit up her kind eyes and her hand warmed Ena's. 'We are delighted such an accomplished young woman is interested in our accommodation, aren't we, Mrs Bundell?' Beatrice nodded, 'yes, Mr Bundell. Mr Todd has told us all about you, Miss Leighton'.

Ena looked at the middle-aged couple, resplendent in their starched white coats. When Jack's uncle learnt the flat was vacant, he offered to speak to Bartholomew Bundell on her behalf. He said they were respectable, friendly people and Ena trusted his judgement. Her slate was clean; the Bundells gave no indication of knowing anything of her shameful start in life, only that she was a hard-working, independent young woman. 'Thank you, I'm looking forward to seeing the flat.' 'Well let's make haste in that case!' Mrs Bundell gestured for Ena to follow her outside while her husband reversed the door sign to indicate they were closed. When he locked the door he started to laugh. 'It's not far!' He pointed at the next door on the bank and spoke proudly. 'You have your own front door, Miss Leighton. You can come and go as you like.'

The milk started to boil and Ena removed it from the heat. She spooned some cocoa into a cup and stirred as she added the hot milk. The Bundells gave her a regular supply of Assam tea, but her favourite bedtime drink had always been cocoa. She smiled, remembering the Bundells' joy when she agreed to rent the flat. She learnt Mr Bundell had lived there until he met and married Beatrice, *somewhat late in life, Miss Leighton. Prior to that joyful occasion, the tea shop was my life'*. He explained once they were married they bought a house on Durham Road. It was walking distance from the tea shop, a house with a garden, suitable for a married couple. The flat was Mr Bundell's home, consequently it was well equipped and furnished much more comfortably than other rooms on Bottle Bank. Ena carried the cocoa to her writing desk and sat. Aunt Ivy had also sent her a new fountain pen and she removed it from the cushioned box on her desk. She pulled a sheet of pale pink writing paper towards her and started to write.

'Dear Rachel,

How happy I was to receive your last letter of 1ˢᵗ December 1922. I am delighted to hear you and William have decided on the date of your wedding. I look forward to returning to Bournemouth with great anticipation. Jack has agreed to accompany me and I am excited for the two of you to meet at last.

Jack and I visited the theatre this evening; a beautiful performance of Puccini's Madame Butterfly. Do you remember how we used to act out the parts when I stayed with your family at Lansdowne Road during the war? We both dreaded playing Butterfly because of her tragic demise! How many times did we each die? The performance was at the King's Theatre, on the corner of Gateshead High Street and Sunderland Road, not too far from my flat. You would love the theatre, Rachel! The exterior is the Spanish Renaissance style, and the auditorium, which can seat 2,000 people in its orchestra stalls, dress circle and galleries, is an Art Nouveau design. It is almost midnight as I write this. Jack and I wished each other happy new year earlier, when he walked me home after the theatre. He returned to his uncle's to be the first-foot there, hopefully he'll bring good fortune to the house. I intend to be my own first-foot and ensure my own good fortune!

I do think I made the right decision in returning to Gateshead, Rac-

hel. I enjoy my work at the flour mill and I am very fortunate to have Jack and his uncle living nearby. Mr and Mrs Bundell ensure I have everything I need in the flat. Aunt Ivy writes regularly with London news and I am hopeful she'll find happiness again, once she has severed herself from her errant husband. I know you keep me in your thoughts although we are further apart these days. I count you as one of my most precious blessings and I remain your very dearest friend, always.

Ena.'

Ena heard a commotion outside and she opened the curtains. The revellers made their unsteady way down Bottle Bank. With arms and hands linked, they sang joyfully.

'Should auld acquaintance be forgot,
And never brought to mind?
Should auld acquaintance be forgot,
And auld lang syne!'

Leaving the curtains open, she grabbed the lump of coal Jack had given her and hurried downstairs. Jubilant new year greetings filled Bottle Bank as the pubs emptied and people continued their carousing on the way home. She waited outside her flat, wishing people well when they passed. When the bells at nearby St Mary's Church announced the dawn of 1923, she walked inside and wished herself a happy new year. Back upstairs, she got ready for bed and pulled the chain on the gas lamp to return her flat to darkness.

Mona

Homeric lurched from side to side as Mona flicked through the dresses in her wardrobe. Vernon had warned her the weather was forecast to take a turn for the worse. He said not to worry, the winds would drop quickly. Still, Mona couldn't shake the fear it was happening again. *Homeric* was going to sink with a catastrophic loss of life.

She'd decided to tell Wilfred about her past. She liked him, and if they were to have any kind of future together, he needed to know. She stared at her reflection in the ornate mirror standing in the corner of her cabin's bedroom. She studied her face; each line told a story of her life. Each wrinkle a sign of a tragedy or a deception. When had she become so hard? How could she tell this kind, apparently straightforward man the shameful things she'd done? He would run a mile. There was a knock on her cabin door and she made her way across the room, swaying unsteadily. She clutched the door frame, 'who is it?' She heard a man's voice and managed a weak smile. 'It's me, Vernon.' She opened the door a fraction. 'What is it?' Vernon smiled. 'I came to see if you were all right.' Mona's lip trembled. He touched her hand. 'Is there anything I can do?' She shook her head, 'it's enough you came'. He put his head on one side, 'are you having dinner with Wilfred tonight?' Mona said she was but had started to wish she wasn't. Vernon frowned, 'don't you think it's time you had some fun? We've had enough misery to last us a lifetime'. She hesitated and Vernon shook his head. 'What? Wilfred is a decent chap and he's good company.' The ship stopped jerking and Mona let go of the door frame, her hand shaking. She looked at Vernon. Her friend. Someone who cared. He'd been right about the weather; the ship was safe. 'Nothing, I was being a silly goose.' 'Should I ask the maître d to give you a secluded table in the restaurant?' Mona nodded, 'yes please, that would be wonderful'. He smiled, 'good. Now, put your best dress on and enjoy your evening!'

At the entrance to the restaurant, the maître d inclined his head politely before leading her to a small table in a softly-lit corner of the room. Wilfred rose to meet her and a warm feeling began in the pit of her stomach. She remembered her sister Ivy telling her about the first time she met her husband Bertie. He'd worn white tie and tails and Ivy said he took her breath away. As she looked at Wilfred, Mona understood. She had thought she was in love with Ena's father Louis, but she was too young. When she discovered she was pregnant, he declared they would be married. He hadn't anticipated his family's reaction to the news, and their hopes of a life together were brutally extinguished. Looking at Wilfred, Mona recognised that running away with Louis set her on a dangerous path. With Wilfred, she had the opportunity to start again, but she needed to be honest.

Wilfred's immaculate dinner suit gleamed and his dark hair was slicked back to show off his handsome features. He spoke quietly. 'You look beautiful.' She smiled, 'thank you'. The tight-fitting black velvet dress was adorned with silver tassels that glistened when she moved. Her glossy hair shone against the silver beaded headband and a silver choker, the centre piece set with small diamonds, completed the look. The waiter pulled out her chair. She sat and he flourished a napkin, placing it gently on her lap. He took the chilled champagne from the ice bucket at the side of the table and filled their glasses. When he left, Wilfred raised his glass and suggested a toast. 'To absent friends?' Mona nodded and raised her glass. She sipped her drink. The bubbles made her nose itch and she laughed. She heard Peggy's giggle in her mind and decided to tell Wilfred about her dear friend.

Somewhere between five courses of delicious food and another bottle of champagne, Mona told Wilfred everything. Abandoning her little girl when she was four-years-old, dancing almost naked for drunken men in a sleazy London music hall, viciously attacking her employer and stealing from another dancer before fleeing to New York City. Wilfred listened quietly as she talked. When she stopped, he leant across the table and took her hands. 'Thank you for trusting me. I'm sorry you've carried this burden for so long.' Mona waited. Would this be the moment he judged her shameful behaviour and left? He continued holding her hands. When she opened her mouth to speak he shook his head. 'No. It's all right. Life can be cruel. Sometimes we find ourselves in situations where we make poor choices. It's happened to us all, but not everyone is honest about it, as you have been this evening, Mona. The important choice is the one you make next.' She nodded, not daring to speak. She had met a man who wasn't shocked by her past, he was only interested in her future. He raised his glass again. 'To new beginnings.' As she repeated Wilfred's toast, the strains of the ship's orchestra began. All around them people linked arms and hands to sing 'Auld Lang Syne'. Above the singing she heard the ship's bell chime. She would begin 1923 in New York City.

Chapter 5

January 1923

Ivy

Ivy returned the telephone receiver to its stand and walked to the window. She watched people going about their everyday business; some hurrying with a sense of purpose, others ambling along without a care in the world. She sighed; her situation weighed heavily now. She turned and looked around her living room. When the war ended, she bought the small flat in a block on Garrick Street because it was close to Endell Street. As the number of wounded soldiers started to decrease, the hospital was confronted by a new problem. An unfamiliar disease crossed its doors, and as the number of patients increased and staff were affected, fear returned to London. The doctors were mystified; the disease wasn't like anything they dealt with during the war. It wasn't typhoid, influenza or meningitis; patients had symptoms of all three diseases. While people all over the world became ill and died, countries involved in the war didn't report it, to avoid affecting morale. Spain, being neutral during the war, hadn't censored its news. Spanish newspapers wrote about the devastating disease, unwittingly providing the deadly strain of influenza with its nickname.

A chill ran up Ivy's spine as she remembered her own experience of the Spanish flu. She had collapsed following a violent row with George. His controlling nature, apparent only after they were married, escalated with alarming speed when Ivy said she wanted to continue working at Endell Street. George argued it was war work and now the war was over, she didn't need to continue. When Ivy stood her ground she saw the full extent of his fury. He slammed out of the flat and she heard his heavy footsteps thumping down the stairs. It was three days before he returned. Their arguments became more frequent and Ivy learnt her best form of defence was silence. George sulked, sometimes for days. Ivy was baffled, unable to question him for fear of another argument. In his rare moments of calm she saw the man she believed George to be. During one of those moments, she told him they had received an invitation to go to the theatre with Grace and Walter. What should have been a wonderful evening turned into a nightmare because of George's jealousy. She felt unwell in the theatre, putting her thumping headache and shivers down to the start of a cold. The night ended with her cowering on the bathroom floor and George pummelling the door in a drunken rage. When a cacophony of crashing and banging told her he was leaving, she pulled herself up. She remembered swaying unsteadily as she hobbled to the telephone to call Grace. The last thing she saw before she passed out was her front door swinging from its hinges, a fist-shaped hole in the middle.

She stared at the door. It had long since been repaired and the locks changed, but George's vicious shadow still loomed. She looked at the telephone. When Lydia's secretary called to arrange her appointment, Ivy heard the barrister's voice in the background and asked to speak to her. She apologised for her insistence but said she needed to know what news Lydia had about her case. 'I've thought about it constantly since I saw you on New Year's Eve.' Lydia spoke quietly, 'yes, of course. I understand'. Ivy sighed, 'can you tell me anything before I come in for my appointment?' Lydia's words made Ivy's blood run cold. 'He's been seen. George is back in London.'

Ena

Ena huddled inside her winter coat and lowered her head against the driving snow. Jack ploughed on ahead, trying to shield her from the worst of the storm. 'We're nearly there, I can see the flour mill.' Ena peered into the white curtain ahead but saw only the back of Jack's overcoat, speckled with snow. 'We should have stayed inside with some of Mr Blundell's strong tea!' Ena's words disappeared into the wet snowy air. She took a deep breath and carried on. When the doors to the flour mill slammed shut behind them. Ena stared at Jack, 'you look like a snowman in an overcoat!' Jack shook himself, leaving puddles of snowy water on the floor. 'Come on, let's get into the office and dry off.' 'Remind me why we've come to work on the coldest day of the year? A day when trams are stuck in the snow on Sheriff's Hill?' Jack turned as he reached the top of the stairs. 'You know why, stocktake.' Ena grimaced, 'I know'. Jack held the office door open and she hurried inside. A small electric heater at one end of the room provided the only source of warmth and she walked quickly towards it. When she reached up to remove her brown bucket hat, melted snow ran down her arms from her sodden gloves. Jack placed some newspaper on the floor and she shook the bedraggled hat and her gloves and coat, before hanging them on the wooden stand near the door.

Jack laughed. 'It looks like some unfortunate creature that's fallen in the Tyne!' Ena put her hands on her hips. 'How dare you insult my poor dead hat, Jack Todd?' Jack moved towards her and she stepped back, laughing. 'No, your coat is dripping wet!' Jack smiled and stopped. He removed his coat and hat and hung them on the stand. 'Hopefully everything will dry out by the time we walk home. Now, should I make some tea?' Ena nodded, 'yes please, that would be very welcome'. As Jack handed her the steaming cup, there was a knock on the door. 'Come in.' Nothing happened. Ena turned; she saw the blurred outline of a small figure through the frosted glass. Jack repeated his instruction, louder this time. 'It's open, come in.' Still nothing happened. The figure didn't move. Ena shrugged her shoulders at Jack and put down her tea. She walked across the office and opened the door, revealing a girl of no more than 15. Ena smiled, 'hello, can I help you?' The girl's bright blue eyes glistened when she moved her hands in response to Ena's question. Ena gasped. She closed her eyes and tried to remember. She felt a hand on her arm and her eyes snapped open. The girl's hands were moving again; this time Ena replied with her own gestures. Ena stood to one side and the girl stared at her as she walked into the office. She grinned when Ena introduced her to Jack, using words and signs. 'Jack, this is Dolly Turnbull. She's been sent with the warehouse records for us to match against our invoices.' Jack looked from Ena to Dolly then back again. Ena watched him; was he remembering their school friend? He held up his cup and raised his eyebrows at Dolly. She smiled and Ena saw her sign, 'yes, please'.

They worked tirelessly until the light began to go and snow started falling again. Ena pointed at the window where fat flakes were already gathered. She signed to tell Dolly she should go home. Dolly shook her head when Ena asked if she had far to go. Alone with Jack, Ena sat in the chair next to the heater. She warmed her hands and spoke quietly. 'Nancy.' Jack took her hands. 'Yes, she's a lot like Nancy.' Ena's lip trembled. 'It was such a long time ago, yet I remember it as if it was yesterday.' Jack nodded. Ena squeezed his hands before getting up and walking to the window. She looked out at the snowy evening, thinking about Nancy. A girl from a different time who taught her sign language. A friend taken away in horrific circumstances. Ena sighed, if she'd done things differently, would Nancy have survived?

Mona

Mona woke early the day *Homeric* was due to arrive in New York Harbor. She had breakfast delivered to her cabin, and finished packing once she'd eaten. After a porter collected her luggage she sat at the writing desk and pulled two sheets of paper towards her. The embossed heading on the paper, *Homeric*, allowed no room for subterfuge. Not that she wanted to be deceitful, she had begun 1923 with a new sense of purpose. She took a deep breath and positioned her pen above the first sheet of paper.

'My dear sister,

I imagine you'll be surprised to receive this letter. I hope you can forgive me for my previous lack of communication and my irresponsibility. I know I have been a burden to you in the past. Please be assured, with the turning of the year I have resolved to change my behaviour. As the notepaper reveals, I am sailing on RMS Homeric. Soon we dock in New York Harbor; then I'll travel to Broadway. You may remember Marv Marvel, the director at the Paradise Theatre? He wants me to play the lead in his production of Sally! He wants to give the show an American feel. I don't know if I'm up to the job, but I'm here to give it a go. I hope life is treating you well in London. I know you have been dealt some ghastly cards in the last few years; I sincerely hope the future holds better for you. I will write again with my address in New York City, once I am settled.

Your loving sister, Mona.'

She stared at the second sheet of paper. When she lifted her hand to start writing the pen shook, dripping black ink onto the pristine paper. She pictured the disappointment in Ena's eyes the last time they met. Her daughter was a stranger. How could she write to a stranger? She shook her head, remembering her resolve to do better. As the nib of her pen touched the paper, there was a knock on her cabin door. 'Miss Leighton? It's time to disembark.' She crumpled the sheet of paper into a ball and threw it into the wastepaper basket before gathering her coat and bag.

She left her cabin without a backward glance.

Wilfred was waiting for her on deck and he offered her his arm as they walked. After she'd confided in him on New Year's Eve, he asked what good choices she'd made in life. She hesitated for a moment. Then she pictured Bella Holliday, the wealthy American she met on her voyage back to England in 1911. She was returning to England a nervous wreck, devoid of self-confidence, when Bella rescued her from the severe maître d, insisting she join her for dinner. Mona met Bella again, on *Titanic*. Mona worried Bella would ruin her reputation by telling the well-heeled aristocrats about her shameful life; surprisingly Bella proved herself the epitome of discretion. When the disastrous events unfolded on *Titanic*, Mona and Peggy ran into Bella amidst the chaos on deck. Bella tried to persuade them to join a group of passengers in the First-Class Lounge. She said they were waiting in the warm until further instructions were received. Mona remembered her actions in that moment, her determination to get off *Titanic* and into a lifeboat. She reached for Bella's hand and the older woman gripped hers. Peggy refused to join them, choosing instead to try and find Edward. Mona stared at the back of Peggy's coat as she hurried away, then she stepped over the side of the huge ship into a small wooden lifeboat. She helped Bella down onto the cold, wet wooden slats, where they pressed together for warmth. Bella screamed when the lifeboat dropped suddenly. It lurched unsteadily towards the black water. Mona looked up and saw people hanging over *Titanic's* rail, shouting at them to wait. She shivered when she remembered the lifeboat hitting the freezing water with a huge splash. Bella's shaking hand gripped Mona's knee. She turned to the older woman. Bella had protected her once and she hadn't forgotten it. Throughout the most terrifying night of her life, Mona reassured and calmed Bella, until the officer in charge gave the order to row. The memory of Bella's sobs was etched into her mind. She concentrated on Bella, trying to distract herself from the screams in the water. Chunks of ice shone in the moonlit ocean and Bella started to shiver uncontrollably. Her speech became slurred and her breathing shortened and Mona implored Bella to stay awake. Mona held her as the lifeboat made its unsteady way between obstacles in the water. She stroked Bella's hair, thinking how angry she would be that it was matted with filth and debris. She did all she could, but Bella didn't survive.

When she stopped talking, Wilfred was silent. Then he took her hand. She smiled at him. He'd helped her to understand that not everything she'd done in life was bad. Now, as they prepared to disembark *Homeric*, Mona looked up at this honest, kind man. Since meeting Wilfred she'd realised how exhausted she was, carrying years of guilt and shame around with her. At the bottom of the gangplank, she turned around. She stared at the ship and nodded; she would leave her anguish there. There was a spring in her step when she linked Wilfred's arm and walked towards a waiting yellow taxicab.

The woman at the top of the gangplank shrunk back when Mona looked back at the ship. She pushed into the crowds, ignoring people's complaints. Out of sight, she reached a hand up to her neck and rubbed an angry scar hidden under her scarf. She glared at Mona and Wilfred. She'd seen them on New Year's Eve and overheard some of their conversation in the ship's restaurant. She whispered under her breath. 'I see you, Miss Mona Leighton. Your fancy clothes and fashionable hairstyle can't change who you are or what you've done. I'm the last person you'll expect to see at the Paradise Theatre.'

Chapter 6

Ivy

Ivy returned her coffee cup to the china saucer. She moved to the edge of the plush armchair and put her hands on her knees. 'I came straight here after seeing Lydia.' Ivy looked at Grace and Walter sitting opposite. Her eyes were drawn to the sofa's slender tapering legs, ending in brass castors. She followed the patterns on the linen fabric, exotic birds intertwined with leaves, a colourful combination of blues and greens. Grace's eye for interior design showed in the two seater sofa and matching armchair she had imported from France; fitting perfectly in their living room. Grace's soft voice snapped Ivy out of her reverie. 'And what did she say?' Ivy shook her head, 'I'm sorry, I was lost in thought'. Her friends waited and Ivy cleared her throat. 'Lydia's private detective has found George living in London.' The words tumbled out one over the other, and Walter asked her to repeat them. 'He's here, that monster of a man.'

Walter stood and walked to the window. 'Where in London?' Ivy sighed, 'Lydia didn't give me the address. She said it's good news; I'm not so sure. I hate the idea of him being anywhere near me'. Grace's gaze moved from Ivy to Walter, her eyes questioning. 'Surely he won't try to contact you? Not after everything that happened?' Walter removed his spectacles and pinched the bridge of his nose. 'I sincerely hope not; perhaps it would be advisable for you to stay here with us for a time, Ivy. We have plenty of room.' Ivy swallowed. 'Thank you, both of you. I'm very grateful. But no thanks, he's not going to scare me out of my own home.' Grace stood and walked towards her. She took Ivy's hands. 'Are you sure? He was so violent on that last evening we were all together.' Ivy nodded and raised her chin. 'Yes. I've faced so much in the last few years; the war brought me into contact with horrors I could never have imagined and the Spanish flu hooked me with its vicious claws, but I survived. I can survive meeting George Scott-Smith again. He doesn't scare me.' Ivy watched Walter pacing behind the sofa. 'What else did Lydia say?' She understood his impatience, she wanted nothing more than for the situation to be resolved. She sighed, 'that they need to continue their surveillance to form a picture of George's movements and activities'.

Grace spoke quietly, 'what about the idea of him being a bigamist?' Ivy shuddered. If evidence of this came to light, it would mean she and George weren't legally married. She turned away from Grace's gaze but her friend persisted, 'this is not your shame, Ivy. His behaviour is at the root of everything' Ivy kept her face averted. Heat burned her cheeks as she considered the consequences of George being proven to be a bigamist. She came from a place where her sister, a pregnant unmarried teenager, decided abandoning her child and running away from home was the best option. They still lived in a world where women were vilified for much less than having a bigamist for a husband. She took a deep breath and turned back. 'Lydia also said she's hopeful a new act will be passed later this year.' Walter stopped pacing. 'The Matrimonial Causes Act?' Ivy nodded. 'Yes. If the legislation goes through, it will make adultery grounds for divorce for either spouse. At the moment only men have this right, women must prove additional fault.' Grace crossed her arms, 'what an appalling double standard!' Ivy rubbed a hand across her forehead. 'It is. Lydia said under the current law a wife's adultery is sufficient cause for a man to end a marriage, but a woman can only divorce her husband if his adultery is compounded by another matrimonial offence.' Walter asked if abandonment could be the other offence. 'He disappeared without trace.' Ivy looked at him, 'he did but the problem is proving it. Lydia needs evidence of his fault before she can proceed'.

Back at her flat, Ivy hesitated outside the door. After George left, Walter arranged for the door to be repaired and the locks changed, yet every time she returned home doubt crept into her mind. Was George inside? She knew it was impossible, still the fear lingered. She shook her head and turned the yale key in the lock. Then she turned the bigger mortice key and as the lock clicked open she hurried inside and shut the door behind her. She used the mortice key again and heard the strong, reliable lock slide into place with a satisfying clunk. She crossed the room and closed the curtains. She went back to the door and checked it was locked. She'd told Grace and Walter that George didn't scare her but she'd lied. She stood in front of the bathroom mirror and studied her face. She narrowed her eyes and stared. This was the face she needed. The one she'd used for the Registrar in Gateshead when she registered her mother's death, and in New York when she discovered Marv Marvel had fired her sister and left her to fend for herself thousands of miles from home. She relaxed her facial muscles and smiled. Her natural face showed her softness. She sighed; she knew which face she'd wear if she ever saw George Scott-Smith again.

Ena

Ena frowned at the small brown envelope in her hand. She tapped it against her palm then turned back to the wages clerk. She opened her mouth to speak but was drowned out by shouting in the corridor outside the office. Someone in the queue asked what was happening. The man behind the desk spoke gruffly. 'It'll be another woman complaining about her wages.' He spat his words. 'They should be grateful we let them work, never mind moaning about their pay.' Before she could respond, the door flew open. Jack stood in the doorway and she saw people running along the corridor behind him. He signalled for her to come quickly. 'What's happening, Jack?' He spoke quietly, 'it's another fire. We need to get outside before it takes hold'.

Ena pushed her wage packet into the pocket of her apron and hurried to follow Jack downstairs. As they made their way through the smoky warehouse, the noxious fumes reached them. An acrid taste caught the back of Ena's throat and she pulled her apron up to cover her mouth and nose. She buried her face into Jack's back and they moved towards the exit. She saw Jack raise his hand to push the door open before a deafening thunder clap forced them outside. Jack stumbled but managed to stay upright, she landed on her knees. Jack pulled her up and she spoke through chattering teeth. 'What was that?' Jack rubbed a hand across his face and stared at the flour warehouse at the east end of the building. Angry orange and black flames licked the side of the warehouse and shards of shattered glass covered the ground. People ran screaming from the space where the doors had been. He turned to face her. 'I'm guessing it's the same as last time, a build- up of flour dust and inadequate ventilation.' She shook her head, 'it shouldn't keep happening, Jack. Someone might be badly hurt'. 'Or worse.' Jack spoke quietly as he looked around. His lips were moving and Ena realised he was counting. She started scanning the crowds. She saw people from the offices and the flour warehouses. Jack had stopped counting. 'I think everyone is here.' An icy chill ran up her spine as she looked at the faces around them. She shook her head; she knew who was missing. She started running towards groups of people, huddled together in shock. 'Where is she? Have you seen her? She's only 15.' Images of her school friend Nancy flashed before her eyes and she started shouting, knowing how pointless it was. 'Dolly? Dolly?' There was no sign of her young friend. She stopped to catch her breath. She turned to look at the burning warehouse. If Dolly was still inside she stood no chance. The flour dust particles in the air stung her eyes and she blinked to shift the grit. When she opened them a woman was standing in front of her. The woman was holding a young girl by the hand. 'Is this who you're looking for?' Ena burst into tears and pulled Dolly into her arms. In between sobs she thanked the woman and signed to her young friend to ask if she was all right. Dolly's hands shook as she signed to say, 'yes, thank you'. Ena saw Jack, tall above the crowds, pushing through the throng towards them. She waved and he quickened his pace. When he was close, he reached for her. 'I've been looking for you. Are you both all right?' His eyes moved from her to Dolly. Ena nodded, 'we are now'. Jack took a deep breath. 'With Dolly, that's everyone accounted for, thankfully. Hopefully the company fire brigade will soon have the blaze under control.' Ena took Jack's hand. 'I'm worried about Dolly; I think we should take her home.' Jack squeezed her hand. 'Of course. I'll tell the Chief Clerk and I'll ask someone to let Uncle John know what's happening.'

Ena signed to ask Dolly where she lived. When Jack returned they set off for Colliery Road. Dolly had told Ena her dad was a miner and their house was close to the pit. When they turned into Colliery Road, Ena saw a sturdy, muscular man marching towards them. He signed to Dolly and she ran to him, immediately enveloped in his bear hug. Ena took Jack's hand and they walked towards Mr Turnbull. His dirty face and hands told of a long, hard day miles underground. He smiled, his teeth gleamed against his sooty face and Ena stretched out her hand to introduce herself. He grabbed her hand in both of his and squeezed. 'Thank you for bringing her home. We've been worried sick since we heard the explosion. I was coming to the Staithes to find her.' Dolly's father turned to Jack and clapped him on the back. He pointed along the street. 'You'll come in for tea? Or something stronger?' The four of them made their way to the small pit house on Colliery Road, where Dolly's mother burst out of the house to greet them. 'I thought the flour mill was supposed to be safe; it turns out to be as dangerous as the pit.' Dolly's father, who introduced himself as Marty, now scrubbed clean of grime and coal dust, took a deep slug of his beer. Jack shook his head. 'I wish I could disagree with you, Mr Turnbull. However, this is the second fire this year and I think the company needs to make some improvements.'

Dolly's mother Olive invited them to stay for tea. 'You'll have some mince and dumplings and mashed potato? I want to thank you for looking after our Dolly.' Ena noticed Marty and Olive signed when they talked, even when the conversation wasn't directed at their daughter. Ena responded in kind and Olive asked where she learnt to sign. 'I had a school friend called Nancy who taught me.' Olive smiled. 'There aren't many people with the skill, pet. I'm very grateful Dolly was fortunate enough to meet you and Jack.' Dolly stopped, holding the potato masher in the air, and signed to say she was very grateful too.

Walking home later, with Olive's recipe for suet dumplings folded safely in her coat pocket, Ena took Jack's arm. He looked down at her, 'are you all right?' Ena nodded, 'yes and no. I'm relieved Dolly wasn't hurt in the accident and I'm pleased to have met her parents'. Jack stopped walking. 'But?' Ena shook her head. Jack continued. 'Dolly's situation is nothing like Nancy's. You can see her parents love her. You're not responsible for what happened to Nancy.' She wanted to believe him, but when she remembered the events leading up to Nancy's death, she always arrived at the same conclusion. It was her idea to run away from Lizzie and she asked Nancy to go with her. If she'd gone on her own, Nancy might still be alive. Jack held her gently by the elbows. 'Only Nancy knows what happened that day. You didn't force her to go with you. You couldn't have prevented it.' Ena pursed her lips. 'Perhaps.' Jack shook his head. 'Dolly isn't Nancy. You've seen how much Marty and Olive love her.' Ena nodded. 'Yes, and I might be able to reassure them of her safety at work.' Jack raised his eyebrows. 'What do you have in mind?' Ena reached into her coat pocket and pulled out her wage packet, forgotten in the drama of the day. 'As well as starting a campaign for women to receive equal pay, I'm going to demand safer working conditions. For us all!' Jack embraced her. 'That's my girl! Now, I'd better get you home. You'll need a good night's sleep before taking on the company tomorrow!'

Jack

Jack looked up at Ena's window and waved. She waved back before closing the curtains. As he walked up Bottle Bank he smiled. He'd met her at school, the scruffy girl who was always hungry. Despite her disadvantages, or perhaps because of them, he was drawn to her. Years later she told him she didn't think she would have survived life with Lizzie without him and Nancy. When her aunt took her to London, Jack thought he'd never see her again.

The dark menace of war hovered at the edges of his mind, fluttering wings of horror that threatened every day of his life. He marched towards Cross Street, each step pushing the memories further away. He reminded himself it was the war that brought Ena back. The newspaper article about the soldiers from his football team who died in one of many horrific Western Front battles. He was the only one to survive. He lowered his head as he walked, determined not to let the memories in. He forced his mind back to Ena. She'd left Gateshead bruised and emaciated, returning an intelligent and beautiful young woman, determined to make something of herself. Ena's tragic start in life strengthened her character and she held no resentment towards those who had wronged her. On the few occasions she mentioned her mother, it was with sadness, not anger. Jack had no sympathy for Mona; he couldn't understand how a mother could abandon her child. Through her actions, Mona deprived herself of knowing the remarkable woman her daughter had become. During the war Ena worked tirelessly, knitting cotton slings for wounded troops and writing short stories for soldiers in the trenches. Jack knew first-hand how any kindness touched a man in those circumstances. He knew many men believed women shouldn't have continued to work after the war, thinking they should be at home doing housework and caring for family. He disagreed. He was proud of Ena's work ethic and her determination to fight injustice. He was delighted she'd agreed to marry him, but they weren't in any hurry. He wanted Ena to have the opportunity to flourish as an independent young woman.

When he turned into Cross Street he saw his uncle sitting on the doorstep. He raised his hands, 'I'm sorry it's late, Uncle.' John Todd shook his head. 'It's all right, you're home now.' The men embraced and went inside.

Mona

Mona looked at Marv's telegram and asked the cab driver to take them to Old Broadway. Wilfred had offered to go with her to the address in the telegram, and she was grateful for his company. New York City was as she remembered; rows of straight narrow streets, bordered on both sides by buildings reaching into the sky. When the cab drew to a halt outside a house on a street of brick tenement buildings, Mona peered out of the window. 'Is this it?' The cab driver's drawl made her smile. 'Sure is, Ma'am. Old Broadway. Favoured residence for Broadway stars!' Mona frowned. 'How far is Broadway? I've lost my bearings.' The driver chuckled. 'See that corner at the end of the street?' Mona turned in the direction of his pointed finger. 'That's it, Ma'am, not far at all!' He glanced at her in his rear-view mirror. 'Are you an actress?' Mona returned his smile. 'Yes. I'm joining the cast of *Sally* at the Paradise Theatre.' The driver whistled through his teeth, 'Well good luck Ma'am, I'm mighty pleased to have met you!' Mona thanked him and stepped out of the cab. The large house had two sloped roofs and dormer windows.

Wilfred paid the cab driver and came to stand next to her. 'I've read about these French-style roofs. The steep roofline and dormer windows allow for additional floors of habitable space.' Mona's lip trembled. 'Do you mean attic space?' Wilfred nodded, 'yes, or some people call them garrets. What's wrong?' Mona shook her head; she didn't trust herself to speak. Wilfred took her arm and turned her to face him. 'You can tell me.' She took a deep breath.

'When I arrived in London, I was taken to a lodging house.' Mona shivered, remembering being led up the rotting staircase, the weak light from the man's candle flickering in the foul, damp air. Up and up they went, until he stopped and opened a door. He pointed a wizened finger at a small, dirty bed and pushed her inside. The stinking, flea-ridden attic bedroom had been the roof over her head for seven years, until she escaped. She spoke quietly but firmly. 'I can't stay in an attic, Wilfred.' As Wilfred started to reply, another yellow taxicab pulled up outside the house. Mona noticed the woman's shoes when she stepped out of the cab. Bright red, high stiletto heels with red silk ribbons fastened at the ankle. The woman's black fur coat contrasted starkly with the snowy street. The cab driver asked if she needed help with her luggage and the woman laughed. 'No thank you, honey. This gal manages just fine on her lonesome!' As the cab drove away, the woman noticed Mona and Wilfred. 'Hello! Are you with the company for *Sally* as well?' Mona nodded. She approached the woman and introduced herself and Wilfred.

'Mighty glad to meet you, I'm Ms Tilly Tucker. Shall we get in out of the cold?' Tilly started walking towards the house then turned back. 'Are you coming?' Mona hesitated. 'Are you staying here too?' Tilly smiled, 'sure! Marv knows how to treat his stars. Only the best penthouse apartment for us!' Mona still hadn't moved. 'Is it in the attic?' Tilly squealed with laughter. 'The attic? Oh honey, it's one of the biggest, most desirable attics in New

York City! Come on, hurry up before we freeze to death on the sidewalk!' Mona followed Tilly into the house, thoughts of the rundown lodging house forgotten.

Chapter 7

Ivy

Ivy flicked through her most recent copies of *The Era* and *The Stage*. Both publications were invaluable sources of information for anyone interested in the London theatre scene. They contained theatrical reviews, news, entertainment information and gossip. She turned to the advertisements for performers, because the last time they spoke, Lydia had advised her to find something to focus on. 'And stop obsessing about George?' 'I didn't say that, Ivy. But this is the fourth time you've called my office this week.' Lydia had agreed to meet her in a café close to her chambers. As Lydia sat, Ivy apologised. 'I'm sorry, it's frustrating sitting around waiting for him to be seen or for him to do something.' Lydia smiled, 'do you want my advice?' Ivy tapped her polished fingernails against her coffee cup then nodded. 'Go back to work.' Ivy raised her eyebrows, 'to Endell Street? It closed at the end of 1919'. Lydia shook her head. 'No. To what you do best. Performing.'

Ivy sipped her coffee, remembering the shows she'd performed in over the years, and the many times she'd been in the audience at one theatre or another. It was her life for a long time, but she hadn't been on stage for years. 'I'm not sure.' Lydia leant across the table. 'I'm going to the Vaudeville Theatre with some friends on Saturday night. We're going to see *Rats!* Why don't you join us? Ask Grace and Walter too, if you like. It might get your theatrical juices flowing again.' Ivy steepled her fingers against her lips. She'd read about *Rats!* and thought the revue, with a mix of comedy sketches, songs and dance numbers, would be entertaining. The cast included Gwen Farrar, one of her favourite English actresses. She and her performing partner Norah

Blaney were members of an entertainment group for soldiers during the war. Initially classical artists, their popularity flourished when they started their ragtime duet. And the four-storey Vaudeville, nestled in the middle of the Strand, was one of her favourite theatres. Its elegant cream-stone façade stood out from other buildings on the street. Inside, a handsome marble entrance hall led theatregoers into an elegant, comfortable auditorium. The seats in the stalls were covered with peacock-blue velvet and placed sufficiently far apart to allow people to pass easily between the rows. The last time Ivy went to the Vaudeville she sat in the stalls, but if Grace and Walter did want to go and see *Rats!*, she would suggest they take a private box. She told herself this had nothing to do with being worried about seeing George, and everything to do with treating themselves. After the horror of the war years and the Spanish flu, they deserved it.

'What do you think?' Lydia looked at Ivy, her eyebrows raised. Ivy smiled, 'I think it's an excellent idea. I'll call Grace this evening.' 'Good. And before then you can start looking for a job!' Ivy returned to her magazines, hoping to spot an opportunity she could tell Lydia about. She had called Grace and she and Walter were keen to see *Rats!* Their box at the Vaudeville was booked for that evening's show.

Ena

Not long after the warehouse fire, Ena visited the library. Hoping to gain support for her campaign from women at the flour mill and adjoining soap works, she wanted to gather some information before approaching anyone. The librarian directed her towards a number of volumes and newspaper articles. She was reading about the Six Point Group, a British feminist campaign group founded in 1921 to make changes to British law, when another article caught her eye. Charlotte Augusta Leopoldine Marsh, a militant suffragette who was born in Alnmouth, around 40 miles from Gateshead. Charlie Marsh, as the piece said she preferred to be known, later moved with her family to Cullercoats, and by 1900 she was living in Newcastle. Ena learnt Charlie joined the militant Women's Social and Political Union in 1907, when she was 20. As a member of the Six Point Group, she was determined to give women a voice in public affairs.

'It's a few years old, that picture.' Ena looked up to see a woman had joined her at the reading table. Her mouth fell open. She stared at the woman then at the picture printed alongside the article about the Women's Sunday Procession in Hyde Park in 1908. Ena opened her mouth to speak but nothing came out. The woman pointed at the small pin attached to Ena's coat; the purple, white and green colours demonstrating her commitment to the suffrage movement. Ena smiled, spotting a matching pin on the woman's coat. 'Charlie Marsh, pleased to meet you.' Ena stammered. 'Ena Leighton, likewise.' Ena looked at the picture again. 'That's you?' Charlie laughed quietly and nodded. 'It was our first major political rally and it was enormous! Much bigger than we expected. It was estimated between 300,000 and 500,000 people attended! Can you imagine that?' Ena shook her head, momentarily struck dumb to have this stalwart of the suffrage movement sitting opposite her. What was she doing in Gateshead Library? 'How old were you in 1908, Ena?' Those were years Ena preferred to forget, and she mumbled, 'I was nine'. 'Were you here in Gateshead?' Ena shifted in her seat. 'I only ask because two years earlier, the suffragists marched down Northumberland Street in Newcastle. I think you would be too young to remember it?' Ena raised her chin and met Charlie's gaze. 'At the beginning of 1912 I was staying in London with my aunt. That's where I started learning about the suffrage movement.' Ena smiled, remembering Clara, the housemaid at Mrs Newbold's guest house. Clara's commitment to the cause made an impression on her and when they moved to Bournemouth she was ready to learn more. Uncle Bertie's sisters fell over themselves to educate her, calling her their very own Geordie suffragist. 'I'm sorry, what are you doing here? Shouldn't you be somewhere in London, campaigning?'

Charlie spoke quietly. 'I still have family in the area. Whenever I visit I call at local libraries and drop off some literature. Although I'm sure some librarians toss them straight into the wastepaper basket.' She gestured towards the surly man behind the desk. Then she looked around before sliding a batch of thin leaflets from her coat pocket. She pushed one across the table to Ena. 'Perhaps you could give some to women you know?' Ena studied the leaflet, feeling Charlie's eyes on her. 'What do you think, can you help us?' Ena nodded, 'I think so. I'm going to start a campaign for equal pay and safer working conditions'. Charlie leant back in her chair and narrowed her eyes. 'I'm very glad to have met you, Ena.' She reached into her coat pocket again and this time she produced a small white card. 'My details,' Ena turned the card over in her hand, her heart racing. When she looked up the chair opposite was empty and a small pile of leaflets lay on the table. She turned towards the library doors. Charlie pointed at the pin on her coat, then she was gone. Ena jumped up and her chair clattered to the floor. The librarian coughed and glared at her. Ena ran outside but Charlie Marsh was nowhere to be seen. She went inside and slid the leaflets into her pocket before righting the chair. She collected the books she wanted to borrow and approached the librarian. 'The woman who sat at the table with me, do you know who she is?' He shook his head and glanced at the clock above the desk. 'It was Charlie Marsh.' The librarian shrugged. 'Do you want these books, Miss?' Ena answered politely, longing to spread the books open on the desk to show him what Charlie Marsh and others had endured for the cause. For every woman in Britain, they were prepared to die in the most horrific circumstances.

Mona

Mona and Wilfred followed Tilly up the driveway to the large house on Old Broadway. Tilly walked quickly but carefully in her high heels and her coat billowed out behind her in the cold wind. She stopped at the front door and reached into her small leather handbag. 'Ta da!' In her gloved hand she held a shiny gold keyring. She unlocked the front door and shepherded them inside. She hurried to close the door behind them then handed a second keyring to Mona. 'Yours for the duration of your stay.' She opened her arms wide. 'Welcome to your new home for the foreseeable, Mona! Wait until you see the penthouse, it's dreamy!'

Mona looked around. The large hallway had a ceramic tile floor, the black and white geometric design stretching the length of the airy room. Large potted palms stood proudly to her left and right, guarding the entrance. Stairs on each side curved gently upwards, meeting on a landing at the top. She took a step towards the stairs but Tilly put a hand on her arm. 'It's a whole lot of stairs up to the penthouse, honey. Let's take the elevator!' Tilly started walking to a recessed area immediately in front of them and Mona saw the silver shine of the elevator doors. She turned to Wilfred and he smiled. Tilly pushed a button and the doors opened silently. Inside, Mona held her breath, remembering another elevator. The first time she came to New York, she stayed with Peggy in her luxurious apartment. Having never used an elevator before, she remembered her rising panic as the noisy contraption clunked towards Peggy's tenth floor apartment. Her confidence grew the more she used it; that same confidence disappeared after the disaster on *Titanic*. That night, the elevator rose all-too-slowly to the Boat Deck, the silence from those packed inside magnified by the thunderous mechanism taking them to an unknown fate. In the elevator in the magnificent house on Old Broadway, the doors closed without a sound. Tilly raised a gloved finger and pressed a button marked PH. The elevator rose silently. When the doors slid open, they stepped out into a long corridor. Mona's heels sank into the plush cream carpet. Tilly crossed the corridor and opened a door marked *'Penthouse Apartment'*. They followed Tilly inside and Mona gasped; this place knocked Peggy's apartment into a cocked hat. The door opened onto a short corridor with polished walnut display cabinets on both sides. Mona removed her boots and gestured to Wilfred to do likewise. She glanced through the curved glass doors of the cabinets. The cabinets were full of theatre programmes and portraits of Marv's star performers. One face stopped her in her tracks. She turned to Wilfred and whispered. 'Peggy.' They stared at the image until Tilly called them to come and see the fireplace. 'Marv had a fire laid for us, it's real cozy in here!' Wilfred touched Mona's arm as they followed Tilly's voice. 'Peggy was beautiful.' She nodded, not trusting herself to reply.

The corridor gave onto a living room which ran the length of the apartment. The high ceiling and plate glass windows filled the room with the last light of New York's late afternoon. A sprawling outside terrace provided breathtaking views of the city skyline. Tilly warmed her hands in front of the elegant Art Deco fireplace. 'This is perfect for the icy New York winter. We'll be snug in here!' Mona joined Tilly at the fireplace and the warmth spread from her stockinged feet and into her chilled fingers. Deep red tiles adorned with white tulips were a perfect contrast to the black cast iron surround of the fireplace, and coals glowed hot in the grate. Mona saw Wilfred had made himself comfortable in one of the large armchairs. An opulent paisley print in gold, red and green covered the chairs and a three-seater sofa, all decorated with tasselled cushions. At the end of the living room double doors stood open, revealing a magnificent mahogany dining table surrounded by matching chairs. Before she could take in the rest of the room, Tilly spoke. 'Where are you staying while you're in New York, Wilfred?' Wilfred laughed, 'an apartment not far away, decent enough for a chap, but a long way from the luxury of this place!' Tilly shook her head. 'Gee, I'm sorry to hear that. You must let me take you both to one of New York City's finest steakhouses this evening. I won't take no for an answer!'

Chapter 8

Ivy

Ivy leant forward in her seat and looked into the stalls. Excited chatter and the rustle of programmes rose to their box as people took their seats. She glanced up, the rows in the dress and upper circles climbed towards the lavish, ornamental plaster ceiling. The walls were white and grey with gold embellishments and elaborate chandeliers hung throughout the auditorium. The carpets and hangings in their box were a dusky rose, the walls a greenish grey. Ivy turned to face the stage, where a striking gold archway framed the rectangle that would be the centre of attention during the show. Heavy velvet curtains hid the stage from view. The black drapes would part in the centre to reveal the introductory scene when the revue began. Ivy sat back and opened her programme. The satirical *Rats!* promised *'a visual spectacle, risqué and irreverent dissection of topical matter, public personae and current fads and a cornucopia of acts alternating between solo performances and dance ensembles'*. Revues, sometimes salacious, often ribald, weren't for the fainthearted or easily offended.

'How long is it since you've been to see a show, darling? Other than mine, of course!' Grace sat to her left with Walter on the end. Ivy shook her head, 'too long. I'd forgotten how much I enjoy the atmosphere'. Grace agreed, 'there's nothing like it, is there?' Ivy closed her eyes and listened to the hubbub. She tingled with anticipation for the spectacle ahead. Grace tapped her arm and she opened her eyes. 'Look, Lydia's waving.' In a box on the other side of the auditorium, Lydia and her friends provided their own spectacle. They were in the cocktail lounge when Ivy arrived with Grace and Walter, and Lydia's friend Teddy wasted no time in ordering more champagne. Ivy's eyes had moved discreetly around the group, taking in their distinctiveness. Lydia's hair was slicked back off her face and her slim figure in pristine white tie completed her androgynous look. Ivy smiled at Lydia's choice of colour for her accessories. Where in London had she found a purple bow tie, gloves and scarf? Teddy's mane of white curls matched the ivory fabric of his dinner suit. His bow tie, in pink and white polka dot, drew glances from around the room. As he filled their glasses, Teddy introduced the others; Vivienne Lawson, Daphne Bloom and Zebedee Scott. Vivienne's full-length ballgown of bright green silk was covered in tassels and sequins, she tinkled when she reached to shake Ivy's hand. Long red tresses piled high on her head showed off her slim neck, decorated with a sparkling diamond necklace and matching earrings. Daphne's outfit was as understated as Vivienne's was ostentatious; a fashionable but plain grey shift dress with a dropped waist and white belt. Until Daphne turned to face her, there was nothing to set her apart from any other woman wearing one of that season's popular numbers. 'I'm very pleased to meet you, Ivy.' Daphne's cut-glass English accent and manicured hands contrasted with her choice of dress. Her bob of yellow curls framed an angelic face and when she smiled, she shone. Ivy tore her eyes away when Zebedee, 'please, call me Zee', bowed in front of her. She immediately warmed to the slightly overweight man with the perfectly curled and waxed handlebar moustache. She learnt later that Zee was an artist. Ivy thought his appearance that night betrayed his profession, presenting himself clad in a paint-streaked tunic. 'My apologies Ivy, I came straight from the studio.' His lisp and good manners, along with the idiosyncrasies of each of Lydia's friends, only added to their appeal.

When Ivy and Grace returned Lydia's wave, Teddy and the rest of their colourful group stood and cheered. Applause echoed throughout the theatre and Ivy laughed. 'Whatever the show is

like, I think Lydia and her friends are going to enjoy themselves!'
'As are we, Ivy.' Grace raised her champagne flute and clinked it
against the side of Ivy's. Ivy nodded and as they sat, the lights
went out and a muted spotlight focussed on the stage. The curtains parted slowly, and the gentle strains of 'I'm Always Chasing
Rainbows' began, teasing the audience with a taste of what was
to come.

Ena

Ena ran down Bottle Bank, desperate to reach the tea shop while
it was still open. The Bundells closed on Wednesday and Saturday afternoons, along with the majority of local traders. She
pushed the door open as Mrs Bundell was preparing to lock up.
'Mrs Bundell! You'll never guess who I met in the library!' Mrs
Bundell's ever-present smile creased into a grin. 'I've told you
before Ena, call me Beatrice.' Ena's words came out in a rush.
'Charlie Marsh! She was in the library! I told her about my campaign for equal pay and safer working conditions. Can you
believe it?' Ena looked around; wondering if Mr Bundell would
approve of their conversation. Beatrice reassured her, 'it's all
right, he's gone home to tend to the garden. Incidentally, he
would be very interested in your news'. Ena wrinkled her nose.
'He would?' She hadn't put Mr Bundell in the suffrage supporter's category. Beatrice nodded. 'Yes. Now, I'll make some tea
and you can tell me about your encounter with the indomitable
Charlie Marsh. We should have cake too, seeing as it's Saturday
afternoon. Incidentally, I can believe you met her in the library.
She comes to the North East regularly and people say she often
calls in. Given how often you're there, and that.' Beatrice pointed
at the pin on Ena's coat, 'I think it's inevitable the two of you
met'. Ena leant over the counter, 'you know about Charlie
Marsh?' Beatrice laughed and tapped the side of her nose. 'I
expect I know a lot more than you think, Ena.'

Back in her flat with leftover chocolate cake, Ena considered what she had learnt that day. She chastised herself for not looking beyond Beatrice's genial appearance. It turned out the matronly Mrs Bundell was a force to be reckoned with. Beatrice was a woman of independent means before she married Bartholomew. She was an accountant and Ena now knew she was responsible for the tea shop's financial affairs. 'Not just a cheery face, you see!' She winked at Ena as she studied Charlie's leaflets. 'The suffragist march on Northumberland Street in 1906; I was there.' Ena almost spat out a mouthful of tea, 'you marched?' Beatrice's face became uncharacteristically serious. 'I did.' Ena struggled to grasp this new image of Mrs Bundell. 'What was it like?' Ena remembered Clara's experience at the Mud March, the demonstration in 1907 where more than 3,000 women marched from Hyde Park Corner to the Strand in support of the suffrage movement. Clara said she returned to Mrs Newbold's drenched to the skin from the incessant rain, and delirious with excitement. During the war, the WSPU called for conscription for women, insisting female workers should enter war industries. Uncle Bertie's daredevil sister Lena joined the 1915 procession of 30,000 women who marched under the slogan, 'We Demand The Right To Serve'. As a result, more factories and businesses started hiring women. Beatrice put down her cup. 'It was frightening and exciting and one of the best things I've ever done!' Ena spoke quietly, 'why was it frightening?' Beatrice took a deep breath, 'I believe you know something about cruelty and hardship, Ena'. It was the first time either of the Bundells had referred to her brutal start in life and Ena shifted in her seat. Beatrice continued, 'as I'm sure you're aware, not everyone is in favour of women's suffrage'. Ena nodded. 'There are those who would seek to, how shall I put it, denigrate our activities. To insist we should "know our place."' Ena smiled at Beatrice's choice of words; 'our', and 'we'. She'd had an ally here without knowing it. 'Some of the po-

licemen were amiable, others noncommittal, but some were...'
Beatrice stopped. Ena met her eyes. 'It's all right, I've read about
the brutality Charlie suffered in prison. Carry on.' Beatrice took
a sip of tea and continued. 'The march started peacefully. We
sang the anthem of course, not aggressively, just loud enough to
be heard.' Ena smiled. Clara had taught her the WSPU anthem
'The March of the Women' and she knew it by heart.

'I saw a policeman grab a woman by the collar and pull her
out of the procession. He shook her and flung her to the ground,
shouting foul language in her face .' Ena raised her eyebrows,
'what did she do?' Beatrice sighed, 'sensibly, she didn't retort. She
curled herself into a ball and waited for his assault to end. A
number of us went to her aid'. Ena whispered, 'was she badly
hurt?' Beatrice shook her head, 'battered and bruised, but she
carried on'. Beatrice leant closer to Ena, 'this is one of our greatest
weapons, Ena. And it's invisible'. Ena frowned and Beatrice
smiled, 'strength, Ena. And in the face of adversity, even greater
strength'. Ena nodded. Charlie Marsh had that in abundance
and when Beatrice took some of the leaflets and said she'd like
to help with Ena's campaign, she knew she did too.

Mona

Mona's eyes widened when she read Keens' dinner menu. Tilly
insisted it was the best steakhouse in the city. When they arrived,
the suited host grinned at the sight of their new friend. 'Ms
Tucker, great to see you back at Keens!' Tilly shook the man's
hand before turning to Mona and Wilfred. 'Ned, please meet my
new English friends, Ms Mona Leighton and Mr Wilfred Henson. Ms Leighton is appearing in *Sally* at the Paradise and I have
a feeling they'll become regulars here while they're in town!'
'Delighted to meet you, folks. Let's find you a table.'

As they followed Ned through the restaurant, Mona's eyes were drawn to the clay pipes hanging on the walls. Hundreds of them. Ned laughed. 'What do you think of our collection, Ms Leighton?' Mona smiled, 'who do they belong to?' Ned stopped at a table and directed them to sit. 'Our patrons. The idea of leaving pipes here has its history in your Old England. Travellers worried that the thin stemmed pipes were too fragile to be carried on the road, would leave them at their favourite inn for safe-keeping.' Mona realised Wilfred had stopped to look more closely at some of the pipes. 'This one says it belonged to J.P. Morgan; is that true?' Ned walked over to Wilfred and pointed at the pipe. 'It is, Sir. You see how the stem has been cracked? That's what we do when a member of our Pipe Club passes away. Mr Morgan was an esteemed associate of Keens.' Wilfred nodded. 'He was a brilliant financier; a driving force behind many successful mergers and acquisitions at the turn of the century.' Ned brought Wilfred to their table. 'You work in finance yourself, Mr Henson?' Wilfred pulled out a chair next to Mona. 'I'm a bank clerk, nothing so grand as Mr Morgan.' Ned signalled for a waiter to bring menus but said they should try Keens' famous mutton chops. Tilly smoothed her napkin over her lap then picked up the menu. 'I adore this place. I wouldn't go anywhere else for steak.' Mona laughed. 'Or mutton chops!' Tilly raised her hand. 'Something Ned failed to mention was that in 1905, your Lillie Langtry took a stand for women's rights here. She walked into what was then a gentlemen's-only establishment and the waiters refused to serve her, so she sued the restaurant. She won her case and swept in here waving her feather boa before proceeding to order, guess what?' They all chorused, 'Keens famous mutton chops!'

With chops and drinks ordered, the friends relaxed. Protected by the winter night in the warm dining room, Mona and Wilfred listened as Tilly told them more of the secrets of Keens.

She said before it opened as a steakhouse in 1885, Keens was part of the Lambs Club, a famous theatre and literary group founded in London. The steakhouse soon became the favourite rendezvous of the rich and famous. 'There was a door at the back used by actors from the neighbouring Garrick Theatre. They would hurry in, wearing full stage makeup and fortify themselves between acts. A lively collection of actors and actresses, dancers, singers, producers and playwrights eat here; this is the place to be seen, darlings!'

Mona was curious about something, and before their food arrived she took the opportunity to ask Tilly why she introduced herself as Ms Tucker, not Miss. 'You introduced me as Ms Leighton too, is it an American thing?' Tilly laughed, 'we're trying hard to make it an American thing, darling! Remind me to show you a *Springfield Sunday Republican* newspaper article, it explains everything'. During their meal, Tilly asked Wilfred what had brought him to New York. 'Other than the delightful Mona, of course!' Wilfred dabbed his mouth with his napkin before speaking. 'She is delightful, but we haven't known each other very long. We met on the voyage.' Tilly raised her eyebrows, 'well blow me down, you two look so cute together!' Mona's cheeks grew warm and Wilfred cleared his throat. 'My sister's fiancé Duncan died at the end of the war. She recently received correspondence from a bank in New York saying he had bequeathed some shares to her. She asked me to come and settle the matter on her behalf.' Tilly stopped eating, her fork in the air. 'Your sister didn't want to visit New York?' 'No. I'm sad to say she still feels her fiancé's lost most keenly, all these years later. The war may be over but its effects are long-lasting. She wrote to the bank asking their permission for me to act as her advocate.' Wilfred shook his head, 'ladies, please forgive me. This is not dinner-table conversation'. Mona reached for Wilfred's hand, 'it's all right. Your sister is very lucky to have you'. Wilfred smiled, 'thank you, I think I'm the lucky one to be in such splendid company. Now, should we polish off these delicious mutton chops and see what Keens has to offer for pudding'. Tilly almost choked on her food. 'Poodin?' Mona laughed, 'it's dessert here, Wilfred'. Wilfred looked at her, 'very well, dessert it is'.

Chapter 9

Ivy

The deafening applause filled the theatre when Gwen Farrar and Norah Blaney took their final bows. Ivy tingled with excitement when people stood and showed their appreciation for the performers. Each cast member played their part; actors and actresses, comedians and musicians. Ivy was mesmerised by The Primrose Girls dance troupe. Some of their moves were extremely risqué and the audience exploded into whistles and cheers at the perfectly choreographed routines. An eccentric comedian called Herbert Mundin caused an uproar with his cheeky jokes, his character acting aided by his jowled features and cheerful disposition. Ivy felt a hand on her arm. 'Did you enjoy it?' Grace leant closer to hear her reply above the din from the stalls. 'Very much, I'm so glad Lydia suggested it.' 'Do you want to go to Teddy's club?' Ivy hesitated. When they met in the cocktail lounge, Teddy had invited them to his nightclub after the show. He'd opened the Redford two years earlier. By all accounts, the private club in a Soho basement was the place to be seen. 'We can go straight home, if you prefer?' Ivy took a deep breath. 'No, I'd like to go. But I need to visit the powder room first.' 'Alright, we'll wait for you in the foyer.'

Ivy made her way down the stairs, humming the tune to the can-can. She smiled, remembering the Primrose Girls' impressive high kicks and cartwheels. At the bottom of the stairs she held on to the last spindle and swung herself around. Her heels clicked on the marble floor of the corridor and she turned towards the powder room. She stopped suddenly; a man was blocking her way. Her stomach lurched and her breath came in quick gasps. The man smirked. 'Well, if it isn't my dear wife.' George's hissed words sent a chill up Ivy's spine. 'How good to see you, Ivy. I heard you were looking for me. Well here I am.'

Ivy stared at the man who had bullied and terrorised her. George's yellow, rheumy eyes and florid complexion told her he hadn't stopped drinking. He staggered as he stepped towards her and she moved out of his way. He raised his fist, his hands shaking. Not with anger, she realised. George was weak, a shadow of the monster she was scared of. She arranged her face and took a step towards him. The stale alcohol on his breath made her want to gag. 'I *have* been looking for you, or rather a private detective has. Rest assured, you pathetic excuse for a man, we aim to find every piece of dirt we can, and ruin your reputation in open court. I won't stop until I'm free of you.' George opened his mouth to reply but was taken by a sudden coughing fit. He bent double and Ivy swept past him. When she reached the door to the powder room she looked back; the corridor was deserted.

'Bravo, Ivy, bravo!' Daphne stood in the doorway. 'I was coming out when I witnessed your altercation with that ghastly drunk. I waited in case you needed help but boy, you did not! You put him straight! Who is he, anyway?' Ivy met Daphne's bewitching green eyes, 'my soon-to-be ex-husband, that's who'. Daphne clapped her hands. 'Excellent. Now, go and powder your pretty nose and we'll head to Teddy's. You deserve champagne after that performance!'

Inside the powder room, Ivy studied her reflection in the mirror. She reapplied her lipstick and brushed her hair, her hands steady. She smiled; she had stood up to George and taken control of the situation. He was small and insignificant. She nodded at this new powerful version of herself and went to meet her friends. By the time Ivy reached the foyer, Daphne had given the assembled group a word for word rundown of her encounter with George. 'Mark my words, friends. There was only one winner in this duel! And here she is, our conquering heroine!' Ivy accepted the cheers, handshakes and pats on the back with good humour. When they started making their way outside, Lydia waited and gestured to Ivy to join her. 'George, did he seem?' Ivy sighed. As much as it pleased her to have triumphed over George in their exchange, it saddened her to see what her husband had become. 'He was drunk and unsteady on his feet; not the man he once was.' Lydia narrowed her eyes. 'Did he reveal anything we could use in evidence?' Ivy shook her head; George's humiliation wasn't evidence. All she wanted was for everything to be settled. 'No. nothing.' Lydia shrugged. 'Never mind, we'll keep the private detective on, hopefully she'll uncover something soon.' Ivy stared. 'Did you say "she"? The private detective is a woman?"' Lydia took her arm. 'You'll like this, darling. She was an actress before the war; such a link between the professions, don't you think?' Ivy nodded, delighted at the idea of George being out-witted by a woman.

The glowing lights outside the Redford turned the pavement a murky shade of yellow as the friends made their way along Soho's Dean Street. Ivy linked arms, Grace on one side and Daphne on the other. Teddy led them to the front of the queue and once inside, directed them to the cloakroom. Hats, coats and scarves safely stored; they followed him towards a beaded curtain. Teddy stopped and turned to his friends. He put a finger to his lips. Daphne whispered to Ivy, 'when in the Redford...' Ivy raised her eyebrows. 'Enjoy yourself and cast off any inhibitions you might have.' Ivy laughed. 'I intend to!'

The beaded curtain opened onto a flight of dimly lit stairs. As they descended, heat rose from the basement club along with a heady perfume. At the bottom of the stairs a solid black door hid the club from view. Teddy knocked and Ivy heard bolts being drawn back and the door was unlocked. Daphne winked at her, 'you can't see it but there's a peephole in the door. No one gets in without Teddy's approval'. Inside, Ivy blinked to adjust her eyes to the dark. The club's interior belied its modest entrance. The lavish room boasted paintings by Auguste Renoir and Edgar Degas, and large leather sofas strewn with cushions lined the walls on both sides. Strains of a jazz band filtered into the room and Ivy looked around to see where the music was coming from. Daphne took her arm and pointed. 'Look, past the bar on the right-hand side; can you see the double doors?' Ivy narrowed her eyes and peered through the smoke. Beyond the well-stocked, gleaming bar of chrome and glass, Ivy caught glimpses of people moving to the music through the slightly open doors. 'Come on darling, let's get some champagne and dance the night away in Teddy's majestic ballroom!' When Ivy followed Daphne to the bar, she saw more of the room where people were dancing. Daphne shouted over the music to order their champagne and Ivy's foot started tapping to the energetic, jazzy rhythm of the tune the band was playing. As they waited at the bar Ivy moved her feet; a small step forward and back then a small step to the side. Daphne handed her a glass and led her towards the doors. 'Come, let's foxtrot! A wall of heat and noise hit them at the entrance to the ballroom. Plum coloured leather booths ran along both sides of the room, with a rectangular wooden dance-floor in the middle. Daphne spoke into Ivy's ear as they squeezed through the crowds. 'This way, Teddy's private booth is in the middle on the left.' Lydia and Vivienne sat close together in the booth, swaying to the music. Daphne put their drinks on the table before taking Ivy's hands and pulling her onto the dance-floor. They stepped and turned and twisted and pivoted and promenaded, singing all the while.

'Toot, Toot, Tootsie, goodbye,
Toot, Toot, Tootsie, don't cry.
That little choo, choo train that takes me,
Away from you, no words can tell how sad it makes me.
Kiss me, kiss me, Tootsie, and then oh baby, do it over again.'

Ena

Ena looked around the room, her stomach rumbling. She'd hurried to the Miner's Welfare Hall after work without eating anything. Jack had helped her set out the wooden chairs in neat rows, and he smiled up at her on the raised platform where she sat behind a small table. She picked up her papers and cleared her throat. 'I'm going to practice, before anyone arrives.' Her voice echoed in the almost empty room. Jack's voice echoed in the empty hall, 'are there enough chairs; do you know how many people are coming?' She shook her head. She'd distributed leaflets at work and Beatrice handed them out in the tea shop, but enthusiasm for the cause was mixed with caution. Women had seen what could happen when they made a stand. Ena reassured everyone she spoke to that the meeting would be peaceful; its purpose was to garner support for her proposal to the manager at the flour mill. She picked up one of her leaflets. She hadn't written anything controversial or seditious, she'd simply set out the details of the meeting and the subject. Where was the harm in that?

She looked at Beatrice, presiding over the refreshments. Her landlady and surprise suffragist had grinned when Ena asked for her help. She and Bartholomew sprang into action, producing a large tea urn and cups and saucers and Beatrice baked pound cake. Dolly's dad solved the problem of where to hold the meeting by suggesting the room at the Miner's Welfare. Now it was her responsibility to present a case the audience would support. She took a deep breath; she'd never spoken in public before. She'd practiced in front of the mirror in her flat and once with Jack and Beatrice; now the day of the meeting had arrived, she didn't know if she could go through with it. Beatrice told her to think about the suffragettes who'd changed history by speaking up, and suggested she write her speech as if she was writing a letter to her aunt. Ena cleared her throat again and started speaking. As she reached the end of her practice speech, the door opened. Two women she recognised from the flour mill stood in the doorway. Jack ushered them inside then pointed towards Beatrice and the refreshments. Ena raised a hand in acknowledgement and the women waved back. The door opened again and her legs shook when she left the platform to greet the next group of women. As more people entered the room, Ena's confidence grew. She thanked people for coming and joined Jack in directing them to Beatrice. The room buzzed with excited chatter and she checked her wristwatch. She nodded at Jack and walked to the raised platform. She picked up her papers and the room fell silent. She turned to face the audience; her papers steady. She saw Jack sitting with Dolly and her parents and Bartholomew alongside Beatrice. Dolly signed to wish her good luck and Ena signed her thanks. She knew Marty and Olive would ensure Dolly understood what was said.

'Thank you for coming. Many of you were caught up in the recent warehouse fire so I don't need to tell you how frightening it was. I've read about other mills and I think we're relatively lucky. We have our own fire brigade who responded to the emergency; many mills don't. The action we take might improve conditions for workers in other mills. Flour, in dust form, can be highly combustible; there are places where women and girls are dying due to the dust. Do you want to allow that?' Ena paused. She heard murmurs around the room and saw some people shaking their heads. She raised her voice. 'Do you?' There were shouts of 'no!' and 'of course not!' and she thanked the audience before continuing.

'An explosion occurs when a cloud of dust particles is ignited by a spark, a flame or another type of ignition. We've all seen the large clouds of flour dust in the air; inadequate ventilation makes an explosion even more likely. We all have a part to play because if we don't follow safety procedures, the risk of an explosion can be increased.' A woman at the back of the room stood up and Ena stopped speaking. 'There are no safety procedures! We do our best and use common sense, but there's nothing written down.' The woman sat and Ena thanked her. She asked if anyone agreed and the room erupted. She allowed people to have their say then held up her hands. The room quietened and Ena smiled. 'This is why we needed to come together. We agree something needs to change. We're in good company; women have been fighting inequality since long before I was born. Women's groups and trade unions encourage us to demand improvements. We must work with our managers to help them understand why we deserve to be safe, to respect what we bring to the workforce. They needed us during the war and they still need us.'

A chair scraped across the floor, setting Ena's teeth on edge. The room fell silent as the man allowed his chair to crash to the floor. He looked around then his gaze settled on Ena. He sneered. 'We don't need you; you need to get back to your house-work! Flaming suffragettes, breaking windows and setting fire to buildings!' Ena recognised the wages clerk and she bit her tongue. All eyes turned to her, waiting for a response. Before she could speak, Beatrice was on her feet. She glowered at the man. 'Don't you know the difference between suffragettes and suffrag-ists?' The man pushed out his chest. 'There's no difference, you're all the same you women, more trouble than you're worth!' Bea-trice smiled, disarming the man. She ignored him and addressed her comments to the room. 'For anyone else who might be wor-ried about violence, I can tell you from personal experience it is more likely to come from men than women. Yes, some suffra-gettes have been destructive and carried out violent acts, but suf-fragist campaigners focus on petitions, pamphlets and peaceful protest. Like our very own Ena Leighton.' She turned to the man. 'Another notable difference is suffragists allow men to join their ranks, while suffragettes do not.' Beatrice stared pointedly at the man and he stood up. 'Well I don't want to join you!' Jack held the door open and the man jostled past people as he hurried to leave. Jack closed the door behind him and Ena continued, 'as I was saying before I was rudely interrupted…' This time the interruption was laughter and cheering and Ena smiled to herself; the ignorant man had done her a favour.

Mona

After dinner at Keens, Walter went to his hotel and Mona and Tilly made their way back to Old Broadway where sleep came easily in their luxurious bedrooms. Over breakfast the next day, Tilly said she needed to run some errands and would see Mona at the Paradise that afternoon. Wilfred had a meeting at the bank, after which he'd arranged to see some of Duncan's acquaintances. Men he'd never met before who'd sent letters of condolence to Mabel. He and Mona agreed to meet for dinner the next day.

Standing on Broadway, Mona looked up at the Paradise. The theatre was as she remembered, the perfect symmetry of the arched windows and doors in the classical Beaux Arts design. Beautiful stone sculptures of the Roman goddesses Venus and Diana sat proudly above the grand entrance. She walked to the side of the building, and entered by the stage door. Inside she turned left, knowing the bright corridor would take her to the entrance hall. She reached a door at the end of the corridor and stopped. She took a deep breath. On her first visit to the Paradise, Peggy had brought her this way to show her the theatre's magnificent lobby. She reached for the door handle, her hand shaking. She was here in this lavish theatre because of Peggy. Without their chance encounter, she would have taken a job at the Casino Theatre, very much *'off-Broadway'* according to Peggy. Mona shuddered; she had stolen that job. She shook her head; she couldn't think about that now. She owed it to Peggy to make the most of her second chance. She turned the handle and exited the corridor into the marble lobby. She took in the majestic paintings and plants before turning to face the elaborate staircase. The white columns at the foot of the staircase gleamed in the morning's sunlight. Her eyes followed the beautifully sculpted detail of the ornate stairs. As she stared at the enormous crystal chandelier, a booming voice echoed around the lobby.

'Well I'll be damned!' Marv's deep American drawl boomed over the balcony. She looked up to the landing but he was already striding down the stairs towards her. He removed a fat cigar from his lips and enveloped her in his massive arms. She smelt smoke and a strong musky aftershave as he held her close. When he loosened his grip he held her at arm's length and looked her up and down. 'Gee, you look well, girl!'

Mona remembered being terrified of this bear-like man when she first met him. They'd had their differences in the past but now she felt an affection for him, a link to Peggy. 'You must miss her; I know I do.' Mona nodded and her lip trembled. She opened her mouth but no words came. Marv coughed gruffly. 'Well, this won't cut the mustard. Come on.' He gently took her arm and led her across the lobby. She concentrated on the sparkling mosaic pattern of the tiles until they reached the door to the corridor. Marv opened the door for her and she smiled up at him. 'That's more like it! That's the smile I remember; the one that wowed this theatre! Roll up folks, Ms Mona Leighton is back in town!'

Pictures of stars past and present lined the walls of the corridor leading to the dressing rooms. Mona spotted Chuck Chancer, a character in Marv's popular production, *The Night Of The Season*. The story followed the success or otherwise of a theatre group. Their trials and tribulations, romances and rivalries throughout a season, and their efforts to continue despite losing their most famous star to a rival theatre. It culminated in the triumphant return of their favourite, Lottie Linton, played by Peggy. Mona was part of the chorus line and she remembered her favourite number, a bright, cheerful song where the chorus line entered the stage on roller skates. The jingle of the bells when the line set off from the wings always made her smile. She kissed her fingertips and reached up to touch Peggy's picture. Marv pointed at the next picture. 'You didn't think much of this fella, did ya?' Mona laughed. 'No, I did not!'

Marv's next production set Mona on a downward path. Peggy had returned to London and she was struggling on her own. *Marv's Fabulous Femme Fatales* proved popular with audiences and they opened to outstanding reviews. Mona's misgivings about the show ran deep; revealing costumes and routines packed with lewd moves, but she needed the work. Marv said he wanted *'to thrill and titillate the audience, particularly the men'*. She tried to lose herself in the rhythms, to delight in being part of a chorus line performing such physical, high-energy dances, but memories of other dances in another music hall distracted her. As they had high-kicked and cartwheeled their way through the routine, a man in elegant black top hat and tails joined them. He came on at the rear and sauntered towards the front of the stage. The man in this picture; Frankie. Marv guffawed, 'you showed him what you thought!' Mona winced, remembering Frankie removing his top hat with a theatrical flourish and holding it out towards the dancers. They sashayed forward in turn, high-kicking the hat as they passed. Mona had hesitated, then the relentless choreographer motioned for her to move. She swished her skirts in time to the gallop and lifted her leg to kick the top hat. Frankie moved the hat, inch by inch, until it was above his head. His smug expression unleashed her fury, and she lifted her leg again and kicked him hard in the face. He collapsed and chaos ensued. She left the stage with her head high, pain searing through her leg to her hip.

She'd returned to the Paradise once more, following the tragic events on *Titanic*. It was their intended destination but being there alone had broken her already fragile heart. Marv and the rest of the production company also found it difficult without their star, and the show didn't run for long. She felt Marv's hand on her arm. 'That's all in the past, right?' She nodded. Marv flung open the door to one of the dressing rooms and hollered. 'Guys and gals, look who's back!'

Chapter 10

Ivy

Ivy had arranged to meet Daphne for coffee before her appointment with Lydia. After their night at Teddy's club, Ivy woke with a renewed determination to get on with her life. Daphne studied her over the rim of her coffee cup. 'Where do you think it came from, that strength you found when George confronted you?' Ivy shrugged, 'I don't know'. She tapped her fingernails on the table. 'Or perhaps I do.' Daphne raised her eyebrows. 'Do tell, darling.' 'Last night at the theatre and later at Teddy's.' 'Yes?' 'Well, it's Grace, you, Lydia, Vivienne, all of you. Making your own choices and doing what you want to do. I was like that. No, I am still like that. George took that from me but it's up to me to take it back.' Daphne clapped her hands. 'Wonderful! Now, go and see our favourite barrister and demand her wretched laws are made to work in your favour!'

Lydia came out from behind her desk and air-kissed Ivy's cheeks. 'A grand night, don't you think?' Ivy smile. 'Yes, thank you for encouraging me to rejoin society!' Lydia laughed. 'I think society had missed you. And I hope your impromptu meeting with you-know-who didn't spoil the evening?' Ivy shook her head. 'On the contrary. Seeing him again was a good thing. In my mind I'd built him up to be a monster but he looked pathetic and defenceless.' Lydia removed her spectacles. 'Don't be fooled, Ivy. However he appears to you now, George Scott-Smith *is* a monster because of his unacceptable behaviour towards you during your marriage. And my job is to defend you against him. Agreed?' Ivy nodded.

Lydia sat back in her leather chair. 'You have excellent grounds for divorce; adultery and abandonment. However, we need strong evidence to prove either one of those faults. Yes?' Ivy nodded again. This was old ground, and as frustrating now as it was when Walter first told her how difficult it would be for her to bring the action against her husband. She should be able to rid herself of George as easily as he could divorce her. 'Look out of the window, what do you see?' Ivy frowned but stood and walked to Lydia's office window. 'Well?' Ivy shrugged. 'What am I meant to be looking at?' She heard Lydia stand and walk towards her then felt the barrister's arm across her shoulders. She pointed. 'There, see?' Ivy looked in the direction of Lydia's finger. Opposite the barrister's chambers was Russell Square, a large public garden. Ivy scrutinised the garden then turned to Lydia. 'The garden?' Lydia laughed. 'The flowers, Ivy! The daffodils!' Ivy turned back to the profusion of yellow in Russell Square, still none the wiser. 'Spring is coming and then summer and what do we expect to happen this summer?' Ivy sighed, 'I don't know, Lydia. What?' Lydia clapped her hands. 'We expect the Matrimonial Causes Act to be passed, making adultery alone grounds for divorce for either spouse. This puts you on an equal footing with him, Ivy.'

Ivy sighed and sat. 'I know that's significant progress, but we still need evidence. Either of his adultery or of him being a bigamist.' Lydia tapped her spectacles on the desk. 'How confident are you that he was unfaithful?' Ivy closed her eyes. The smell of stale perfume on her husband's clothes, his unexplained disappearances and secretive behaviour. She opened her eyes. 'I'm confident.' Lydia leant across the desk. 'You know there are ways of ending a mutually unacceptable marriage?' Ivy shook her head. 'You mean arranging for him to be caught in a compromising situation with another woman?' Lydia nodded. 'I know it's tasteless, yet it might be a way to achieve what you want. It's my job to set out all possible options.' Ivy rubbed the back of her neck. 'No. That would be letting him off too easily.' Lydia picked up her pen. 'Very well. I'll put the private detective on 24-hour duty outside George's address until she sees something we can use. Now, tell me how your job search is going.'

Vernon

Vernon had mixed feelings about visiting his brother's grave. He came for their mother, who found it too overwhelming. He cleaned and polished the headstone then arranged a bunch of daffodils in the small flower pot at the base of the grave. He brushed his hand across his brother's name.

In loving memory of a dear son and brother, Private Albert Revill 1st January 1891 – 1st December 1918, died from his injuries, served with valour.

When Vernon learnt his brother was at Endell Street Military Hospital, he ran to be with him. Vernon considered himself lucky, he was one of *Titanic's* few survivors. When war broke out he signed up and his regiment was dispatched to France. Four years later he had witnessed more horror than he wanted to remember, but he came home, alive and relatively unscathed. His mother believed he had been saved for some greater purpose and when they received word of Albert, Vernon knew what it was. His brother lost his legs, his sight and his soul during the war. He visited Albert regularly and was delighted when the doctor said he could take him home. The doctor apologised, saying they had done everything possible, sadly it was unlikely Albert's condition would improve. Vernon and his mother cared for Albert the best they could, but the war had already taken him. One night Albert went to sleep and didn't wake up. Vernon continued to visit Endell Street after his brother died and he tried to do his best for other wounded soldiers. He looked up; rows and rows of lives lost. Such a waste. He stood and rubbed the dirt from his hands.

When he left the graveyard, he crossed the road and walked to the Poetry Bookshop. It opened the year before the war began and the welcoming atmosphere made it one of his favourite places to visit. He pushed the door and the bell tinkled above his head. A man's cheery voice called from the back of the shop. 'Be with you momentarily, please browse to your heart's content.' Vernon called back. 'Thank you Harold, I will.' Vernon heard Harold chuckle. Harold Monro sold and published poetry and readers were encouraged to spend time in the shop. Poets were often ensconced there, chatting to Harold or sitting writing in one of the big, comfortable armchairs positioned on either side of the roaring fire. During the war, when Harold was serving in the armed forces, the shop was run by his assistant, Alida Klementaski. Harold and Alida got married after the war and continued to run the bookshop together.

'Ah, my good man, I thought it was you.' Harold wandered into the shop, his angular nose in a book. 'How are you?' The men shook hands and Vernon explained he'd been visiting his brother's grave. Harold put his hand on Vernon's shoulder and led him to one of the armchairs. 'Let me show you something our friend Robert is working on.' Vernon sank into the chair and Harold handed him a sheet of paper. The title of the poem was 'Nothing Gold Can Stay'. As Vernon started to read, the bell above the door rang. He looked up, thinking about the first line of Robert Frost's new poem. *'Nature's first green is gold, her hardest hue to hold.'* The woman took a step into the shop then stopped. She smiled and her piercing blue eyes shone. Eyes he'd never forgotten; eyes exactly like her sister Mona's.

Ena

When the meeting ended, Jack stayed behind to help Ena put the chairs away. Along with the Turnbulls and the Bundells, they made short work of clearing up. Beatrice and Ena handed out pieces of pound cake for people to enjoy as they worked. 'This last piece is yours, Ena.' Beatrice handed Ena the cake, wrapped in greaseproof paper. 'Thank you, I'll take it home for supper.' Beatrice touched her arm. 'No, you should eat it now. You've had nothing since you finished work.' Ena smiled, 'I know, but my hunger has disappeared. I think it's the excitement of the evening!' Beatrice laughed. 'Yes, I don't think we'll see that angry man again in a hurry!' Ena sighed. 'Unfortunately, I'll see him all too soon at work.' Beatrice tutted. 'It's so frustrating that some people fail to see the invaluable contribution women can make.' Ena pursed her lips. 'Or deliberately refuse to see it?' Beatrice stopped what she was doing, 'what can we do about him?' Ena shrugged, 'perhaps we don't need to do anything. If the management agree to improve safety at the flour mill, we will have achieved our objective'. Beatrice put her head on one side. 'And equal pay?' Ena smiled, 'I think that's a fight for another day, don't you?'

After everyone else left, Ena and Jack sat together on the edge of the raised platform. Jack reached for Ena's hand. 'I was very proud of you tonight.' She laughed, 'I was terrified!' He raised his eyebrows. 'You seemed very calm.' She tapped the side of her nose before standing and stepping up onto the platform. 'You see this table?' He nodded. 'There was a cloth over it earlier.' Jack said he hadn't noticed. 'Beatrice put it there before anyone arrived. Watch.' Ena stood behind the table and pointed at her legs. 'You couldn't see my legs when I was speaking, but I was shaking like a leaf!' He smiled. 'Beatrice knows what she's doing, doesn't she?' Ena nodded, 'she certainly does'.

When Ena opened her front door, two white envelopes lay on the mat. She looked at the handwriting and a warmth spread through her, like comforting arms. Upstairs, with her slippers on and cocoa made, she opened Aunt Ivy's letter. When Beatrice suggested she should write her speech as a letter to her aunt, she went one step further and sent it to her. She was excited to see what she thought of it.

'My dear girl,

How proud I was to read your speech. I think by now your meeting will have taken place; I hope it was everything you wanted. With your words, I'm sure you'll have won your colleagues support for such an important cause. Safe working conditions are essential and employers must be made to recognise that. You know to your cost, there are those in life who seek to keep women down and debase our actions. With young women like you taking up the mantle, I'm confident for our future success. We've achieved much but we must continue.

I met with my formidable barrister earlier this week. Lydia is a woman who will fight until she draws her last breath; she's exactly who I need to rid myself of George. I hope to be divorced from that awful man by the end of the year.

I visited the theatre with Grace and Walter recently, we saw a colourful revue called Rats! It reminded me of my love for performing and I intend to look for opportunities in the theatrical magazines. I think it would do me good to be back on stage.

I was delighted to receive an invitation to Rachel's wedding in Bournemouth. I know we suffered immense loss when we lived there; we also made steadfast, loving, friendships. I know Meta Leaman treated you like another daughter and I'll be eternally grateful to her for that. Perhaps we can arrange to travel together from London? Write soon with news of your meeting and plans for the grand wedding.

Your loving aunt, Ivy.

P.S. I enclose an article I read recently; I think you'll find it interesting!'

Ena unfolded the *Time and Tide* magazine article. Her aunt had written a note at the top. 'Something you might want to consider!' Ena smiled; she could always rely on her aunt to further their cause.

The use of Ms. as a title was first proposed in 1901 in the American Springfield Sunday Republican. Time and Tide is disappointed but not surprised to discover the item made only a minor splash, getting picked up and discussed over the course of a few weeks in other newspapers around the country, before the proposal faded from the public eye. The article advocated for a mechanism to address a woman without reference to her domestic situation. Fortunately, we no longer live in a world where a woman's worth is defined by her husband or lack thereof. To call a maiden Mrs. is only a shade worse than to insult a matron with the inferior title Miss. Yet it is not always easy to know the facts. How to avoid this potential social faux pas? The writer suggested 'a more comprehensive term which pays homage to the sex without expressing any views as to their domestic situation', namely, Ms. with this 'simple' and 'easy to write' title, a tactfully ambiguous compromise between Miss and Mrs., 'the person concerned can translate it properly according to their circumstances'. Time and Tide calls for its readers to consider this proposal.

Aunt Ivy's words about their time in Bournemouth rang in her ears. Their first years there were the happiest of Ena's life, before the war changed everything. She and Aunt Ivy kept themselves busy after Uncle Bertie's departure. She didn't allow herself to imagine he wouldn't return. When the news came, her world was destroyed. She hadn't thought her aunt would ever recover, but despite their own loss the Leamans rallied round. Together, they survived the darkest days of their lives and now there was a reason to celebrate. She turned to the second envelope, smiling at the neat handwriting on Rachel's invitation.

MR AND MRS EDWIN LEAMAN
EXTEND AN INVITATION TO THE MARRIAGE OF
THEIR DAUGHTER RACHEL
TO MR WILLIAM LOVE
TUESDAY, JULY TWENTY-FOURTH
NINETEEN HUNDRED AND TWENTY-THREE
ONE O'CLOCK IN THE AFTERNOON
IN THE GARDENS OF
THE RICHMOND PARK SYNAGOGUE,
BOURNEMOUTH

Rachel had included a letter.

'Dear Ena,

I am delighted to send you and Jack this invitation to my wedding. I am looking forward with great excitement to being called "Mrs Love"! You know William is not of the Jewish faith; this means our ceremony is a little different, including not being able to have it inside the synagogue. However, the gardens are magnificent and I feel no sense of loss or being second-best by this situation. William's father and mine are working to construct a beautiful white bridal canopy, beneath which our marriage ceremony will be conducted. I dearly hope you'll be allowed time off work to attend. In our history, the third day of the week was considered a particularly auspicious day for a wedding; in the account of the third day of creation, the phrase "and God saw that it was good", appears twice. This means Tuesday is a doubly good day for a wedding!

Your very dearest friend, now and always.

Rachel.'"

Ena slept soundly that night. In her mind she set out two letters; one about improved safety at the flour mill, the other a polite request for time off to attend Rachel's wedding.

Mona

Once the fuss ended, Mona moved around the dressing room, greeting old acquaintances and meeting the new additions to Marv's company. Thankfully, there was no sign of the odious Frankie. Marv rapped his knuckles on the dressing table. 'Ok folks, now you've said your howdies, let's get down to business!' The room fell silent as Marv held court. 'Who here has heard of *Sally*?' The room erupted with shouts and cheers until Marv lifted his hands. 'Ok, I guess that's everyone! Our *Sally* will be the best *Sally* New York City has ever seen!'" More whoops and hollers followed until Marv called for quiet. 'Now, you've seen that our favourite English performer has returned to us. Ms Mona Leighton needs no further introduction, guys and gals, she is our *Sally*!' Marv looked at Mona and she performed a little curtsy. She quickly cast her eyes around the room but all she saw were smiles and nods of approval. For some of them, Peggy had been their favourite English performer and she always would be. If there were reservations about Mona's rise to prominence, no one voiced them.

'So, what's it about, this *Sally*? Well, the plot hinges on a mistaken identity; Sally, a waif, is a dishwasher at the Alley Inn in New York City. She poses as a famous foreign ballerina, rising to fame (and finding love) through joining the Ziegfeld Follies. It's a rags to riches story with a ballet for the centrepiece, and a wedding for the finale. Sound good?' Everyone agreed but the chatter stopped suddenly with Marv's next words. 'Ok, this is a big production and I need you here, all day and every day, until I'm satisfied you're good enough. And I'm still holding auditions, so y'all better be at the top of your game! Got that?' Marv's eyes swept the room, capturing the reluctant nods and half-smiles. When Marv was looking the other way, Mona glanced at her wristwatch. She had arranged to meet Wilfred and she didn't want to be late.

Chapter 11

Ivy

Ivy stared at the man sitting in the Poetry Bookshop. Vernon got up and walked towards her, smiling. 'Ivy, what a wonderful surprise.' Ivy held out her hand. As she did, Vernon moved closer and air-kissed her cheeks. She laughed nervously and dropped her hand. Vernon apologised and an awkward silence followed. Into the silence stepped Harold Monro, brandishing a volume of poetry. 'Vernon, please do introduce me to your friend.' Ivy saw relief cross Vernon's face as he made the introductions. 'And how do you two know each other?' Harold's question returned them to silence until Vernon spoke. 'Ivy worked at Endell Street during the war. My brother was a patient there.' Ivy smiled at her friend; grateful he'd given Harold the less-complicated version of their acquaintance. Endell Street was where they'd met, but there was more he could have said. Apparently satisfied, Harold went to make tea and Vernon gestured to the armchairs on either side of the fire.

Ivy pointed at the sheet of paper Vernon had placed on the table next to the armchair. 'What were you reading when I came in?' Vernon handed her the paper. 'It's something Robert Frost is working on.' Ivy raised her eyebrows. 'And you've seen it before it's published?' Vernon nodded, 'Harold is a wonderful benefactor and supporter of poetry; he publishes and sells it'. Ivy handed the paper back, her eyes glistening. 'He's saying the most beautiful things are the briefest. I'm sorry, I didn't mean to intrude.' Vernon shook his head. 'It's all right. I was feeling sorry for myself after visiting my brother's grave and Harold gave me this to read.' Ivy smiled, 'couldn't he have chosen something cheerful?' They both started to laugh and Harold joined in when he reappeared with tea and biscuits. 'Laughter is exactly what he needed, Ms Leighton.'

Ivy looked at Vernon over the rim of her teacup. He seemed the same, as if no time had passed. They'd met five years ago, in the strangest circumstances. Vernon told Harold they met at Endell Street and that was true; the full nature of their connection wasn't clear for some time. She learnt later Vernon thought he recognised her, but it was Mona he'd met. On *Titanic*. He said he returned to the hospital hoping to see her and learnt she was away on her honeymoon. Ivy smiled at him now. 'The note you left me changed everything.' Vernon shook his head, 'you must have thought it odd, a complete stranger leaving you his address'. Ivy nodded, 'I did, but I was also curious'. Vernon sipped his tea. 'I didn't understand our connection at that point, yet I believed we had one.' Ivy smiled, 'I was cautious about meeting you'. She stopped then took a deep breath and spoke quickly. 'I was having a difficult time in my marriage; unsure who I could trust.' Vernon leant forward and spoke quietly. 'I'm very sorry to hear that, Ivy.'

She remembered plucking up the courage to go to his mother's house in Highgate. She'd hesitated, but her friend and fellow nurse Victoria said Vernon was compassionate towards many of their injured soldiers, particularly those other visitors chose not to talk to. Ivy smiled, remembering the warmth of Irene Revill's home, her welcome despite her own sadness. Their connection was Mona. She and Vernon had met on *Titanic* where he was a ship's steward. Miraculously, they both survived and thanks to letters Mona wrote to Vernon, she and Ivy were reunited. Without Vernon, Ivy might still be looking for her sister now. 'How is she, your sister?' Ivy laughed. 'How much time do you have?'

Ena

Ena stood at the window, watching the deliveries coming and going. She tapped her fingers on the window sill. Behind her, Jack sighed. 'What is it?' She shook her head. 'Nothing.' Jack walked across the office. 'You still haven't had a reply?' 'No, and I can't keep Rachel waiting much longer. She needs to know if I can go to her wedding.' Jack was silent away and Ena narrowed her eyes. 'Have you been told you can have the time off?' Jack studied his shoes. 'I'm sorry, I didn't know how to tell you. I was hoping you would get it too.' Ena sighed. 'You know what this is about, don't you? Not time off to attend my best friend's wedding, it's about my request for safer working conditions.' Jack hesitated. 'You don't know that for certain, do you?' 'It's something of a coincidence though, isn't it?' Jack nodded slowly. 'What will you do?' Ena narrowed her eyes. 'Stop waiting, that's what.'

With each step, she rehearsed. She knew the words in the letter she had sent to Mr Young by heart, and she repeated them to herself as she thumped down the stairs. Beatrice had helped her to compose the letter and Jack looked at it before she left it on Mr Young's desk. Marked private and confidential, Ena believed her letter made the case for improved safety measures in a clear and compelling way. Initially, she listed the faults and inadequacies with the current safety measures but Beatrice advised her against that approach. 'Better to identify one significant improvement and ask for it. What's the one thing you think would make a difference?' Ena had stared at her list, unable to pin-point one thing. 'Picture the meeting; what immediately springs to mind?' Ena saw the rows of women in the hall. An image of the irate wages clerk hovered and she pushed it away. She turned to Beatrice. 'Two things.' 'What are they?' 'Inadequate ventilation and no written safety procedures.' 'Very well, ask for them to be improved.' 'As simply as that?' 'Yes, don't give them a reason to say they don't understand what you want. Write it as you would to a child.' Ena laughed and started writing.

At the bottom of the stairs she turned right. Mr Young's office was immediately in front of her. She saw two figures through the frosted glass, and her heart sank when the door opened and Mr Young shook the hand of the wages clerk. 'Thank you for coming to me with your concerns.' The man gave Mr Young a strange half-bow and Ena cringed. His obsequious smile made her stomach turn as he crept away. She stared at Mr Young, was she too late? 'Ah, Miss Leighton, how fortuitous. Do come in and take a seat.'

'It's Ms.' The words were out before she could stop them. She wanted to kick herself but Mr Young's eyes were steady. He straightened a pile of papers on his desk and cleared his throat. She was expecting to be fired or at the very least, demoted. Her head pounded and her throat was dry. Mr Young picked up the top sheet of paper and Ena's heart hammered against her chest when she recognised her own handwriting. 'Your letter.' She opened her mouth and managed a croaked, 'yes'. 'You do realise not everyone is in favour of these proposals?' Ena sighed; the hateful wages clerk had beaten her to it. By stating his case to Mr Young first he'd put her on the backfoot. Then she pictured Beatrice standing up to him at the meeting and her confidence grew. She needed to make the most of this opportunity. 'I do, and I appreciate people are entitled to hold different opinions.' She sat up straight in her chair. 'However, even those not in favour of these proposals will benefit from their introduction.' Mr Young raised his eyebrows as she continued. 'With written safety procedures everyone will understand their individual and collective responsibilities, should an emergency arise. And with better ventilation, the number of emergencies must surely decrease.' Ena took a breath and Mr Young filled the space with a question. 'Can you write them?' Ena blinked. 'I beg your pardon?' 'The new safety procedures, can you write them?' Ena spoke clearly. 'I can.' She heard a rumbling noise outside and Mr Young looked towards the window. 'Perfect timing.' Ena craned her neck to try and see what was happening. Mr Young stood and gestured for her to follow him to the window. 'It's the company who are installing the new ventilation system. You put your case across very well.' Ena watched the equipment being unloaded then back to Mr Young. He extended his hand and she shook it firmly. 'Thank you, Mr Young.' He opened the door to see her out. 'Oh, I hope you enjoy your trip to Bournemouth to attend your friend's wedding.' Ena almost tripped over her own feet in surprise. She turned back. 'Thank you.' He smiled, 'you're welcome, *Ms* Leighton.'

Mona

The group that left the Paradise later were very different to the enthusiastic, cheerful recipients of Marv's news about their new production. The director started with 'exercises to make sure you're all in good shape!' Some of the younger members of the company and those who'd performed rigorous routines more recently approached the exercises with gusto. Others, including Mona, struggled. Her work in repertory theatre had involved more sedate musical numbers without a cartwheel or high-kick in sight. When they were released, she moved carefully and slowly towards the stage door. Tilly called to her to wait and she took the opportunity to rest. She leant against the wall and closed her eyes. Pain shot up her right leg and into the small of her back and she adjusted her position. Salty tears stung her cheeks and she rubbed her face with her hands.

'Gee honey, what's up?' Tilly held her arms, concern etched across her face. Mona ran a hand across her forehead. 'Nothing, I'm just tired.' Tilly started leading her towards the stage door. 'I know what you need, a pick-me-up!' Mona shook her head. 'I need to go back to the apartment and sleep.' Tilly studied her friend. 'Don't you have plans to meet Wilfred?' Mona sighed. 'Yes, and I don't want to let him down but I'm exhausted.' Tilly nodded. 'Should I call his hotel and leave a message with reception?' Mona managed a smile. 'Would you?' Tilly put an arm across Mona's shoulders and they walked outside. 'Of course darling, leave it with me.' As the door was closing, Marv's familiar boom reached them. 'Tilly Tucker, are you still in the building?' Tilly laughed. 'I'd better see what he wants. I'll catch you up.' Mona stepped into the street. Behind her, Tilly called out. She turned and saw her friend's manicured hand moving in the air as if conducting a piece of music. 'Remember darling, 'Look for the Silver Lining!' Despite her pain, Mona smiled. After the torturous exercises, the director insisted on setting out the choreography for one of the show's songs. She pulled her coat tighter and made her way to the apartment, singing to herself.

'Look for the silver lining,
Whene'er a cloud appears in the blue.
Remember, somewhere the sun is shining,
And so the right thing to do,
Is make it shine for you.
A heart full of joy and gladness,
Will always banish sadness and strife,
So always look for the silver lining,
And try to find the sunny side of life.'

With each step she winced. Had she made a terrible mistake in coming back? Then she thought about her new, unexpected friendship with Tilly and her growing fondness for Wilfred. She could see Old Broadway a few blocks away and she carried on.

*

Tilly pulled the stage door shut behind her. She knew the image Marv liked to portray, how he wanted his performers to see him. The big, brusque New-Yorker who would fire them in the blink of an eye if he saw fit. She also knew the real Marv, where he came from and the reason for his tough-guy image. He'd called her back inside to ask how Mona was, if Tilly thought she was up to the show. Tilly would never tell anyone, but Marv cared. A woman bumped into her as she started walking along the street. 'Gee I'm sorry, I didn't see you.' The woman re-arranged her scarf around her neck before meeting Tilly's eyes. 'It's all right, I wasn't watching where I was going. I'm looking for the stage door of the Paradise.' Tilly laughed. 'You've found it honey, right there! Are you here for the auditions?' The woman nodded. 'Go right on in and ask for Marv. Show him what you're made of!' The woman smiled but her eyes were steely. Tilly shrugged and turned away.

Chapter 12

Bournemouth
Monday 23rd of July 1923

Ena and Jack travelled to Bournemouth with Ivy, Grace and Walter. They had taken the train from Newcastle to London the previous day, ready to make an early start on Monday. Ivy wrote to say Walter had booked and paid for their train tickets. Jack objected, saying he wanted to cover the cost, but he reluctantly agreed when Ena showed him Ivy's letter.

'...I'm sure Jack will disagree, please explain this is something Walter feels very strongly about. He knows the losses we have all suffered in recent years and he wants to ensure we have a wonderful, carefree trip. Travelling first-class is part of that.'

Warmth from the summer sunrise filtered into Waterloo Station as Ena and Jack made their way through the throng of travellers. Ena spotted Ivy, beautifully dressed in a fitted white jacket and straight black skirt. Her white linen cloche hat was decorated with a lace band and a silk flower on one side. Ena's heart soared at the sight of her aunt. Ivy turned when they approached and Ena flew into her arms. 'My dear niece, how I've missed you.' Ivy reached out a hand to Jack. 'I'm delighted to see you again, Jack. It's been a long time. How is your uncle?' Jack took Ivy's hand and moved closer. 'He's very well and he asked me to give you his best wishes.' Ivy smiled, 'John Todd, the Gateshead postman with the big heart'. Jack nodded, 'he is that'. As Ena introduced Jack to Grace and Walter, an announcement informed them of the platform their train was scheduled to depart from. Walter signalled for a porter to take their luggage and they made their way to the platform. Ivy linked her arm through Ena's and Jack walked alongside, his head held high.

The elegance of their first-class compartment took Ena's breath away. There was plenty of room for the five of them and they made themselves comfortable on the luxurious upholstery. Ena removed her hat and coat then ran her hand along the red and gold padded cushion before sitting down. Walter cleared his throat. 'When everyone is hungry, we can visit the dining car.' He sat closest to the window; his long legs stretched out in front of him. Ena smiled at the man who had so generously arranged their trip. She knew he and Grace had helped her aunt in many ways over the years, including finding the brilliant Lydia Stamp. Her aunt leant closer and Ena smelt jasmine, rose, vanilla and sandalwood. 'That perfume is beautifully sweet; what is it?' Ivy held out her wrist and Ena breathed deeply. 'It's called Chanel No. 5. I read that Coco Chanel decided to launch a scent for new, modern women. Her mother was a laundrywoman and she was brought up with the smell of soap and freshly-scrubbed skin. Apparently, she arranged to have ten samples of scent produced by a perfumier called Ernest Beaux in Grasse, France. They were numbered one to five and 20 to 24. She picked No. 5.' Ena nodded, 'she made a good choice'.

'Tell me what happened at work, Ena. In your last letter you said you thought the weaselly-sounding wages clerk had got to the manager before you. Ena grinned, 'when I saw him coming out of Mr Young's office I thought the worst. But he was either there for a different reason or Mr Young saw through him. Either way, he agreed to our proposals. Ivy smiled, 'what, no argument?' Ena laughed. 'I suspect wheels were already in motion, but when he saw the strength of feeling among the workforce he took action.' Ivy patted Ena's hand. 'You made that happen, Ena. Bravo.' Ena shook her head. 'It wasn't just me; I had a lot of support.' Ivy looked around the carriage. 'We all need it, my dear. If you continue to fight injustice as I think you will, you'll come up against other detractors. You'll need your friends and you'll need…', Ivy gestured towards Jack and Ena took her fiancé's hand. 'I've always needed Jack.' Jack squeezed Ena's hand. 'And I you.'

Over lunch, Ena asked Ivy about Vernon. Her aunt had mentioned him during the journey and Ena was curious. 'Where did you meet him, this Vernon?' Ivy stopped eating and met Ena's eyes. 'I met him through your mother.' Ena frowned; her aunt didn't often mention her sister. 'Do you still want to know?' Ena nodded. Ivy explained Vernon met Mona on *Titanic*. 'Isn't it miraculous that of 2,224 souls on board, only 735 survived and two of them were Vernon and your mother?' Ena shrugged; her mother's ability to emerge unscathed from such a tragedy was uncanny. And having had a horrific near-death experience, did she make it a priority to be reunited with her daughter? No. Ena sighed; 'yes, I suppose so'. Ivy continued, explaining about Endell Street and the letters Mona wrote to Vernon. 'He was very kind; he could have ignored the similarities between me and your mother and written them off as coincidence. Vernon is a clever man; he suspected there was a connection. Until that day, I believed Mona was dead.' Ivy took a deep breath and reached for Ena's hand. 'I know your mother has disappointed you, but I believe she has a good heart. Perhaps you can find some compassion for her in yours?' Ena put her head on one side. 'Perhaps. Tell me more about Vernon.' Ivy leant across the table in the dining carriage; her eyes bright. 'I was surprised to learn how much we have in common. When I saw him by chance most recently, he was in the Poetry Bookshop on Devonshire Street. Imagine meeting someone who loves poetry or books as much as you do?' Ena smiled; she couldn't remember when she'd last seen her aunt so cheerful, Vernon brought out the best in her.

When Bournemouth Central Station came into view, a high-pitched whistle signalled their arrival. Ena gazed at the colourful floral displays stretching along the length of the platform. She remembered another arrival, when Uncle Bertie was waiting to meet them. She caught her aunt's eye and smiled sadly. Then the sadness was gone, replaced by a cheery announcement. 'Come along, everyone; Bertie's sister Lena will be waiting to meet us!'

Lansdowne Road

Bertie's eldest sister waited for them outside the station. The statuesque Lena Primavesi leant against her motor car, one foot resting on the black running board. Elegantly clad in a dark blue chauffeur's uniform, she strode towards them and doffed her cap. Ivy embraced her. 'Lena! How good to see you. I adore the outfit!' Lena jangled her car keys. 'Well I thought I'd better look the part! Now, I know Walter, so you must be Jack.' Lena pumped Jack's hand. 'It's great to meet you at last.' Jack smiled, 'likewise, thank you for being our chauffeur'. Lena laughed. 'My pleasure. Let's get your luggage loaded and head home. Mother and Father can't wait to see you all.'

Walter and Jack helped Lena fit their luggage into her car and they climbed inside. Before she put the key in the ignition, Lena turned to her passengers. 'Is everybody comfortable?' Murmurs of assent filled the car and Lena ran a gloved hand along her seat. The black leather upholstery gleamed and Lena nodded. 'She's a beauty, the 1922 Packard Series 126, with plenty of room for you all! And, the *pièce de résistance?*' Lena jumped out of the car and reached up to the roof. With a few clicks and a folding motion, the canvas top was rolled back to create an open-air driving experience. Lena sat in the driver's seat and started the ignition. 'Let's hope it doesn't rain!'

When they reached Lansdowne Road, Ena looked at her aunt. She remembered the first time Aunt Ivy brought her here to meet Uncle Bertie's family. Ena, still emotionally scarred from living with Lizzie, hadn't known what to expect. She had watched Catherine Primavesi, Bertie's mother, walk up the garden path before embracing Aunt Ivy. She soon realised this elegant, generous, sophisticated woman was the polar opposite of Lizzie. Years later, Catherine's shiny coils of dark-brown hair wound at the back of her head were shot through with grey, but her warm smile and kind eyes were the same. Catherine waited in the doorway and as Ena got closer, the familiar wave of sweet, lemony cologne reached her. 'Ena, how delightful to see you again, my dear.' Ena embraced Catherine and thanked her. 'You must all be thirsty after your journey. Come in and we'll have some tea.'

The house was as Ena remembered, the front door opening onto a long, bright hallway with a high ceiling. A man stood at the foot of the curved staircase. Bertie's father, Giulio Cesare Primavesi, or 'Julius Caesar' as Ena had called him when she was a teenager. Lines cut through his ruddy cheeks and his bushy moustache and eyebrows were white as snow. He stepped towards her, his bright eyes sparkling. 'Dearest Ena, welcome back into our home.' Ena embraced Bertie's father and whispered into his ear. 'Dear Julius Caesar, I'm delighted to be back.' Giulio laughed and hugged Ena a little tighter. When Catherine directed them towards the lounge, Bertie's other sisters appeared at the top of the stairs. Isabel and Gertrude shouted their hellos and hurried down to greet everyone. Ena looked around; they'd all seen so much sadness, but today, cheerful noise and laughter filled 75, Lansdowne Road.

Over tea and cake Ena learnt that Bertie's brother Leo had returned to the Air Force. He was an instructor, training new recruits and pilots. Unfortunately, he hadn't been able to take time off from his job at the Central Flying School in Wiltshire to attend Rachel's wedding. When Catherine was talking about Leo, Ena watched her aunt. It was Leo who told Ivy the truth about George. As Ivy slowly convalesced from the Spanish flu, she learnt to live with her grief at losing Bertie and her shame in marrying George. When summer made an appearance in the garden, Ena had suggested they should have a picnic. That was the last time they were together. At the picnic Leo told Ivy he knew George. He said the man she knew as Squadron Leader George Scott-Smith was the lowest ranked Warrant Officer in the RAF. He and his fellow airmen were warned to avoid him. When Ivy asked why, Leo explained George was a known con man, a gambler and fraud who tried to borrow money from anyone he could start a conversation with. When Leo exposed George's lies, the picnic fell silent. George's claim of being a barrister was discredited when the private detective Walter hired found no trace of him anywhere in the legal profession. Now, looking at her aunt in conversation with Bertie's mother, Ena longed for better news from Lydia's private detective, something that would free Ivy from George forever.

Ena studied Bertie's sisters. Lena, Isabel and Gertrude were deep in conversation and Ena remembered how excited she was when they talked to her about the suffrage movement. They helped her to realise that women could do anything, if they were determined enough. Lena looked at her, 'Ena, we've heard about your campaign at work. Well done for standing up for what's right!' Ena's cheeks grew warm when the sisters turned to her. 'What's next for our Geordie suffragist?' Ena smiled, proud of the nickname the sisters had given her years ago. She sat up straight and spoke clearly. 'Equal pay for women!' Everyone cheered and raised their tea cups in agreement.

'Grace, we read your reviews regularly and are so proud to say we know you. What are you rehearsing for now *The Cabaret Girl* has ended?' Catherine Primavesi was the perfect hostess, skilled at ensuring everyone was included in conversation. Grace, their stunning star of the show on any given stage was happy to sit quietly in company, allowing others their moment. She came to life when Catherine asked about her career. 'I've started rehearsals for a new show called *The Street Singer.*' 'Can you tell us anything, or is it under wraps?' Grace touched a beautifully manicured finger to her lips. 'I'll have to swear you to secrecy if I tell you!' Catherine laughed. 'My lips are sealed.' Grace nodded. 'Very well. It's the story of the Duchess of Versailles who falls in love with a poor and untalented artist named Bonni. She disguises herself as a street singer in order to meet the artist and by the end of the first act they are a couple. Through an art dealer, she proceeds to buy Bonni's pictures.' Grace stopped. Catherine motioned for her to continue and Grace shook her head. 'No, you'll have to come up to London and see the show. I'll reserve a box for you!' Catherine looked across the table at her husband. 'What do you think, Giulio? We haven't been to London for a long time.' Giulio twirled the end of his moustache. 'Well how can we ignore a personal invitation from the one and only Lady Grace Opal?' Catherine clapped her hands and looked around the table. 'We should all go!'

When they finished their tea and cake, Lena offered to drive them to their hotel. Rachel had told Ena there was a meal the night before the wedding, to which they were all invited. The meal, called the Shabbat Kallah, was a joyful occasion where family and friends gathered to celebrate the upcoming wedding. Rachel said some of the religious aspects would be omitted, but they were having a kosher feast followed by singing and dancing. They had been asked to arrive at the East Cliff Hotel by 7 o' clock that evening and Lena shepherded them to her car, determined not to be late.

The hotel sat proudly at the top of the cliffs overlooking Bournemouth's breathtaking coastline. Ena breathed deeply, the tangy air making her tongue tingle. She linked her arm through Jack's as they walked towards the entrance. 'I can't wait for you to meet Rachel.' Jack smiled, 'I'm looking forward to meeting her too, and William.' Pink and white roses and lilies curled round the steps up to the entrance and cascaded from the hotel doors. Their scent led them into the marble lobby where Rachel and William waited to greet them. Ena fell into Rachel's arms, immediately transported to their girlhood friendship. Grinning, Ena introduced Jack to Rachel and William before turning to her friend. 'Can you believe you're getting married?' Rachel laughed. 'I know, and you'll be next!'

Ena saw a woman standing behind Rachel and she hurried towards her. Rachel's mother, Meta Leaman, opened her arms. 'My other daughter, how I have missed you.' Ena blinked back tears, remembering Meta's warmth the first time they met. Her smile sent Ena back in time; to being surrounded by a love so strong she could hardly breathe, to safety, to a feeling of family. Ena was happy to call Meta '*Ma*', after all, her own mother was nowhere to be seen. When Aunt Ivy was offered a job at Endell Street during the war, both Catherine Primavesi and Meta Leaman said they were happy for Ena to stay with them. She chose the Leamans. Meta smiled, 'this is such a joyous occasion, isn't it?' Ena agreed but saw the deep-seated sadness lurking beneath Meta's smile. 'He would have been delighted to see his sister so happy.' Meta nodded. 'He was such a generous young man.' Ena pictured Donovan, Rachel's brother with the mischievous smile. At 16, Donovan wasn't old enough to sign up but he was determined to follow his elder brother Cyril and do his duty. Ena hadn't acknowledged the strength of her feelings for Donovan until Rachel told her he'd disappeared. She was in love with Rachel's fearless, stubborn brother and his letters told her he felt the same. If he'd survived the war, would the pull to return to Gateshead have been so strong? In his final letter he encouraged her to live. To find Jack, or someone else who made her happy. To find the pretty village she dreamt of and her house with a garden. He told her to live well, to make sure there was a point to the madness of the war. He said to do it for him and those who wouldn't return. She watched Jack, deep in conversation with William. She had loved Jack since childhood. She would never know if her love for Donovan would have withstood the horrors of war. She looked around the room, picturing the people who were missing; Uncle Bertie, Donovan and her mother. Then she counted her family, gathered to wish Rachel and William well. Aunt Ivy, her only blood relative; the others hers by marriage, chance or circumstance. People who'd known horrific loss but who loved her and would support her no matter what. And Jack, the boy who'd helped her and now the man she was going to marry.

Chapter 13

Tuesday 24th of July 1923
Wedding Day

Ena took her time on the familiar walk to Capstone Road. She had agreed to help Rachel get ready then travel to the wedding with her, her parents and her brother Cyril. Jack was meeting her there, along with Aunt Ivy, Grace and Walter. She looked around, remembering her walks with Uncle Bertie and Aunt Ivy when she lived in Bournemouth. Bertie encouraged her to see the beauty of nature, and Ena started to note details of what she'd seen. She had kept her notebooks and now she resolved to revisit them and remind herself of those happy days. When she turned into Rachel's street an image of Donovan leaping over the front gate flashed through her mind. She smiled; he'd done what he longed to do by signing up. None of them could have known the tragedy that would follow.

'Hello!' Ena saw Rachel leaning out of her bedroom window. 'Hello, Mrs Love to-be!' Meta opened the front door and ushered Ena inside. 'You know where she is!' Ena hurried upstairs, 'I do!' When Ena burst through Rachel's bedroom door she stopped suddenly. Her lip trembled at the sight of her best friend's wedding dress hanging on the wardrobe door. 'Oh Rachel, that's the most gorgeous dress I've ever seen.' Rachel blushed and took Ena's hand. 'Feel the silk, Ena. It's so soft.' As Ena ran her hands across the delicate fabric, she studied her friend. One of the things she'd always loved about her was her humility. Rachel was a beautiful young woman. They both had auburn hair but Rachel's curled in soft loops. For her wedding day, Meta had pulled her daughter's hair back off her face and clipped it on top of her head. The clip was hidden by a white lace headband and Rachel's curls cascaded down her back. Her dark-brown eyes sparkled and Ena thought she had never looked happier. 'Will you help me with my gown? Mother is meant to be coming but I think Cyril may have waylaid her.' Ena took Rachel's hand. 'Of course I'll help you, it's my pleasure. How is Cyril? I didn't see him at the hotel last night.' Rachel looked down. 'He's suffering, Ena. He can't drive and doesn't leave the house much. He still has nightmares about gas, barbed wire and fighting. His screams pierce our nights like daggers. He is a shadow of himself.' Ena put her hand under Rachel's chin and lifted her head. She took her handkerchief and dabbed her friend's beautiful eyes. 'Cyril will want you to be happy; don't you think?' Rachel sniffed then wiped her eyes with Ena's handkerchief. 'Yes.' Ena nodded. 'Good. In that case, let's get you into this beautiful wedding gown.'

Ena lifted the gown off its hanger and held it out, ready for Rachel to step into. The white silk taffeta rustled when Ena moved. The close fit on the top and the long full skirt showed off Rachel's slim figure to full effect. The bodice was cut straight against Rachel's chest and the waist dropped to the middle of her hip. When Ena moved to the back of the gown to pull up the zip, she saw the plunging backward bodice. 'This is rather daring, Ms Leaman!' Rachel laughed and pointed at a box next to her bed. 'Shoes next, Ms Leighton.' Ena gasped when she removed Rachel's wedding shoes from the box. They were the fanciest Mary Jane's Ena had ever seen. The popular style usually came with a single strap across the top, fastened by a button. Rachel's had ribbons in place of straps, passed into eyelets at the sides and tied in a bow at the top. The white shoes were decorated with tiny applique flowers and the heels were high enough to show off Rachel's ankles. As Ena fastened the ribbons, there was a light knock on the door and Meta came into the room. She started to speak but stopped when she saw Rachel. Her eyes brimmed with tears and she shook her head. 'I'm sorry. I knew the moment you were born you were going to be beautiful inside and out; today is proof of that. Meta came towards her daughter and they embraced. 'I've brought your bouquet.' Meta moved back to the door to collect the flowers and the delicate aroma floated into Rachel's bedroom. 'Your father insisted on adding some of his sweet peas from the garden.' The bouquet's multi-coloured centrepiece sang with fragrance. The pink, purple, blue, white and yellow petals added a soft, sweet touch to the arrangement. Nestled in the middle of Rachel's favourite pink and white roses, they completed the bouquet. 'They're beautiful Ma, thank you.' Meta took a deep breath. 'Are you ready?' Rachel nodded and they made their way downstairs. In the hallway it was Edwin's turn for tears. Ena and Meta collected the posies and buttonholes, leaving Rachel and Edwin to follow separately; Ena, Meta and Cyril left Capstone Road to travel to the Richmond Park Synagogue.

The gardens were on two levels and from the top, Ena saw the full effect of the bridal canopy lovingly constructed by William's father Seymour and Edwin. Rachel had explained the significance of the canopy to her. It symbolised a home being established beneath it, and she would keep it to use as a wall hanging or a bedspread after the ceremony. Left open on all sides to indicate visitors were welcome, Rachel and William's canopy was festooned with garlands of flowers. Neat rows of white chairs were positioned on either side of the path leading to the canopy. Ena spotted Jack and when he turned she waved. He waved back and she started making her way towards him. Before she reached him, Aunt Ivy appeared and said she needed to speak to her. Her cheeks were flushed and Ena hoped she wasn't ill. She promised to find her once she and Meta had handed out the posies and buttonholes. As guests arrived, the sun shone warmly on their happy group. Before Ena could speak to her aunt, the music began, signalling Rachel's arrival. She and Jack hurried to take their places. Aunt Ivy was sitting further along the row, deep in conversation with Grace. Ena tried to get her attention but was distracted by Rachel's choice of music. Ena smiled; it was always going to be something her friend's favourite pianist had performed. Arabella Goddard enchanted audiences around the world with her rendition of Sigismond Thalberg's 'Home Sweet Home'. Rachel arrived under her wedding canopy with Seymour Love playing the piano and his son William waiting to take his bride's hand.

Rachel had explained the ceremony and Ena watched William agree to be bound by the terms of the ketubah, the marriage contract, in the presence of two witnesses. The ketubah detailed the groom's obligations to the bride, including providing her with food, clothing and love. Once rings were exchanged and religious blessings offered, Rachel and William each took a sip of wine from the proffered cup. Ena knew members of the audience who expected Rachel and William to kiss at the end of the ceremony were in for a shock, when William stomped his foot on the wine glass. Rachel had told her there were various interpretations of the symbolic act. Her favourite was the fragility of glass suggesting the fragility of human relationships. The glass is broken as an incantation; *as this glass shatters, so may our marriage never break*. Rachel said it was the perfect way to end the hushed time under the canopy and begin the celebrations. The moment William broke the glass, Seymour started playing 'Siman Tov u'Mazel Tov', the traditional Jewish chant declaring good fortune, used to congratulate the newly married couple. Everyone stood and clapped along, revelling in Rachel and William's happiness. When the song drew to a close, they were directed towards another area of the garden for toasts, speeches and food. Tables groaned with a kosher feast; chicken soup with matzo balls and noodles, roast beef or lamb with sweet potatoes and carrots, braised brisket on sautéed onions and mushrooms, challah bread filled with raisins and nuts and stuffed cabbage rolls with beef and rice.

Ena felt a hand on her arm and she turned to see her aunt's animated face. 'What is it?' Ivy thrust a piece of paper into her hand and Ena stared at the stark words on the white telegram. 'TREMENDOUS NEWS. STOP. WE'VE GOT HIM. STOP.' 'Does this mean what I think it means?' Ivy clasped Ena's hands. 'Yes! It's from Lydia. It's about George. The Matrimonial Causes Act was passed last week, meaning Lydia has some evidence to enable me to divorce him.' Ena embraced her aunt. 'I'd say that calls for a glass of champagne, wouldn't you?' Ivy laughed and they went to join the wedding party. As afternoon turned to evening, lights came on in the garden and the singing and dancing began. At their hotel later, Ena and Jack joined Ivy, Grace and Walter in the lounge. They reflected on the day; the joyous ceremony and the surprise of the smashed glass. Ena lay back in one of the large armchairs and kicked off her shoes. 'I couldn't eat another thing or dance another dance!' Jack laughed. 'Me neither!' Walter signalled for a waiter. 'No, but I think we could all manage another glass of champagne!' He winked at Ivy and they agreed they had something to celebrate.

Chapter 14

Ena

On the train from Kings Cross to Newcastle, Ena told Jack she knew where she wanted to get married. 'Is it under a canopy in a garden where I have to smash a glass afterwards?' She punched him playfully on the arm. 'No, you silly goose. But it is in Bournemouth.' Jack turned to her, his eyebrows raised, 'not in Gateshead or Whickham? We'll be living there once we're married'. Ena shook her head, 'we don't know anyone in Whickham yet. The people I'd want to be there were with us in Bournemouth, apart from your uncle and perhaps the Turnbulls and the Bundells. Would that be all right with you?' Jack took her hand. 'I'd marry you anywhere, I just want you to be happy. But what about your mother?' Ena shrugged, 'I don't even know where she is'. Jack frowned, 'does your aunt?' Ena sighed, 'she said she'd received a letter, sent from some ship. She's on her travels again, back to New York'. Jack persisted, 'and you don't want to contact her?' 'No. If she could write to her sister, why not her daughter?' She held Jack's gaze until he changed the subject. 'Very well. Where in Bournemouth?' Ena smiled. 'St. Paul's Church, I passed it on the way to Rachel's and there was a wedding taking place. The bride and groom were coming out of the church and the bells were ringing; everyone looked so happy.' Jack doffed his cap at her, 'just name the day and I'll be there!'

Back in her flat that night, Ena started reading her old notebooks, reminding herself how much Uncle Bertie had taught her about nature and valuing everyday sights and sounds. He was part of the reason for having her wedding in Bournemouth; she'd been at her happiest when she lived there with him and Aunt

Ivy, it was where her friendship with Rachel began and she was part of the Primavesis' and the Leamans' extended families. After her grandmother died and her mother and aunt left Gateshead, Bournemouth was the first place that had felt most like home. She turned the page in her notebook and saw her last entry, made a year ago when she returned to Gateshead. She'd written it on the day Jack proposed. They were at work and she found Jack sitting outside the flour mill. He was drawing the garden he'd pictured when they saw the house they'd named Littlecroft. They agreed the name was evocative of the small house; somewhere they would feel safe and secure. Ena remembered them standing outside the flour mill with their arms around each other. Her eyes had followed the bends of the river, back in the direction of Pipewellgate, where she knew such misery. She reminded herself of her future; her life with Jack and the house they planned to live in. She read what she had written a year ago, 'The Village on the Hill', and underneath, one word. 'Home.'

At work the next day, Ena wasted no time in starting to gather support for her equal pay campaign. During her lunch break she spoke to as many women as she could; women who came to the meeting at the Miner's Welfare Hall. She was careful, remembering how discreet Charlie Marsh was when she met her in the library. Beatrice also warned her to be wary, not everyone was an ally. Ena approached her conversations by saying she believed they were generally well cared for at work, but (and at this point she would ensure she wasn't being overheard) that shouldn't stop them asking for more. When she ran the gauntlet of disapproving male eyes, she reminded herself what she knew about Charlie. As a paid organiser of the WSPU, Charlie was one of the first women to be force-fed while in prison for militant protest. After being force-fed 139 times, she travelled to Newcastle in a seriously emaciated condition to be at her dying father's bedside. By the time she arrived, he was already unconscious and died several days later without knowing she was there. Charlie and countless other women like her had given Ena's generation the freedom to campaign and the strength to persevere when the odds were stacked against them. Ena ignored the detractors and carried on.

Ivy

Ivy went straight to Lydia's chambers when she got back to London. She didn't want to waste a moment now her case was progressing. Lydia's secretary invited her to wait, saying the barrister was with another client but would see her afterwards. Ivy thanked her and said she was happy to wait. She sat outside Lydia's office and closed her eyes. She replayed the last few days in her mind. Her reunion with Bertie's family and the Leamans was bittersweet; there was a chasm where her beloved Bertie should have been. She smiled to herself; he would have taken such pleasure in Rachel and William's happiness. And it would have delighted him to see the strong, determined young woman Ena had become. She sighed; the war was cruel; it took so much from so many people. She opened her eyes; she needed to stop wallowing. Despite her heartache, their time in Bournemouth was wonderful. The wedding was beautiful and nothing could undermine the joy of the bride and groom.

Lydia's door opened and she came out with a small, grey-haired lady. They shook hands and as the older woman left, Lydia ushered Ivy into her office. Once the door was closed, Lydia embraced her and repeated the words in her telegram. 'We've got him, Ivy!' Ivy narrowed her eyes. 'Are you sure?' Lydia gestured to Ivy to take a seat. 'Yes, look at these photographs my private detective took.' Lydia pushed a brown folder across the desk and Ivy hesitated. She put her hand on the folder then stopped; were these images she wanted to see? She looked at Lydia and her barrister shrugged. She took a deep breath and opened the folder.

The images were grainy but irrefutable; it was her husband in an extremely compromising position with another woman. She closed the folder and pushed it back to Lydia. 'Is it enough?' Lydia leant back in her chair and put her hands behind her head. 'It's evidence of adultery. If he agrees to be divorced it should be enough.' Ivy sighed. 'And if he doesn't? In my experience, George won't do anything unless it benefits George.'

Lydia positioned her pen above her legal pad. 'Let's take this one step at a time. Our first move will be to write to George setting out our position.' 'Which is?' Lydia twirled her pen in the air. 'Something along the lines of, *"After much contemplation and consideration, I have decided to seek a divorce. This decision has not been made lightly, and it comes after a long period of reflection on our marriage.*"' Ivy scoffed. 'Our marriage was a sham; can't we say that?' Lydia tutted. 'You know we must approach this from a professional, legal perspective. I know what you'd like me to write, but we must do this objectively. Ivy sighed. 'It's so frustrating having to be nice to him.' Lydia leant forward. 'Try and think of it this way. You're not being nice, you're being clever.' Ivy frowned. 'What do you mean?' Lydia tapped her forehead. 'Ok, do you remember *Aesop's Fables?*' Ivy nodded, 'yes, our mother read them to us when we were little'. Lydia continued, 'great. What about "The North Wind and the Sun?"' Ivy nodded again, 'the power of persuasion over force'. Lydia smiled, 'yes. You and George can argue over who is stronger, trade blows via letters, or you could adopt a higher position, appear gentle rather than threatening, be persuasive not forceful. Can you approach it that way?' Ivy took a deep breath, 'yes, I think I can'.

Lydia made some notes on her pad and said she would let Ivy see a draft letter before sending it to George on her behalf. 'One thing we must do is protect you financially. The Married Women's Property Act includes a wife's right to own, buy and sell property independent of her husband. We'll ensure your flat sits outside any settlement.' Ivy hugged Lydia before she left. As she walked along the Strand she resolved to be an iron hand in a velvet glove if that's what it took to rid herself of George Scott-Smith.

Mona

After a few days of rehearsals, during which Mona thought she would never walk again, her muscles slowly started to strengthen. Her aches and pains disappeared and she began to enjoy dancing again. She'd known Wilfred wasn't staying in New York long, and when the time came for him to leave, she realised her affection for him had grown in the short time she'd known him. His meetings with Duncan's bankers proved fruitful; his sister's fiancé was a shrewd investor and Mabel was now a woman of independent means.

At dinner on his last night, Wilfred said it was comforting to know his sister was well provided for, but no amount of money could make up for her loss. Mona put down her knife and fork, 'it's reassuring to know there are people who think of others, isn't it?' He nodded. 'It is. Duncan was a first-rate chap; I think he and Mabel would have had a very happy life together.' Mona sighed. 'None of us know what might be round the corner, do we?' Wilfred reached across the table and took her hands. 'That shouldn't stop us making plans. I know you have to stay, but we can write to each other. And I promise to come back for your opening night.' She smiled, 'you'll be here?' He kissed her hands. 'I will.' Mona's lip trembled; she couldn't remember when someone had last made her a promise and kept it. She looked at Wilfred as he continued eating. Could she trust him?

They said their farewells that night, having agreed Mona wouldn't go to wave him off. Rehearsals were in full swing and he wanted her to focus on the show. She agreed reluctantly, not wanting him to go. When they parted, he repeated his promise to return. 'You'll be here on opening night?' He embraced her. 'Yes. And you'll be magnificent, I have no doubt.' She drew back slightly and met his eyes. 'Thank you for believing in me.' He kissed her softly then turned and walked away. As his figure receded, she crossed her fingers, hoping this time things would be different.

The next day she woke early. As the coffee percolated she put some slices of bacon on a skillet on the stovetop. She warmed some muffins and poured grapefruit juice into two glasses. The bacon was turning crispy and golden brown when she heard Tilly padding into the lounge in her bright red sheepskin slippers. 'Gee, that smells good! You can cook more often!' Mona gestured for Tilly to sit in the lounge, saying she would bring her breakfast on a tray. She watched Tilly sit then curl her long legs up under her dressing gown. 'I might get used to this, Mona! What's got you up and at 'em?' Mona came into the lounge, carrying their coffees. 'I didn't think I would sleep after Wilfred left, but I did. I woke feeling hungry and decided to make breakfast.' She went back into the kitchen and returned with the muffins and juice. 'Well I'm not complaining, this smells wonderful!' Mona sat and took a sip of her coffee. 'I do miss Wilfred but I'm excited about the show.' Tilly spoke in between bites of muffin. 'Let's see how excited you are following this afternoon's rehearsal!' Mona laughed. 'Oh yes, Marv wants us to rehearse "You Can't Keep a Good Girl Down", doesn't he?"' 'He does! Are you ready for it?' Mona stood up and twirled around, bacon muffin in her hand. 'You know what, my friend? I am!'

On their way to the Paradise, they agreed how remarkable it was that a modern Cinderella story should still be in vogue. Tilly linked her arm through Mona's as they walked. 'You're a lot like the character of Sally, you know?' Mona looked sideways at her friend. 'Do you think so?' Tilly nodded. 'Yes, you're typical of the liberated, upwardly mobile new woman. Think about Act I;

after getting a job as a dishwasher, your character reveals her boundless drive in the song we're going to rehearse this afternoon.' Mona smiled to herself, rehearsing the lyrics to 'You Can't Keep a Good Girl Down' in her head. Perhaps there were similarities between her and Sally. She hummed the tune, thinking she preferred the song's alternative title, 'I Wish I Could Be Like Joan of Arc'.

'She had no stairs to wash,
with soap suds and a pail;
'She just cut out domestic bosh,
and bought a suit of mail.'

There were times in her life when she'd longed to be braver, to stand up to those who threatened her. She'd learnt to wear an invisible suit of armour, in order to survive. She shook her head; she could never have imagined playing a role like Sally. She looked up at the entrance to the Paradise, determined to perform to the best of her ability and make the most of the opportunity Marv had given her.

Chapter 15

Ivy

As Ivy poured tea, Grace asked how things were going with Lydia. 'How many letters is it now?' Ivy sighed. 'Three in the last three months.' 'And he still hasn't responded?' Ivy shook her head, 'no, and I'm starting to think he never will'. Grace stirred her tea then rested her spoon on the china saucer. 'Isn't he obliged to, legally?' Ivy sat back in her chair and crossed her legs. 'I'm sure he thinks he's above the law.' 'What does Lydia say?' 'That we should proceed regardless. The judge can summon him to attend court and if he doesn't turn up he could be arrested.' Grace tutted, 'I don't understand it. Why wouldn't he want to draw this sorry situation to a conclusion, to let you both get on with your lives?' 'He's arrogant, Grace. And I'm convinced he thinks he can ignore Lydia's letters and carry on with his debauched existence.' 'Well he might be in for a nasty shock, if that is the case.'

After Grace left, Ivy looked back at the letters Lydia had sent since their meeting in July. She was starting to question the power of persuasion over force approach, and voiced this at her most recent appointment with Lydia. Her barrister put her head on one side , saying in her experience, men like George didn't respond well to being put under pressure, especially by a woman. Ivy rubbed her temples; would she ever be rid of him? She picked up a volume of poetry Vernon had given her the last time they met. Vernon, as different from George as it was possible to be. She'd discovered they had a lot in common; in addition to poetry and books, Vernon shared her love of the theatre. He'd told her he was learning to cook. His mother hadn't been well and he was trying different recipes to tempt her appetite. He had invited Ivy to eat with them but she declined; the last thing she needed was to give anyone reason to suspect her of anything inappropriate. She read the first line of a poem then put the book down. The telephone rang and she sighed. Lydia's voice was shrill with excitement. 'We have new evidence! If this doesn't bring George creeping out from under his rock, I don't know what will!' Ivy replaced the receiver, then immediately picked it up and called Grace. 'Ivy? Is everything all right?' She laughed, 'better than all right, darling. Can I come over?'

Grace sipped her drink, listening to Ivy relay her conversation with Lydia. The private detective had come up trumps, apparently as frustrated by George's inaction as they were. Despite having photographic evidence of his adultery, the detective knew it would be difficult to persuade the other party to give evidence against him in court. The resulting notoriety and damage to her reputation would be too great to risk it. The detective decided on a different course of action. She could be the witness herself; if she convinced George she was genuine. She waited outside his address, where she'd been for months, unrecognisable from the suited, hatted individual who'd lurked in the shadows with her camera. She wore a bright red dress and high-heeled shoes, arranged a fur wrap around her shoulders and walked straight into George as he stumbled along the street. She took the blame for the collision, flattering him and pandering to his ego. When he invited her inside for a nightcap, she accepted.

Grace's eyes were wide and Ivy sat forward in her chair, 'I asked Lydia if that wasn't incredibly dangerous'. Grace nodded, 'I would have thought so too'. Ivy shook her head, 'Lydia said the woman was an actress before the war, but her work during the conflict was much more interesting. She was appearing at the Lyceum in Charing Cross when a Zeppelin raid forced both cast and audience into an underground station to shelter. A man approached her in the tube station and recruited her to the secret service. She thought he was a con man but when he recited her education and career back to her she realised he'd done his research. He knew she'd excelled in languages including Latin and Greek, was fluent in Dutch and had a good grasp of French and German. He said he'd been watching her performances for months and her acting was of a standard that could be very useful to the war effort. On stage, she'd been a very credible reporter, a battlefield nurse, a teacher and a politician. He'd observed her lack of fear during the Zeppelin raid. He said she appeared defiant, which was perfect for their requirements. Lydia said the woman joined an intelligence unit that reported to the Secret Service Bureau, and carried out covert work behind enemy lines. As a skilled linguist and a speaker of Dutch, she was an obvious candidate for operations in Flemish-speaking Belgium. Her first mission was to pose as a reporter and infiltrate enemy lines. She encoded messages into news broadcasts and passed encrypted missives to a network of contacts. She did everything in her power to gain information, risking her life to gather and pass on intelligence.' Ivy paused to have a drink and Grace waited. Ivy smiled at her friend then continued. 'Lydia said she had reservations about the detective's actions, because she'd wanted them to win by taking the higher ground, but finding a way to get inside his house turned out to be the best thing she could have done.' Grace waited. Ivy drummed her hands on the table, 'because, his wife was inside!' Grace almost choked on her drink, 'his wife?' 'Yes! The idiot was so drunk he'd forgotten she was there when he invited our detective inside!' Ivy laughed at something she had never expected to find amusing; her husband was a bigamist. Her marriage to George Scott-Smith was invalid and if she instructed Lydia to do so, he could be prosecuted. Grace shook her head, 'and will you instruct her?' Ivy pursed her lips, 'I haven't decided yet, but the power lies with me'.

Ena

Ena hadn't expected to be holding another meeting at the Miner's Welfare Hall so soon, but when she canvassed opinion at the flour mill it became clear women were impatient for change. After years of partial progress, equality remained out of reach. At the beginning of the war, the WSPU established a truce with the government when Mrs Pankhurst asked, 'what is the use of fighting for a vote if we have not got a country to vote in?' Instead, the WSPU threw their weight behind the war effort and in return, an amnesty was granted to suffragette prisoners. Women were urged to keep industries, and thereby the country, going. Ena remembered what she'd read about Charlie Marsh. During the war, she worked for the Prime Minister David Lloyd George. He was aware of her militant background, but made a strategic decision to employ her because he was campaigning for women to join the workforce to replace men who'd gone to war. In 1918, the Representation of the People Act gave over eight million women in Great Britain the vote; women over the age of 30 who owned property.

The evening was a repeat of the meeting earlier in the year, with Jack and the Bundells helping to set out the room. Ena expected Dolly and her parents, along with a good proportion of the flour mill's female workforce. When everyone had refreshments and was seated, she began. 'This is about us having the right to equal pay for equal work. It's not a new campaign; the suffragettes saw gaining the vote not as an end in itself, but as a way of influencing the government on issues that are important to all our lives. Equal pay is key, especially to working class women. Many of us took on jobs during the war; jobs previously reserved for men, jobs the country needed us to do. The Prime Minister employed a woman, and a militant suffragette at that, as his motor mechanic and chauffeur! And what happened when the war ended? It's not so politically convenient now, is it, when we're fighting for equal rights including equal pay for equal work? Some men would happily see us all back in the kitchen!' Ena scanned the room; the wages clerk was nowhere to be seen.

'And yes, some of us now have the vote, thanks to the efforts of our courageous forebears, but how many of us? Around two-thirds of the total population of women in the country. What about the rest of us? The same Act of Parliament made things better for men! It abolished property and other restrictions for them, and extended their vote to most men over the age of 21. Men in the armed forces can now vote from the age of 19. So tell me friends, are things becoming more equal or not?' Ena took a breath and in the space, the applause began. She raised her hands and the room quietened. 'Those of you who have a vote, women died to give you that right, you must use it intelligently. The Prime Minister has decided to call an early general election in December. Whatever your political affiliations, ask your candidates for their views on issues that are important to you. Make it clear you want to prevent any undercutting of our male colleagues' standard of living. That's not what this campaign is about. Tell them you want equal pay for equal work!' A woman towards the back of the room stood up and Ena nodded to indicate she should ask her question. 'Could we go on strike? Female tram and bus conductors did it in London at the end of the war and they got a bonus payment to make them equal.' Ena smiled at Jack, sitting in the front row. He knew she'd read about this because with the help of Aunt Ivy and Lydia, she'd managed to get hold of one of the letters the company sent the women the following year, dismissing them. They'd protested against women being excluded from a war bonus awarded to male transport workers. Their protest escalated into a nationwide strike of 17,000 female bus and tram workers who also demanded equal pay. After a week of strikes, the women received the war bonus, but were still not given equal pay. 'I can't advise you to take strike action; only your trade union can do that. What I would say is, in my opinion, the decision of the company to give the women the war bonus was an act of cynical appeasement.' The woman was still standing and she raised her hand. 'They got it, didn't they?' Ena nodded. 'They did, and the following year they were all dismissed. I can show you one of the letters if you like.' The woman sat and Ena sighed. 'I'm sorry, the last thing I want to do is dampen anyone's enthusiasm for action. We need to be tactical and use the right sort of action, most likely to be effective, to achieve our goal. And we need to be single-minded about that goal, equal pay for equal work!' She looked at Beatrice who was nodding and mouthing, 'ask for one thing'.

Mona

After Wilfred left New York, Tilly told Mona they should let their hair down and enjoy themselves. 'There's never been a better time for it, honey!' Mona hesitated; 'but aren't there restrictions?' Tilly laughed, 'do you mean Prohibition?' Mona nodded and Tilly put an arm around her shoulder. 'Sweetheart, let me tell you about Prohibition!' They left the Paradise and walked along Broadway. Tilly explained that while the production, importation, transportation and sale of alcoholic beverages was currently prohibited in the United States, many people had stockpiled alcohol for legal home consumption. 'Some enterprising individuals bought complete inventories from liquor retailers and wholesalers, emptying their warehouses, saloons and club staterooms. Even the President is rumoured to have moved his own large supply into the White House. So if it's good enough for him, it's good enough for me!' Mona stopped walking. 'But where can we go?' Tilly tapped the side of her nose with a long red fingernail; 'stick with me, kid. I'll show you!'

It took them 20 minutes to walk to West 44th Street, where Tilly said the best speakeasy was. Before Mona could ask, Tilly explained speakeasies were clandestine establishments that illegally sold alcoholic beverages. They were usually disguised as restaurants and hidden in alleyways, as was the case with Tremblay's. A plain blue awning advertised only that the establishment sold burgers and hot dogs. Inside, a sleek countertop with high stools to the left and a number of small tables and chairs to the right afforded the only seating. A sign above the counter advised customers hamburgers and hot dogs cost five cents while milkshakes and ice cream sodas, the only drinks on offer, were six cents each. A couple of stools were occupied, along with a few tables and the smell of grease hung in the air. Tilly walked straight to the back of the diner and stopped at a plain black door. Mona stared; the door had no handle. Silently, the door opened and they slipped inside. When the door closed behind them, Tilly pointed at a tiny hole towards the top of the door and winked. Someone must have seen them from this side of the door but there was no sign of anyone now. They were in a small, silent vestibule with one dim lightbulb hanging from the ceiling. Tilly took Mona's hand. A few steps led them to a second plain door without a handle. Again the door opened silently; this time it swung back with a strong metallic thud. When Mona stepped over the threshold she noticed the solid door was several feet thick, like the door to a bank vault. Another silent vestibule and another bare lightbulb, then a door with a brass handle. As Tilly turned the handle, she gave Mona a smile as if to say, wait until you see what's on the other side of this door.

The assault on Mona's senses was immediate. The air was thick with smoke and loud jazz music bounced off the walls of the secret underground world. Competing with the smell of smoke was a muskiness that took Mona back to the music halls in London. As her eyes adjusted to the gloom, she looked around. Tilly touched her arm. 'See anyone you recognise?' Mona shook her head, but Tilly assured her the club was a favourite of movie stars, show girls, aristocrats and the wealthy elite of New York City. Of course, some of them will be in Charlie's VIP Room!' 'Charlie?' Tilly led her towards the bar. 'Charlie Tremblay; it's his club. He was a small-time bootlegger before Prohibition, now he's the proud owner of this little oasis of entertainment. Tremblay's is open all day and most of the night; during the day the city's writers, poets, playwrights, journalists, and activists gather here, and at night, it's all ours! Ok, what's your poison? How about a nice glass of wine?' Mona frowned, 'how is this possible?' Tilly gave a deep delicious laugh, 'what's wine made from?' Mona furrowed her brow. 'Holy moly Mona, grapes! And grape juice isn't restricted by Prohibition, yet if you let it sit for 60 days it ferments and turns into wine with a 12 percent alcohol content!'

Mona's head spun; the sounds and smells and the mere existence of Tremblay's threatened to overwhelm her. She didn't know what to drink in a country where drinking alcohol was illegal. Tilly pointed at a sign behind the bar which listed the options. There was gin and tonic and a variety of cocktails. The Bee's Knees; gin, honey and lemon juice, the Mary Pickford; rum, grenadine, pineapple juice and maraschino liqueur, the Southside; gin, mint, simple syrup and lime juice or the Sidecar; brandy, orange liqueur and lemon juice. 'And if none of those are to your liking, there's always this!' Tilly lifted her long skirt to reveal her knee-length leather boots. Mona burst out laughing; secreted inside was a thin silver flask.

'Well blow me down, if it isn't Ms Tilly Tucker of Island Park, Newport County, Rhode Island! A little place with a lot of character, in a greasy spoon café with hygiene issues kind of a way!' 'Charlie!' Tilly and Charlie embraced, then the owner of Tremblay's stood back and looked at his friend. 'Gee, it's great to see you. What fortunate wind blows you this way?' Tilly turned and took Mona's arm. 'Charlie, please let me introduce you to Ms Mona Leighton, English stage star and currently rehearsing for the one and only Marv Marvel's Broadway production of *Sally*!' Charlie shook Mona's hand and said it was a pleasure to meet her. 'Now ladies, can I get you a little hooch to drink before you have a swell time dancing up a storm?'

Chapter 16

January 1924

Ivy

Ivy's stiletto heels clipped rhythmically down the stone steps outside the court building on the Strand. Clutching the cream envelope, she held her head high and breathed deeply. At the foot of the steps she stopped and slid the envelope into her green leather handbag. She snapped the silver clasp shut. That was the last time she would think about George Scott-Smith. 'Halloo!' Ivy smiled broadly at her friend. 'Hello, Grace. Thank you for coming to meet me.' 'My pleasure, darling. Where's Walter?' Ivy looked around, 'he's talking to one of the barristers. Someone from his old chambers, I think'. Grace nodded, 'shall we?' Ivy hesitated, 'shouldn't we wait for Walter?' 'Don't worry, he'll know where to find us!' Ivy raised her hand to hail a taxicab, 'The Langham?' She couldn't imagine they would celebrate anywhere else. Grace laughed, 'of course!'

By the time Walter joined them, they were sipping their first glasses of champagne. He kissed Grace softly on the lips and Ivy watched her friends; their love had grown stronger over the years. He kissed Ivy on both cheeks before filling his glass, then he raised the champagne flute and made a toast. 'To darling Ivy's brilliant, happy future!' Ivy and Grace raised their glasses and repeated the toast. Walter put down his glass, 'how does it feel?' Ivy nodded. 'Lydia gave me a letter setting out the details of our agreement. Under the law I can't divorce him because we were never legally married, but I want to ensure he can't touch the Garrick Street flat or my future earnings. Providing there are no objections from his side, that should be the last I see or hear of him.' Walter scoffed, 'I can't see them daring to raise any objections after the judge's summing up, can you?' Ivy shook her head, 'I hope not'. Grace turned to her husband. 'What did the judge say, darling?' Walter laughed, 'he took a very dim view of George impersonating a Squadron Leader and not bothering to turn up at court'. Ivy tutted, 'I'm relieved he wasn't there, but it's frustrating the judge was more concerned about George's lack of respect for the armed forces and the court than his behaviour towards me'. Grace laughed cynically, 'that's the patriarchy for you, darling. It's alive and well in London'. Ivy smiled, 'despite that, Lydia said his first wife is seeking a divorce and is very keen to see him prosecuted for bigamy. And I've got this!' She took Lydia's letter out of her bag and slapped it on the table. They cheered and Walter called for more champagne.

Back in her flat later, Ivy kicked off her shoes. She walked to her gramophone and placed a record on the turntable. It was one of her favourites and perfect for today. She wound the handle then lifted the arm and placed the needle on the edge of the record. She closed her eyes and waited for the familiar crackle. Her spine tingled as the music surrounded her and she began to dance. She kicked her legs out in front and then behind, copying the moves of Norah Blaney and Gwen Farrar. She sang at the top of her voice, without a care in the world.

'Oh, you don't need a barometer to pick a rainy day,
You always know it's gonna rain when the weather experts say:
Oh it ain't gonna rain no more no more, it ain't gonna rain no more,
Don't listen to what the old folks say, it ain't gonna rain no more.'

When the record finished she returned the needle to the beginning and started dancing again.

Ena

Saturday morning found Ena reading the newspapers at the library. She was looking for national news about the equal pay campaign; anything she could use to further their cause at the flour mill. She shook her head as she read the headlines about the general election. The Prime Minister's decision to call an early election had backfired. He'd hoped to achieve a mandate to impose taxes on imported goods and encourage people to buy domestically produced products instead. Ena frowned, where would the price increases have left the Bundells? They imported all their tea from abroad. The rationale for the taxes was to drive down unemployment. Ena knew after the war ended the economy faced significant challenges as businesses struggled to get back on their feet. The post-war recession and industrial unrest contributed to a sharp rise in unemployment. Ena thought about the women who had gone on strike in London. She didn't believe that was the answer but neither were import taxes. Stanley Baldwin had expected to unite his party, instead he divided it. He'd held on to the party leadership but some colleagues continued to call for his resignation. Now, with an unstable minority Labour government, Ramsay MacDonald was in charge of the country. She sighed and turned the page. The headline sent a shiver up her spine.

'MEN AND BOYS DEAD IN PIT EXPLOSION'

It was the third accident at the Aire Colliery in as many years. The newspaper article said the explosion was caused by firedamp (a flammable gas such as methane) and coal dust being ignited by a defective safety lamp. The majority of miners working the nearest seam managed to escape before realising some of their number were missing, including two boys. Despite warnings, a group of men went back in. When they disappeared into the mine, a cloud of dust rose up the shaft and a second explosion knocked anyone standing nearby off their feet. It was days before the bodies were recovered and identification was almost impossible because of damage to their faces; Ena read one boy was so badly disfigured he could only be identified by his belt and trousers. She covered her face with her hands; the war might be over, but they faced daily battles much closer to home. Unemployment, dangerous working environments and for women, the ongoing fight for equality.

She remembered Beatrice telling her about the Bryant & May match workers. The female workforce, many only 13 years old, faced a life of hard toil for very little reward. They earned a pittance while the company's shareholders received huge dividends. Every day endangered the girls' health, reportedly being told to "never mind their fingers" when working with machinery, even if it led to serious injuries. It was generally accepted they would suffer occasional blows from the foreman. With no separate facilities, they ate at their benches. The possible result, Beatrice said, was "Phossy jaw", a disfiguring and painful disease affecting people working with white phosphorous without proper safeguards. The girls experienced toothache and swollen gums as vapour from the phosphorous destroyed their jaw bones. Over time they lost teeth and had recurrent abscesses. Following a shocking exposé of the conditions the girls worked in, Bryant & May tried to bully the match workers into denying its revelations. Their heavy-handed tactics riled the match workers, and 200 of them downed tools. The action spread quickly, and soon around 1,400 had walked out in sympathy. The women called for others to be organised and show solidarity.

Ena thought of the WSPU's motto, 'Deeds not Words'. The match workers had shown they wouldn't allow themselves to be put in a dangerous position at work, they acted positively against an oppressive employer. She looked at the headline about the pit accident again and took out her notebook. If she couldn't progress the equal pay campaign, what were more practical things she could do? She knew the CWS had spent a significant amount of money on buildings and state-of-the-art machinery; could she use that as leverage for some space of her own? Somewhere for people to come if they needed help. She started to make a list of the help she and others might be able to offer.

Jack

Jack looked into the oily river as he walked across the High Level Bridge to Gateshead. Heavy industries crowding both sides of the riverbank created a bustling hub of activity. The River Tyne was used to transport coal from the area's many mines to ships, where it was exported to countries around the world. The river remained one of the world's most important shipbuilding centres, with local shipyards building a variety of vessels from cargo ships to warships. The dark buildings housed manufacturing and engineering works that produced machinery and tools to support the shipbuilding industry. Chemical industries producing plastics were also starting to take root in the region. All brought much-needed jobs; with them came pollution.

He'd called to see Ena at the library on his way into town and heard her latest idea, to set up a welfare centre at the flour mill for people in need. She'd realised the fight for equal pay wouldn't be won quickly, if at all, and ever-resourceful, she'd come up with a different, more practical way to help people. He'd offered to go to the Grainger Market in Newcastle to ask if traders would be prepared to donate goods late on a Saturday afternoon, which would otherwise go to waste. He was carrying two brown paper bags full to the brim with fruit and vegetables. Ena's latest project hadn't got off the ground yet, but he was sure their neighbours and friends could make use of the unexpected haul. As he adjusted the position of the bags, he bumped into a woman walking in the opposite direction across the bridge. 'Sorry, Miss, I wasn't looking where I was going.' 'It's all right, no harm done.' Jack met the woman's eyes as they stood on the path in the middle of the bridge. She smiled slowly and her dark eyes lit up. 'It's Jack Todd, isn't it?' He nodded. 'Yes, and you're Shirley…?' 'Kindred. I was in the year above you at school.' Jack moved one of the bags and extended his hand to Shirley. 'Of course. How are you?' Shirley smiled again. 'I'm well, thank you, but my mother is ill. That's why I'm back in Newcastle.' 'Back? Where have you been?' Shirley laughed. 'Where haven't I been? I'm a dancer and I've worked all over the world since leaving school. What about you, do you still live in Gateshead?' Jack gestured to the opposite side of the bridge. 'Yes, I live on Cross Street with my uncle and I work at the flour mill on the Dunston Staithes.' Jack looked along the river towards the mill, suddenly thinking how small his world was, compared to Shirley's. Then he remembered his time in France and Turkey during the war and he was grateful to be exactly where he was. 'Do you ever see anyone from school?' Jack started to shake his head then stopped. 'Do you remember Evie Brown?' Shirley gasped. 'Of course, the little bright spark. That poor girl; what became of her?' Jack laughed and put down his bags. 'I can tell you, and she's no longer called Evie Brown.'

Walking away, Jack hoped he'd done the right thing. Ena rarely mentioned her past; would she want Shirley to know what had happened to her since they were at school? He hoped she wouldn't be angry, because Shirley had invited them to see her performing in a play called *Pot Luck* at the Grainger Music Hall on Nelson Street in Newcastle. She'd told him to look out for her stage name; Shirley Sparkle.

Mona

Mona and Vernon wrote to each other regularly. He told her when he arrived back in London, the manager at his bank asked to see him. Word had travelled fast about his meetings in New York and the manager complimented him on his negotiation skills. 'It turns out, Mr Henson, we have an opening for a deputy branch manager and I think you're the man for the job.' Wilfred wrote that the vacancy was at the bank's Sutton Coldfield branch in Birmingham, less than 20 miles from Dudley, where his parents and sister lived. 'It's perfect, Mona; I think the time is right to move. And the job opportunity is too good to turn down!' He gave her his parents address in Dudley, saying he intended to give up his London flat. She read his words again. She hadn't thought further ahead than seeing him again on opening night, but this news changed things. She'd imagined returning to London when *Sally* ended and enjoying life there with him. Tilly advised her to forget it and talk to him when he came back. Mona put the letter away. She missed Wilfred, but she and Tilly quickly fell into a regular routine of rehearsals, eating out and visiting Tremblay's. Tilly could always suggest somewhere new if they weren't in the mood for mutton chops or steak (if they were it was always Keens), New York had an endless variety of restaurants. They worked their way through the cocktail list at Tremblay's then started again at the beginning, including new concoctions Charlie invented every other day. They became part of a group of performers who worked hard then danced until dawn, enjoying everything New York had to offer.

Mona squeezed into the booth next to Tilly. She picked up her cocktail glass and toasted her friend. 'This is the life!' Tilly laughed. Mona took a drink before speaking, 'this Prohibition is a lark, isn't it?' Tilly raised her eyebrows. 'What do you mean?' Mona leant closer, 'I thought we wouldn't be able to get alcohol anywhere, that anyone found drinking would be immediately arrested and thrown in jail. Look at us!' Tilly looked around Charlie's speakeasy. 'Prohibition has only driven the alcohol industry underground. Ask Charlie how much better he's doing since his business became illegal! He told me some moonshiners produce millions of gallons of illegal hooch, and there are tens of thousands of places like this all over the country.' Mona chewed her bottom lip. 'But isn't it dangerous? What if Charlie gets caught?' Tilly winked, 'if he gets caught, we all do, honey! Speakeasies and bootlegging operations are raided all the time. The trick is to make them appear innocuous, as our dear friend Charlie has done with his "diner". Now, are you ready for another dance?"' The band started playing Eddie Cantor's popular hit, 'No, No, Nora'. The light-hearted, vaudeville-style routine suited the friends perfectly and people crowded onto the dance floor to join their comedic, energetic moves.

Outside, the woman pulled her coat tighter; it had grown cold since Mona and the American actress went inside the diner. She narrowed her eyes but the windows were steamed up, all she could see was the counter and a few tables and chairs. They'd been in there for ages and unless there was another exit, they hadn't left. She rubbed her neck. That loud director at the Paradise had refused to take her on. He'd said her scars would frighten any audience members who were of a nervous disposition. 'Sorry honey, you'll give them the heebie jeebies!' She'd scoffed and told him his audiences were full of stuck-up snobs. When she turned to leave she heard him laughing, and her anger rose.

She punched her gloved fist against the wall, wishing it was Mona's face; this was all her fault. She saw two young men going into the diner and she hurried across the road. They stopped suddenly when they saw her. She affected her best English accent. 'Excuse me, I do beg your pardon, I'm looking for my friends. I'm sure I saw them go into this diner. Might I come in with you and see if they're inside?' They shrugged, 'sure, why not?' One of them opened the door and allowed her to go in first. There was no sign of Mona and the other woman. She frowned; the diner was tiny but they must be here somewhere. She squared up to the men; her pretence gone. 'Where are they?' The men looked at her, their expressions blank. 'They must have left. Would you like a milkshake?' She stared at them then turned and threw the door open. 'No, I would not like a flaming milk-shake! They're here somewhere and I'll find them! Mark my words, you'll be sorry you crossed me!' She stomped outside and stopped just past the diner. She turned back and wiped her gloved hand across the window. She narrowed her eyes and saw the two men disappearing through a door at the back of the diner. She smirked.

Chapter 17

Ivy

Ivy threw herself into life after George. No longer anxious about the future, she reminded herself of who she was and the things she liked to do. In addition to the Poetry Bookshop, she became a regular at Hatchards on Piccadilly and Foyles on Charing Cross Road. Visitors to all three shops were welcome to browse and sit and read for as long as they wanted. There were always publications to discover and Ivy found herself reading new authors in addition to old favourites. One day, as she stood in Hatchards trying to choose between Agatha Christie's new short story collection, *Poirot Investigates*, and P.C. Wren's *Beau Geste*, the door opened and she heard a familiar voice. 'I'd get them both if I were you.' Ivy looked up; Vernon's friendly, easy manner always made her smile. They'd seen each other a number of times since she'd declared herself officially single; once or twice in the Poetry Bookshop and they'd met for coffee at the Café Royal on Regent Street. Their conversation flowed easily and she enjoyed his company.

She smiled at him. 'I might! How are you Vernon, how is your mother?' Vernon spoke slowly. 'She's a little better but still very melancholy.' Ivy touched his arm. 'It's understandable after everything she's endured.' Vernon sighed then pointed towards the back of the bookshop. 'That's the section I need! Come on, help me with something.' Ivy followed him to the cookery books. 'I want to cook something my mother hasn't had before; I need a delicious new recipe. Can you suggest anything?' Ivy put her head on one side and browsed the shelves. Something occurred to her, 'does your mother like tomatoes?' Vernon nodded. 'What about spaghetti?' He shrugged. 'I'm not sure she's tried it before.'

Ivy took Vernon's arm and turned away from the bookshelves. 'If you trust me, I'll help you cook something I think she'll enjoy.' Vernon smiled, 'does that mean you'll come and eat with us, or do you already have plans for today?' Ivy laughed. 'Yes, it does, and no, I have no plans other than reading a new book.' When they left the bookshop, Ivy said they would need to buy some ingredients on the way back to Vernon's mother's house. 'What are we cooking?' Ivy tapped the side of her nose. 'It's an old family recipe from Italy.' Vernon raised his eyebrows. 'I didn't know you had Italian relatives; I thought your mother was French.' Ivy nodded. 'She was; the Italian connection belongs to my first husband. Bertie's father's family were Italian immigrants who came to England around the same time as my mother arrived here from Paris. Bertie's mother Catherine used to make this delicious spaghetti recipe, but we'll need some nice fresh tomatoes and a few other things. We can take the underground train and go to Borough Market.'

The market's noise reached them as they walked along Borough High Street. Trains rumbled overhead, crossing the railway viaduct above the market. Barrows clattered and traders competed with each other; greengrocers, fishmongers and butchers all claiming to have the bargain of the day, the week, the century. Their friendly chaos filled the air and Ivy smiled. She took Vernon's arm and attempted a Cockney accent. 'come on darlin', this way for the very best fruit and vegetables in London!' Vernon laughed, 'which part of London are you from?' Ivy put her hands on her hips, 'there's manners f'yer!' Vernon stopped walking, 'if I close my eyes, I could swear that was Eliza Doolittle!' Ivy smiled, '*Pygmalion* is one of my favourite plays; I love the idea that someone can achieve something others thought impossible. Eliza and her accent are a perfect example'. Vernon nodded. 'I agree. We should keep our eyes open for a showing of it.' 'I'd like that. Now, which of these tomatoes look best?'

On the train to Highgate, Ivy and Vernon sat together with the shopping bags on their knees. Along with the beautifully ripe, fresh tomatoes, they'd bought spaghetti and a variety of other ingredients Ivy remembered Bertie's mother using in her recipe. 'It was always delicious when she made it, I hope your mother enjoys it.' Vernon looked at her, 'I hope so too. I do know she'll be delighted to see you.'

The last time Ivy visited North Road; it was to be reunited with her sister. Irene Revill's large terraced house was as she remembered it. High ceilings allowed the last light of the afternoon to fill the long hallway and her shoes sank into the luxurious carpet. Vernon took her hand. 'This will be a wonderful surprise for her.' He opened the lounge door quietly, keeping Ivy hidden behind him. Irene greeted her son; her voice was smaller and quieter than Ivy remembered. 'I've brought a guest home with me, mother. Do you know who it is?' Irene didn't reply. Vernon moved to one side and Ivy stood where Irene could see her. She averted her eyes and concentrated on unbuttoning her coat, hoping Vernon's mother hadn't noticed her shocked expression. Irene Revill's pretty blue eyes were cloudy and unfocussed and the large armchair emphasised her thin frame. Her smile, when her gaze rested on Ivy, was weak. She pushed herself out of the chair and moved towards her. 'My dear, I am so happy to see you again.' The women embraced and Vernon held up the shopping bags. 'And you'll never guess what we're having to eat!'

Catherine Primavesi's spaghetti with tomato sauce was a resounding success, with Irene managing to eat a medium-sized portion. Ivy suggested to Vernon they keep it relatively simple, hoping to tempt Irene's palate. She heated some olive oil in a pan then added a few cloves of finely chopped garlic. Vernon chopped the tomatoes and Ivy cooked them until they broke down into a sauce. She added a pinch of salt and a few fresh basil leaves before stirring the pan then letting the sauce simmer. In another pan, Vernon cooked the spaghetti in salted boiling water until it was, in Ivy's words, *'al dente'*. He raised his eyebrows and she laughed. 'Still a little bit firm, Vernon.' After draining the spaghetti and adding it to the sauce, Ivy mixed everything together then garnished the dish with basil leaves and a drizzle of olive oil. When they finished eating, Irene sat back in her chair and thanked Ivy for the meal.

Over coffee, Irene asked Ivy about her career. Ivy sipped her drink, considering her reply. She had returned to London after recuperating from the Spanish flu in Bournemouth, fully intending to return to work at Endell Street if they still needed her. Before she managed to contact the doctors, she was thrown off course by her disastrous marriage. More recently, she'd been checking the theatrical magazines with a view to returning to the stage, but now realised her efforts were half-hearted; she wasn't sure it was what she wanted to do with her life. She looked at Irene. 'I'm very glad you asked me; I think it's time for something new.'

Ena

Ena knocked on Mr Young's office door. She'd made a list of help she thought she and others could offer to people in need. Now she needed a space to provide the help. She and Jack drew a map of the buildings making up the flour mill and adjoining soap works, and she had a suggestion to put to Mr Young. The flour warehouses were situated at the east end of the building, along with offices, the boardroom and committee room. A blacksmith's shop and a sack repair shop stood at the rear of the building, but what Ena was interested in were the nearby storage rooms. She was hoping to persuade Mr Young al allow her to use one of the rooms. He called for her to come in. He stood up and wished her good morning then invited her to sit. He gestured towards her list and asked how he could help. She opened her mouth to speak but he interrupted.

'I do apologise Ms Leighton; may I say something?' Ena nodded. She looked at her lap and crossed her fingers under the piece of paper, hoping her plan wouldn't be thwarted before it had begun. 'I wanted to thank you for the comprehensive safety procedures you drew up following our last meeting. I understand they're proving very effective in reducing the risk of accidents.' Ena raised her head. 'I'm pleased to hear it, Mr Young.' He steepled his fingers across his lips. 'Now, what can I do for you today? I heard something about a campaign for equal pay?' Ena shook her head. 'No, it's not that. I think given the country's economic challenges we need to be realistic and accept that is a long-term objective.' Mr Young nodded. 'That's a very pragmatic approach, Ms Leighton. And is what you have written down more of a short-term objective?' Ena sat up straight and cleared her throat. 'I hope it can be achieved in the short term, but it's an initiative I believe could have a long-lasting impact on our community.' Mr Young leant forward. 'I'm all ears, Ms Leighton.'

Back at the tea shop, Ena told Beatrice about her meeting. 'I'm not giving up the equal pay campaign, it's infuriating we should have to fight for it, especially after our efforts during the war. I think there need to be fundamental changes in government policy before we stand a chance of getting anywhere close to effective debate. I've been reading other, equally worrying news reports about unemployment and poverty and I think we can do something to help.' Beatrice nodded. 'Very wise. Better to fight for something you think you have a chance of achieving. So?' Beatrice pointed at Ena's notebook. Ena smiled. 'Mr Young agreed to us using one of the CWS storerooms to set up a welfare centre.' Beatrice clapped her hands. 'Well done, Ena. That's tremendous news. Please allow me to make the first donation to the cause.' She reached under the counter and produced a large bag of loose tea. 'I'll divide it into smaller bags to give out to people. We can ask families with allotments to donate whatever they can in the way of vegetables. And we can make batches of soup and divide it among people.' Ena agreed. 'The cost of meat and dairy produce continues to rise, it's a disgrace some families are relying on soup kitchens to survive.'

Beatrice reached under the counter again. This time she produced a half-knitted garment hanging off two knitting needles. 'This was going to be Bartholomew's Christmas present but I think the wool can be put to better use!' Ena smiled, remembering the knitting army she'd been part of in Bournemouth. 'That's a good idea; I can knit some items too.' She embraced her friend, confident that between them they could make the welfare centre worthwhile.

Mona

As opening night approached, Mona became increasingly nervous. Tilly and Marv reassured her rehearsals had gone well and there was no reason the show shouldn't go off without a hitch, 'Besides, Wilfred will be in the audience, cheering you on.' Mona helped Tilly with her zip before turning around for her friend to do the same. 'Yes, he said in his last letter he would be here.' 'Well then, no need to worry, is there? And afterwards we can show Wilfred the delights of Tremblay's!' Mona smiled then turned away. She still found it unbelievable Marv had offered her the lead in his show. She saw the guilt and sadness in his eyes every day. Guilt for sacking her and grief for the loss of Peggy. She sighed; he was trying to make amends. She owed it to him, to Peggy and to herself, to do her best. She thought about Wilfred's last letter; he'd said he missed her and couldn't wait to be back in New York. He told her he could stay longer, because the bank had allowed him some time off before starting his new job. He wanted to go back to Keens and for her to show him the other places she'd discovered. He also wrote that he wanted her to meet his parents and sister, *'I think you'll get along famously'*, and to make plans for their future.

Mona stood in the wings, readying herself for her opening scene. She hadn't dared to look out while the curtains were down but Marv assured them it was a full house. She knew what the audience would have seen when they arrived and she envied anyone visiting the theatre for the first time. The auditorium walls, adorned by gold silk wallpaper, glittered. Red velvet drapes and rugs and polished brass railings added to the opulence of the luxurious stalls. A huge Wurlitzer organ dominated the space on the right-hand side of the stage, and an orchestra pit reached the performance level. The ceiling's coloured gilt frescos shone, illuminating Greek statues and busts hidden in wall niches. Wherever theatregoers sat, on each of the Paradise's three levels, their surroundings were equally beautiful, with rest rooms and waiting rooms as grand as any cathedral.

Mona tapped her foot in time to the music, waiting for her cue. She is playing one of a group of foundlings who have come to the Alley Inn in Greenwich Village to apply for the job of dishwasher, escorted by Mrs Ten Broek, a wealthy widow and social worker. The Inn's proprietor chooses Mona's character, Sally Green, known as 'Sally of the Alley', but she isn't happy with her new position. Alone with her fellow waifs, she admits what she wants more than anything is to become famous. When the familiar tones of the piano began, Mona relaxed into her role. The set was an empty dining room where she and four other maids were clearing dishes away. She gathers the others around her and kneels. Although she has to start at the bottom, Sally is determined nothing will keep her down, just like Joan of Arc. She leads the group in a merry dance, declaring, 'You Can't Keep a Good Girl Down!' The audience joined in, clearly on the side of ditching the notion of down-trodden women, and thunderous applause filled the auditorium. In between her numbers, Mona scanned the boxes; there was no sign of Wilfred. She tried to peer into the stalls but glare from the stage lighting made a clear view of any one individual impossible.

As the story progresses, Sally catches the eye of Blair Farquar, a millionaire's only son. She dances at the Inn, impressing a theatrical agent called Otis Hooper. Seeing Sally dance gives Otis an idea; he knows his client, Madame Nookerova, a famous French ballet dancer, is unable to make a forthcoming appearance. Since no one knows what Madame Nookerova looks like, he decides to pass Sally off as the ballerina. While Sally goes off with Otis to plan the deception, Blair returns with his friends. Everyone is curious about his latest love, and he reveals his plans to take his Sally away from the alley. During the ball at the Farquar's Long Island estate, the host, in introducing *'Madame Nookerova'* to the press, describes her looking as innocent as a primrose. To which madcap Sally snaps, 'I am zee opposite of a primrose. Zere is nossing 'prim' about me!' With that as her musical cue, she sails gaily into the revelation that she is a 'Wild Rose'. Blair, puzzled by the ballerina's close resemblance to Sally, finds himself falling in love all over again. Sally's dancing impresses everyone and Otis gets her an engagement in the new Ziegfeld Follies. In the 'Butterfly Ballet', amid choruses of butterflies and moths, Sally dances and emerges a fully-fledged Ziegfeld star. In the finale, Sally and Blair make their wedding vows as joyful bells ring out for the final number. *'The Little Church Around the Corner'.*

Mona enjoyed the notion of being 'madcap', singing about her vibrant and untamed spirit and comparing herself to a wild rose. Much of the show reflected her desire to break free of her humble beginnings and embrace a life full of excitement and adventure, and she lost herself in the routines. It was only when the company took their encores that she had the opportunity to scan the boxes again. Her heart sank but she kept smiling. Tilly caught up with her on the way back to their dressing room. 'Perhaps he didn't come to see you beforehand because he thought he'd make you nervous. He's thoughtful like that.' Mona shook her head. 'He's not here.' Cheers rang out when she pushed the dressing room door open. 'Here's to our star!' Mona thanked people and smiled but her heart was like a rock in her chest. Wilfred had broken his promise.

Chapter 18

Ivy

Ivy had considered doing something new when she was flicking through theatrical magazines looking for opportunities to start performing again. She didn't find anything that interested her and she started questioning herself. Was there something else she could do? When she and Vernon visited Borough Market, she noticed they had a charitable trust. She'd looked into their operation and discovered it was run by volunteer trustees. The market was more than somewhere to buy and sell goods; it was a social hub where people gathered, shared news and built community ties. She contacted the trust to ask if they needed more volunteers, and within a few days she was busier than she'd been for years. The cost of living and the price of food were concerns for many people; staple items like flour and bread fluctuated in price, putting them out of reach for some. The community kitchen where Ivy volunteered ensured no one in need went without.

She enjoyed her own company and spent time with her friends. Since their meal at North Road, she and Vernon had worked together to come up with new food for his mother to try. Every time Vernon sailed, he came home with ideas for new recipes. There was colour in Irene's cheeks for the first time in years, and Ivy managed to persuade her to visit Waterlow Park; a 26-acre park on a steep hillside less than half a mile from her house. Irene's steps were shaky, but she told Ivy it was worth the effort for the spectacular views over the city. Ivy missed Vernon when he was away but she continued to spend time with Irene. They talked about books, listened to music and played cards. She socialised with Grace and Walter and became a regular at

Teddy Parr's Redford club, along with Lydia, Daphne, Vivienne and Zee. Life was good.

At the community kitchen one day, Ivy was struck by a particular group of women. She didn't remember seeing them before and her eyes were drawn to them when another of the volunteers said they were music hall dancers. 'Apparently the place fell on hard times and they were thrown out of their accommodation.' Ivy's mind flew to her sister's time working at a sleazy music hall in London, and the flea-ridden excuse for a lodging house her employer used for his dancers. She knew Mona was in New York but still scanned the shocked, drawn faces of the women, looking for her sister. She started walking towards them. 'We should give them some soup and help them to find alternative accommodation.' The other woman stayed where she was. 'Good luck. There's a never-ending supply of theatricals like them.' Ivy knew out-of-work performers faced significant challenges; she also knew what support was available to help them. The Actors' Benevolent Fund provided financial assistance, helped with living expenses, medical costs and other necessities. In addition to financial aid, the Theatrical Guild provided help in finding work. And there was them, the community kitchen. Ivy quickened her step; she would do whatever she could to help.

She stopped dead in her tracks when one of the women turned to face her. She'd seen her before. Her long hair had lost its sheen; now it hung over her shoulders and down her back; lank, dry and streaked with grey. The woman tried to smile; the angry bruising across her cheek and jaw turned her expression into a grimace. She leant towards Ivy and narrowed her eyes. She spoke softly; 'I recognise those eyes. You're my friend's sister.' As the woman said Mona's name, she collapsed into Ivy's arms.

Mona

At Tremblay's, Mona drank and danced and laughed. Inside, she despaired. Tilly said she was sure Wilfred would have a good reason for not being there. 'There must have been some emergency. Something to do with his parents or sister.' Mona shrugged and ordered another cocktail. She'd believed Wilfred was different; that they had the chance of a happy future together. Bur like almost everyone else, he'd let her down. If there was an emergency, why hadn't he sent her a telegram? She sighed and pushed her way onto the dance floor. She closed her eyes and lost herself to the music.

She moved to the rhythm of 'Everybody Loves My Baby', her arms and feet getting faster and more frantic as the saxophone and piano reached their crescendos. Sharp nails dug into her arm and she cried out. Her eyes flew open and she turned, ready to confront her assailant. The words dried in her mouth. 'Nellie Pilkington. How did you get in here?' Nellie sneered, 'you think you're so clever, don't you? Like you're the only one who can drink in secret?' The woman jabbed at the angry red scar on her neck. 'That arrogant Marv wouldn't employ me because of this. Your brand new life, all at my expense. You stole this life from me and now I'm here to take it back.' Mona looked around but everyone on the packed dance floor was lost in their own jazz-fuelled world. Nellie sneered. 'Looking for your new American friend, are you? She's over there but I don't think she's interested. She's only got eyes for her latest fella.' Nellie tilted her head in the direction of the bar and Mona spotted Tilly, Charlie's arm slung across her shoulders. Nellie moved closer and yelled in Mona's face, 'see? Who's going to protect you now? Not your sister, she was in London the last I knew. And not your precious Violet. Remember her, eh? She saved your skin more times than I care to remember. Where do you think she ended up?' Mona saw the glint of a blade and stepped back. Nellie moved forward again and as Mona felt the cold steel on her neck, there was a thunderous pounding on the vault door. The music stopped, then three deep blasts from the trombone player threw the club into chaos. Nellie snarled and grabbed Mona's arm, 'you're not getting away this time!'

Mona tried to move but Nellie tightened her grip. Mona tried to make herself heard over the pandemonium. 'We can't be found drinking in an illegal speakeasy, Nellie.' They were almost knocked off their feet as people ran towards the exit. A burly man barged into them and Nellie raised the knife in his direction. A deafening crash silenced everyone; the vault door was down. High-pitched, screeching whistles told them the New York Police Department had breached Tremblay's defences. Mona screamed when a policeman grabbed her and held her arms behind her back. She winced as cold metal handcuffs dug into her skin. The policeman snapped the handcuffs shut and Nellie cackled, 'looks like good old law enforcement has saved me a job!' The policeman told her to shut up and produced a second pair of handcuffs.

Ena

When Ena opened the door to the storeroom Mr Young had offered to let her use for the welfare centre, her mouth fell open. Jack folded his arms across his chest. 'This is why he didn't mind giving it up.' Ena cast her eyes over the dusty room, rubbish and boxes littered the floor. She took a deep breath. 'We'll clear it out, clean it up and make it shipshape and Bristol fashion in no time!' Jack shook his head. 'I admire your optimism Ena, but I think it's a lost cause.' Ena rubbed her hands together. 'Well, let's see, shall we?'

Two weeks later, thanks to the efforts of an army of friends, the rubbish was gone and new shelves were in place. Shelves that now groaned with donated produce, knitted garments and outgrown toys. They were ready to help. Ena had asked people to spread the word about the centre; saying it would be open in the evenings and at weekends. Beatrice, Dolly and Olive offered to help when they could, and Ena hoped to extend their opening hours. On the first day, she hurried to the centre when she finished work. She unlocked the door and turned on the light. She heated some soup and sat behind the counter. After half an hour she walked to the door. The flour mill and the soap works were active throughout the evening and into the night, and she watched and listened to the sounds of deliveries and machinery. As the sun set and darkness fell, she heard footsteps outside and stood up, ready to help however she could. Jack ducked as he came through the door and she sighed. 'I'm sorry, am I a disappointment?' She shook her head. 'No,' Jack looked around. 'No one came?' 'No. It's pride, isn't it?' Jack shrugged. 'Possibly. Or shame.' Ena tutted. 'People don't need to be ashamed in front of me.' Jack touched her arm. 'I know that, but they don't. Very few people know how you went without. Come on, let's get you home.' Reluctantly, Ena put on her coat and hat and locked the door behind them.

Two weeks later, Ena could count on one hand the number of people who'd visited the welfare centre. A woman arrived one night, as she was locking the door. Her black woollen shawl was threadbare across her thin shoulders and she coughed when she tried to speak. Ena understood enough to know she had young children at home who were starving. She made a point of not asking the woman any personal questions; instead she offered soup and bread which the woman grabbed with grubby hands. Ena picked up a brown paper bag and placed a number of items inside; soap, a scrubbing brush, homemade biscuits and some of Beatrice's tea. 'Come again, please. And tell anyone else who's struggling. Please.' Ena's words fell into the cold air as the woman disappeared into the night.

Incessant rain pounded the roof of the storeroom all morning on Ena's third Saturday at the welfare centre. Dolly joined her as the midday bells rang at St Mary's Church. She brought beef dripping sandwiches and while they ate they signed, asking each other what more they could do to encourage people to accept their help. Ena was signing, 'I don't know and I'm starting to think I should give up', when a massive explosion rocked the storeroom. A crack appeared in the roof then dust and debris started to land on their heads. As Ena grabbed Dolly and signed, 'we need to get out of here,' a roaring sound like thunder rolled along the riverbank towards them. Ena put her arm around Dolly's shoulders and bent low as they hurried outside. Through a curtain of rain, her eyes were drawn to the horizon, where the pit had stood. Ena felt a tug on her arm and turned. Dolly's hands moved quickly. 'My dad; he's at work.' A black avalanche of rocks and dust careered down the hill from the entrance to the pit head. Ena pulled Dolly away and they ran.

ACT TWO

Chapter 19

Ivy

The women from the dance troupe gathered around Ivy and their friend. 'Violet? Vi? What happened, is she all right?' The woman's anxious eyes searched Ivy's, hoping for reassurance. 'I don't know but she needs to be seen by a doctor.' The woman shook her head. 'We can't afford doctors, Miss. We haven't got any money.' Ivy hailed a taxicab. 'You don't need money; we're going to the Samaritan Free Hospital for Women. Are you coming?' The woman hesitated for a moment then helped Ivy lift Violet into the cab. Violet's eyes were unfocused and her legs shook as they sat her in between them. Her head rested on her friend's shoulder and she closed her eyes. The driver turned to look at them, narrowing his eyes at Violet. Ivy met his gaze. 'She's ill and we need to go to the Samaritan Free Hospital for Women on Marylebone Road, as quickly as possible.' The driver stared at them. Ivy opened her handbag and took out her purse. 'I can pay; now please start driving.' The cab started to move and Violet's friend sighed. 'It never ceases to amaze me what money and nice clothes can get you.' Ivy turned to her. 'I know it's wrong, but the important thing is your friend is seen by a doctor. Don't you agree?' The woman looked at Violet, her eyes sad. 'Yes, I do.'

'Who are you, anyway?' Ivy extended her hand. 'Ivy Leighton, I'm pleased to meet you, Ms…?' The woman wiped her hand on her dress before taking Ivy's. 'My name is May.' Ivy heard the trace of a Scottish accent in May's soft voice and frowned; what had brought her to London? The dirt under her fingernails and the dark circles beneath her eyes told Ivy life hadn't been easy for May. 'How do you know about this hospital?' Ivy smiled. 'A friend of mine is a doctor there. Trust me; she'll look after Violet.' 'She?' Ivy nodded. 'When I was an orderly at Endell Street Military Hospital during the war I learnt we have a lot of extremely skilled female doctors and surgeons. The war gave them the opportunity to practise because so many male clinicians went to the front. Some female doctors were prevented from practising fully once the war ended; many male doctors returned and reclaimed their positions and women were expected to return to their pre-war roles or leave the profession altogether. Some were told they could only treat women and children, so Vivienne found a hospital where her skills would be put to good use and she's been at the Samaritan ever since.' 'Vivienne?' 'Yes, Dr Vivienne Lawson.' Ivy pictured her friend, with her outlandish fashion sense and long red hair. Lydia had told her about Vivienne's expertise in treating vulnerable women; she looked at Violet's bruised face and May's worried expression and nodded. 'I think we're exactly where we need to be.'

When the cab pulled up outside the hospital, Ivy took out her purse and paid the driver. She looked up at the red brick building with its bow windows. They walked inside slowly, supporting Violet between them. A friendly receptionist directed them to a waiting area and said she would contact Dr Lawson. Ivy heard Vivienne's footsteps on the tiled corridor; her one concession to the obligatory white coat uniform were bright orange heeled strap shoes. They matched her hair, pulled back into a tight bun, her curls tamed for the duration of her shift. 'Ivy.' She had never seen Vivienne in her professional capacity and marvelled at the change in her friend's demeanour. She couldn't imagine this starched doctor shrieking at one of Teddy's lewd jokes, cocktail and cigarette in hand. 'Hello, Vivienne. This is my friend Violet. She needs medical attention.' Vivienne gave a short nod. 'She does.' Vivienne gestured towards a hospital porter who wasted no time in producing a wheelchair. With Violet seated safely, Vivienne turned to Ivy and May. 'I'll need to conduct a thorough examination; you may as well come back in an hour or so. There's a decent café round the corner.' Ivy thanked her and the porter wheeled Violet away. She looked at May. 'Come on, I'm sure you can manage something to eat and I'm in need of a cup of coffee.'

Settled in the café, with May's breakfast ordered and Ivy's hands around a cup of strong coffee, the women considered each other across the small table. Ivy spoke first. 'Well, this isn't how I expected my day to turn out.' May's eyes darted from one table to another. 'I honestly don't have any money, not one penny; is that doctor going to treat Violet for nothing?' Ivy nodded. 'Yes, the Samaritan provides free healthcare to women who can't afford private medical treatment.' May's lip trembled. 'Thank you, I don't know what would have happened to Violet today if you hadn't been there.'

Ivy sipped her coffee. 'What brought you to the community kitchen?' May sighed, 'it's not something I'm proud of'. She stopped and Ivy waited. 'One of the other dancers, she...' A waitress arrived with May's breakfast and the interruption gave her an opportunity to take a breath. As she picked up her knife and fork she spoke quickly. 'It was a stallholder in the market. One of the girls stole an apple and he yelled after her that she didn't need to rob him, not when there was free food round the corner.' May stared at her plate and Ivy saw a tear roll down her cheek. She reached across the table and took May's hand. 'It's all right, you have nothing to be ashamed of.' May shook her head. 'But I do. My whole life has been shameful.' May's shoulders shook as she sobbed and Ivy moved her chair to sit next to her. She gave her a handkerchief and squeezed her hand. 'Dry your eyes and take some deep breaths. And don't let that delicious breakfast go to waste.' May smiled through her tears and Ivy ordered another cup of coffee.

When they returned to the hospital, the receptionist directed them to a ward, saying Dr Lawson had decided to admit their friend. They walked into a large room with rows of beds lined up along the walls. Curtains were drawn around some of them for privacy and Ivy saw Vivienne standing at the side of one. They approached slowly and Vivienne opened the curtain for them. Violet's hair fanned the white pillow, framing her pale face and hollow cheeks. Her eyes were closed but they flickered when Vivienne started speaking. 'Violet has a severe case of malnutrition along with a number of cuts and bruises. I'd like to know how she acquired them, but that's for another day. We have some wonderful new antiseptic medicine to prevent her worst wounds becoming infected. I'll keep her under observation for a couple of days; a few good meals and clean hygienic surroundings should help her to heal.' Vivienne turned to May. 'You can sit with your friend for a while if you like. One of our nurses will dress your own wounds while you're here. Ask her to give you some carbolic soap before you leave. It's strong and astringent and a marvellous antiseptic.' May thanked Vivienne and sat on a chair next to Violet's bed.

Vivienne opened the curtain and indicated Ivy should follow her. Outside the ward, she led her to a seating area. 'As a charitable hospital, our admission process is relatively strict; I'll need a letter of recommendation from a doctor or benefactor. Would you provide that, darling?' Ivy nodded. 'Of course; I'll draft something when I get home.' Vivienne looked towards the ward. 'I'm guessing there are others and I'm questioning what happens when I discharge Violet. Will she go back to the same vulnerable situation?' Ivy sighed. 'They're homeless and unemployed. They need a more permanent solution or this will continue to happen.' Vivienne took Ivy's hand. 'Yes, and next time there may not be a guardian angel nearby.' Ivy smiled, 'I'm glad I was there and able to help. I've met Violet before, as it happens.' Vivienne raised her eyebrows. Ivy stood up. 'That's a story for another day.' They returned to the ward where Ivy gave May money for a cab and a bed for the night. 'Come to the community kitchen tomorrow and bring your friends. We need to talk about getting you some help.' May thanked her then took Violet's hand. Ivy opened the curtain to leave then turned back to look at the women. Either of them could so easily have been her sister.

Mona

Mona lifted her skirt off the filthy floor of the small, dingy cell. The weak lighting cast gloomy shadows on the stone walls and she pulled her coat tighter. 'You new here, honey?' Mona looked at the woman sitting opposite. Her easy manner told Mona she was a regular visitor to the New York Police Department's holding cells. She nodded and the woman leant closer, revealing more of her diamond-decorated décolletage. She smelt of coffee and cigarettes and despite their location, Mona warmed to her. 'Listen, honey. These suckers', she gestured towards their armed guard, 'they're not interested in you and your friend. It's the likes of me they love to make an example of. Ain't that right, suckers?' The guard moved closer, 'keep it down, Texas'. The woman chuckled and sat back, her fur coat against the cold wall. She lit a long cigarette and inhaled deeply. She pointed the cigarette at Mona and Nellie, 'So, how do you gals know each other?' The cigarette rested on Nellie. 'You; you look as though you've been in the wars.' Nellie adjusted the scarf around her neck then glared at Mona. 'It's all her fault, I shouldn't even be here.' Texas grinned. 'No? Where should you be?' Nellie raised her chin. 'I followed her into that place because I wanted to have my say, to get my revenge.' Texas motioned for her to continue. 'We've got all the time in the world for your, "the world-owes-me-something story"'. Texas mimed a yawn and Mona stifled a giggle. Nellie stood up and put her hands on her hips. Texas clapped her bejewelled hands. 'That's what I like to see, a woman who means business! Let's hear it!'

Mona almost felt sorry for Nellie, then she pictured her holding the knife in Tremblay's and her pity disappeared. Nellie hissed, 'I saved her life and she repaid me with this.' She pulled the scarf away from her neck and Mona recoiled; had she done that? She spoke softly, 'Nellie, I'm sorry, I didn't think I'd hurt you, not that badly.' Nellie scoffed. 'You might have only broken the skin but I took the punishment for both of us after you ran! His henchmen found me and carried on where you left off.' Mona stood and moved towards her but Nellie turned away. Texas blew smoke rings up to the ceiling, 'jeez, this is the best entertainment I've had in all the times I've cooled my heels here! What happened next, gals?' Mona looked at the sassy American. 'I think it's what happened beforehand that's more important, don't you, Nellie?' Nellie glared and Mona took a deep breath. 'We were working at a sleazy music hall in London and I was desperate to make some extra money at Christmas. Nellie had a second job dancing at Billy's Club…' Texas interrupted, 'one of the *other* kinds of dancing clubs, was it?' Mona nodded. 'It was dangerous and Nellie did her best to protect me but he, our boss, wouldn't take no for an answer. Until…' Mona stared at Nellie. 'You saved my life and I'll always be grateful. I don't know what happened; I saw a way out and I took it, then you suffered as a result. Please forgive me.' Nellie crossed her arms. Texas tutted and pointed her cigarette at Nellie, 'look, we gals need to stick together, especially when we find ourselves in trouble. How about it?' Nellie shrugged. Texas sighed, then gestured towards the front of the cell. 'This conversation ain't over, but it looks like you two might be getting out of here.'

Mona heard keys jangling and turned to see the guard unlocking the cell. He pointed at her and Nellie. She looked at Texas, 'what about you?' Texas tutted, 'don't worry your pretty head, honey. I'll be back atop the piano at the El Fey Club on West 47th before you can say *"Hello, Suckers, come on in and leave your wallet on the bar."* Do come and see me there, sometime!'" The guard took Mona's arm and led her out of the cell. Texas laughed as Mona and Nellie made their way into the corridor. 'Toodle-oo, gals. Try not to fight, now!' Tilly was waiting for them. Mona opened her mouth to speak but Tilly put a finger to her lips. The guard positioned Mona and Nellie in front of a high desk, where a uniformed officer stared down at them. 'You two were in Tremblay's diner earlier tonight, yes?' Mona and Nellie nodded. 'And do you know the American alcohol laws?' They nodded again. 'Have either of you manufactured, sold or transported intoxicating liquor?' Mona glanced sideways and Tilly shook her head. A second officer appeared and whispered something to the first. He raised his eyebrows, 'did either of you see someone with a knife in Tremblay's?' Mona shuffled her feet and Nellie coughed then they both shook their heads. 'Ok, get outta my sight and don't let me see you again, understand?' Mona and Nellie thanked the officer and Tilly hurried them outside.

Mona grabbed Tilly's arm. 'What happened to Charlie? Are you all right?' Tilly carried on walking. 'Not here.' 'Where are we going?' Tilly laughed. 'Tremblay's! Where else?' Back in the warm cocoon of the speakeasy, Tilly said police raids were a regular occurrence. 'If you're caught drinking, you can be arrested. It's much more common for owners and operators of speakeasies to be targeted by law enforcement. I think they were making a point tonight, but I'm surprised because Charlie keeps a few lower-ranking officers happy so they look the other way. They enjoy a regular drink and usually tip him off when raids are planned; perhaps he's upset someone. The discovery of a knife could have landed him in serious trouble. Good job he's got friends on the force!' Mona and Nellie exchanged a glance; knowing the true story of the knife needed to stay between them.

'What'll you have to drink, darlings?' Mona stared; 'wasn't the alcohol confiscated in the raid?' Tilly pointed at a section of wall behind the bar. It looked exactly like the rest of the wall but Tilly explained it hid a secret wine cellar. 'At the sign of a raid, bartenders know to stash everything away!' As they sipped their cocktails, Mona asked Tilly about the El Fey Club. Tilly raised her eyebrows, 'how do you know about the El Fey?' Mona laughed, 'there was a woman in the cell with us who said she worked there'. Tilly almost choked on her drink, 'was it Texas Guinan?' Mona nodded, 'yes, she invited us to visit her at the El Fey sometime'. Tilly raised her glass in a toast. 'Well, something incredible came out of your first experience of a police raid, girls. A personal invitation from the one and only Texas Guinan, the queen of the New York speakeasy. That'll be a night to remember!'

Chapter 20

Ena

Ena held Dolly back when she tried to run towards the pit. She signed to say it was dangerous, that they needed to go to Colliery Road and find her mam. They kept their heads low as filthy coal dust swirled around them. A powerful push at her back threw them to the ground. Ena managed to pull her coat over Dolly as she waited for the thunderous second explosion to end. Shielding her eyes, she peered up towards what remained of the pit head. The coal face, exposed by the explosion and weakened by the torrential rain, had collapsed. A landslide of mud, coal and rubble slid down the hill with frightening speed and thunderous violence. Ena heard a voice and looked up to see Jack coming towards them through the rain. He pulled them up and with Dolly in between them, they stumbled to Colliery Road. Ena felt a tug on her coat sleeve and turned to Dolly, needles of rain stinging her face. Dolly signed, asking if Jack knew anything about her dad. Through heavy rain and air thick with coal dust, Ena moved her hands, 'not yet'.

As they reached Colliery Road, Ena raised her head. Olive Turnbull stood outside their house, along with a group of miners' wives, shawls pulled over their heads and huddled together for comfort. Olive broke free of the group and ran to her daughter. Dolly fell into her mother's arms and Ena turned away from their frantic signing. Jack took her hand, 'I'm going to the pit to see if I can help.' Ena nodded. 'I'll come with you.' She told Olive. 'Please Ena, bring us good news.' Olive stared at the group of women, many of whom Ena knew had been in this situation before. 'Some have gone to the pit but those with children, we stayed behind. Thank you for bringing Dolly home; please find

Marty for us.' Ena hugged Olive, without promising anything. She took Jack's arm and they retraced their steps, heads low against the foul air. When they reached the foot of the pit, the landslide suddenly came to a halt. The rain continued and a huge mound of slurry blocked their way. Flour mill and soap works staff, along with local residents, battled against the elements to get somewhere close to the pit head. The CWS fire brigade was soon joined by Gateshead engines, and firemen in heavy blue tunics, rubber leggings and protective helmets scrambled to put equipment in place. Ena and Jack moved to the side of the slurry mound and watched the rescue effort. A fireman directed people away from the pit head and Ena shielded her eyes against the rain to try and lip-read. 'Move back; it could blow again!' The firemen used thick, heavy hoses to pump the slurry out then took huge axes to the piles of rubble blocking their access into the pit. 'I feel helpless Jack, what can we do?' Jack shook his head. 'Nothing at the moment, best to let the experts work.' She took his hand and they stood in silence.

'Hello, Ms Leighton, Mr Todd; I came as soon as I heard. Is there any news?' Ena turned to see Mr Young making his way towards them. He'd replaced his usual smart office suit with thick dark overalls, sturdy hobnail boots and a black sou'wester. She shook her head, 'nothing yet. Do you know what happened?' Mr Young sighed. 'I received a message at home to say there had been an explosion and miners were trapped underground.' Jack gestured to the pit head. 'One of the miners told me there was a chronic problem with flammable gas, and as a precaution, explosives were never used. They rely on picks to manually extract the coal. They also carry special safety lamps to prevent gas being ignited accidentally. They're meant to be explosion-proof.' Mr Young tutted. 'Well something has clearly gone terribly wrong. I'll go and see if I can talk to the Colliery Manager.' Ena put her hand on his arm. 'Please, let us know what you discover. Miners' families are desperate for news.' He patted her hand. 'I will, Ms Leighton.'

Ena watched Mr Young picking his way closer to the pit head then she turned to Jack. 'Was it Marty who told you about the gas?' He nodded, 'it's been worrying him for some time'. 'He has to be all right, Jack. Dolly and Olive need him.' He took her in his arms. 'I know. We have to hope, Ena.' She took a deep breath. 'I need to do something; I can't stand here waiting.' Jack looked at her. 'What are you thinking?' She managed a weak smile. 'If people won't come to the welfare centre, we can take it to them.' Jack took her hand and they walked back to the flour mill. The door to the storeroom swung on its hinges, a victim of the explosion and torrential rain. 'Luckily there's nothing perishable near the door.' Jack ducked as he walked in behind her. 'What can we take that will help?' Ena's eyes moved around the room. 'Blankets and shawls, biscuits and barley sugars. We'd need an urn of hot water to make tea.' Jack started taking items off the shelves. 'Perhaps Beatrice could help with that?' On cue, the door creaked open and the Bundells appeared, tea urn in hand. 'We thought you might do this, so here we are.' Ena thanked her friends, and between the four of them they gathered anything they thought might help both the rescuers and those they hoped would be safely brought up.

On their way back the rain stopped. When they reached the foot of the pit, they saw firemen carrying ladders to the pit head. Bartholomew bit his lip, 'they'll need to go down a fair way to rescue anyone with those'. Jack nodded. 'Men might be trapped on different levels. Look, they've also got heavy-duty ropes and harnesses and those smoke helmets will protect them against any toxic gases; hopefully they can reach any survivors.' It was the first time anyone had suggested there might be fatalities; although they all knew it was likely. Ena closed her eyes and prayed for Marty and anyone else trapped in the bowels of the earth. As she handed out tea and biscuits, she spotted Mr Young talking to the Colliery Manager. She asked Beatrice to pour two more teas and made her way towards the men. Mr Young turned when she approached. 'Ah, Ms Leighton, doing something positive, very good.' Ena handed them the tea and asked the Colliery Manager if he knew what had happened. The man's large gloved hands shook as he took the tea and his grave expression made Ena's stomach lurch. 'As I was telling Mr Young, the best explanation of the presence of gas appears to be its escape from a notoriously dangerous coal seam much deeper in the mine. We don't know the reason for the ignition at this stage.' Ena took a deep breath before asking her next question. 'Are there any survivors?' The Colliery Manager lowered his head and spoke quietly. 'We don't know yet.' Mr Young pointed towards the group of firemen. 'You can't see from here but that man has three bars on his epaulettes; he's the Superintendent in charge of the rescue operation. If anyone has the experience to find survivors, it's him.' Ena narrowed her eyes. All she could see of the man was a shock of bright red hair when he removed his helmet. 'What's his name?' Mr Young looked in the man's direction and touched the brim of his sou'wester in salute. 'That's Tommy Dawson.'

The day grew colder and as the sun set, the crowds gathered at the pit head were silenced. Some of the firemen who descended had been brought back up, their ventilation apparatus only being good for so long against the continued presence of gas. Ena saw one of the firemen coughing violently when he removed his breathing equipment. When he bent double in an attempt to breathe, a first-aider went to help him. Suddenly there was a shout. 'Clear the way! We're bringing them up!' The crowds started to cheer but people quickly moved away. The firemen brought men to the surface, but the bodies on stretchers were so badly mutilated as to make identification impossible, Ena couldn't imagine any of them were still alive. The smell of burning flesh turned her stomach and she gagged, trying not to be sick. Jack put his arm around her shoulders. 'Come away, Ena.' She shook her head. 'No, I need to know what's happened to Marty. I need to tell Olive.' Jack turned her to face him. 'I'm so sorry Ena, I don't think anyone is being brought out of there alive.' The silence was deafening as stretchers were loaded into ambulances.

Chapter 21

Ivy

When Ivy left the hospital, she went to see Grace. At the sight of her friend, Ivy broke down. Grace held her and waited for her sobs to subside. She dabbed Ivy's face with a handkerchief until her friend managed to speak. 'Oh Grace, what was suffrage for if women continue to be hurt and debased by men? Brave women died to make things better for us all, but things are not better.' 'What happened, Ivy?' Ivy took a deep breath and told Grace about the women at the community kitchen. 'They've been beaten and thrown out onto the street, left to starve or freeze to death.' Grace sighed, 'some men in our business consider women dispensable. It's ironic, given the same women make money for them'. Ivy agreed, 'sadly, our society provides them with a continuing supply of vulnerable women, so they move on to their next victim'. Grace nodded, 'it makes me realise how lucky I was, years ago. I could easily have been in the same position as the women you met today, if I hadn't met Ursula when I did'. Ivy turned to her friend, suddenly realising she knew very little of Grace's life. 'Ursula?' Grace laughed, 'I'll go and put the kettle on'.

Once they were settled with tea and cake, Grace told Ivy about Ursula Innes, the woman she credited with her rise to fame. 'She protected us, Ivy. No man in our business was a match for Ursula Innes.' Ivy frowned. 'I've never heard of her, is she still working in London?' Grace shook her head. 'No, she took her dance troupe to America years ago and I believe she's still there. She treated her dancers well, made sure we ate properly and had somewhere decent to stay. Of course, the worst of the male directors hated her for it; she didn't give them the time of day. She worked us hard but gave us time off too. Her view was being cared for would make us better at our jobs, which of course is true.' Ivy sighed. 'Why don't some men see that? It makes perfect sense.' Grace shrugged. 'I don't know; some men can't seem to shift the old attitude towards women with a theatrical career, that we're fair game for whatever treatment they want to dole out.' Ivy tutted. 'Or they choose not to change their attitudes. Are you still in touch with Ursula?' Grace shook her head. 'No, I haven't heard anything of her for years.' 'And do you know of any other female directors who work in the same way to protect women?' 'No. We need a new Ursula Innes, don't you think?' Ivy nodded then realised Grace was staring at her. 'What?' 'Well, why not? You're well connected and have years of experience in the business.' Ivy stood up. 'Me?' Grace laughed. 'Yes, I think you'd make a perfect Ursula!'

Ivy, Vernon and Irene had a picnic in Waterlow Park the next day. It had become one of Irene's favourite places to walk, and she breathed deeply as they made their way around the three ponds, all fed by natural springs. 'It always feels so clean here, Ivy. I was shut up inside myself for so long, the fresh air is wonderful.' Ivy took Irene's arm. Vernon's mother still hadn't been able to visit her younger son's grave, but she was slowly regaining some measure of herself. The lush green trees and borders full of colourful blooms never failed to make her smile. She told Ivy she'd started gardening again and found comfort in bringing flowers and plants to life. They stopped at one of the grassy slopes and Vernon opened the wicker picnic basket. He shook the woollen blanket and laid it out for Ivy and his mother to sit on. The red and blue tartan contrasted with the verdant grass and Ivy smiled up at Vernon as she made herself comfortable. He had just returned from New York; his ship didn't dock for long but during his short shore leave he visited Katz's delicatessen in Manhattan's Lower East Side. He was very excited about a new sandwich he'd tried; pastrami on rye. 'I went to Smithfield Market to find the pastrami and Rinkoffs for the rye bread, so I hope you both like it.' Ivy and Irene watched Vernon lay out china plates and glasses. 'I've brought iced tea and lemonade because I know you like both. And there's mustard and dill pickles to accompany the sandwiches.' Vernon continued removing items from the basket; small homemade pork pies and potato crisps in greaseproof bags with a twist of salt, and for afters he'd brought fresh fruit and a cream sponge cake. Ivy laughed. 'When did you do this? You only came home yesterday.' Irene tutted. 'He hasn't slept, have you, son?' Vernon shook his head, 'it's worth it for my two favourite ladies. Now, tuck in!'

After they'd eaten, Irene said she wanted to take a stroll to Sydney Waterlow's statue. 'When he was Lord Mayor of London, he donated the park to the public in 1889 as "a garden for the gardenless". His generosity means we can sit here today, enjoying this beautiful spring sunshine.'" Vernon helped his mother up. 'I won't be long.' Ivy took Vernon's hand. 'Thank you for arranging this, the picnic was delicious.' Vernon smiled, 'you're very welcome, it's heartening to see my mother eating well these days. Did anything exciting happen while I was away? How are things going at the community kitchen?' Ivy held out her glass, 'pour me another iced tea and I'll tell you'.

Back at Garrick Street, Ivy started to make a list of everything she needed to do, if she was serious about establishing herself as the director of a dance troupe. A director like Ursula Innes, where the dancers' welfare was paramount. Vernon had encouraged her, saying he thought she was perfect for the job. 'You've been a performer yourself and you've seen the underbelly of the industry. You can be the antithesis of that; I think dancers will flock to you.' He also said he knew a few London hoteliers through his job as a ship's steward. 'I'm sure one of them will talk to you about negotiating a deal on accommodation.' She would ask Vivienne to be the provider of regular health checks, in return for a regular donation to the hospital. That left her with investment. She tapped her pen against her notepad; that was the all-important starting point, she needed up-front capital to set the wheels in motion.

Mona

After their time in the police cell, Mona hoped Nellie would soften towards her, perhaps even agree to call a truce. She was disappointed; Nellie seemed angrier than ever. She tried to ask her about the knife but Nellie refused to speak to her, and flounced out of Tremblay's without finishing her drink. As she left, Mona called after her, 'I'll be at Toney's Ice Cream Parlour for breakfast tomorrow, please come.' Nellie didn't respond. Tilly stared after her, 'where will she go?' Mona sighed. 'I don't know, but she's been looking after herself for a long time. I'm sure she'll be all right.' Tilly frowned as the door closed behind Nellie.

The next morning, Mona arrived at the ice cream parlour early. It was near the Paradise, and Tilly had taken her there for what she said was the very best ice cream and candy in the city. Mona looked around before she went inside, but there was no sign of Nellie. She pushed the door open, still hopeful. The parlour was full of light, with shiny brass railings, wood panelling and mirrored walls. Wire chairs with leather seats were positioned around small white marble tables. Cooling fans purred quietly, providing respite from the ever-increasing warmth of spring in New York's enclosed streets and avenues. She sat at a table near the window. Nellie couldn't miss her. She ordered coffee and waited.

Across the street, Nellie watched Mona going into the ice cream parlour. She wiped her brow with her scarf. Even this early in the morning, New York's muggy heat filled the streets. She ran her tongue over her cracked lips, tasting yesterday's drink in

Tremblay's. Her head pounded and her heart ached. She yawned and a coughing fit took hold. She shrunk back into the alley and waited for the coughing to end. She glanced along the alley. Some of the anonymous huddled shapes were starting to move, others could have died in the night. No one cared about New York's homeless, it was no different to London. She rubbed her shoes against the back of her stockings and straightened her coat. She ran her hands through her hair and pinched her cheeks. Her stomach rumbled and she walked to the end of the alley. Mona hadn't moved. Nellie watched as she lifted a drink to her lips. She salivated. She didn't want to talk to Mona, but she was thirsty and hungry. She sighed. Mona wanted her forgiveness, but if she let go of her vengeance and anger, what would she be left with? She couldn't remember a time when she hadn't felt angry towards someone; resentment fuelled her and helped her to survive. Her earliest memory was her father beating her mother. The day he first raised his hand in her direction, her mother screamed at her to run. She took her anger with her, along with a deep-seated fear. Initially, she struggled on the streets, but a powerful survival instinct kicked in, replacing her fear. She learnt how to live without love or protection. She did whatever work she needed to, in order to survive. When Mona had arrived at the Diamond all those years ago, Nellie saw her as yet another woman who thought she deserved better. Nellie didn't think that; she'd had no choice in life and she accepted her fate. Mona's poor choices led to her downfall, and Nellie had no sympathy for her. Until Mona asked for her help. She'd wanted to earn more money and send something home for her daughter. An image of herself as a little girl, cold and hungry on London's streets at Christmas flashed through Nellie's mind, and she agreed. And she'd regretted it ever since, because Mona turned on her. That was her reward for helping someone. She scoffed and started walking away from the parlour.

Mona sighed. She had finished her coffee and there was still no sign of Nellie. She stood up to leave and saw a figure across the street. She hurried out of the parlour and shouted. 'Nellie! Please wait!' Nellie didn't stop. Mona ran after her, sweat running down her face. Nellie ducked into an alley and Mona followed. Sharp nails raked Mona's face in the dark space and she screamed. Then she heard a dull thud and a dishevelled man thumped across her feet. She peered into the gloom. Nellie's wild eyes glistened and she dropped a blood-stained brick on the man's head. She threw her head back and laughed, 'what is it about you, Mona? Why do I keep on protecting you?' Mona shook as she tried to speak. 'I don't know, Nellie. I don't deserve it.' Nellie stared and something shifted. She'd thought Mona believed she was entitled to something in life, that it should be given to her rather than having to work for it. Nellie had never received anything unconditionally. Mona dabbed her cheek with a lace handkerchief. She reached her arm out to Nellie. 'Are you hungry?' She led Nellie to the back of the parlour and a private booth of beautifully carved wood. They sat opposite each other, sinking into the soft leather cushions and resting against the high-backed seats. Mona's eyes were drawn to Nellie's scarf, carefully arranged to hide her scarred neck. Under Mona's scrutiny, Nellie adjusted the scarf. Mona leant across the table, 'it's all right, no one can see'. Nellie's eyes glistened. Mona remembered what Violet said years before, when she arrived at the Diamond. She'd told her not to worry about Nellie, she acted tough as old boots, but wasn't all bad. Mona had seen both sides of Nellie over the years but this was new; a vulnerability in a woman she'd thought invincible. She pushed a menu across the table. 'See what you fancy; they serve breakfast and have all kinds of ice cream, milkshakes and banana splits.' Nellie sniffed and picked up the menu.

When they'd ordered; eggs over-easy with hash browns and sausage and a vanilla ice cream soda for Nellie, and a root beer float for Mona, they fell silent. Eventually, Mona spoke. 'What happened, Nellie? After I'd gone?' Nellie adjusted her scarf again. 'After you left me in Billy's Club, with that monster bleeding all over the floor and me with only your rags to wear?' Mona looked down, 'I'm so sorry, Nellie. I shouldn't have left you like that; I snapped.' Nellie sighed and took a deep breath. 'It was all right, for a little while anyway. Billy had heard the ruckus and he came into the room to see what was happening. He rushed me away and locked me in his office then one of the other dancers brought me some clothes. She told me to stay where I was until the coast was clear.' Mona frowned, 'what did she mean?' Nellie sniffed. 'It was to give Zettler's henchmen time to clean up. When Billy came back for me, the club was operating as normal; as if nothing had happened.' Mona frowned. 'Where was Zettler?' Nellie shrugged. 'I didn't know and I cared less; I was just glad to be getting out of there alive.' Mona looked around the ice cream parlour then leant across the table and whispered her next question. 'Did I kill him?' Nellie hesitated then shook her head. 'No. He's dead but his blood isn't on your hands. Your handiwork gave us a good laugh for months; watching him trying to hide his ugly scars. But it was those nasty little cigarettes that finished him off.' Mona pictured their odious, chain-smoking director. The toxic stench from his drug of choice, *'Cigares de Joy'*, had followed him to his death like a malevolent cloud.

There was something else Mona wanted to ask Nellie and her cheeks grew warm as she formed the words. She'd stolen Nellie's money and her passage to New York; she was responsible for what had happened to her. She took a deep breath, 'where did you go?' As Nellie started to speak the waitress brought their order. Nellie stared at the tall crystal glass. Layers of chocolate syrup and vanilla ice cream suspended in iced soda water and topped with whipped cream. She smiled sadly, 'I'm guessing you want the truth, not some polished version of it?' Mona closed her eyes and nodded. Nellie leant across the table. 'I had nowhere to go. None of the other dancers would help because they knew Zettler's men were looking for me.' Mona hesitated, 'what about Billy, couldn't he help you?' 'No. 'He'd already risked enough by hiding me straight after it happened. Zettler put a lot of business his way and he could just as easily have ruined him.' Mona poked her straw into her drink. 'And Violet had disappeared by then.' Nellie met Mona's eyes, 'sometimes she turned up for breakfast at the Diamond, but one of Zettler's thugs was always with her. I was homeless for a while, until they found me'. She touched her scarf and looked away. Mona reached across the table and gently moved the scarf. She stared at the jagged red wheels criss-crossed along the front of Nellie's throat. 'Did they do that to you?' Nellie pushed Mona's hand away before replacing the scarf. Mona narrowed her eyes, 'but you're here; you escaped'. Nellie laughed, 'yes, and that's the funny side of this whole sorry affair'. Mona frowned, 'what do you mean, funny?' Nellie reached into her handbag and produced a large knife. 'Remember this?' Mona gasped and started to stand up. Nellie grabbed her arm, 'sit down'. Mona kept one eye on the door but did as Nellie said. Nellie raised her left hand and pushed the blade of the knife into her flesh. Mona screamed and Nellie laughed when the blade disappeared, not into her hand, but back into the handle of the knife. Nellie laughed again, 'it's fake!' Mona stared and Nellie performed the trick again. It was Mona's turn to laugh then Nellie handed her the knife. Mona held up her left hand and plunged the knife into her palm. The rubber blade shot backwards, disappearing into the handle once more. She smiled, 'it looks like steel!' Nellie nodded, 'I know, it looks like the real thing! Even the New York Police thought so!' Mona shook her head, 'come on then, what's the story?'

Nellie took a deep breath. 'After this', she pointed at her neck, 'they kept me under lock and key in one of his brothels. Most of the men were straightforward enough; a few were nasty. I started to think I'd be there forever, then Kenny appeared.' Mona put her glass down. 'Kenny?' Nellie smiled. 'He saved my life, did Kenny Earnshaw. Most of the men, they took what they wanted and left; not Kenny. He asked how I came to be there and there was something about him that made me tell him. I haven't experienced much in the way of kindness in my life, but Kenny was kind. He came back the next day and said he had a job for me. I didn't trust him at first, I thought he was another one of Zettler's cronies, but he wasn't. He took me to a theatre where he produced comedy shows. He thought I could make people laugh, that it would be a better position for me than working for Zettler.' Mona smiled, 'that's unbelievable! How did he persuade Zettler to release you?' Nellie shrugged, 'all he said was he knew things Solomon Zettler wouldn't want getting out. I couldn't believe my luck, and the shows were hilarious. Full of fake props like that'. Nellie pointed at the knife lying on the table in between their glasses. Mona put her head on one side. 'You *can* make people laugh; I remember when you had everyone in stitches at the Diamond, doing your impression of Zettler.' Nellie smirked, 'turns out I'm good at something after all.'

Mona frowned, 'why did you come here with that?' Nellie picked up the knife and plunged the blade into the table. 'I wanted to scare you. I hated you for what you'd done. I managed to save some money and figured I'd see what New York City was like.' Mona smiled, 'and now? Do you think you can forgive me?' Nellie shook her head. 'I'm not sure I know how to forgive, but I don't think I'm in a position to judge you or anyone else. I've done plenty of things I'm ashamed of.' Mona sighed, 'will you at least let me help you to find somewhere to stay?' Nellie nodded. 'Good. Before that I think we should go somewhere and have a proper drink.' Mona stood up, 'come on, I know just the place!'

Chapter 22

Ena

The flour mill closed for two days following the disaster, as a mark of respect to those who had died. Six men lost their lives and 20 more were seriously injured by the force of the explosion. Eight miners were unaccounted for, and people gathered at the pit head to help the fire brigade by digging through the rubble. They moved material by hand or with garden tools. They worked quietly, listening for signs of life beneath the muddy earth. Attempts to locate the missing men were hampered when rain started falling again.

Ena barely slept and she was at the welfare centre before sunrise. When she approached the flour mill she looked up the hill to the site of the pit. She saw figures moving; black silhouettes against the grey sky. Jack and Bartholomew had done a makeshift repair to the storeroom door the previous evening, and she pushed it open carefully. Inside, she started cleaning up and getting ready to help. As a weak sun tried to break through the thick clouds, Jack and the Bundells arrived, carrying all manner of supplies. Ena smiled; between them they would try to make the desperate situation a little better for people. She and Beatrice were folding blankets when the first people appeared. A woman put her head around the door and spoke quietly, 'we heard there was hot tea, is that right?' Ena approached the woman to welcome her and gasped at the sight outside the centre. A crowd of people stood in silence; a community brought together in the face of disaster. Some were empty-handed and in need. Others, she saw, had brought what they could to add to the centre's supplies. Allotment vegetables, homemade children's toys, jars of jam; Ena's lip trembled at their generosity. 'Yes, please, come inside.' As people warmed their hands round cups of tea, they started telling their stories. A husband, brother or son hurt or missing, a neighbour grieving an unnecessary loss. A sense of bewilderment hung around them and Ena kept busy, trying not to think about Marty. Dolly's dad was one of the missing; eight men who'd gone to work the previous day and not come home. Mr Young had it on good authority from the Colliery Manager it was unlikely they would be found alive. She'd kept that information to herself, telling Dolly and Olive every effort was being made to find the missing men. That much was true, when one group of exhausted searchers laid down their tools, another took up the job. Children, oblivious to the despair, whipped up their wooden-top toys outside the welfare centre. By the end of the first day's light, the shelves were almost empty. People promised to return the next day with whatever they could offer to replenish Ena's stock. Ena and Jack walked to Bottle Bank in silence. There was no sign of the missing men.

On the second day after the explosion, Ena called at Colliery Road on her way to the centre. The Turnbull's front door was open and Ena found Olive sitting on a chair just inside. Dolly's sprightly mam had gone grey overnight. She looked up when Ena approached, her eyes dull and her lips drawn. Ena shook her head. 'There's no news, Olive. I'm so sorry.' Olive stared at her lap and Ena placed the kettle on the stove to make tea. Dolly appeared at the foot of the stairs and raised her hands in question. Ena signed her reply and Dolly turned away. Ena made tea then left, promising to return with any news. Jack was waiting outside the centre when she arrived and he pointed at the bags and boxes near the door. 'People have left donations overnight.' Despite her sadness, Ena smiled. 'We're part of a generous community, Jack.' He nodded and opened the door, 'and this is now the heart of it'.

As they were filling the shelves and marvelling at the kindness of strangers, they heard shouting outside. They stopped what they were doing and hurried to the door. People were running towards the site of the pit, shouting. Ena grabbed Jack's arm, 'what's happening?' Jack shook his head. 'I don't know, something has got people excited. Come on.' He took her hand and they joined the crowds. At the foot of the pit, they stopped. Above them, Superintendent Dawson was calling for calm. 'Everyone must be quiet. We need to listen for sounds of life.' Ena gasped, 'life? Jack, is it possible? Could Marty be alive?' Before Jack could reply, the ground beneath them started to shake. Ena squeezed Jack's hand, 'what's that?' A voice behind her answered. Mr Young was scrambling up the hill towards them. 'It's another explosion. If there is anyone still alive in there, they need to get them out. Now!' They got as close as possible to what remained of the pit head then stopped. The air was thick with coal dust and silence. Mr Young whispered to Ena, 'the Colliery Manager said one of the firemen thought he heard something from underground'. Ena frowned, 'what sort of something?' Mr Young pulled her and Jack to one side, 'like a chink'. Jack's eyes widened, 'a chink on tin?' Mr Young shrugged, 'perhaps, I don't know. It might be wishful thinking'. Ena looked up at the firemen. She knew the miners took tin cups down with them, for drinking water or tea during their breaks. She turned to Mr Young, 'but after nearly 48 hours, is it likely anyone is still alive in there?' Jack answered. 'It's possible. I read about a case in America where a group of miners survived a pit collapse. They were in an air pocket that provided them with enough oxygen to keep breathing until they were rescued.' Suddenly, one of the firemen called for silence. Then they heard it. Faint but unmistakable. Tin on tin. Ena's lip trembled as she pictured Marty and his colleagues toasting each other in their dark underground prison. She shivered and Jack put his arm around her shoulders.

Chapter 23

Ivy

Summer brought stifling heat to London and Ivy opened the dance studio windows to let in some air. She looked around the large room, remembering her conversation with Teddy when she started looking for investors. 'Darling, what a splendid project! You'll be perfect.' 'The thing is Teddy; I need some help.' Her friend's white curls were combed back off his face and dimples formed in his cheeks when he smiled. He handed her a cup of tea in a beautiful china cup. 'I'm all ears, darling.' When Ivy set out her plans for her dance troupe, Teddy went straight to his desk and reached for his cheque book. Ivy gasped, 'Teddy, that's too much!' He shook his head. 'I don't know how much Lydia has told you about my situation, Ivy, suffice to say, I have more money than I could ever hope to spend. My father; richer than Croesus but colder than Antarctica, left me everything when he put a gun in his mouth a few years ago.' Ivy put her cup down. 'I'm so sorry, Teddy. I didn't know.' Teddy waved her concern away. 'Fret not, darling. He never allowed me to know him so he died a stranger.' 'Your mother?' Teddy sighed. 'Ageing aristocratic heiress, drinking herself to death in the crumbling family pile in Chiswick. I visit infrequently.'

Ivy studied her friend; Teddy's unfailing bonhomie hid a tragic family background. In the Redford he'd created a club where bohemians mingled comfortably with the upper crust. Those calling themselves 'Bright Young Things' and 'Flappers' were also welcome. Despite their exuberant and outrageous behaviour, or perhaps because of it, Teddy encouraged this generation of bold, sexually liberated young people to eschew the authorities' hatred of jazz and make a night of it, and a morning, and an afternoon, if they had the stamina. Daphne told Ivy about a party he organised in a Burlington club. It had a Mozart theme and the guests were told to dress in eighteenth century costume. Another, that she attended with Lydia, Vivienne and Zee was Teddy's pyjamas and bottle party, where they were instructed to come in nightwear and bring their own alcohol. Daphne had laughed. 'Zee didn't need to change, coming straight from his studio as he often does. His tunic doubled up perfectly as a nightgown! Whatever people brought to drink; Teddy made sure there was a steady supply of it for the duration of the party. I remember walking home at dawn, stopping at an all-night café for bacon and eggs. What a night it was! That's Teddy; the perfect host.'

Walter and Daphne also put money into her venture and a contact of Vernon's offered hotel rooms for Violet and May. The women insisted on it being a temporary arrangement; once they started receiving wages as dancers in Ivy's new troupe, they were determined to be independent. Grace helped her to find the studio. It was located on the top floor of an office building on St Martin's Lane, in the middle of London's vibrant theatre land, not far from the magnificent Coliseum Theatre. Ivy stood with her back to the window. The oak hardwood flooring gleamed and she imagined the sound of tap shoes; metal toecaps clicking in time to the music. Floor to ceiling mirrors graced the walls and a brand new wooden ballet barre ran along the length of the studio, opposite the window. A piano was positioned in the corner and next to it, a brand new gramophone. Ivy bought the best she could afford. She went to Broadwood & Sons for the piano, knowing their long-standing reputation for high-quality instruments meant they were favoured by prominent musicians and composers. The pianos were known for their excellent craftsmanship and rich sound. She'd bought the gramophone at the Columbia Graphophone Company, famous for their high-quality sound reproduction and stylish designs. Ivy smiled; here she would instruct her dancers in ballet, tap and stage. Her approach would be to ensure her dancers' physical and mental well-being was catered for, they would live in decent accommodation and have regular health checks at the Samaritan. Ivy clapped her hands; now all she needed were dancers.

She decided to keep her dance troupe relatively small. It made sense in order to ensure the women were cared for in the way she wanted. She thought six dancers was enough to begin with and if the venture proved successful, she would hold more auditions. She already had Violet and May and asked them if there were any other women they could suggest. This conversation took place when Violet was discharged from hospital, under Vivienne's strict instructions to 'eat properly, keep a decent roof over your head and come back for regular check-ups'. Ivy took Violet and May to the café near the Samaritan, where they were in time for lunch.

'Have whatever you like; your new healthy eating regime hasn't started yet!' The friends thanked Ivy and studied the menu. Once they'd ordered; a pot of tea, three scotch broths, two steak and kidney puddings with mashed potato, one roast lamb with boiled potatoes and carrots and three bowls of semolina pudding, Ivy sat back and looked at her potential new recruits. Before she told them about her new dance troupe, she asked the question she'd wanted to ask ever since Violet collapsed into her arms at the community kitchen. There were two reasons she'd waited; she wanted Violet to have recovered and she was scared to hear the answer. She took a deep breath, 'would you tell me how you came to meet my sister?' The friends exchanged a glance and Ivy shook her head. 'I'm sorry, I shouldn't have asked. I'm sure that's a time you would prefer to forget.' Violet sipped her tea then spoke slowly. 'You came to the Diamond looking for her years ago, didn't you?' Ivy nodded, 'yes, I'd been told she was working there and that's when I met you'. Ivy shuddered, remembering the desperate-looking group of women, huddled together round the corner from the sleazy music hall. Violet's words were gentle. 'But she'd already gone, hadn't she?' Ivy nodded again, 'yes, and the other woman…?' Violet sighed. 'Nellie.' Ivy sipped her tea. 'Yes, she said Mona had hurt her, and stabbed someone else. I found out later when my sister wrote to me, that she attacked a man called Solomon Zettler.' Violet and May put their cups down and stared at her. Ivy put her hand to her mouth, 'I'm sorry, is he the man who threw you out onto the street?' The women looked at each other and for a while no one spoke. Then May raised her chin and met Ivy's eyes. 'That man harmed so many women, I'm glad he's dead.' Violet touched Ivy's hand. 'Your sister was applauded by most of us for what she did to him.' Ivy sighed, 'but not Nellie?' Violet shook her head. 'No, he and his violent henchmen punished Nellie for Mona's actions, because she was there and Mona had disappeared.'

Ivy spoke quietly, 'I think my sister believes she killed him'. Violet leant across the table, 'your sister is a good person; you need to let her know she didn't kill him, and she didn't hurt Nellie, not seriously'. Ivy shrugged, 'I wish I could but I don't have an address for her. Her last letter said she was sailing to New York to join a production company at the Paradise Theatre on Broadway. She said she would write again with her address in New York, but of course she didn't'. May smiled sadly, 'could you write to her at the theatre?' Ivy nodded, 'yes I could, thank you. I can't always think straight when it comes to Mona'. May nodded, 'she sounds a little like Nellie'. Violet said she had told Mona not to mind Nellie, that she acted tough but wasn't all bad. Ivy frowned, 'where's Nellie now? She wasn't at the community kitchen with you'. Violet shook her head, 'no, she hasn't been with us for a while. The last we heard; she was working in Kenny Earnshaw's comedy show at the Hippodrome'.

Mona

Mona breathed a sigh of relief when she and Nellie stepped through the door to the house on Old Broadway. The building's state-of-the-art air conditioning system delivered an icy blast of welcoming air after the stifling heat outside. The matinee had gone well and Marv said the evening was a sell-out. 'Take a couple of hours folks, then back here for more!'

Mona kicked off her shoes and sank into one of the large armchairs. Nellie went into the kitchen and Mona heard her chipping off pieces of the ice block to make ice cubes. She returned with two tumblers of water, with ice and a slice of lemon in each. 'I'm so grateful you and Tilly invited me to stay here, Mona. This place is like a palace!' Mona ran a hand across her brow. 'It's been a long, hot summer.' Nellie poured more water then sat down. 'You know I'm grateful Marv relented and gave me a position in his ensemble, don't you?' Mona sipped her water. 'I do, I think he realised he'd acted hastily.' Nellie hesitated, 'the thing is…I think it's time to go back'. Mona raised her eyebrows. 'To London?' Nellie nodded. 'Yes. I've enjoyed being here and I never thought I'd say this, but I miss the grey old place. We're nearly at the end of this run of shows so it might be a good time to leave.'

Mona stood up and walked to the window. She would never tire of the view from the penthouse. Tilly said it didn't matter where a penthouse was; overlooking Central Park, the Hudson River or any of the busy city streets, New York's apartment views were spectacular. Mona watched the hustle and bustle below. She thought of the places she'd seen and everything she'd experienced since she arrived; the restaurants, cafés and clubs. She smiled, remembering their visit to the El Fey; it was like nowhere she'd ever been. As Mona and Nellie knew first-hand, due to the illegal nature of her business, Texas was regularly arrested for violating Prohibition laws and causing public disturbances. She was at liberty the night they visited the El Fey, and true to her word, the flamboyant hostess had left word at the door that they should be brought straight to her private booth. Texas was lying across the top of the piano. When she saw them she drawled, '*Hello, Suckers*', and the room erupted. The El Fey was known for its tropical, exotic cocktails and the friends took full advantage of the extensive list; feeling themselves transported to an island paradise. In addition to the lively atmosphere, up-tempo jazz music, and Texas's witty jokes and stories, the El Fey was the perfect club for spotting celebrity clientele. They'd only been inside for a few minutes when Tilly tugged at Mona's sleeve. 'Look, over there, it's Grace Moore.' Mona knew the woman nicknamed the 'Tennessee Nightingale' was one of the most famous operatic sopranos and actresses in musical theatre and film at the time. She'd come to New York in 1919 to pursue her singing career, and performed in nightclubs to earn enough to pay for singing lessons.

Mona had ridden in a trolley car and visited Bloomingdales and Macy's. She'd taken a horse-drawn carriage ride through Central Park and would always remember her first view of the Statue of Liberty. She pictured London's dirty, busy streets. An image of Violet appeared in her mind. The woman she'd met when she was unceremoniously dumped at the lodging house near the Diamond. Not long before the ever-hopeful Violet disappeared, she tried to convince Mona things were changing for women in Great Britain. Mona questioned how the changes could reach women like them, working for a pittance in a run-down music hall. What had happened to Violet? She leant against the penthouse window. Up here they enjoyed complete privacy; the penthouse provided an escape from the city's noise and dirt. She turned to Nellie. 'Do you have somewhere to go back to in London?' Nellie shook her head. 'No, but Marv might give us letters of recommendation; I'm sure we'd soon find jobs and somewhere to stay. And you could look up that Wilfred fella, if you're still interested in him.' Mona looked out of the window again; was she still interested? She hadn't heard anything from him since before opening night. Perhaps it was time to forget Wilfred Henson. Mona yawned, 'This heat has taken it out of me, I'm going to have a nap before it's time to go back to the Paradise.' Nellie nodded, 'Alright, I'll wake you up in time.' As she made her way to her bedroom, Mona tried not to think about Wilfred.

The night before they were due to sail to Southampton, Mona and Nellie arrived at the Paradise to find the place deserted. They had performed their last show the previous evening and had come to collect their final wage packets. When Mona pushed the stage door open, the silent corridor was in darkness. 'That's odd, Marv would usually be here shouting orders at everyone.' As they walked towards the dressing rooms, the sound of the orchestra tuning up reached them. Mona headed for the entrance to the stage; the door, usually open at this time, was closed. She frowned at Nellie then pushed the door open. They were met by a cacophony of noise; the orchestra struck up and Tilly's dulcet tones rang out.

'Toot, Toot, Tootsie, goodbye,
Toot, Toot, Tootsie, don't cry,
That little choo, choo train that takes me,
Away from you, no words can tell how sad it makes me,
Kiss me, kiss me, Tootsie, and then oh baby, do it over again.'

When her friend finished singing, Mona joined her on stage. Tilly laughed, 'you didn't think you'd get away without a party, did you?' 'I should say they won't!' Marv handed out drinks, 'from his own private stash', according to Tilly. He instructed everyone to give three cheers for their English buddies as they left for London. 'Come back anytime, gals, I'll always find a place for you!' Marv raised his glass and Mona smiled; the man who'd terrified her years ago had become a friend.

The next morning, Mona and Nellie stood in the salty air at the rail of RMS *Cedric*. Nellie touched Mona's arm. 'I'm not dragging you away, you know. I could have travelled alone.' Mona shook her head. 'No, I think it's time to go back. And I've decided; I'm going to find Wilfred and give him a piece of my mind.' Nellie cheered as the deep bellow of the ship's horn signalled their departure.

Chapter 24

Ena

The crowd at the pit head held their breath. Ena whispered to Jack, 'how will they get them out?' He shook his head, 'whatever they're going to do, they need to do it quickly'. He looked up and Ena followed his gaze. Black clouds scudded across the horizon, the strong wind pushing them towards the pit. As fat drops of rain started to fall, Mr Young arrived. 'I've spoken to the Colliery Manager and he says Superintendent Dawson thinks the men are perched on a ledge at least 60 feet down. His experience tells him the pocket of air that's saved them up to now is disappearing rapidly.' Ena pictured Dolly and Olive. 'Can they save them?' Mr Young pointed towards Tommy Dawson, 'if anyone can, it's him'. They watched Tommy Dawson's every move; they would learn the detail of the rescue operation later.

Superintendent Dawson's first instruction to his men was to ensure their protective helmets and breathing apparatus were working correctly. 'We don't know about the air quality in there; the chances are it's contaminated.' Dawson had the respect of his men, having successfully carried out a number of dangerous rescue operations during his career. The men did the necessary checks to ensure their equipment and clothing were satisfactory. 'The rain is our enemy; if it continues, conditions will become increasingly dangerous. Expect it to be slippery underfoot and proceed with caution. The sounds we've heard from underground suggest some of the missing miners are positioned on a ledge, likely a ledge of rock, some distance down the mineshaft. Their electric cap-lamps will have afforded them some light, but the charge only lasts for 12 hours at most; they'll have been in darkness for some time now. We need to reinforce the walls with boards to create a stable surface for our descent, and for our exit with the men in tow.' There was no aspect of Dawson's instructions that brooked the possibility of failure; positives littered his monologue. 'The steel wire ropes are strong and durable; they can withstand whatever conditions we encounter in there. The body harnesses are designed to support your breathing apparatus to enable you to move freely, to carry oxygen and other tools. Use the breathing apparatus the second the atmosphere becomes irrespirable. Remember, irrespirable air is unfit for breathing and it doesn't have the qualities necessary to support human life. If the men are where we think they are, your ventilation apparatus will withstand the rescue operation. You will all survive and bring to the surface of this mine men who will live to tell their tales.'

Far below the firemen, Marty prayed. He wasn't a religious man; he didn't insist on his family going to church every Sunday. His faith rested in the power of kindness and community. He believed when people worked together, incredible things could happen. Ena was the perfect example. He and Olive knew about her start in life, and following her disappearance, they'd feared for her safety. It didn't take long for the news to filter through; Jack and his uncle had helped her to escape her unsuitable guardian's clutches and her aunt had taken her away, to safety. The young woman who returned to Gateshead wasn't defined by the cruelty inflicted on her as a child, the opposite was true. Ena Leighton was a force for good in their community and with their beloved daughter. As soon as Dolly met Ena at work, she was different; more confident and outgoing. And happy. He and Olive never considered not keeping their daughter, although it was commonplace to hide those with disabilities away. They learnt to sign and showed their neighbours how proud they were of her. With Ena as one of her strongest allies, Dolly's place in their community was assured.

Marty knew mining was a dangerous occupation from the moment his father took him to the pit head and asked if he'd like to dig for his own coal. There were boys in his class at school whose fathers forced them down into the darkness, but Marty wasn't one of them. He was proud to be crowded into the metal cage next to his father and the other miners, proud to be serving his community. Pride wasn't the emotion crushing his chest as he perched on the narrow rock shelf halfway between daylight and certain death. This was panic; pure, breathtaking panic. When the first explosion ripped through the mine, he was lying on his back, horizontal to a particularly valuable coal seam. They'd been mining its haul for days. The thunderous roar deafened him and he saw but couldn't hear the river of rocks that flew past, careering into the dark levels below. He pressed his arms against his sides and exhaled deeply to flatten his chest cavity, hoping the coal seam to his right would hold him like a straightjacket. When the level he was working started to fill with noxious coal dust, he knew he had to move. His electric cap-lamp glowed with a dull light and he used his right hand to position it carefully at elbow height to his left-hand side. A weak shaft of light spread a short way along the ravine created by the explosion, and he rolled onto his front to see what lay ahead. A narrow tunnel, peppered with sharp rocks and a sheer drop into a cavernous hole on one side. He shifted the lamp to look in the other direction and wished he hadn't. The image of a wall of rocks and disembodied limbs would stay with him forever.

He was about to start crawling along the tunnel when a low rumbling signalled a second explosion was imminent. He flattened himself against the coal seam and tried not to breathe. Filthy coal dust and deadly rocks flew past him and he held his breath, waiting for the avalanche to end. When the tunnel fell silent he turned and found his exit blocked by fallen rubble. He was trapped. His heart hammered in his chest and his breath came in ragged bursts. He pictured Dolly, his beloved daughter. Her strength and determination had astounded them all and he chastised himself. He ripped the arm of his heavy jacket on a piece of sharp rock when he removed the pick axe from one of the pockets. He started chipping away at the rubble that blocked his route into the tunnel, working down and moving the pieces towards his feet. With each bit of space he created, he moved a tiny way out of the coal seam and into the tunnel. His hands and wrists burned but he kept on chipping. Eventually, and being mindful of jagged rubble and the loose ceiling of crumbling rocks not far above his head, he started to crawl along the tunnel. Muddy rain dripped methodically onto his head and body as he moved. Steam rose out of the drop to his right, and he covered his mouth and nose. If he was to survive this he needed to find clean air. They were trained to search for air pockets in situations like this, to find oxygen. He kept his head turned to the left and continued to crawl, his lamp leading the way with a thin, flickering light. He tried to hold on to the passage of time, to understand how long he'd been crawling. He'd been on day shift on Saturday, entering the cage just after 6 o'clock in the morning. He remembered hearing St Mary's midday bells and then the explosion. Not long after, the second explosion trapped him. He didn't know how long it had taken him to chip away at the wall of rubble. He continued, not looking back and not looking down. As he crawled, dust swirled around him and he started to cough. He stopped to unbutton one of the large pockets in his jacket and remove his tin flask and cup. With filthy lacerated hands he slowly removed the screw-top lid and poured a tiny amount of tea into the cup. 'Don't you spill it, Marty-boy.' His hands shook as he sipped the sweet tea. He pictured Olive filling his flask that morning, before kissing him goodbye. She'd called from the doorway and when he turned she put a protective hand on her stomach and said, 'let's tell Dolly tonight'. He nodded then ran back and kissed her.

He replaced the lid on his flask and carried on crawling. Suddenly, he froze and cocked his head to one side. His ears were still ringing with the sound of the explosion and he wasn't sure what he'd heard, if anything. He resumed his slow, wearisome crawl then stopped again. A chink. Tin on tin. Somewhere above and to his left. He removed his flask and tin cup again but this time he didn't take a drink. Instead he knocked the cup against the flask. He knew not to shout; reverberations could cause more rockfall and possibly lead the precarious ceiling to collapse. The chink above came again in reply and he continued to crawl. A little way along the tunnel he heard another noise, this time a slither, something sliding down the wall of coal and rock to his left. He moved his head and saw a strong, thick rope. Whoever was making the chinking sound had thrown the rope in his direction. He got onto his knees and grabbed the rope. He tugged it and waited. The rope moved up slightly, a tug from whoever was above. He grabbed the rope again and lifted his legs. His knees scraped the jagged muddy wall as he tried to get purchase on the rope. His muscles screamed in agony but his body rushed with adrenaline when he started to rise. With each of his efforts being matched by someone above, he made slow, steady progress. His fingers trembled and rivulets of sweat burned his eyes as he reached a ledge. He peered over the top and saw three pairs of feet. He laughed, 'I'd recognise those plates of meat anywhere!' Cockney-John sniggered, 'come on, Geordie-boy, pull yourself up here with me and the Parker twins'. When the men hauled Marty onto the ledge, their lamps went out. That told them they'd been underground for at least 12 hours, making it Saturday evening or later.

Superintendent Dawson's men worked as a team to slide the boards into place. Jack and Mr Young joined others at the pit head, forming a human chain to pass the boards and other materials along to the firemen. The rain worsened when Ena returned to the welfare centre for items she was sure the trapped men would need; blankets, ham sandwiches, tea and biscuits. She talked to Marty as she hurried down the hill, her feet slipping and sliding in the mud. 'Hold on, Marty. They're coming for you. Hold on.'

Trapped on the ledge, Marty and the others lost all sense of time. They spoke quietly, trying to reassure each other rescue couldn't be far away. 'We saw your light, that's how we knew where to throw the rope.' Cockney-John smiled at Marty but his eyes were wild, he'd already been underground for longer than he could bear. 'Thanks, mate. We'll be getting out of here before you know it.' The Parker twins were 20 years old and had worked down the mine since they were 14. Golden-haired young men who spent most of their lives in the dark. Marty knew that like him, mining was what their family had always done; their father and grandfather before them. 'You all right, lads?' The twins nodded in unison. They said little, but Marty knew they were strong as the proverbial ox. 'Did you help Cockney to pull me up?' The twins grinned, 'aye'. Marty managed to smile, of anyone to be trapped with, the Parker twins and their brute strength were the two he would have chosen every time. 'We need to conserve our energy, take it in turns to sleep.' Cockney-John and the twins suggested Marty should go first. He didn't object, the long slow crawl along the tunnel had taken every ounce of his stamina and his bones ached like those of a much older man. There wasn't enough room to stretch out on the ledge but Marty made himself as comfortable as possible. He closed his eyes and sleep claimed him. When he woke, it was pitch black. Through his ringing ears he could hear a low rumbling. He blinked and his eyes adjusted to the dark. The Parker twins' eyes shone and they pointed at Cockney-John. The big man's snores reverberated gently around their underground prison. Marty whispered to the twins that they should sleep. They leant into each other and closed their eyes.

Above ground, Tommy Dawson encouraged his weary men to keep going. 'We know there are men trapped underground. It's our job to bring them out alive.' He looked from man to man, defying anyone to say what was in his own mind. They hadn't heard anything for hours and in all likelihood, the trapped miners were already dead. 'Let's get down there!' The firemen strapped their body harnesses to their chests and clutched the steel wire ropes, nailed into place at the pit head. Four of them formed a chain and were slowly lowered into the opening at the pit head. Dawson crouched at the top and watched his men descend, supported by the wooden boards that formed the mineshaft's temporary walls. The men carried oxygen bottles along with extra harnesses and breathing apparatus. The remaining firemen formed a circle around the opening and slowly let the steel wire ropes out. They held the ropes and waited for their colleagues' signal.

'Angels, Marty. I saw them. They were wrapped in clouds and rode blazing red chariots. They left a trail of mouthwatering smells in their wake; liver and onions and a tankard of yeasty beer. Where are they, Marty? I'm starving.' Marty lifted his flask to Cockney-John's chapped lips. He grabbed for the flask but Marty rationed the tea, knowing how little they had left. As his friend hallucinated, he and the Parker twins were forced to watch his deterioration. Marty's arms were heavy when he chinked their tin cups together again. The twins shook their heads; 'I don't think anyone is coming, Marty'. As Marty lowered his head, Cockney-John whispered, 'stay with me, please don't leave'. There was a moment of silence and then another voice, a long way above them. 'This is the fire brigade. How many are you?' Marty and the Parker twins laughed and called back. Cockney-John smiled, 'it's the angels. They're here for us'. He began to sweat and then started shivering, until exhaustion swept him to sleep.

The firemen lowered themselves onto the ledge one at a time. They took turns to give the trapped men oxygen before fitting harnesses, breathing apparatus and the all-important steel wire ropes. Then they tugged on the ropes, signalling to their colleagues on the surface to pull them up. Above ground, Dawson clutched each rope in turn when his men received their signal. On his count, they pulled the rope. Gloved hand over fist, until their muscles were on fire. Cockney-John went first then the Parker twins insisted Marty should go next. As he was hoisted to the surface, heavy with mud and his limbs limp, he spoke to their rescuers under his breath. 'I'm sorry I'm too weak to help, but I know you've done everything you can. Thank you.' He blinked as a glimmer of light appeared above him. His eyes and throat burned and his fingers froze inside the protective gloves the fireman had given him. He gasped when his body was elevated from the underground tomb. He put out his tongue to catch cold drops of rain, his heart racing. He heard cheers and then there was silence as he allowed his ordeal to claim him. When Ena realised Marty was among the survivors being loaded into the ambulances, she ran to Colliery Road. She shouted when she turned into the street and Olive ran out of the house to meet her. 'Marty's alive!' Olive screamed and fell into her arms. 'Quick, get Dolly. We need to go to the hospital.'

Chapter 25

Ivy

Ivy's plan was to prepare her dance troupe for the autumn and winter seasons of London shows. She knew from experience that disciplined, well-turned out troupes were always in demand, and she had contacts at many of the nearby theatres. Her training sessions were rigorous, with the initial focus on mastering the fundamentals of ballet. Once her dancers were proficient, they would be able to easily apply what they'd learnt to contemporary dance routines. Her position, with her back to the large window, provided a clear view of the six women as they placed their right hands on the barre in front of the mirrors. These warm-up exercises, designed to improve their strength, flexibility and technique, were second nature to them now. They followed Ivy's instruction, to 'observe and correct', to the letter.

One day, after the dancers left, Grace called at the studio. 'Put the kettle on darling, I'm parched!' Sitting with their tea, Ivy told Grace of her surprise that all six dancers had picked everything up so quickly. Grace shook her head. 'Think about what some of them have been through. I'm sure they're grateful to be doing what they love in your magnificent studio and being cared for. Without your intervention, who knows what they would be doing. You hear of theatricals having to take all manner of work to stay afloat; waitressing, typing, shop-work. Thanks to you they've been able to pursue their passion for performing and you've given them back their dignity.' Ivy nodded, 'so far, so good. I need to secure our first booking and I'm in competition with some well-established directors'. Grace tutted, 'none of them can hold a candle to you. What did you decide to call your troupe?' Ivy smiled, 'that was easy, "The Leighton Girls"'. Grace put her head on one side, 'that wasn't always your surname, was it'? Ivy laughed, 'no, I was born someone very different'. Grace raised her eyebrows, 'do tell'.

Ivy said she was born Dinah Jane Brown in Gateshead on the 2nd of January 1883. 'Gosh darling, after my birthday next month we'll be the same age! We don't look it though!' Ivy smiled, 'it's only a number, isn't it?' Grace nodded, 'look at us. I'm still getting rave reviews and you're embarking on a new career as a director!' Ivy laughed, 'yes, I wish I could tell the young Dinah Jane Brown she'd be doing this 41 years later'. Grace sipped her tea, 'you were Dinah when I met you at Hampson Hall, weren't you?' Ivy nodded, 'yes, the name change came when I moved to London and Mrs Newbold told me I would need a stage name'. Grace smiled, 'you took her first name, didn't you?' Ivy said she had. 'Armed with your introduction, she welcomed me into her guest house. I was green as grass, knew nothing about the theatre or London life, and she took me under her wing. I was very lucky. You arranged my audition at the West London Theatre, and thankfully Monsieur le Grand was confident he could cast me.' Grace laughed, 'I remember he wasn't too impressed by your name, *"Mees Brown"?"* Ivy smiled, 'you remember correctly'. Grace frowned, 'and the surname Leighton? Where did that come from?' Ivy sighed, 'you'll remember I came to London to try and find my sister?' Grace said she did and Ivy continued. 'I'd received a letter from her and she signed it, *"Mona Leighton, (my new name for the stage in London)"*. Mrs Newbold had talked about a name's significance, saying it could be chosen to set something right or in memory of someone. Using the same surname as my sister helped me to feel a little closer to her.'"

Grace studied her friend over the rim of her teacup. 'Do you know where she is now, your sister?' Ivy sighed and looked out of the window. For all she knew, Mona could be one of the people hurrying along the Strand. 'The last I knew she was on her way back to New York. She wrote she'd been asked to play the lead in a production of *Sally* at the Paradise Theatre on Broadway.' Grace whistled, 'that's some part!' Ivy smiled, 'I know, but that was months ago and I've heard nothing since so it's anyone's guess where she is now'. Grace leant forward and spoke quietly, 'was she ever reunited with her daughter?' Ivy shook her head. 'They met up a couple of years ago but Ena said it was like having a conversation with a stranger, and they parted without plans to meet again. She finds it easier to accept her mother will never be part of her life.' Grace sighed, 'how sad'. Ivy nodded, 'it is, but I understand Ena's point of view; Mona keeps disappointing her'. Grace took Ivy's hand, 'why do you think she left her? I remember you saying Ena was only four at the time'. Ivy took a deep breath. 'I don't know. She's been running from one thing or another for most of her life. I'd love to think she could be at peace with herself.' Grace sighed, 'yes, let's hope wherever she is, she's happy. And your dancers? What are their backgrounds?'

Ivy sipped her tea, 'terrible things happened to some of them, Grace. And it could easily have been any of us'. Grace raised her eyebrows, 'me, if not for Ursula Innes'. Ivy agreed, 'exactly, and my sister found herself in a terrifying situation through no fault of her own, other than trusting a man'. Grace scoffed, 'we both know how careful we need to be on that score'. Ivy sighed, 'as you know, I have four dancers who came to me via your recommendations, two sets of sisters, both from dance backgrounds'. Grace nodded, 'ah yes, the Millers and the Woods. How are they getting along?' Ivy smiled, 'very well. I think because both sets of parents are performers, their route to the stage was much smoother. They only have basic education, but what they don't know about the theatrical world isn't worth knowing. And their rhythm is tremendous!' Grace asked her about the two dancers from the community kitchen and Ivy's face darkened. 'It makes me so angry, Grace; what those women have suffered. I now know May was born in Edinburgh, where her doctor father and wealthy socialite mother entertained the cream of Scottish society. Her life changed the day she went with them to Waverley Station, to wave off some visitors. She became separated from her parents and remembers being grabbed and pulled onto a train. A strong-smelling cloth was placed over her mouth and everything went black. She woke to find herself in that disgusting lodging house Solomon Zettler used for his dancers, where Mona was.' Grace gasped, 'did no one come looking for her?' Ivy sighed. 'No, her parents met with tragedy the day their daughter was abducted. As they searched in desperation outside the station, May's mother stepped into the road. When her husband tried to pull her clear, a tram hit them. They died at the scene, and it wasn't until later, when their housekeeper told the police May was missing, that the search for her began, but the trail was cold.' Grace shook her head, 'that poor young woman'. Ivy nodded, 'she only told me recently, but I think it shows she's starting to trust me'. Grace smiled, 'I'm glad she has you to support her now.'

Ivy poured them both another cup of tea. 'Violet's story is equally frightening, perhaps more so given its simplicity.' Grace frowned, 'what do you mean?' Ivy sighed. 'She thought she was auditioning for a part in an ensemble, plain and simple. Everything appeared above board when she arrived at the theatre, a decent place just off Drury Lane. She couldn't see the director sitting in the stalls because the stage lights were blinding. She heard his voice and was delighted to be offered a spot in his next show. It was only when she met the rest of the troupe she realised something was seriously wrong with the set-up. By then it was too late, she was trapped. She quickly found herself in debt to Zettler; there was always some garish new outfit to pay for and they earned next to nothing. They were half-starved and regularly beaten. If I hadn't seen her at the community kitchen, I dread to think what might have happened.' Grace scowled, 'it's appalling these things are allowed to go on'. Ivy sighed, 'I know, but at least Violet and May are out of harm's way now'. Grace nodded, 'thanks to you'. Ivy reached for Grace's hand, 'and you'. Grace squeezed her friend's hand, 'now, tell me how that lovely man of yours is doing'. Ivy laughed, realising she started to smile when she thought about Vernon.

Mona

Mona and Nellie's voyage to Southampton was relatively un-eventful. They ate delicious food in the restaurant and drank their way through the cocktail list, *'not a patch on Tremblay's or the El Fey!'* They danced to the ship's orchestra and showed off their New York fashions. They'd both embraced the flapper style and owned a number of short-skirted dresses, elbow-length gloves and headbands. Their long necklaces bounced as they moved their arms and legs to the Black Bottom. They revelled in the disapproval of people in the ship's restaurant, who clearly thought their love of jazz inappropriate.

One evening, as they sipped their Bees Knees cocktails, *'gin, lemon juice and honey, darling'*, Mona saw Nellie's attention wavering. She'd been talking about going to Wilfred's bank to confront him when they got back. Nellie was looking at her and nodding, then Mona saw her put her head on one side, in the direction of the table next to them. She glanced at the two young women. When they left the restaurant, Nellie grabbed her hand. 'You'll never guess what they were saying!' Mona shook her head and Nellie continued. 'They're going to some studio in London where a woman is recruiting dancers for a new troupe!' Mona gasped, 'a woman?' Tilly laughed, 'yes! We're so used to sleazy men wanting us to dance for other sleazy men. I've never met a female director, have you?' Mona said she hadn't. 'Did they say what she's called?' 'No, but it shouldn't be hard to find her. They said she provides hotel accommodation; clean, comfortable rooms. Imagine that!' Mona gestured in the direction of the women, 'should we ask them where the woman's studio is?' 'No, we don't know how many dancers this director wants; we might be up against those two. Let's go to the Hippodrome when we get off the train, someone there will know.' Mona nodded, excited by the prospect of the unexpected opportunity.

Sitting opposite Nellie on the train to London, Mona asked something that had been on her mind for a long time. She hesitated, part of her was scared to ask, but it was something she needed to know. She took a deep breath. 'Nellie, do you know what happened to Violet and May? They'd both disappeared by the time I left London.' Nellie sighed, 'are you sure you want to hear this?' Mona said she was, 'I can't stop thinking about them'. Nellie nodded. 'Alright. As you know, we hadn't seen May for a while.' Mona waited. She remembered May being with them one day and gone the next. They wanted to believe she'd escaped, but knew it was unlikely. There were whispers Zettler was imprisoning women in his new brothel. The addition to his depraved empire was much worse than his other establishments. The men frequenting his new club demanded horrific acts. They paid Zettler and occasionally he gave the women a paltry sum. The women tried to make themselves invisible when his henchmen came calling, but they believed May had been caught. Mona leant across the table, 'and Violet?' 'The same, I think. I told you she sometimes turned up for the excuse of a breakfast at the Diamond; but one of Zettler's nameless thugs was always with her.' Mona moved closer, 'did you ever see May there?' Nellie shook her head.

When the train pulled into Waterloo Station, Nellie was one of the first on the platform. 'I'd forgotten how much London feels like home, this is where I belong!' Mona looked around;

what did London have to offer her? Ivy was here but her stomach lurched when she realised she'd never written with her address in New York. Anything could have happened to her sister while she'd been away. London didn't feel like home to her. She closed her eyes, considering when she'd last been truly happy. An image of Wilfred formed in her mind and she smiled. Nellie tugged at her coat sleeve and her eyes shot open. 'Come on, let's go to the Hippodrome and find out where that woman's studio is.' Nellie started walking along the platform but Mona didn't move. Nellie turned back. 'Come on, we need to get there while this director still wants dancers!' 'I'm sorry Nellie, I'm not coming.' Nellie hurried back to her, 'what do you mean? This is the opportunity of a lifetime; dancing for a woman who, by the sound of it, will take care of us.' Mona bit her bottom lip, 'I need to find Wilfred and ask him why he broke his promise'. Nellie scoffed. 'Why? He's like every other man we've ever met, Mona. He's a liar. Don't waste your time running after him, come with me.' Mona sighed. 'That's the thing. I don't think he is like every other man; I think there must be a good reason he didn't turn up for my opening night.' Nellie shook her head. 'Yes, a wife hidden away somewhere. Look, come with me to the Hippodrome, then see how you feel about finding this Wilfred.' Mona smiled sadly. 'I know you don't understand, I'm not sure I do. But I need to know, one way or the other.' Nellie scoffed, 'and if I'm right?' Mona laughed, 'if you're right I'll come and find you and this remarkable female director, all right?' Nellie punched Mona lightly on the arm, 'you better had! Right, I'm off to the Hippodrome to see Kenny. Where are you going?' Mona put her head on one side, 'first stop, the bank where Wilfred said he worked'. Nellie raised her hand, 'best of luck!' Mona returned the gesture, 'and to you!'

Chapter 26

Ivy

In the wings, Ivy stood tall with her shoulders back and her chin up. She watched her Leighton Girls take their final bows. When they left the stage, she saw their smiles and bright eyes. She touched each of their hands as they filed past her. 'That was fantastic. Exactly as we rehearsed it.' In their dressing room, the excited chatter rose when Ivy opened the door. Violet came towards her, 'how many encores?' Ivy laughed, 'I think it was three!' Violet took her hand, 'thank you for making this possible'. Ivy shook her head. 'You six do the hard work out there. So much of the magic the audience see on stage happens in the dance studio and behind the curtain.' May turned from the mirror and smiled at her as she removed her heavy stage makeup. 'But you make sure we're well enough and happy enough to perform to the best of our ability.' Ivy nodded; her dance troupe was a resounding success.

When she'd started pitching for West End shows, she met solid resistance from the industry's traditional core. She was mistaken for a secretary or a dancer and asked where her director was. When she explained it was her dance troupe, one producer looked her up and down and sneered. 'A female director? A woman trying to do a man's job?' She remembered Grace saying Ursula Innes experienced similar prejudice and she persevered. She found herself facing a brick wall, until she met Alfred Atherton. She and Vernon were at the bookshop, drinking tea with Harold and Alida. They were sitting around the fire, discussing how T.S. Eliot's *The Waste Land* shifted between satirical and prophetic voices. As Vernon said he enjoyed the abrupt, unannounced changes of narrator, location, and time, the bell above the door tinkled. Harold turned, 'Alfie my good man. Come and join our critique of Eliot!' The smartly dressed man smiled and walked towards them. Harold offered him his seat and disappeared into the back of the shop, returning with a striped deck chair. 'Now, introductions are in order before we continue dissecting Eliot.' When Vernon shook Alfie's hand, he asked what he did for a living. Harold answered on his friend's behalf, 'I'll tell you, because he'll hide his light under the proverbial bushel!' Ivy saw Alfie blush and when she learnt of his accomplishments, she liked him for his modesty. Harold continued, 'Alfie is a theatre impresario, known for his spectacular revues and musical comedies. He organises and finances musical shows, plays and operas'. He turned to Ivy, 'I'm surprised you haven't met, given your occupation'. She shook her head, 'no, I'm sure I would have remembered Mr Atherton'. He smiled, 'please, call me Alfie. What do you do, Ms Leighton?' Ivy sat up straight and told him about The Leighton Girls. As she talked, he took a notebook and pen from his inside pocket and started writing. She stopped mid-sentence, and he gestured with his pen for her to continue. 'What are you writing?' He looked up, 'just a few notes about your Leighton Girls; I might have the perfect opportunity for you'.

Ivy later discovered the show Alfie had in mind was his production of *Lady, Be Good!* Before he left the bookshop, he gave her his business card and asked her to call to arrange an audition. He said he needed a lively ensemble for a number of routines in the show. 'A talented ensemble will help to bring the show to life; they'll need to master some intricate dance parts and add their voices to a few full-company musical numbers. Can your dancers do that?' Ivy assured Alfie they could. Now, as her dancers left the theatre, she reminded them to get a good night's sleep and eat a hearty breakfast before returning for rehearsals the next day. 'Wrap up, there's an autumn chill out there.' Violet touched her arm as she was leaving, 'I've got my health check with Dr Lawson in the morning, but I'll come straight here afterwards. I'll be as quick as I can.' Ivy shook her head, 'don't rush. It's important you take the time to be thoroughly checked over'. Violet smiled, 'thank you, Ivy. You'll never know how grateful I am to you. I can't imagine what might have happened if you hadn't been there that day'. Ivy nodded, 'and I'll always be grateful to you for looking after my sister when she arrived in London'.

Violet closed the door behind her and Ivy smiled. She pulled on her coat and looked round the dressing room; her dancers had removed their makeup and changed out of their costumes then tidied up and cleaned the mirrors. Ivy caught her reflection in the mirror. She reached into her handbag and reapplied her lipstick. She rubbed her lips together then fastened the large buttons on her black side wrap coat. She turned the fur collar up to protect her neck from the autumn wind and pulled on her gloves. As she reached under the mirrors to switch off the spotlights, she heard the door open. A shadow fell across the room and she smiled, 'I wasn't expecting you back until tomorrow'. Vernon stood in the doorway; arms outstretched, 'the captain decided to sail a day earlier than scheduled, there were storm warnings and strong winds forecast along the Atlantic coast'. Ivy walked towards him and he enveloped her. 'I'm very glad you're home safely. Did you catch the show?' He smiled, 'just 'Carnival Time' and their numerous encores'. Ivy looked up at him, 'they're perfectly in sync for that final number now, aren't they?' He nodded and kissed the top of her head.

Somewhere in between chatting about books, cooking for Irene and picnics in Waterlow Park, their friendship had grown into love, and Ivy had decided to trust this beautifully ordinary, yet extraordinary man. He'd helped her sister, his brother and complete strangers at Endell Street. Victoria was right. She'd said Vernon was the only thing that kept some men at the hospital alive. He was endlessly patient and spent hours wheeling them around, talking to the worst of them, men who got no other visitors, men who couldn't reply. She'd described Vernon as the bright light in an otherwise incredibly dark place for the men. His humility and desire to help others made him extremely attractive. When she'd told him about George he scoffed, saying the man must have been blind not to see her value. He said she deserved to be with someone who appreciated her for everything she brought to the world. Now, standing in the dark dressing room, Ivy relaxed into his embrace, 'shall we go for supper, Mr Revill?' Vernon took her arm, 'that would be marvellous, Ms Leighton'.

Ena

Summer was over and Gateshead's trees were wearing their autumn colours by the time the pit reopened. The extent of the damage and the measures required to ensure the miners' future safety had been assessed. The owners of the coalfield held a number of public meetings following the tragedy, restating their commitment to safety and the prevention of further incidents. When Marty was lifted onto a stretcher at the pit head, he pulled his oxygen mask away from his mouth and tried to tell the firemen what he'd seen underground. He'd heard people saying four men were still missing, and he wanted to help those who had saved his life. He was told to try and relax, that everything possible was being done to find those unaccounted for. When the stretcher was loaded into an ambulance, his breath came faster and a first-aider tightened the oxygen mask around his face. He told Marty they were going to the Gateshead Dispensary, where he would be looked after. Marty closed his eyes as he was driven away. Mr Young brought his Austin Seven to Colliery Road and Ena watched him help Dolly and Olive inside. The Gateshead Dispensary, on the corner of Nelson Street and West

Street, provided emergency care. It was 20 minutes away and Ena silently urged Mr Young to drive as fast as possible. The rescue effort continued; Tommy Dawson refused to end the search until they'd brought every last miner to the surface, dead or alive.

Marty spent two weeks in hospital. Once he could, he told a doctor about his gruesome discovery underground. A message was relayed to the fire brigade and focussed searches were undertaken in the area Marty identified. The families of those unaccounted for clung to faint hope that another air pocket might have saved their loved ones. The firemen's search snuffed out their hope. When Dolly and Olive returned to Colliery Road after visiting Marty on the first day, they found Ena and Jack waiting. A pan of ham and vegetable broth simmered on the stove and Ena served the warming soup to her friends. Olive's eyes were full when she spoke, 'where did the ham shank and vegetables come from? I didn't have anything in'. Jack smiled, 'the Colliery Manager brought the ham and your neighbours left carrots, turnips and leeks outside. Ena found lentils and split peas in your kitchen cupboard'. Olive nodded, 'it's perfect, thank you'. She had a couple of mouthfuls then put down her spoon and took a deep breath. 'The doctor thinks Marty will be all right. He's got some congestion on his lungs but they don't expect it to develop into pneumonia.' Her lip trembled and Ena reached for her hand. She noticed Dolly signing and turned to watch. She was asking her mother if they should tell them the news. Olive signed to say yes, she could. Dolly's face lit up as her hands moved to tell them she was going to have a little brother or sister. Ena looked at Olive, 'you're pregnant?' Olive grinned, 'yes, the baby is due in March next year'.

The reopening of the pit coincided with the annual Harvest Festival celebrations at churches throughout Gateshead. Ena and Jack had agreed to accompany the Bundells to St Mary's on Oakwellgate. Their arms were full as they made their way up Bottle Bank. The bright blue cloudless sky and autumn crispness told them colder weather wasn't far away. When they turned the corner at the top of the bank, Ena smiled at the sound of the church bells, calling them to celebrate the gathering of crops and the bounty of the season. Inside, the church was festooned with fresh flower garlands and corn dollies. Tables groaned with produce. Ena's eyes roamed across the donations; luscious, colourful fruit, vegetables and grains, then homemade goods; jams, preserves, bread and cakes, to be distributed to those in need in their community. They handed their contributions over and squeezed into a pew alongside the Turnbulls. Jack nudged Ena, 'next year, we'll be able to celebrate Harvest Festival at St Mary's Church in Whickham'. She squeezed his hand. After the pit disaster and learning about the new baby, they'd decided to set the date for their wedding. They all needed reasons to celebrate. On the 17th of August 1925, she would become Mrs Ena Todd. The vicar opened his arms in welcome and the rich, powerful harmonies of the church organ surrounded them. They stood and started singing.

'All things bright and beautiful,
All creatures great and small,
All things wise and wonderful,
The Lord God made them all.'

A few weeks later, life was calmer for those whose loved ones survived the disaster. The community cared for the bereaved, who in most cases had lost their breadwinner. Neighbours knocked, making sure families had enough to eat and coal for the fire. After work one day, Ena opened the door to see a letter from Aunt Ivy on the mat. Her aunt's last letter had mentioned her dance troupe and Ena was excited to learn more. Upstairs, she boiled milk for cocoa and opened the letter. It was dated Thursday the 6th of November 1924.

'*Dearest Ena,*

I do apologise for my tardiness in replying to your last; suffice to say life has been extremely busy! I was comforted to hear Marty's injuries were not severe and the good news about the baby. How wonderful to have new life to celebrate. You kindly enquired as to my progress with "The Leighton Girls". I'm delighted to report we've been successful in securing numerous engagements in some of London's fabulous West End theatres (hence my lack of time to write). My second delight is being able to invite you and Jack to my wedding! You may recall me telling you about my friend Vernon; well our friendship has grown and deepened and when he returned from his latest voyage yesterday, he proposed and I accepted! We were at a fireworks display in Hyde Park and I'll never forget the lights and explosions in the sky that heralded his question! We do hope you and Jack will be able to come to London and celebrate with us. We booked the wedding today; it is on the 6th of December at Paddington Register Office. All for now, my darling niece. I hope to see you in a few weeks.

Your loving aunt, Ivy.'"

Chapter 27

Wednesday 6th of December 1924
Wedding Day

Ivy and Vernon's wedding was a small, intimate affair. They kept the guest list short, inviting only Ena, Jack and Irene to the service, and a group of their close friends to the wedding breakfast. Ivy wrote to Mona at the Paradise as May suggested, but there was no reply. She didn't know where else her sister could be, and reluctantly accepted her absence from the celebration. Ena and Jack travelled from Gateshead the day before, and they joined Ivy and Vernon for an evening meal. They were staying in a hotel close to the Register Office which Ena reported was 'small, clean and comfortable'.

Ivy's silk ecru dress fell to just below the knee, the cummerbund around the dropped waist emphasising her slim figure. A lace appliqué sewn onto tulle decorated the cummerbund, the motifs featuring intricate floral designs. Matching ecru low-heeled T-strap shoes completed her outfit. Her auburn hair had been trimmed, and her hairdresser used a heated curling iron to create Marcel waves. The result was a refined, wavy style that framed her beautiful face. Pear-shaped diamond drop earrings matched the ornament at the end of her long sautoir necklace. Irene was a picture of elegance and sophistication in a soft blush chiffon calf-length dress, with matching elbow-length satin gloves. Her bell-shaped cloche hat, also in soft blush, was adorned with small pink feathers on one side. Ivy smiled at her soon-to-be mother-in-law's transformation. Irene would always grieve for her lost son, but Ivy knew Vernon's happiness had helped to lessen her sadness.

The service called for two people to witness the bride and groom signing the wedding certificate; Ivy and Vernon asked Ena and Irene to perform the task for them. Afterwards, they took a taxicab to the Redford, where Teddy had laid on a lavish wedding breakfast. They were welcomed at the door to a private function room by waiting staff holding trays of sparkling champagne. Inside, Teddy and the rest of their friends were lined up ready to congratulate them. Grace and Walter, Lydia, Daphne, Vivienne and Zee all raised their glasses and toasted the new Mr and Mrs Revill. Vernon was delighted to see Harold had closed the bookshop so he and Alida could be there. A long rectangular table, draped with a pristine white cloth, was positioned in the middle of the room and set for 14 people. The silver crockery gleamed and crystal glasses sparkled. Next to each place setting was a small name card and a menu. Teddy's staff directed them to their seats and topped up their champagne flutes; he spared no expense with the catering, hiring a private chef to provide a mouthwatering feast. There was shrimp cocktail or devilled eggs, followed by Oysters Rockefeller. The main courses were Chicken à la King, Beef Rib Roast with horseradish sauce, or Lamb with broiled potatoes, peas and carrots. For dessert there was Pineapple Upside-Down Cake or ice cream. Ivy raised her glass to Teddy in thanks, and he called for a toast to the happy couple.

As people sat back in their chairs, replete and content, Teddy got up and walked to the end of the function room, where huge curtains stretched from one side of the room to the other. He pulled a heavy tasselled cord attached to the curtains and they opened slowly, revealing a small stage and a jazz band. Ivy and Vernon's guests cheered when Teddy shouted, 'hit it boys!' The band went straight into a lively Charleston, and Lydia and Daphne immediately stepped onto the small dancefloor. After a few moments, Teddy called to the band to stop. Lydia, Daphne and the band members feigned surprise and Ivy started to laugh.

Teddy cupped a hand to his ear, 'what's that you say? The happy couple haven't had their first dance? Well, we ought to rectify that, don't you think?' Everyone clapped in agreement and Vernon stood up. He offered Ivy his hand, 'Mrs Revill, may I have the pleasure?' Ivy smiled and took her husband's hand, 'you may, Mr Revill. They stepped onto the dance floor and the band started playing.

'It had to be you, it had to be you,
I wandered around, and finally found,
The somebody who,
Could make me be true,
And could make me be blue,
And even be glad, just to be sad,
Thinking of you.'

Ivy told Vernon it was one of the happiest days of her life. He understood Bertie was her first love, and her happiness that day too. She explained this felt different; she was older and because they'd all lived through so much tragedy she appreciated happy days more now. 'None of us know how many we'll have.' Vernon agreed, 'let's make the most of this one!' Ivy laughed and got ready to toss her bouquet. 'Is everybody ready?' Her guests cheered and she stood with her back to them, hands raised above her head. The posy of roses, lily of the valley and violets flew into the crowd and a hand shot up to catch it. Ivy turned to see who would be blessed with good luck and happiness. Her heart sang and she hurried over to Ena. 'That's perfect; you deserve it!'

Ena

Ena's boots crunched in the snow as she walked up Bottle Bank. It had snowed every day since she and Jack returned from London, and it was now frozen solid underfoot. She pictured her aunt and smiled; the wedding was wonderful and Aunt Ivy had written to say she and Vernon enjoyed a few days away in Brighton before he sailed again. She was busy with her dance troupe, *'booked solid until February, darling'*, and settling into their new flat on James Street in Paddington. They had suggested to Irene they could live with her, but she insisted on them starting married life in their own home. Ena shivered as she unlocked her front door; secure in the knowledge her flat would be warm. When autumn shifted into winter, Bartholomew asked if he could light a fire in the flat so it would be warm by the time she got home. The agreement in place, each morning Ena cleared the grate and laid a new fire and Bartholomew lit it when he and Beatrice closed the shop.

Upstairs, she removed her coat, boots and hat and poured milk into a pan for cocoa. While she waited for the milk to simmer, she took a roll of brown paper and a ball of string out of her shopping bag. She placed the gifts she'd bought on the table. Warm woollen scarves for the Bundells, replacing the half-knitted one Beatrice donated to the welfare centre. A tin of Black Bullets for Jack's uncle, who enjoyed the strong-flavoured, long-lasting mints. Jack was more difficult to buy for; saying he had everything he needed and would prefer Ena to buy something for herself. She'd found the perfect place in the Grainger Market; the Marks and Spencer Penny Bazaar. It had been there for almost 30 years and many products were offered for sale with the slogan, *'don't ask the price, it's a penny'*. She thought Jack would be content with that, and as her eyes moved along the shelves she spotted just the thing; a dark blue and grey striped necktie. She opened her mouth to ask the assistant the price, then stopped and handed over a shiny penny. It was much easier to choose a gift for Aunt Ivy and Vernon. She'd already sent them a parcel, inside were two neatly wrapped books; *The Collected Poems of Emily Dickinson* and P.G. Wodehouse's *Ukridge*. She'd been delighted to meet the proprietors of the Poetry Bookshop at Ivy and Vernon's wedding, and found time to ask them to suggest volumes the couple hadn't read. Following their conversation, she hoped they would both enjoy the American poet's collection, and the English humourist's short stories about Stanley Featherstonehaugh Ukridge's none-too-successful schemes to make money. For Dolly, Ena cast her mind back to being the same age. What would she have liked to receive for Christmas? At Dolly's age, she was living in Bournemouth with Aunt Ivy and Uncle Bertie and had everything she could wish for. Christmases came and went when she lived with Lizzie. There were no presents and no delicious food. Christmas Day was a day like any other; cold, miserable and long. She shook her head; those memories didn't belong in her life now. She rarely thought of Lizzie, despite her erstwhile guardian living only a few streets away. When she returned to Gateshead, Jack took her to Cobden Terrace to see Lizzie but the older woman didn't recognise her, the girl who'd lived with her for nine years. She took a deep breath and reached for Dolly's gift; a 1925 diary. Somewhere to record her memories of the arrival and first nine months of the new addition to the Turnbull family. And, as Ena wrote on a small gift card, *'a place for you to record your memories of being a bridesmaid at my wedding to Jack in August next year'*.

Ena walked to the window and looked at the grey, snowy sky. Tomorrow was Christmas Eve and Jack would come to meet her to walk to work as usual. The difference tomorrow was they could finish early, and she would spend the evening decorating the Christmas tree with Jack and his uncle. John Todd had invited her to stay on Christmas Eve and eat with him and Jack on Christmas Day. She remembered one of Donovan's letters where he'd written about the Christmas truce in December 1914. He said they were huddled in a filthy trench when late on Christmas Eve, they heard voices drifting through the air. They realised the Germans were singing Christmas carols. Raising themselves slightly to peer over the parapet, they saw lights in the darkness. German soldiers had placed candles on tiny Christmas trees and displayed signs proposing a temporary ceasefire the next morning. As the sun rose on Christmas Day, something extraordinary happened. Small groups of unarmed Germans climbed out of their trenches. Donovan and his comrades laid down their guns and stepped forward to meet them. They heard later their commanders shook hands, exchanged gifts and agreed the terms of a truce. For a short time they were not at war with each other. They were in a place called no-man's land, a strip of land between opposing trenches. They chatted and swapped gifts of tobacco, food and buttons they tore from their uniforms. Donovan wrote that he had played football with German soldiers and one German, a barber before the war, offered men free haircuts. They were able to collect their dead from the battlefield without being fired upon, as the Germans were able to collect theirs. At dusk, the truce ended. They returned to their posts and guns were soon firing again. Since the end of the war, a belief Christmas should be a time of peace and companionship had taken shape. Ena knew this would be the case at Cross Street.

As she got ready for bed, she remembered her visit to the theatre with Jack the previous weekend. He'd seen a poster advertising a pantomime at the Empire Theatre in Newcastle, and someone they went to school with was one of the performers. He said Shirley Sparkle's name was printed near the top of the poster. 'She plays Cinderella.' Ena hadn't remembered Shirley, even when Jack said Sparkle was a stage name and her real surname was Kindred. Ena recalled Jack saying he'd bumped into her months ago, when she was in a play called *Pot Luck* at the Grainger Music Hall. They'd talked about going along but hadn't made it. Ena didn't know if she wanted to see Cinderella; a young girl's rags to riches story acted out on stage. She'd lived it and knew how painful it was. Afterwards, she was delighted she'd gone. The moment the young Cinders appeared; Ena was mesmerised. Shirley embodied the forsaken character, and told the story of her ascension to the throne via marriage with empathy and flair. Her skilful dance moves portrayed every harrowing emotion the young Ena had experienced, and she recognised herself in the story. Someone who went unnoticed, then unexpectedly achieved recognition after being neglected. For many years she believed she had been forgotten; that her mother and aunt left her without a backward glance. She now knew that wasn't the case where her aunt was concerned. Her mother was a different matter. When the show ended, Jack asked if she wanted to go backstage and see Shirley. Ena hesitated; she wasn't sure she wanted to be reminded of her dismal school days. 'Is it all right if we go straight home?' Jack nodded and took her arm.

Shirley

Shirley's heart raced when the applause rang out for her encore. She would never tire of the adrenaline rush; the surge of energy as her breath came faster, a sense of being strong enough to perform the whole show again from beginning to end, an invincibility that came from performing, more powerful than any other emotion. She blinked when the house lights illuminated the auditorium. She curtsied once more and her feather-light feet carried her off the stage. Back in her dressing room, her hands were steady as the director handed her a glass of champagne. 'Bravo, Shirley Sparkle; you never let us down!' She affected a bow and sank into a chair in front of the mirror. She started to remove her makeup then stopped. 'Has anyone come backstage and asked for me?' The director shook his head. She turned to the mirror and ran a piece of cotton wool across her eyelids. She'd seen them in the stalls and hoped they would come and see her. There was something she wanted to tell Ena. Something she'd seen at her lodgings on Springbank Lane. A picture of someone from long ago, someone who looked just like her.

Chapter 28

Friday 27th of March 1925

Ena

Ena stamped her feet to return them to life; she shook snow off her coat and small puddles of water gathered on the office floor. Jack gestured towards the heater and she hurried over, rubbing her numb hands together. The year had begun with more snow and frost, with below-freezing temperatures causing dangerous ice on the paths and roads throughout Gateshead.

The weather wasn't the only problem facing the North East. The post-war period of prosperity was well and truly over, and unemployment was rising. The region was badly affected, as the once-thriving shipbuilding and coal mining industries continued to fall into decline. Coal reserves were depleted during the war and the country was importing more coal than it was mining. Poverty among the unemployed contrasted sharply with the affluence of the middle and upper classes. Ena saw both sides of the divide, recognising that while for some it was a time of Bright Young Things, Flappers, jazz and new, daring fashions, it was also delivering great hardship to many around her. She took some comfort from the help she provided at the welfare centre, but her concern continued to grow for those who stayed away. Their close community talked and she knew of people, most likely those greatest in need, who for whatever reason, didn't ask for help. Beatrice told her about a small group of suffragists who had opened a soup kitchen in Newcastle, to ensure children didn't starve. Ena pictured herself as a girl, hungry and neglected, and resolved to double her efforts.

In February, severe gales and heavy snow blizzards contributed to the treacherous conditions. Trams and buses were delayed or got stuck in the snow; resolute flour mill staff set off to walk to work, chilled to the bone by the time they arrived. Many, already suffering from colds and chesty coughs, gave up and went home. Ena and Jack had been setting off earlier, determined to help keep the mill running, despite the severe weather.

Towards the end of March, a blizzard swept across the North East, making roads impassable and even short journeys unsafe. Ena got ready for work as usual and watched for Jack from her window. She rubbed her hand across the glass as snow built up on the outside and there he was. His unmistakable silhouette, head low against the driving sleet, boots crunching on sheets of ice. She pulled her coat and boots on and hurried downstairs to open the front door. She smiled at her fiancé, a tall snowman in an overcoat. Through chattering teeth, he said he was going to try and get to work but she should stay at home. When she started to object he shook his head. 'No, Ena. I'm only going to make sure there's been no damage to the buildings overnight. I'm sure if Mr Young is there he'll be advising everyone to stay at home today. I'll come and let you know how everything is.' Reluctantly, Ena agreed. She wished Jack good luck and went back upstairs to light the fire. As flames started to lick the coal, she removed her coat and placed the kettle on the gas ring to make tea. While she waited for the kettle to boil, she swapped her boots for slippers and pulled on her new cardigan. The Bundells' Christmas present, more like a heavy knitted woollen jacket than a traditional cardigan, had kept her warm during the harsh winter. She fastened the large green mother-of-pearl buttons running down the front and pulled the collar up around her neck. The thick, dark green cardigan sat low on her hips and she arranged it underneath her as she made herself comfortable with her tea. The snow continued to fall outside and she tried to relax as she waited for Jack to come back. She picked up her presents from Aunt Ivy and Vernon, trying to decide which of the two books to read. She'd started Leo Tolstoy's *Anna Karenina* when she got back to her flat on Christmas night, and was savouring each chapter. She sipped her tea and opened the other book, *Stopping by Woods on a Snowy Evening* by Robert Frost. She'd read the eponymous poem a number of times and turned to it again now.

'Whose woods these are I think I know.
His house is in the village though;
He will not see me stopping here
To watch his woods fill up with snow.'

A thunderous knocking at her front door made her jump and spill her tea. She hurried to the window, her mind racing to Jack and thoughts of an accident. The knocking continued and she heard a shout. 'Ena! Are you in?' She saw the figure of a man hunched in her doorway, sheltering from the snow. It was Marty. She ran downstairs and pulled the door open. The wind howled around them but his anguished words reached her. 'Olive is asking for you. I think the baby is coming!' The storm raged as she and Marty fought their way to Colliery Road. Icy snowflakes stung her face and soaked through her coat and boots. Mid-morning masqueraded as darkest night and she pulled her hat down, lowered her head and moved slowly forward, step by slippery step through the deserted streets. Eventually, Marty gasped, 'we're here'. He pushed the door open and the fire's heat surrounded them. He threw his boots off and ran up the stairs two at a time. Ena heard Olive's desperate breathing and she set water to boil on the stove. She turned at light footsteps on the stairs and Dolly ran towards her. She tried to sign to say her coat was soaking but Dolly didn't stop. Ena held the teenager as she sobbed, then stepped back to speak with her hands. 'What happened?' Dolly's hands worked quickly and Ena concentrated,

'Mam, sudden pain, baby coming'. Ena signed, 'where's Nurse Brown?' She knew the plan was for the local midwife to attend Olive and deliver the baby. Dolly shrugged then signed, 'snow'. Ena nodded. She signed, telling Dolly to gather as many towels together as she could, and to keep the hot water coming. Then she washed her hands and climbed the stairs to Olive's bedroom.

With each stair, she rehearsed what she knew about delivering a baby. Her scant knowledge came from novels. She knew to time contractions and help the mother to breathe properly and tell her to push at the right time. She pushed the bedroom door open; Olive lay back against the pillows, her hair was stuck to her forehead and her breath came thick and fast. Ena hurried to the side of the bed and started mopping her friend's brow. Olive grabbed her hand and squeezed, 'it hurts, Ena'. Ena sat on the edge of the bed. 'I'm here now. We'll get through it together.' When Olive started to speak another contraction gripped her and she screamed. Ena told her to breathe and push when she felt the urge. When the contraction eased and Olive's breathing steadied, Ena asked how long it had been since her waters broke. Olive managed a croaked, 'early this morning'. Ena nodded, 'it shouldn't be too much longer then'. She busied herself with the towels Dolly had brought, hoping she'd convinced Olive. She didn't know how long it would take.

The cycle continued; a contraction, breathing and pushing. And throughout, Olive's piercing screams. She'd lost track of time when she heard the front door open and heavy footsteps on the stairs. She turned, longing to see Nurse Brown. Marty gestured to her. She laid a damp cloth across Olive's forehead and tiptoed across the room. 'She's at another birth, way over on the other side of Gateshead.' Ena looked at Olive then at Marty, 'let's pray she gets here soon; I think your baby is coming'. The colour drained from Marty's face and Ena took his arm. 'Keep the fire in and look after Dolly. Has she eaten?' Marty shook his head and Ena pushed him gently towards the top of the stairs. 'Make some soup.' Marty mouthed the word as he went back downstairs. She returned to Olive and another contraction. As the smell of vegetable soup drifted up the stairs, the front door opened again and she heard Jack's deep voice. It helped to know he was there.

The room grew brighter and she looked out to see the moon full in the sky. As she turned back to Olive, she heard a noise outside. She returned to the window and laughed at the sight of a tractor rumbling along Colliery Road, its steel wheels cutting a sharp path through the snow. She saw Nurse Brown jump out of the tractor, clutching her medical bag. She saluted the tractor driver and hurried to the Turnbulls' front door. Ena heard her ask for a pan of boiling water. Then Olive screamed and Ena saw the baby's head emerging. The door opened and Nurse Brown bustled in, holding the pan with a pair of scissors sticking out of the top. She told Olive to stop pushing and breathe, 'in through the nose and out through the mouth, dearie'. She motioned for Ena to do likewise and she kept time with Olive. Nurse Brown held the baby's head as Olive endured one final contraction, pushing her son out into the world. The midwife used the sterilised scissors to cut the umbilical cord, wrapped the baby in a towel and handed him to Olive. The bedroom was silent and the three women stared at each other. Then Dolly's baby brother cried and cheers rose from downstairs. Olive started to cry as she kissed her new son and Nurse Brown shook Ena's hand, 'you did a fine job, pet'. Ena shook her head, 'I'm just glad your tractor arrived when it did!' The midwife looked at Olive, 'shall I tell baby's dad and sister to come up?' Olive nodded and Ena kissed her friend and the new baby before going to join Jack.

Three weeks later, Ena and Jack stood alongside Dolly as godparents to Robert Martin Turnbull. The christening took place at Christ Church on Wellington Road in Dunston. Marty delighted in saying his strong healthy son would attend the Boys Brigade in Wood Street Chapel, a short walk from the church. Olive laughed, 'give him a chance Marty, he's only three weeks old!' Marty cradled his son, to be known as Bobby, in his muscular arms. 'Wor Bobby is a proper bobby dazzler!' He held tight to Bobby and put his other arm around Dolly's shoulders. His voice broke as he held his children, 'I'm the luckiest man alive'. After the service they went back to Colliery Road for tea and sandwiches and, 'something to wet young Bobby's head, Jack?' Olive took the baby upstairs to be fed and Dolly signed to say she wanted to ask Ena something. Ena sat opposite and watched her hands. 'On my gift card at Christmas you said the diary was for me to record my memories of being your bridesmaid.' Ena signed, 'yes?' Dolly smiled, 'can we go shopping for my dress? I think Mam is a bit busy at the moment!' Ena signed back, 'of course; we can go this Saturday if you like'. Dolly nodded cheerfully and signed her thanks.

Ivy

Ivy smiled when she opened the white envelope with Ena's neat hand-writing on the outside. She read the invitation then passed it over the breakfast table to Vernon.

MS ENA LEIGHTON
INVITES YOU
TO HER MARRIAGE TO MR JACK TODD
WEDNESDAY, AUGUST SEVENTEENTH
NINETEEN HUNDRED AND TWENTY-FIVE
ONE O'CLOCK IN THE AFTERNOON
AT ST. PAUL'S CHURCH, BOURNEMOUTH

Vernon paused between mouthfuls of toast. 'Why Bournemouth? It's a long way to travel. Wouldn't it be more traditional to get married in Whickham, where they're going to live?' Ivy put her head on one side, 'Ena said they don't know anyone in Whickham yet. She had her happiest years in Bournemouth, and everyone she'd want to invite was at her friend Rachel's wedding, other than Jack's uncle and perhaps some friends from Gateshead. She walked past St. Paul's when we were there last year and decided that was where she wanted to get married.' Vernon passed the invitation back, 'what about her mother; shouldn't she be sending the invitations?' Ivy sighed. 'In an ideal world, yes. But Mona hasn't been part of Ena's life for a long time. I don't even know where she is these days.' Vernon frowned, 'I told you I saw her on RMS *Homeric*, didn't I?' Ivy sipped her coffee before answering, 'yes, you said she'd met a man; was he called Wilfred?' Vernon nodded. 'Wilfred Henson. I introduced them. He was a Flight Commander in the Royal Naval Air Service during the war and I met him at Endell Street when he visited his sister's fiancé. He started working as a bank clerk in London after the war.' Ivy pictured her sister; flighty Mona who never stayed in one place long. Was it possible she and this Wilfred had kept in touch? 'Do you know where Wilfred lives?' Vernon shook his head, 'I think his family hailed from the Midlands; precisely where, I don't know. I'm sorry'. Ivy reached for Vernon's hand, 'it's all right, darling. My sister has been missing in one way or another for years'. There was also a letter in the envelope, and Ivy laughed when she learnt her niece had helped to deliver Olive's baby. Ivy had told Vernon about Ena's start in life and now she was delighted to describe her niece as an independent, determined young woman. She told him about Nurse Brown arriving on a tractor and he smiled, 'they're made of strong stuff up there!'

Vernon poured more coffee before asking what her plans were that day. 'I must go to the studio and put the dancers through their paces once more before Alfie's new revue opens tomorrow. And you?' He sighed, 'I need to pack so I'm ready to leave for the station early tomorrow morning'. Ivy put her head on one side, 'are you all right, my dear?' He sighed again, 'yes, but since we got married, each time I've sailed I've wanted to leave less and less'. Ivy smiled, 'well I'll be busy while you're away and when you come back we'll make sure we spend time together'. Vernon kissed her, 'I like the sound of that. How long will you be at the studio?' Ivy checked her elegant silver wristwatch, his wedding present to her. The small delicate face was adorned with tiny marcasite stones; she was reminded of their wedding day every time she looked at it. 'I should be finished by midday.' He nodded, 'meet me in the usual place and we'll have a picnic'. Ivy embraced her husband, 'I'll look forward to it'.

At the studio, the Leighton Girls were ready for their final rehearsal. Ivy appraised the six women; they were perfect for Alfie's latest production, *Charlot's Revue*. They had several numbers including 'How d'you do?,' 'Ready to Work' and Violet's favourite, 'Dancing all over the town'. Violet loved to shimmy, and Ivy applauded her dancers as they glided in unison across the studio. After a few hours, she was satisfied they were ready. She advised them to sleep and eat well and said she would see them at the Prince of Wales Theatre the next day. She locked the studio and hurried to meet Vernon at St. James's Park. It had become their favourite place for a picnic; there were a number of spots around the curved lake where they could sit unobserved under the picture-perfect cherry trees. Today, Ivy hoped to catch the last of the cherry blossom, before spring started to give way to summer. She walked to the lakeside meadow where there were black and white mulberry trees and fig trees by the water; one fig tree was believed to be the biggest in the country. She always walked past Duck Island at the east end of the lake, hoping to see the pelicans. The large water birds were introduced to the park in 1664; a gift from the Russian Ambassador to King Charles II.

She spotted Vernon and waved. He'd laid the contents of the wicker picnic basket out on the tartan blanket and Ivy sat, stretching her long legs out in front of her. Vernon produced a bottle of champagne and two glasses and proposed a toast. 'To my beautiful wife.' Ivy chinked her glass against his, 'and to my wonderful husband'. They ate their way through the contents of the picnic basket then lay back on the blanket, hands touching. Ivy closed her eyes and the spring sunshine warmed her face. Vernon kissed her cheek and asked her to dance. She smiled but didn't move, 'here? In the park?' He pulled her to her feet, 'why not?' She laughed, 'there's no music!' Vernon embraced her and started singing.

'Yes, sir, that's my baby,
No, sir, don't mean maybe
Yes, sir, that's my baby now.
Yes ma'am we've decided,
No ma'am we won't hide it,
Yes, ma'am you're invited now.'

He sang softly as he twirled her around on the grass; nestled in his arms she moved without a care in the world. When he reached the end of the song he whispered that he loved her. She held him close and said she loved him too.

Chapter 29

Wednesday 17th of August 1925
Wedding Day

E na's white matte silk wedding gown fell to just below the knee. She favoured the loose, boxy fit to anything more sculpted, but insisted on a satin ribbon around the dropped waist. The long net sleeves with a floral pattern ended in cuffs trimmed with white beads and pearls, matching the gown's slightly scooped neckline. A white lace headband completed her understated, striking look. The flowers in the posies, along with the corsages, came from William Love's garden. Ena took a deep breath, the fragrant white gardenias, along with purple and white roses and green foliage, brought a touch of the suffrage movement to her wedding. The gentle scent wafted through the group gathered outside the church.

The wedding party had stayed at the East Cliff Hotel the previous night and the wedding breakfast would be served there after the service. The Loves, Leamans and Primavesis, along with the Turnbulls and Bundells, came together to celebrate with Ena and Jack. In the absence of either her mother or father and given her aunt was the consistent parental figure in her life, Ena asked Aunt Ivy to walk her down the aisle and give her away. They agreed the origin of the tradition, the idea of transferring responsibility and care of the bride from her father to her new husband, had no place in their society now. However, Ena asked Ivy to do it in recognition of her constant love and support, saying she thought it more representative of the joining of two families than a transfer of ownership. Ivy was delighted to accept and stood at her side as the organ began, leading them into church with 'The

Trumpet Voluntary'. Jack turned slightly as she walked down the aisle, and she smiled at him. He stood tall in a smart dark blue suit and pristine white shirt and handkerchief. His necktie, in an elegant paisley pattern, was Ena's wedding present to him. Jack said he'd wanted to buy her a fur coat but thought she'd prefer to choose it herself, so he gave her the money instead. Ena thanked him and said she would go shopping after the wedding.

When they reached the end of the aisle, Ivy stepped back and Jack took his place next to Ena. The vicar nodded at the organist and the music stopped. Before the vicar spoke, Ena leant into Jack and whispered, 'you saved me all those years ago, thank you'. Jack shook his head. 'No, Ena. You saved yourself. I feel honoured to stand alongside the strong, independent woman you've become. You're a force for good in a world that treated you very badly.' The vicar cleared his throat and the service began.

Back at the hotel, the wedding party was welcomed with glasses of champagne, ale or fruit juice. Conscious of the hardship she knew many people were suffering in parts of the North East, Ena chose a relatively simple menu for her guests. They were served cream of mushroom soup, then roast beef with Yorkshire puddings, vegetables and gravy, a cucumber, gin and mint sorbet and sherry trifle to finish. Once their drinks were replenished, John Todd stood and tapped a teaspoon against his glass. He ran a hand through his greying hair and cleared his throat. 'I'm not used to making public speeches; being a postman never called for it.' He smiled at the friendly laughter, 'but in my role as uncle of the groom and best man, I want to say a few words. I've known Ena and her family for a long time and I couldn't be happier with my nephew's choice of bride. Life tests us; through hardship, battle, illness or loss, we've all been challenged. What matters is how we respond to those challenges. The two young people here, who have today vowed to love and cherish each other always, will face those challenges together and be better for it. Please, join me in a toast to the happy couple, Mr and Mrs Todd!' John raised his glass and the room rose as one. John sat and wiped his brow with his handkerchief. As he sat, Jack rose.

Jack turned to face his uncle. 'I want to thank you, not just for that humbling speech but for bringing me up.' He addressed his and Ena's guests. 'My uncle said we've all suffered loss; what he would never tell you is that his was great. As some of you know, my parents died when I was a baby and my aunt and uncle took me in. Tragically, my aunt died not long after, but my uncle never considered not keeping me. I was loved, well-fed and cared for. Not everyone is so fortunate.' Ena sipped her drink and waited for her husband to continue. 'I was brought up to appreciate what I had and to be kind to others, following my uncle's example. When I met Ena, I saw a girl determined not to be defined by her circumstances, to meet whatever challenges life threw at her with strength and resolve, and she's been doing it ever since. I'm proud to call Ena my wife.' Jack raised his glass and bent to kiss her.

After the kiss, Ena stood. The room fell silent and all eyes turned to her. She smiled, 'I know this is unusual and contrary to tradition, but it's my wedding and I want to say something'. Her guests applauded. She looked at the Turnbulls and saw Marty signing for Dolly. She signed herself to thank her friend for being a wonderful bridesmaid. Dolly's hands moved to say she was welcome. 'I hope you all enjoyed the food; I think the hotel staff have done a marvellous job.' She saw nods and heard murmurs of agreement. 'As Jack thanked his uncle, so I want to thank my aunt.' Her eyes moved to Ivy. 'Without you, my life would have been very different. You helped me understand how I could make a difference in a world that can be brutal. It's also a beautiful world, full of friendships and love, as we've seen today.' She opened her arms and gazed around the room, looking at each of her guests in turn. She stopped at Jack. 'Thank you for seeing me, all those years ago. I'm proud to call you my husband.' Ena sat and Jack leant across to embrace her. In the powder room later, she smiled at herself in the mirror as she washed her hands. She used the creamy, sweet-smelling soap and soft, fluffy towel. Her narrow gold wedding band gleamed, a perfect fit on the third finger of her left hand, and she swore never to take it off.

Ivy

When Ivy and Vernon arrived back in London after Ena's wedding, they only had 24 hours before Ivy was due at the studio and Vernon had to leave for his next trip. 'Picnic, darling? I'll go to Portobello Road Market to see what's fresh.' Ivy nodded, 'yes, and see if your mother wants to come; we can tell her about the wedding'. It was warm as they walked to Waterlow Park, still Irene's favourite. They found a spot and the women waited for Vernon to unveil their feast. They watched people; families and friends, enjoying the fresh air and music drifting from the bandstand. Irene listened as Ivy described Ena's wedding dress. 'I do apologise that I didn't feel up to coming along, it was very kind of your niece to invite me.' Ivy shook her head, 'she said not to worry, she knows it's an arduous journey. I'm sure she'll write to you herself but she asked me to thank you for your letter and kind gift'. Irene waved the thanks away. 'It wasn't much, just some crocheted doilies.' Ivy touched her mother-in-law's hand. 'Handmade gifts are very personal; she said she couldn't wait to use them.' Irene smiled, 'I'm finding my concentration for crocheting and embroidery has returned'.

The next day, Vernon left and Ivy made her way to the studio. She'd given her dancers some time off while she was away, now they would need to rehearse for their next engagement.

When she turned the corner into St Martin's Lane, she saw Violet and May waiting outside the building. When she reached them, they both started talking, their animated chatter drowning each other out. Ivy laughed, 'hold on, I can't make out what you're saying. What's got you so excited?' May touched Violet's arm, 'you tell her; it was you that saw her'. Ivy frowned, 'saw who?' Violet spoke clearly. 'Nellie Pilkington. May and I went to see Kenny Earnshaw's comedy revue at the Hippodrome while you were away, and there she was, bold as brass and just as comical.' Ivy stared, 'the same Nellie you danced with at the Diamond?' Violet smiled, 'one and the same, and the best part is we went to see her backstage afterwards and she knows where your sister is'.

ACT THREE

Chapter 30

Ena

Ena and Jack spent a few days in Boscombe after their wedding, then they made the long journey to Whickham. Ena had told the Bundells she would be moving out of the flat above the tea shop once she was married, and boxed up her belongings before the wedding. Jack's uncle and Bartholomew had moved everything to West Street for them. On the Saturday following their wedding, the Todds arrived home and began married life in the house they named Littlecroft. Jack held the garden gate open for Ena to walk in. She thanked him and walked up the path to their front door. Jack unlocked the door then waited. She laughed, 'you don't believe that old superstition, do you?' Jack didn't move, 'what, that by carrying you over the threshold I'm protecting you from any evil spirits lurking at the door of our new home?' Ena nodded then squealed when Jack lifted her up. 'No, I don't believe it, but I thought it would make you laugh!' Safely inside, Jack pushed the front door closed with his foot. The curtains twitched in the front room of the house next door. 'Happy newly-weds by the sound of it, Mr Fox.' The man in the armchair shook his newspaper, 'come away from the window, Winnie'.

Ena and Jack walked around the house. Two reception rooms and a kitchen led off the hallway; the late afternoon sun streaked in through the large bay window at the front, warming their faces as they stood in the airy room. Someone, Ena thought Bartholomew, had laid a fire for them in the fireplace on the left-hand wall. Ena frowned when she looked at the remaining two walls. Jack laughed, 'I know that expression, what do you have in mind?' Ena tapped the side of her nose, 'it's a surprise'. French doors led to the garden from the reception room at the back of the house, and Ena saw a second fire was ready for their return. 'We have good friends, don't we, Jack?' Jack didn't reply and Ena turned to see him staring out of the French windows. He pointed outside, his eyes bright, 'Look.' She followed his gaze, 'what is it?' He smiled, 'it's a blank canvas'. He reached into his inside pocked and produced a piece of paper. It was the drawing he'd made of his ideas for the garden after they'd seen Littlecroft for the first time. In the drawing, Jack had sectioned the H-shaped garden off into vegetables, flowers and lawn, bordered on all sides by bushes and trees. He'd written the names of certain vegetables in the top half of the H; turnips, potatoes, cauliflower and some berries; strawberries, raspberries and currants. In the bottom half of the H, the flowers included roses and pansies. She took his hand, 'we're here now Jack, and that blank canvas is all yours. Now, let's see if our kind friends have left us any food; I'm ravenous!' Jack laughed and they walked into the kitchen.

They used boxes to create a makeshift table and laid out the bread and cheese from Beatrice. There was a note welcoming them home, along with the Bundells' wedding gift; a year's supply of tea. Once they'd eaten, Jack asked her to come into the garden with him. When they stepped out of the back door, he took her hand. Because Littlecroft was at the very bottom of West Street, they had gardens all around their house. As they walked into the back garden, Jack set out his plans for the space. A low stone wall bordered the garden on the right-hand side with a gap at the top. Jack pointed at the fields, 'do you remember me saying I thought we could walk to the Seven Sisters from here?' Ena nodded, 'yes, and you said once we reached the row of ancient oak trees we could carry on, along the banks of the River Derwent to the Butterfly Bridge'. Jack took her in his arms, 'shall we do that tomorrow?' Ena smiled, 'I'd like that. Now, let's start unpacking'.

From her bedroom window, Winnie Fox watched the young couple walking round their garden. She admired the woman's smart dress and the gentlemanly way her husband held the gate open for his wife. Her own husband snored loudly downstairs and she tutted. The next morning, Ena and Jack woke early. After tea and toast with jam they put on their walking boots. They took a flask of tea and some ham sandwiches and stepped over the wall at the end of their garden. Winnie's bedroom curtain twitched, 'where are they going this early in the morning, Mr Fox?' Her husband sighed heavily, 'I'm sure I don't know, woman, now close that curtain and let me get back to sleep'. The fields were wet with dew as Ena and Jack made their way to the Seven Sisters. They craned their necks as they looked up at the old oaks. The trees stood tall and proud, sentries to times past. 'The stories they could tell, Ena.' She breathed deeply, 'I know; I wish they could talk'. A warm summer breeze rustled through the ancient branches and Ena laughed, 'I think they heard me'. Jack took her arm, 'have you heard the saying?' Ena shook her head, 'no, what is it?' Jack smiled, 'well I think the oak leaves must have been out before the ash this year, because it hasn't rained much, has it?' Ena wrinkled her nose, 'what are you talking about?' Jack pointed at the top of the tree. 'I found this piece of folklore; it says the emergence of the leaves predicts the weather for the summer.'

'If the oak before the ash,
Then we'll only have a splash.
If the ash before the oak,
Then we'll surely have a soak.'

Ena laughed, 'we'd better keep a close eye on these old oaks, then!' Jack put his arm around her and they continued walking through the quiet beauty of the ancient woodlands. 'I think our visit to these trees will be the first of many, Ena.' They walked to the Butterfly Bridge, where the river meandered slowly. The flowers in the hay meadows were perfect for attracting common blue and meadow brown butterflies, and the air was busy with colourful wings. Jack took her hand, 'I read that the original bridge was built in 1842 by a local stone mason called John English. He lived on Woodhouse Lane, not far from West Street. He was known as Lang Jack because he was strong as an ox and six feet four inches tall!' Ena smiled, 'we could use his help with the rest of our furniture, when it arrives!' Jack nodded. 'We could. We still need to find some armchairs for the front room and something to stand against the wall opposite the fireplace.' Ena smiled slowly, her eyes twinkling. Jack took her hands, 'there's that look again; what are you thinking?' Ena shook her head, 'come on, let's go home and carry on unpacking'. Jack turned to start walking back, realising whatever his wife had in mind, she was keeping it to herself for now.

When they stepped back over the wall at Littlecroft, a woman waved from the garden next door. 'Hello! I'm Mrs Fox, delighted to meet you.' Mrs Fox pointed to a low gate at the end of the shared garden fence, where their houses met. Ena and Jack introduced themselves and shook hands with the apron-clad woman over the gate. 'I'm Winnie. I hope you'll be very happy living here, myself and Mr Fox are.' She gestured towards the house, where a small, thin man stood at the back door. He raised a hand and they waved back. Winnie continued, now, I know you won't have everything you need yet, so I took the liberty of making extra Sunday dinner. Mr Fox!' The man jumped and hurried inside the house. He returned carrying a dish covered with a checked tea towel. Winnie took it from him, 'it's only a small piece of beef, some Yorkshire puddings and a few potatoes, pet'. Jack took the dish and Ena thanked Winnie. 'That's very kind of you. We're hungry after our walk so this will be marvellous.' Winnie nodded, 'you're welcome; knock if you need anything'. Ena thanked Winnie again and promised to return the dish later in the afternoon. Winnie smiled, 'just come to the back door'.

Ivy

As Ivy approached the Hippodrome, she tried to picture Nellie. She'd only met her once before, when she went to the Diamond to look for Mona. Nellie was one of the women, along with Violet and May, who gathered for breakfast close to the sleazy music hall. While Violet had tried to help Mona, Nellie's anger at the mention of her sister made Ivy take a step back. She'd grabbed Ivy's arm with a filthy hand and spat words at her, the rough accent and bitterness dripping into the cold London air. She'd yanked a scarf away from her neck to reveal an angry, red weal, saying Mona had cut her with a knife. Now, thanks to Violet and May, Ivy knew Mona hadn't caused Nellie any serious harm. Still, she was prepared for the woman's anger; after all, Mona stole her money for passage on the ship to America. Violet and May offered to come with her, but Ivy said she wanted to talk to Nellie on her own. Violet reminded her of Nellie's temper and Ivy was on her guard.

Ivy didn't know Kenny Earnshaw but Alfie said he was a decent chap who lived and breathed musical comedies and revues. 'His sole aim in life is to make people laugh!' Outside the theatre, posters advertising the current show, *London Calling!*, included Nellie's picture and the exclamation, 'Our very own Nellie Pilkington as Miss Hernia Whittlebot!' Ivy smiled when she stepped into the Hippodrome; entry was gained through a bar decorated as a ship's saloon. The performance space featured both a traditional stage and an arena that sank into a huge water tank for aquatic spectacles. The tank had a circle of fountains around the side, and eight in the centre. Entrances at the side of the auditorium could be flooded, and used for the entry of boats. Shows included equestrian acts, elephants and polar bears, and acrobats would dive from a minstrels' gallery positioned above a sliding roof, in the middle of the stage's arch. The auditorium was covered by a retractable glass roof, often illuminated at night, sending beams of light down Cranbourn Street and Charing Cross Road.

Ivy took her seat in the stalls and waited for the lights to dim. Despite her nerves about meeting Nellie, she enjoyed the show. The revue sketches made light of London society; Nellie's appearance in ' The Swiss Family Whittlebot', poked fun at the Sitwell siblings, known for their avant-garde poetry and ideas. Ivy smiled at the unlikely Nellie embodying the role of the formidable, eccentric poet, Edith Sitwell. When the cast took their encores, Ivy stood up and moved to the end of the row. She walked down the side of the stalls until she reached the black curtain separating the auditorium from the area of the theatre reserved for performers and staff. She was ready to introduce herself in her capacity as the director of a dance troupe, but no one challenged her. She made her way along the dimly-lit corridor, towards where she expected the dressing rooms to be. She heard voices behind her; the cast's excited chatter as they left the stage. A loud, comedic voice rang out above the others and she stood to one side. When Nellie passed her, she reached out and touched the sleeve of her dress. Nellie jumped back. 'Who are you?' Ivy raised her hands and apologised, 'I'm sorry, I didn't mean to startle you'. Nellie narrowed her eyes, 'I know you'. Ivy nodded, 'yes, I'm Mona's sister, Ivy'. Nellie glared at her, 'what do you want with me?'

People pushed past them, colourful costumes and voices filled the narrow corridor as Ivy tried to explain why she was there. Nellie shook her head, 'I can't hear you, come this way'. Ivy followed Nellie along the corridor, towards the back of the theatre. When they reached the door, Nellie pushed at the handle and cool air rushed inside. She held the door open and Ivy hesitated, remembering the other woman's nature. Nellie smiled; 'it's all right, me and Mona sorted our differences'. Ivy stepped outside, finding herself in a back lane. Nellie followed and closed the door behind them. 'This way, there's a decent café on the corner of Charing Cross Road; I could murder poached eggs on toast and a cup of strong tea.' Once Nellie had ordered her supper, Ivy asked about Mona. 'Violet said you know where my sister is?' Nellie nodded, 'it's strange; I followed her to New York wanting to confront her, hating her for what she did to me, but things worked out differently'. Ivy frowned, 'what do you mean?' Nellie shrugged, 'we reached an understanding. That's not what you were expecting me to say, is it?' 'No, I thought you wanted revenge for Mona attacking you and stealing your passage to America.' Nellie sighed, 'I did, but things changed after the raid'. Ivy blinked, 'raid?' Nellie laughed and in between mouthfuls of poached eggs and toast, she told Ivy about her time in New York with Mona and Tilly.

As Nellie talked, Ivy asked for their teapot to be refilled and she listened, transfixed. She interrupted when Nellie said Wilfred hadn't turned up for Mona's opening night. 'What, he promised to be there, then let her down?' Nellie waved a hand dismissively, 'another man and another broken promise. Although…' Ivy leant across the table, 'although what?' Nellie pursed her lips, 'Mona didn't think he was the same as every other man; she thought there must have been a good reason he didn't show.' Ivy sipped her tea, 'you disagreed?' Nellie nodded, 'yes, I thought his good reason was a wife hidden away somewhere'. Ivy took a deep breath, 'do you know where she went?' Nellie shook her head, 'not exactly. All I know is she was going to the bank where Wilfred worked'. Ivy raised her eyebrows, 'which bank?' 'No idea, sorry.' Ivy sat back in her chair and sighed; she was back to square one. Once she'd paid the bill, she followed Nellie to the door of the café. Nellie thanked her for supper and said she needed to be on her way. 'Sorry I couldn't help more; she's all right, your sister, once you get to know her.' Ivy smiled sadly; 'yes, she is'. Ivy had gone a few steps when Nellie called out, 'one thing Mona did say…' Ivy stopped and turned back, 'what?' 'Well, she said if I was right about him, she'd come and find me.' Ivy narrowed her eyes, 'and she hasn't?' 'Nope.' At home later, Ivy took up her pen to write to Vernon. He was her only hope, he'd introduced Mona to Wilfred and was the one person who might know which bank his friend had worked for. She sealed the letter with a kiss and propped it up on the sideboard near the door, ready for posting the next morning.

Chapter 31

Ena

In the weeks following their wedding, Ena and Jack made Littlecroft their own; gradually adding furniture, decorations and ornaments. In September, Jack planted spinach, which he said could be harvested throughout winter. The onions and broad beans would result in crops in early spring. Ena watched him plant handfuls of daffodil bulbs; he'd said they would shoot roots before winter set in, allowing them to bloom in the spring.

One Saturday morning, she looked out of the French doors as a shimmering haze gathered across the garden. A lack of rain and mild temperatures had resulted in an unseasonably warm month. Jack ran a hand across his brow as he dug. She went into the kitchen and took a jug of lemonade out of the cold pantry. The pantry, to the left of the back door, was out of direct sunlight on the north side of the house, where the temperature was lowest. A small, high window covered in mesh ventilated the pantry, allowing cool air to circulate. Ena returned the jug to the stone shelf, alongside the milk, butter and cheese. Winnie was hanging washing out and Ena greeted her neighbour. 'It's another lovely day.' Winnie took two pegs from her apron pocket and fixed them to a wet towel on the line. 'It is, pet. These clear skies make perfect drying days. I think we're having one of those Indian summers, don't you?' Ena agreed, 'yes, I think so'. She walked to the vegetable patch and gave Jack his drink. He stuck his spade in the soil then mopped his brow, before taking a gulp of the cool lemonade. 'Thank you, this is warm work.' Ena smiled, 'how is the planting going?' Jack looked around the newly-dug area, 'we'll have some of our own vegetables for winter, and potatoes and tomatoes in early spring'. Ena nodded. 'I'll make some sandwiches at dinner time and we can eat them out here. We should make the most of this weather.' A voice piped up next door, 'Indian summer, pet. That's what it is!' Ena and Jack laughed and agreed with Winnie. Towards the end of the month, Jack asked Ena about her fur coat. 'I thought you might have gone into town to buy one by now.' She smiled; 'I'm not ungrateful, it's been so warm that I couldn't imagine trying heavy coats on'. Jack nodded, 'I understand, but I hope you'll treat yourself, when the time is right'. Ena took his hand, 'I will, I promise'.

In October, Winnie's Indian summer disappeared overnight, replaced by wet and stormy conditions. With the change in the weather, Ena decided to take a bus into Newcastle. She held her umbrella in front of her face as she walked up West Street to the bus-stop. When the bus came, she climbed the stairs to the top deck and sat at the front. After the conductor took her fare, she rubbed her sleeve on the inside of the window for a better view of Whickham Front Street. The bus passed the baker's and the Swalwell Cooperative Society and towards the end of Front Street, it stopped outside the church and more people got on. Two middle-aged women clomped up the stairs, breathing heavily and shaking drops from their umbrellas as they took the seat behind Ena. 'What are you taking to the Harvest Festival?' Ena heard the other woman sigh before answering. 'I don't know. He was going to dig up some vegetables; I'll have to get on at him.' The other woman tutted, 'if you want something doing… ', the women laughed and Ena smiled. She was looking forward to the Harvest Festival celebration at St. Mary's; Winnie said it was an important community event that brought the village together.

When the bus arrived in Newcastle, Ena rang the bell to alight on Grainger Street. The brown envelope nestled in her handbag, and a bell tinkled when she opened the door to the second-hand furniture shop. 'Good morning, Madam, how can I help you?' Ena smiled and pointed at the piano. She left the shop with an empty envelope and a delivery arranged for the following Saturday. She opened her umbrella and walked to the Grainger Market. On the bus home, she took a brown paper parcel out of her shopping bag. The stall holder had wrapped it up for her and she opened it carefully, not wanting to damage the fragile sheet music. She traced the title with her finger, 'long and tapering, pianist's fingers', Aunt Ivy had said'. Ena hadn't played since she moved into her own flat in Bournemouth more than seven years ago, and she hoped she remembered how. She wrapped 'The Blue Danube' by Johann Strauss up again and smiled, imagining Jack's face when she told him.

When she got home, Jack raised his eyebrows, 'where's your fur coat?' Ena took his hand and led him into the front room. She pointed at the empty wall opposite the fireplace. 'It's going to go there.' Jack frowned, 'what is?' Ena laughed, 'my fur coat! Only I didn't buy a fur coat, I bought a piano!' Jack shook his head, 'I should have known you had something planned!' Ena looked up at him. 'I've missed playing, and I would've only worn a fur coat occasionally; I'll play the piano all the time. I spotted it in the shop when we were looking for furniture.' Jack kissed the top of her head, 'the money was for you to buy yourself a present; I'm glad you chose something you wanted'. Ena took the sheet music from her bag and put it on the floor in front of the wall. She stood back and Jack embraced her.

When the piano arrived, the delivery men stood it against the wall. Ena opened the lid and placed her sheet music on the wooden stand. Jack put his head on one side, 'there's something missing'. He nodded at the delivery man then turned to Ena. She frowned, 'what are you up to?' Jack tapped the side of his nose, 'you'll see'. When the delivery man returned, he was carrying a piano stool and two brown paper packages. He placed the mahogany stool in front of the piano and handed Ena the packages. She thanked him and Jack saw him out. Alone in the room, Ena put the packages down then ran her hands across the stool's cushioned seat. She lifted the lid of the hinged seat, revealing a storage space for sheet music. She picked the stool up by its wooden handles and re-positioned it slightly before sitting. She looked up at the music then placed her hands on the keys and started to play. The slow, graceful waltz began and she smiled. When Jack came back into the room she stopped playing and pointed at the stool, 'you?' Jack shrugged, 'well you hadn't mentioned a stool, so I went into the shop and asked if they had one'. Ena stood and embraced him, then picked up the packages. She handed one to him and he frowned, 'for me?' She nodded, 'I saw it when I bought the piano and I thought you'd like it'. He placed the heavy package on the table and unwrapped it. The needle on the banjo-shaped barometer hovered between 'dull' and 'wet', and he laughed, 'it works!' He turned to her, 'thank you. What's in the other package?' Ena raised her eyebrows, 'I don't know. I only paid for the piano and the barometer. Perhaps the shop made a mistake.' Jack said she should open it. 'If it's their mistake, we can take it back, whatever it is.' Ena unwrapped the package carefully then she gasped, 'it's a metronome! I saw it in the shop but I didn't have enough money left. Look, there's a note with it'. Jack peered over her shoulder to read the note from the shop owner.

'Dear Mrs Todd,
This metronome needs a piano. I thought you might be able to help.
Yours sincerely,
Mr Storey (Storey's second-hand goods, Newcastle.)'

'Oh Jack, that is such a kind gesture. I'll call in and thank him the next time I'm in Newcastle.' Ena placed the pyramid-shaped metronome, in its wood-grain finished case, on top of the piano. She unfastened the thin pendulum and the metronome started to click. She smiled, 'I can set it at the required tempo for the piece I'm practising!' Jack asked her to continue playing 'The Blue Danube'. When the waltz finished, he went into the hallway and hung the beautifully crafted wooden-framed barometer on the wall. He started checking it every day, often a number of times each day.

October continued with constant rain and flooding in some parts of the North East, and by mid-November winter had set in with frost and fog everywhere. Jack kept a fire going, making sure Littlecroft stayed warm. In the evenings and at weekends Ena played the piano or knitted. They played cards; Gin Rummy, Newmarket or 21, and listened to the news, music and plays on their new wireless. Occasionally, they visited the Whickham Picture House and had seen *The General*, a silent comedy starring Buster Keaton, and *Flesh and the Devil*, a romantic drama with Greta Garbo and John Gilbert.

By November, Jack's barometer appeared to be stuck on 'stormy', and while Ena wouldn't have swapped her piano for anything, she longed for a fur coat. Arctic air brought severe frosts and heavy snowfall, and by Christmas Eve they were snowed in. Jack's uncle managed to get to them earlier in the day before the snowstorm worsened, but their plans to go to the carol service at St. Mary's were thwarted. Instead, they kept warm in front of the fire and sang along to the wireless.

On Christmas morning they exchanged season's greetings with Winnie and Mr Fox over the fence, and were soon back inside, sheltering from the elements. Snow continued to fall outside as the mouth-watering smell of roast turkey filled the kitchen. Ena decorated the table with sprigs of holly and ivy and the three of them sat down to a feast. John Todd sat back, having cleared his plate of turkey, stuffing, roast potatoes, carrots, parsnips and Brussels sprouts, all covered in thick, meaty gravy. 'Thank you Ena, that was delicious. I couldn't eat another thing.' Jack laughed, 'well you'll have to, because there's Christmas pudding and custard!' Later, after exchanging gifts, Jack put more coal on the fire and they toasted each other with sweet sherry. Ena sat back and opened her new book, her Christmas present from Jack. As she read the first page of Emily Brontë's *Wuthering Heights,* she gave silent thanks for her loving husband and their warm home.

Ivy

After she'd posted her letter to Vernon, Ivy waited impatiently for his reply. She counted the days then realised he'd be there in person before anything arrived. She knew he'd started to dislike being away, and if she was honest, she didn't like it much either. When she wasn't at work she saw her friends and Vernon's mother and she was content. When he was home they had picnics in the park, went for afternoon tea, visited the theatre, cinema and opera, or stayed in the flat playing records and dancing. A letter landed on the mat the day before he was due home. She opened it carefully, longing for news to lead her back to her sister.

'My darling Ivy,

I was delighted as always to receive your last letter. I'll begin with the news I know you'll be waiting for, although sadly it will disappoint you. Unfortunately, I have no further details about Wilfred Henson, only that he worked as a bank clerk somewhere in London. I'm deeply sorry I can't help you to find your sister. Perhaps when I arrive home we can put our heads together to think of a way forward?

In other news, this voyage has been largely uneventful, although I have some new recipes courtesy of a marvellous French chef who boarded at Cherbourg. I look forward to presenting some new dishes

*to you! I know from Mother you've visited regularly and walked to
her favourite park together. Thank you for spending time with her,
she gains so much from being in your company. I hope everything is
continuing to go well for you at work; it sounds as though Alfie's new
show is a resounding success!*

*As always, I miss you, love you, and I'm longing to be back in your
arms.*

Your loving husband, Vernon.'

Ivy pinched the bridge of her nose. After meeting Nellie, she
was hopeful about finding Mona, but it proved to be a dead end.
Vernon was her last chance. She sighed; she'd spent so much of
her life looking for her sister. She realised she needed to put
thoughts of finding Mona to the back of her mind. Vernon
would be home the next day and she wanted to make the most
of their time together, before he left again. A series of autumn
concerts were starting on Clapham Common; there would be
jazz bands and cocktails. And the magnificent British Empire
Exhibition was on at the Empire Stadium until the end of October, an event she knew Vernon was keen to attend. She stood
up; determined to concentrate on her happy life with her wonderful husband, instead of chasing her sister's shadow. By the
time Vernon walked through the door, Ivy had read the British
Empire Exhibition brochure from cover to cover, and had a
number of suggestions for him.

Vernon embraced her then stood back, holding her arms.
'I'm so sorry I couldn't give you any more information about
Wilfred; I don't know which bank he was working for when he
met your sister.' Ivy shook her head, 'it's all right, I shouldn't
have built my hopes up. I know from past experience she doesn't
always want to be found'. Vernon took her hands, 'we can ask
around, see if anyone has seen either of them in London'. 'No, I
want to focus on having a good time now you're home. Look at
this.' She handed him the brochure and his eyes widened when

he read the list of events. 'I've made a note of things I think we'd enjoy.' Vernon read Ivy's list, 'there's a lot here that sounds like fun. Should we start with the pleasure park?' Ivy laughed, 'Yes! The dance hall is rumoured to be three times the size of the Royal Albert Hall, and the funfair is filled with hair-raising spectacles including a water ride called The Chute, and a funhouse with a fan hidden in the floor that blows air up women's dresses!' Vernon feigned shock, 'It sounds hilarious! Look at this; I think we'll avoid the "Seven Ages of Woman" exhibit, don't you?' Ivy nodded, 'yes; haven't the organisers heard of women's independence? Which liberated woman wants to see a series of rooms depicting the various gas appliances used during her life?'

On their way to the Empire Stadium the next day, they overheard people discussing the elaborate exhibits. The grand pavilions, a life-sized butter sculpture of the Prince of Wales and his horse in a huge, refrigerated unit, a working model of Niagara Falls and a recreation of Tutankhamen's tomb. Over the coming weeks, before Vernon had to leave again, they watched a rodeo, Roman chariot-racing and a re-enactment of the Great Fire of London. They also saw a performance of the very grand-sounding Pageant of Empire, with a cast of around 15,000 amateur performers along with 300 horses, 500 donkeys, seven elephants, llamas, bulls, 730 camels, 72 monkeys, three bears, 1,000 doves, hawks and a macaw. Ivy was mesmerised by the spectacle, saying even Kenny Earnshaw's Hippodrome couldn't compete with it. When the time came for Vernon to leave, he held her close and whispered that he longed to stay. She took a deep breath and gave him a cheery farewell; inside she was desperate for him not to go. He was away at New Year and Ivy celebrated Big Ben's chimes at the Redford, along with Grace and Walter and Lydia's colourful friends. As 1926 dawned, she hoped it might be the year her husband came home for good.

Chapter 32

1926

Ena

Ena invited Winnie and Mr Fox to Littlecroft to see in the New Year with her and Jack. Winnie refused to let Mr Fox come inside until they'd heard Big Ben's chimes ring out on the wireless. Ena hurried to the door to admit a shivering Mr Fox holding a lump of shiny coal. She handed him a warm drink and his teeth chattered as he tried to say something, 'good, good'. Ena frowned; not understanding. Winnie shouted, 'he's saying you're a good neighbour, pet, and you are! Now close that door, come inside and play this piano!' Ena smiled and sat at her piano. They sang along to 'Auld Lang Syne' as 1926 dawned on Littlecroft.

Aunt Ivy's first letter of the year included the news that Vernon was planning to leave the White Star Line and look for a job in London. Ena smiled at her aunt's words, 'he can spend more time with his mother and enjoy our wonderful, fun-filled life in London. It will be marvellous to not always be thinking about the next time he has to leave. His final voyage is in March; by Easter he'll be home for good'. She called for Jack and showed him the letter, 'we could invite them to stay, perhaps for my birthday in May?' Jack agreed, saying the garden would have yielded lots of vegetables by then and they could cook up a storm, 'to use sailors' slang!' Ena laughed, 'will your elderflower champagne be ready by then?' Jack shook his head. 'Unfortunately not. I'll pick the flowers in late May or early June, but the champagne has to ferment then age for a few months.' Ena folded the letter and slid it back into the envelope. 'Not to worry, they can have some the next time they visit. Once Vernon is working in London, hopefully they can come up more often.' Jack tapped the barometer, 'let's hope the weather improves by the time they visit; January has been nothing to write home about so far'. Ena nodded and warmed her hands in front of the fire. According to Jack, the extreme cold was due to a high-pressure system over western Russia. It rained incessantly until the end of the month, when temperatures started to rise. 'Should we take the opportunity and walk to the Seven Sisters while we can?' Ena smiled, 'yes, I'll make a flask of tea and some sandwiches'.

The walk was second nature to them now, and they knew how lucky they were to have such an array of natural beauty on their doorstep. Ena remembered the stinking back lanes of Pipewellgate, where she'd lived with Lizzie when she was little. An ever-present dirty, grey mist hung over the area, and smells from the heavy industry on the banks of the river wafted up the streets. Crumbling slums threatened imminent collapse and rats scurried among the filth. She shook her head to dislodge the memories and breathed deeply as they walked across the wet springtime carpet leading to the ancient oaks. Since they'd moved into Littlecroft, Jack had read about the flowers and birds they might see on their walks. He knew which flowers would be blooming and which birds might be feeding, and he delighted in describing everything to her. Today he said they might see some celandines and possibly early wood anemones. Ena pointed excitedly at the shiny, yellow, star-like celandine blooms, their long stalks and glossy, dark-green heart-shaped leaves reaching up from the woodland floor. Jack took her arm and led her to a shaded part of the meadow. 'Look, the anemones are coming. By next weekend, this meadow will be full of them.' Ena stared; the delicate white petals with a light pink tinge moved slowly in the cool breeze, balanced precariously at the top of their long stalks.

They sat on the riverbank to eat their sandwiches, enjoying

the cool, clean air. Suddenly, Jack pointed up into one of the birch trees. He put a finger over his lips and cupped his ear. She listened. She knew the bird; Jack had described the siskin to her on another walk. This flock had gathered to feed on the plentiful seeds in the birch and alder woodlands, and the trees lifted with their activity. Their shrill, steady, mechanical-like sound filled the air, and Ena put her hands over her mouth to stifle a laugh. Jack placed his binoculars in front of her face and she gasped. The small, yellowish-green birds had a dark streaked belly and a striking yellow rump. Their forked tails bobbed as they fed. She recognised the male birds from Jack's description; the black cap and bib and bright yellow cheeks set them apart from the females. On their way home, they talked about work. They were both grateful to work at the flour mill where thus far, there were no job losses. Other industries in the region continued to decline, and unemployment, particularly among men, was rising at a terrifying rate. The welfare centre was busier than ever and Ena worried she wouldn't be able to meet demand; some people who'd donated in the past weren't in a position to do so now. Marty had held onto his job and the Bundells' tea shop was still open, but Beatrice and Bartholomew were paying much higher prices for their imports. Ena sighed, 'where will it end, Jack?' He took her hand, 'I don't know; we can grow more of our own vegetables; that can help us and our neighbours'. Ena squeezed his hand, 'you're right, and I can help people by baking bread and cakes and knitting'.

In February, Jack didn't need to look at his barometer to know he would have to clear their front path. Snow had been falling for days, and he and Ena found themselves trudging to work in wellington boots. Dolly, now 18, had been promoted and was working in the office, alongside Ena and Jack. She smiled as she signed, telling them how Bobby kept them entertained; today he'd copied her as she brushed her hair. Her hands worked quickly, 'he used his spoon, covered in scrambled egg, to brush his hair! Mam had to wash him all over again!' Ena laughed; she looked forward to Dolly's tales about her baby brother. Ena and Jack did their best to support the Turnbulls, knowing falling exports and mass unemployment were creating difficulties throughout the mining industry. Jack offered to speak to Mr Young to see if there was a job for Marty at the flour mill or the soap works, but Marty was adamant; he came from generations of mining stock and was a miner through and through. The situation worsened when some mine owners refused to modernise the industry as other countries were doing, failing to mechanise pits and increase efficiency meant Britain was falling behind. When some owners started cutting miners' pay and increasing their hours, real fear set in. Miners including Marty were suffering: the work was difficult; injury and death were commonplace, and the industry refused to support its workers.

The snow and frost continued into March, but Ena was excited to visit the new library on Prince Consort Road in Gateshead. It was opened at the end of the month by The Earl of Elgin, Chairman of the Carnegie Trust. Ena read that the trust was actively involved in funding the construction of public libraries across England. She was proud the initiative to promote education and literacy by providing communities with access to free public libraries had been extended to the North East, too often overlooked by the authorities. The Earl himself was instrumental in the inauguration of Gateshead Central Library, marking a significant contribution to the community's access to knowledge and information. Ena wanted to be there and show how much she appreciated the acknowledgement of her birthplace. When she left the library, the snow had started to thaw and by the time she arrived home, children were skipping in the street. Spring was coming and perhaps with it, hope for an improvement in all their fortunes.

A letter from Aunt Ivy was waiting for her at home. Her aunt's joy jumped off the page. 'Exciting news! Teddy has offered Vernon the job of maître d at the Redford. He's introducing an afternoon tea service and with Vernon's experience as a ship's steward and his love of good food, he'll be ideal. He'll be back by the end of the month, and we'll visit you and Jack at Littlecroft for your birthday in May.' Ena smiled as she handed Jack the letter, 'things might be looking up'.

Ivy

Ivy strolled around Covent Garden Market with her shopping basket slung over her arm. She'd decided to cook a celebratory meal for Vernon to welcome him home permanently. She hadn't realised how much she wanted him to leave the White Star Line, until he accepted Teddy's job offer. Now it was settled, she couldn't wait for him to walk through the door. She'd found a recipe for Lemon sole Véronique and had already been to Billingsgate Market, near the Thames. The market's location near the river meant it carried the freshest fish, with catches being unloaded straight off the boats every morning. She'd bought the sole and some langoustines to elevate the dish. Now she was looking for white grapes, fresh tarragon, mushrooms and samphire. She ticked the items off her list as she visited the various stalls, singing to herself as she walked. She knew she had vermouth at home for the sauce, but wanted a nice bottle of white wine to accompany the dish. The stall holder wrapped the Chablis in brown paper and she placed it carefully in her shopping basket. Lastly, she bought two big bunches of flowers; roses and lilies, to brighten up the flat, before taking a taxicab back to James Street.

The afternoon light was fading when the cab dropped her off. She unlocked the door to their flat and reached for the light switch, juggling shopping bags and flowers. One of the bunches slipped out of her arms and as she bent to gather the blooms, she saw a small yellow square on the mat. She stared at the envelope, her ears ringing. Nausea rose into her throat and her hands shook as she reached for the Post Office Telegram. She tore the envelope open and sank to her knees, the words blurring in front of her eyes.

'Deeply regret to inform you Mr Vernon Revill died of pneumonia on Saturday the 13th of March 1926. All at the White Star Line express their deepest sympathies.'

Ena

Ena arrived home to another letter from Aunt Ivy. Excited to read about hers and Vernon's forthcoming visit, she opened it before taking her coat and shoes off. As she read the short letter, her heart raced and her head swam. She bumped down into a chair and dropped the letter on the floor. She put her head in her hands and wept. Jack's footsteps were heavy on the stairs and then she was in his arms, sobbing. He held her until her shoulders stopped shaking, then he picked up the letter. Ena saw his expression change when he read her aunt's words. He shook his head and took her in his arms again.

Chapter 33

Ivy

Ivy's friends supported her after she received the news. When she managed to pick herself up off the floor, she crawled to the telephone and called Grace. Time was an irrelevance; all she knew was it was dark when Grace and Walter arrived. Walter retrieved her shopping and Grace enveloped her as she wept. In between sobs, Ivy said she needed to tell Vernon's mother about her remaining son. 'Oh Grace, that poor woman. To lose one son was bad enough, now both of them. I dread to think what this will do to her.' Grace patted her hand, 'not tonight, darling; tomorrow'. They drank hot, sweet tea and sat in silence. When the clock struck midnight, Walter spoke, 'perhaps you should come home with us tonight, Ivy?' She shook her head; everything she had of Vernon was here in their flat. Grace took her hand, 'I'll stay here with you, in that case, all right?' Ivy sniffed, knowing wherever she was, sleep wouldn't come. She watched Grace walk her husband to the door and say goodnight. Her friends' marriage had outlasted her own three failed attempts to find happiness, where was the fairness in that?

The next morning, the telephone started to ring. Walter, who offered to visit Irene and give her the news, then Lydia (whom Walter had told), then Teddy with Daphne in the background, then someone from the White Star Line. Ivy asked the man to repeat his words, her head pounding. She gestured to Grace for a pen and paper and made some notes. When she replaced the receiver, Grace pointed questioningly towards the paper and Ivy nodded. Grace read Ivy's notes. 'A company representative will call and return his belongings to you. Is that the best they can do?' Ivy shrugged, 'he was sympathetic about my loss, and said Vernon was taken ill very suddenly, there wasn't time to contact me. What could they have done, realistically? The ship was in the middle of the Atlantic Ocean when he died'. Grace took her hand and spoke quietly, 'and his body?' Ivy's lip trembled, 'they buried him at sea'. Grace pulled Ivy into her arms and held her as she sobbed.

A few days later, the White Star Line representative visited Ivy. Grace and Walter were with her and offered tea, which the young man politely refused. He was sympathetic and efficient, delivering what Ivy suspected were scripted lines for the situation. Before he left, he asked Ivy to sign for Vernon's belongings. Walter saw him to the door then came back and poured three large glasses of brandy. He raised his tumbler, 'to our magnificent friend and Ivy's devoted husband, Vernon Revill'. Ivy and Grace copied the gesture. As Ivy toasted her husband, she looked towards the gramophone, the last record they'd played still lay on the turntable. She closed her eyes, picturing her last dance with him.

'I'm sitting,
On top of the world,
I'm rolling along,
Yes, rolling along.'

When Grace and Walter left, with a promise to telephone later, Ivy closed the door, drew the curtains and went to bed. She pulled the covers over her head, but all she could picture was Vernon's blue, sausage-shaped kitbag lying unopened on the living room floor. She dragged herself out of bed and grabbed the bag. She opened the wardrobe and pushed the bag all the way to the back, on the side where Vernon's redundant clothes hung. Then she went back to bed.

Ena

The day after she received the news about Vernon, Ena wrote to her aunt. She started the letter then stopped and put her pen down; no words could ease her aunt's suffering. After losing Bertie, Ena and Ivy grieved together in Bournemouth. Ivy had lost her first love and Ena the only father figure she'd ever known. Ena cared for her aunt and threw herself into her work at the community hall. In time, Ivy returned to work and focussed on continuing to help injured soldiers at Endell Street. Everyone agreed George was a mistake, but when Ivy met Vernon, Ena knew her aunt had another chance of happiness. For it to be snatched away in such cruel fashion, just as their plans for the future were coming to fruition, was beyond anything Ena could understand. She pictured her aunt on her wedding day, the epitome of joy. She picked up her pen again.

Dear Aunt Ivy,

There is nothing I can write to lessen your loss. All I can say is how very sorry Jack and I were to learn about Vernon. Life has dealt you such a cruel hand; and you do not deserve to have had your happiness snatched away. Throughout my life you were the one steadfast, loving person I could always rely on. I hope now to offer you that same support. I will come to London as soon as I can, and please know when you feel up to it, you are welcome here at Littlecroft.

Your loving niece,

Ena.'

She looked up at Jack. 'I can't believe this is the letter I'm writing to her; it should be full of plans for hers and Vernon's visit next month.' Jack sighed, 'I know, but I'm sure your aunt will be grateful to hear from you'. Ena sighed and sealed the envelope.

Jack was frustrated by April's unexpected snow and frost. 'I wanted to harvest the rhubarb, broccoli and spring cabbage.' Ena nodded, 'let's hope the weather improves soon. I know you wanted the vegetables for the welfare centre'. Jack pursed his lips, 'I worry it still won't be enough; some families are becoming desperate'. Ena sighed; the newspapers were full of stories about the possibility of industrial action, as workers grew increasingly dissatisfied. The gripes weren't confined to one area; anger was widespread among different occupations throughout the country. Marty said the miners were desperate; savage wage reductions and worsening working conditions had led many of them to consider upping tools and leaving. 'Owners keep their profits but send us down for longer and longer. The conditions are treacherous and show no sign of improving. I nearly died in there once; it feels like a matter of time before there's another disaster. What would we do, Jack? It's all we know. I have mouths to feed; one a 14-month-old baby. I have to put up with whatever they choose to dole out. Unless the Federation can do something this time.'

During the war, the government had intervened in the coal mining industry to keep the fires of war burning. When the war ended, mine owners took back control, insisting on reduced pay and lesser conditions. The Miners' Federation of Great Britain, of which Marty was a member, was formed to represent and coordinate the affairs of local and regional miners' unions in England, Scotland and Wales. The Federation appealed to the National Union of Railwaymen and the Transport Workers' Federation to bring the idea of a general strike to life, by joining them in action. They refused and the miners were defeated. Britain's coal exports continued to fall, and the owners informed the Federation that because they were making a loss they intended to reduce pay and conditions dramatically, yet again. This time, transport workers agreed to support the miners by imposing an embargo to stop all movements of coal. As a coordinated strike of mine, railway and transport workers was due to begin, the government announced the establishment of a Royal Commission to examine the coal industry's problems. While it met, the government agreed to provide the coal industry with a subsidy, to cover the gap between the production and market price of coal. While everyone waited for the Commission to report, Marty and his fellow miners hoped for the best, but feared their demands would be ignored. Their fears were realised when the Commission's report was issued. Last minute attempts by the government to persuade the Federation to agree to cuts in pay and conditions were rejected, before the subsidy ended on Friday the 30th of April. With the Federation's refusal and its general secretary's resolute response, 'not a penny off the pay, not a minute on the day', the owners locked out more than one million miners. On the 1st of May, the miners found themselves unable to work. The national trade union centre, the TUC, promised to support the miners in their dispute.

On Monday morning, the streets were eerily quiet as Ena and Jack walked to work. 'Something's different Jack; what is it?' Jack looked around, 'buses.' Ena stopped, 'buses?' Jack nodded, 'yes, we normally see a few going into Gateshead or Newcastle at this time; this morning we haven't seen any'. Then they saw the miners. The men, usually deep underground by the time Ena and Jack arrived at the flour mill, were gathered on street corners, deep in conversation. They saw Marty on Colliery Road and he hurried towards them. 'The TUC has called a general strike and the government has declared a state of emergency! Perhaps now Baldwin will realise how important our industry is!' Ena frowned, 'what does that mean, a general strike?' Marty punched his fist in the air, 'it means we've got support! The country will come to a standstill!'

Ivy

For the first week after Vernon's belongings were returned, Ivy hardly got out of bed. Grace and Walter visited Irene; tragically the news proved too much and she was hospitalised for melancholia. Vivienne said Irene had been admitted to one of the best psychiatric wards in London, and she would visit to monitor her progress. Violet sent her a note saying she mustn't think about work; Alfie Atherton had offered the Leighton Girls studio space for rehearsals. He'd also found them an engagement, 'for as long as necessary'. Ivy read the note and went back to bed. Her curtains remained closed. When Ena's letter arrived, her tears started again. Her beloved niece, who comforted her when Bertie died, now doing it again. They had helped each other over the years, in the absence of other close family. Ivy pictured her sister; someone she should be able to turn to. Where was she?

Ivy read Ena's letter again. She and Vernon had been planning a trip to the North East for her niece's 27th birthday on the 22nd of May. She straightened her shoulders and raised her chin; she was an aunt and Ena deserved to have a happy birthday. She pulled her curtains open then went to have a wash. Once she'd dressed, she walked to the window. She watched people going about their everyday business. That was her, a week ago, before her world imploded. She looked around; the flat was tidy, there was no sign of the flowers she'd brought home that fateful day, or the fish and vegetables, thankfully. She went into the kitchen and opened the wooden icebox. She managed to smile, remembering Vernon's excitement when it was delivered. He explained a large block of ice needed to be placed in the compartment at the top of the icebox. When the ice melted, the cold air circulated down into the storage compartments below, keeping the food cool. He'd said the melted ice water was collected in a drip pan, which needed to be emptied regularly. Ivy saw with relief that the icebox was empty. Someone, she guessed Grace, had removed the block of ice. She made coffee and drank it black as she picked up her pen to reply to Ena.

Ena

When the strike began, their community was buoyant. Miners were cheered and applauded as they took to the streets in support of their cause. People gave whatever they could, to help families without a wage coming in. Food, clothes and blankets appeared at the welfare centre and Ena worked quickly to stock the shelves, going straight there every day after work.

On the 4th of May, there were reports of strikers stretching from John O'Groats to Land's End, and transport had come to a standstill throughout the country. Marty said the reaction to the strike call was immediate and overwhelming, declaring, 'that'll show the owners!' The next day, amidst government criticism, *The British Worker*, the TUC's newspaper wrote 'We are not making war on the people. We are anxious ordinary members of the public shall not be penalised for the unpatriotic conduct of the mine owners and the government.' Marty was ecstatic, 'it's time people knew what's going on!' The government put a militia of special constables in place; volunteers who would maintain order in the streets. Jack came across one of them wandering near the flour mill, he'd become separated from his group and asked for directions to the pit. As Jack walked with him, the man said he'd found sympathy with the miners, not the employers. 'If I'd known about the appalling poverty here, I would never have become a special constable. This conflict shouldn't have been allowed to happen.'

On the 6th of May, the atmosphere changed. *British Gazette*, the government newspaper, suggested transport into London had improved due to motor car sharing, cyclists, private buses and strike-breakers. The next day, the TUC met with the Royal Commission and worked out a set of proposals designed to end the dispute, but the Federation rejected the proposals. There was a mixed reaction around Dunston a few days later, when news of a group of striking miners in Cramlington derailing the Flying Scotsman reached Marty's pit. The intention was to take up a rail, then stop a blackleg coal train the miners believed was undermining the strike. Unfortunately, the miners inadvertently derailed a train carrying 281 passengers. The miners' reputations were salvaged when people learnt the volunteer driver was warned of trouble ahead and slowed down. When the train engine and five carriages were derailed, there was only one minor injury to a man's foot. Most people were treated for shock and bruises and continued their journeys. The *British Worker* claimed, 'the number of strikers has not diminished; it is increasing. There are more workers out today than at any moment since the strike began'.

Unfortunately for Marty and his friends, a High Court injunction ruled no trade dispute could exist between the TUC and the government, other than the miners' strike. The general strike was not protected in law. The other unions became liable for incitement to breach of contract and faced potential sequestration of their assets by employers. On the 12th of May, the TUC visited the Prime Minister to announce its decision to call off the strike, if the proposals worked out by the Royal Commission were respected, and the government offered a guarantee there would be no victimisation of strikers. The government stated it could not compel employers to take back every man who had been on strike, and the TUC agreed to end the dispute without such a guarantee. The general strike had lasted for just nine days, and with the miners isolated once again, Marty raged 'we're worse off than before!'

Chapter 34

Ivy

Ivy collected her suitcase from the luggage rack and stepped off the train onto the platform at Newcastle Central Station. It was the day before Ena's birthday and she was on her way to Whickham, to stay at Littlecroft for a couple of weeks, perhaps longer. Ena had told her to buy a single ticket; she was welcome to stay as long as she wanted. A porter offered to take her suitcase but she smiled and said she was all right, it wasn't heavy. She hadn't brought much; the dress she was wearing and one other, two blouses and a skirt. Since Vernon died, she'd found herself caring less about material things. Tastefully decorated and furnished as it was, she'd wandered aimlessly around their flat, looking for something. Looking for him. Memories of him haunted every inch of the place and she'd been relieved to lock the door behind her and leave. She walked to the front of the station and made her way to the taxi rank outside.

Ivy stood at the garden gate, looking up at Littlecroft. Ena opened the front door and hurried out to greet her. Inside, Jack took Ivy's suitcase and Ena made tea. While they waited for the kettle to boil, Ena asked after Vernon's mother. Ivy sighed, 'it was always going to be impossible news for her to bear. Vivienne assures me she is in the best hands and being very well cared for'. Ena nodded, 'and what about you?' Ivy shook her head, 'I don't know, I feel lost. He was my best friend as well as my husband'. Ena embraced her aunt, 'I'm so sorry'. Ivy took a deep breath, 'but I'm here now and I'm looking forward to celebrating with you tomorrow'. Jack came into the room and Ivy asked what plans they had for Ena's birthday. Jack frowned, 'well it depends on the weather. If it's fair, we can show you one of our favourite walks and if not, we can have a birthday picnic indoors'. Ivy looked at her niece; this was where she'd needed to be.

Ena

'Happy birthday to you, happy birthday to you, happy birthday dear Ena, happy birthday to you!' Ena leant forward and blew out the candles on her cake. She smiled as Jack and her aunt applauded. Jack cut three slices of cake and passed them over, along with a sweet sherry each. Ena looked at her aunt; her best present was seeing the rosy glow in Ivy's cheeks.

Their walk to the Seven Sisters was breezy, but Ivy said it had blown the cobwebs away. Ena asked if she'd ever consider coming back for good. Ivy hesitated before answering. 'I don't know. I have my work in London and it's where my friends are, but you're here.' Ena took her aunt's hand, 'I'm sorry, it's too soon'. Ivy shook her head, 'it's all right, I'm taking things one day at a time at the moment. And today is about you!' She handed Ena a present, beautifully wrapped in pale blue paper, tied with a shiny blue ribbon. Jack nudged her, 'whatever can it be?' Ena turned the rectangular package over, 'I have no idea!' When she undid the ribbon and unwrapped the package, the first book Ena saw was Fyodor Dostoevsky's *Crime and Punishment*. She thanked her aunt, saying it was one she'd wanted to read for some time. Jack laughed, 'and after you've read it, we can use it as a doorstop!' Ena picked up the tome and made as if to hit Jack with it and they all started to laugh. The second, lighter volume was Charlotte Brontë's *Jane Eyre*. 'I remembered you saying how much you enjoyed *Wuthering Heights*.' Ena nodded. 'I did, thank you. I'm fascinated by the Brontë sisters, I think they were a long way ahead of their time.' Ivy agreed, 'they were. And how interesting they used male-sounding names to get published, so their books would be judged on the merit of their writing alone'. Ena raised her eyebrows, 'yes, I read they

believed female authors were liable to be looked on with prejudice'. Ivy sighed, 'we've made some progress, haven't we?' Ena
reached across the table, 'we've come a long way, thanks to
women like you'. Ivy smiled, 'and you, my dear. Oh, I have
something else for you'. The second package was wrapped in the
same blue paper but was much thinner. When Ena saw the sheet
music for Harry Dacre's 'Daisy Bell (Bicycle Built for Two)' she
jumped up. 'Come on, gather around the piano.' She started
playing and singing; she smiled at her aunt and husband as they
joined in.

'Daisy, Daisy, give me your answer true,
I'm half-crazy over the love of you,
It won't be a stylish marriage,
I can't afford a carriage,
But you'll look sweet,
Upon the seat,
Of a bicycle built for two.'

Next door, Winnie shook her husband's arm to wake him
up, 'let's go round and wish Ena a happy birthday, Mr Fox. We
might get a slice of cake!'

Ivy

While Ivy was staying at Littlecroft, Ena took her to the welfare
centre. Ivy's eyes moved around the well-stocked shelves, 'what
you've done here is marvellous, Ena. Your community must be
very grateful'. Ena placed packets of biscuits on a shelf, 'people
are very generous, it's a combined effort'. 'Still, it was your idea,
wasn't it?' Ena didn't reply. Her aunt continued, 'it must be such
a help to the families affected by the strike; am I right in understanding some miners still haven't returned to work?' Ena sighed,
'yes. When the general strike collapsed, some miners refused to
go back under the same conditions'. 'Is Dolly's father one of
them?' Ena faced her aunt, 'yes. Marty is steadfast in his belief

they need to hold firm. In the meantime, they only have Dolly's wage coming in. Jack and I are doing what we can to help'. Ivy took Ena's hand, 'I'm sure you're a great support to them'.

Ivy turned away and walked to the door. She stood with her back to Ena, 'I was thinking, while I'm here…' Ena looked up, 'yes?' 'Lizzie.' Ena bristled, 'what about her?' Ivy sighed, 'I'm in two minds because of how she treated you, but I'm thinking of going to see her'. Ena laughed bitterly, 'I went with Jack, when I first came back'. Ivy stared, 'did you?' Ena nodded, 'she didn't recognise me'. Ivy's mouth fell open, 'how could she not recognise you? You lived with her for years'. Ena's lip trembled, 'no, I merely existed. Thanks to Jack and my friend Nancy and you, I survived'. Ivy walked over to Ena and took her in her arms, 'I'm so sorry; you didn't deserve that start in life.' Ena sniffed and blew her nose, 'no'. She took a deep breath, 'but it was all a long time ago, and I'm happy and safe now. You go and see her if you want; I have no wish to'. Ivy shook her head, 'no, I agree with you'.

Ivy returned to London in the middle of June. She moved slowly among the crowds at King's Cross Station, people pushed past her as she made her way to the underground. Commuters jostled for position on the crowded platform and she stood her ground. A train squealed into the station and she adjusted her handbag on her shoulder before picking up her suitcase. The train doors swished open and she stepped forward into a wall of heat. She pushed her way into the stuffy carriage, positioned her suitcase in between her feet and grabbed a handrail. Passengers stared straight ahead as the train swung and clunked between stations. She alighted at Paddington and walked along the platform. She looked at the seemingly endless stairs stretching up to street level. Someone barged into her as she paused. The man pushed past her without apology. She pictured Whickham and her walks with Ena; neighbours and strangers passing the time of day with each other. Her heart swelled with pride when she saw people's reactions to her niece; thanking her for everything she was doing for the community. She started walking up the stairs, grateful for her light suitcase; she hadn't brought back much more than she'd taken. At the top she turned right out of the station. She breathed heavily in the oppressive heat of London's busy streets. She knew the walk to James Street would take around 15 minutes, but with every step her fatigue grew. She switched her suitcase into her other hand and carried on.

Her legs were leaden by the time she opened her front door. She dropped her suitcase on the carpet and opened the windows. London's muggy heat rushed into the room. Her mail was stacked on the table and she made a mental note to call Grace and thank her. She kicked off her shoes and went into the kitchen. She poured a glass of water and drank it in a few gulps. She poured a second glass and took it into the living room. Their flat, once a haven of fun and security, was empty. They'd chosen an Art Deco design and spared no expense with furnishings. The sumptuous upholstery featured black and white geometric patterns, sleek lines emphasising the modern look. Plump, red cushions were scattered on the armchairs and the sofa, and a repeating diamond shape crisscrossed the red Persian rug. Ivy sighed; their once lively flat was silent. She jumped when the telephone rang, splashing water onto the rug. When she hung up, she stood with her hand on the receiver and didn't move. Vivienne hadn't known she was home but took the chance and called, because she needed to tell Ivy about Irene. Vernon's mother had died in her sleep the previous day. Vivienne said it was peaceful and Ivy should take comfort from that. She asked if Ivy had keys to Irene's house, saying arrangements would need to be made for her funeral, 'not yet, when you're ready'. Ivy couldn't think straight, did she have keys to the house in Highgate? Vernon would have had a set. Where were they? As she tried to order her thoughts, the telephone rang again. At the sound of Grace's voice, she sat and cried, her heart breaking all over again.

After a fitful sleep, she woke to the sound of the milkman clinking bottles on steps nearby. She reached out and stroked Vernon's undisturbed pillow. She replayed her conversation with Grace in her mind. Her friend wanted to come over when she learnt about Irene, but Ivy said no. Once she'd stopped crying, she blew her nose and told Grace she intended to get some sleep and pull herself together. 'But darling, you've had a shock, it's all right to grieve.' Ivy thanked Grace, saying she'd appreciate her company more the next day. She swung her legs around and her feet sank into the soft carpet. She smiled, remembering dancing barefoot with Vernon. She padded into the kitchen and made coffee. Then she sat at her writing desk and started making a list. At the top was, 'find keys to Irene's house'. She stood in the middle of the living room. She and Vernon were creatures of habit; a place for everything and everything in its place. Her keys to the flat were in a bowl on the small mahogany table near the door. Where were his? An image flashed in front of her eyes and a wave of nausea rose. Vernon's kitbag, returned to her by the White Star Line representative. She'd pushed it to the back of the wardrobe. Her legs shook as she walked into the bedroom. She opened the wardrobe door and knelt down. She reached into the wardrobe and grabbed the bag. She sat on the bedroom floor with the bag in front of her. She took a deep breath and opened the bag. A wave of Vernon's cologne hit her and she wailed.

Ena

After her aunt returned to London, Ena replayed their conversation about Lizzie. She tried to put that part of her life to the back of her mind. Lizzie had forced her to live in poverty and her life now felt like another existence. But every time they visited Jack's uncle, her mind drifted to Lizzie, living a few streets away. Her aunt was surprised when Ena said Lizzie hadn't recognised her. At the time, Ena was saddened. Lizzie's appearance told Ena her life was still bleak. Ena held no resentment or anger towards Lizzie, she'd moved past that years ago. She wished Lizzie could have made better choices for herself, but she had no other feelings for her. Her thoughts drifted to her mother. Her actions led to Ena being sent to live with Lizzie. If she'd stayed in the North East, what would have happened to her? She knew her mother was unmarried and only a teenager when Theodosia died. Her mother's choices would have been limited; abandoning her daughter wasn't her only option. At Rachel's wedding, she'd included her mother in her list of missing people; was she missing or did she choose to stay away? Ena shook her head; how could she miss a stranger? She needed to concentrate on the here and now. Her happy life with Jack and her place in their community.

She had enjoyed having her aunt to stay. They discussed books and music and Ivy told her about the Leighton Girls and their shows. She said how difficult it was to get theatres to take her seriously, until she met Alfie Atherton. 'And ever since, we've been booked solid!' Ena asked her aunt if she intended to go back to her job as a director when she returned to London. Ivy hesitated then nodded, 'yes, I expect so'. She took her aunt to Chase Park and they sat near the old windmill. Aunt Ivy looked around and said how pleased she was to see Ena and Jack living in such a beautiful place. An image of Pipewellgate flashed through Ena's mind and she pushed it away. Her aunt was right, Whickham was beautiful and it was her home now.

Ivy

Ivy's shoulders shook as she emptied Vernon's kitbag. Each item was a memory of him. She took her time, savouring the links to her beloved husband. She remembered him packing the bag, the last time he left her. The shirt, trousers and shoes he was wearing when he left, and a clean shirt to return home in. Except he hadn't come home. She sighed and continued. His shaving kit and cologne and the book he'd been reading; *A Tale of Two Cities* by Charles Dickens. At the bottom of the bag she found two sets of keys, his for their flat and a set for his mother's house. And underneath the keys, an unopened letter. Her hands shook as she lifted it out of the bag. It was addressed to Vernon, but she didn't recognise the handwriting. She turned it over and the name and address of the sender swam in front of her eyes. Mr Wilfred Henson of 96 Waterloo Road, Wolverhampton.

Chapter 35

Ivy

Ivy frowned at the name and address on the envelope. Vernon had said he didn't have any more information about Wilfred, that he didn't know which bank he was working for when he met Mona. Her lip trembled; had he lied? She refused to believe that of her steadfast husband; what reason would he have had? She turned the envelope over; it wasn't addressed to her, but she was Vernon's next of kin. She walked to her writing desk and reached for her letter opener. She slit the envelope open and removed the letter. When she unfolded the piece of pristine white paper, a beautifully embossed card fell out.

MR AND MRS CHARLES THOMAS HENSON
REQUEST THE HONOUR OF YOUR PRESENCE
AT THE MARRIAGE OF THEIR SON WILFRED
TO MS MONA LEIGHTON
SATURDAY, JUNE FIFTH
NINETEEN HUNDRED AND TWENTY-SIX
ONE O'CLOCK IN THE AFTERNOON
AT WATERLOO ROAD BAPTIST CHURCH
WOLVERHAMPTON

Ivy's head swam. Every time Mona had disappeared or done something reckless, she'd been there to pick up the pieces. For months now, she'd imagined Mona had fallen on hard times, that she was working in another rundown music hall, not knowing where her next meal was coming from. Ivy shook her head and laughed, none of that was true, according to the glossy wedding invitation lying on her writing desk. It appeared her flighty, unreliable sister had settled down. Ivy read the invitation again and her stomach lurched. The wedding had been the previous weekend, when Ivy was in Whickham with Ena and Jack. She swallowed to shift the lump in her throat. If Vernon hadn't died, they would have gone to Wolverhampton for Mona and Wilfred's wedding. The room swayed as something else dawned on her; if she'd opened Vernon's kitbag earlier, she could have been there to celebrate with her sister. She sighed; she could only deal with what was in front of her now. She read the letter Wilfred had sent to Vernon along with the invitation.

'My dear friend,

I do hope this letter finds you well and enjoying an incident-free voyage. I am also sending this letter and invitation to your mother's address in Highgate, in the hope that one of them reaches you. I know the General Post Office works to ensure letters are delivered, even when you're at sea. I must thank you for introducing me to Ms Leighton; as you can see from the enclosed invitation, the introduction proved extremely successful! We hope you will be able to join us to celebrate our marriage.

Yours sincerely,

Wilfred Henson.'

Ivy remembered Nellie saying Mona believed Wilfred was different, that he must have had a good reason for not turning up to her opening night in New York. The letter and wedding invitation suggested her sister was right about him. Vernon died before he could read the letter and the one sent to his mother's address would be lying there still. Ivy sighed, now she'd found the keys to Irene's house, she needed to arrange her mother-in-law's funeral.

Ena

Ena and Jack settled into a satisfying routine, working at the flour mill during the week and the welfare centre in the evenings, alternating weekends with Dolly and other volunteers. When it was dry, they stepped over their garden wall and walked to the river or took a picnic to Chase Park and sat near the old windmill. By the end of the summer, they were familiar figures in Whickham, stopping to chat to people when they visited the shops and the park. The miners were still on strike and the longer they stayed out, the more difficult it became for the families. Ena knew Olive was struggling to make ends meet and she and Jack helped as much as they could. They stocked the centre's shelves with tinned food and vegetables and Ena knitted, thinking about the months ahead.

As summer turned to autumn, villagers started to prepare for the annual harvest festival celebrations and Armistice Day commemoration. To mark the end of the war, people gathered around the memorial near St Mary's Church on the closest Sunday to the 11th of November. This year, Ena and Jack walked along Front Street on Sunday the 14th, to remember the valiant hearts who gave their lives during the bloody conflict. Ena held tight to Jack's arm, all too aware of his contribution. He never mentioned the war and Ena didn't ask. She looked up at him, his head high as they approached the village green. Local community groups, including ex-servicemen, scouts and the Salvation Army, stood in ordered silence near the memorial. At precisely 11 o' clock, a single bugle player from Whickham's Brass Band stepped forward to play the 'Last Post'. The hairs on the back of Ena's neck bristled and tears filled her eyes as she remembered those who had died for them, particularly Bertie and Donovan. She clutched the hand of the man at her side, knowing it could so easily have been him. The vicar's surplice blew in the cold November wind, and he cleared his throat before giving the exhortation.

'They shall grow not old, as we that are left grow old,
age shall not weary them, nor the years condemn.
At the going down of the sun, and in the morning,
we will remember them.'

The crowd responded. 'We will remember them.' During the two-minute silence that followed, marking the exact time the armistice was signed, Ena closed her eyes, remembering her own war years in Bournemouth. The work that kept her mind from wandering to the horrors of the conflict, the measured joy of being with the Leamans and the Primavesis, the letters that brought news they all feared, the day it ended. The bugle player ended the silence with the 'Rouse', and everyone bowed their heads, joined in ensuring the sacrifices of those who served and died were remembered and honoured. The silence continued as representatives of local groups and organisations laid poppy wreaths at the foot of the memorial. At home later, Ena and Jack sat quietly in front of the fire. The war had changed everyone.

At the end of November, Marty and his fellow miners reluctantly gave up their fight and returned to work. They were on strike for seven months before hardship forced them back underground, begrudgingly accepting longer hours and lower wages. Ena thought ahead to Christmas; in addition to Jack's uncle, she intended to invite the Turnbulls and the Bundells to have Christmas dinner with them. She hoped celebrating with friends would do them all good. As she started to collect coloured paper to make decorations and foil and ribbons for homemade cards, she smiled to herself. She and Jack had something else to celebrate this Christmas; the doctor had confirmed she was pregnant.

Ivy

Ivy arranged for Irene to be buried next to her elder son, Albert. She hoped it was what Irene would have wanted, and thought Vernon would have approved. Their friends gathered to say farewell to Irene, and afterwards Teddy provided afternoon tea at the Redford. As they took their seats, Lydia touched Ivy's arm. 'I've been meaning to ask; do you need help with the legal side of things? Did you find the necessary paperwork at Irene's house?' Ivy smiled, 'it's all right, thank you. Irene was very well organised. She'd made a will leaving everything to Vernon, or in the event of him pre-deceasing her, to me'. Ivy shook her head, 'it doesn't seem right, to benefit in this way'. Lydia nodded gravely. 'I understand, but those were her wishes. You were a loving daughter-in-law; you looked after her.' Ivy sighed, 'I loved her; she was a kind, gentle woman'. Lydia raised her teacup, 'to Irene'.

Back at James Street, Ivy filed documents and letters away, relating to Irene and anything she'd needed to address when Vernon died. It was straightforward; they'd bought the flat together and upon Vernon's death, it became hers. She'd told Lydia she didn't feel comfortable about the inheritance from Irene, but she'd thought of a way to assuage her guilt. Once she'd sold the house in Highgate, she would make a significant charitable donation. She'd decided on the Royal British Legion, which supported ex-servicemen and their families, and the Enham Village Centre. The centre was established in the wake of the war, for the treatment of ex-servicemen suffering the effects of amputations, neurasthenia and shell shock. If Alfred had lived, it might have been the perfect place for him. As she ordered her paperwork, she found the letter Wilfred sent to Vernon at his mother's address. She tapped the wedding invitation on her writing desk; after years of trying to find her sister, she had an address for her. So much had happened since they were last together; where would she start? As the first signs of autumn's crispness arrived outside, Ivy picked up her pen to write to Mona.

Ena

Christmas carols rang out from the house at the bottom of West Street. Littlecroft was a riot of colour, with red and green paper streamers stretching from wall to wall, and a giant red paper honeycomb bell hanging in the middle of the living room ceiling. A small, bushy Christmas tree stood in the corner of the living room, next to the French doors. Ena and Jack had called at the market in Dunston on Christmas Eve and carried it home together. She'd decorated it with streamers, glittery garlands, coloured glass balls and festive-shaped ornaments. She'd added some small chocolate treats and biscuits but drew the line at real candles, worried about Bobby's chubby hands. The tree was topped with a silver angel she made using a piece of cardboard and strips of lace. Ena hung one of Jack's socks above the fire for Bobby, saying Father Christmas had left it there for him. Dolly picked her brother up and helped him lift the sock down. Bobby sat on the rug and emptied the sock. He laughed gleefully and pointed at each of the gifts in turn - an orange, an apple and a small wooden train. Then he held them up one by one for everyone to see.

They squeezed around the table to enjoy a Christmas feast, roast turkey with all the trimmings then Christmas pudding and custard. They exchanged gifts then gathered at the piano for a singalong. Ena looked at the people who had filled Littlecroft and made it a joyous Christmas. Sitting at the piano, she moved her hands across her stomach. Next year there would be a baby in the house, her son or daughter. She smiled and started playing.

Ivy

When Ivy wrote to her sister, she didn't expect a reply. Mona had spent most of her life running away from her family; Ivy had no reason to think that would have changed. She was wrong. A reply arrived within days. Ivy laughed when she opened the envelope. She could count on one hand the number of letters she'd received from her sister, and those Mona had bothered to write had been brief and to the point. This was the longest letter she'd ever had. She made a pot of tea and sat comfortably on the sofa. As she started to read, she pictured Mona. Before their mother died, when they lived together on Seymour Terrace in Gateshead. Before Mona found herself pregnant when she was just 16. Before everything changed. She smiled; her sister was always wilful and she could be selfish; but at the heart of her was a naïve, trusting dreamer. She put her faith in the wrong people time and again. When she read Mona's letter, Ivy started to think that this time, Mona's trust had been rewarded. Nellie hadn't believed Wilfred was genuine, she thought he was yet another man who'd let Mona down. But Mona's instincts proved to be correct when she eventually found Wilfred.

'*Dear Ivy,*

You cannot imagine how delighted I was to receive your letter, and how saddened I was to read about dear Vernon. I am pleased you found such happiness together, but what a cruel world to take him from you so soon. I had no address for you other than Garrick Street, hence Wilfred's letters to Vernon. I am so sorry you only received the letters and wedding invitation after the fact; we hoped to ask you and Vernon to witness our signatures at the ceremony. It was a very small affair, just us, Wilfred's parents and his sister Mabel.'

Ivy paused to sip her tea. She shook her head, trying to grasp her sister's change in circumstance. Mona was married, happily it seemed, and living in Wolverhampton. She carried on reading.

'*You mentioned your meeting with Nellie, and knowing I intended to look for Wilfred at the bank in London. The bank was resolutely unhelpful; refusing to give me any information about Wilfred's whereabouts, only that he wasn't there. My next stop was his flat in London; again, I drew a blank. The place was deserted. You might ask why I continued looking and I must be honest, I almost didn't. I considered going to the Hippodrome to find Nellie, but something stopped me. What did I have to lose? If I discovered Wilfred was a cheat as Nellie thought, at least I would know. So I returned to the station and asked which train would take me to Dudley. It was late when I arrived at his parents' address. There was no answer at the door and the cab driver asked if I wanted him to wait. I looked up at the dark house and shook my head then asked him to drive me to a hotel. That night, I realised how tired I was, Ivy. I'd been running away and searching for something all my life. I started to believe I'd found it; someone who genuinely cared for me, now I wasn't sure.'*

Ivy put the letter down and went into the kitchen to boil water to refresh her tea. While she waited for the kettle to boil, she pictured her sister in the hotel, wondering about Wilfred. She must have felt so alone. Carrying a hot cup of tea, she returned to Mona's letter.

*'I went back to Wilfred's parents' house the next morning, having decided to stop looking if there was still no answer. When my cab drew up outside the house, a woman was coming out of the front door. I started getting out of the cab, and the woman stopped. **Our eyes met and the woman smiled. It was Wilfred's sister Mabel, and she asked if we could take my cab. I agreed but when she asked the cab driver to take us to a hospital in Dudley, I felt nauseous. On our way to the hospital, Mabel told me what had happened to Wilfred.** I didn't take in what she said, only that Wilfred was seriously ill and couldn't move, never mind travel to New York. All I could understand was he had some sort of sleeping sickness. He'd had a sore throat, nausea, headache and a fever. His parents insisted on the doctor seeing him when he started having double vision. While the doctor was there, Wilfred closed his eyes and by the time I got to the hospital in Dudley, he'd been asleep for months. **The ward's sharp,***

clinical smell caught the back of my throat and I thought I would faint, but Mabel held me steady. I learnt she and their parents had taken turns to be at Wilfred's bedside. I joined them in the daily vigil, longing for him to wake up. The doctors said it might never happen, but we kept faith. Mabel and I read to him or talked, hoping our voices would permeate his sleeping brain. I booked a hotel room close to the hospital, terrified of being too far away. I refused to believe he would never wake up.

The doctor offered no solutions, saying the disease needed to run its natural course. The day Wilfred woke for the first time, there was no obvious sign anything was about to change; he simply opened his eyes. Mabel and their parents had gone home for the evening, and I was reading the latest copy of The Era when he spoke. I dropped the newspaper and stared at him. He asked if we were in New York then went back to sleep. The doctor said it was a positive sign; if he'd woken once, chances were he would again. And he did, every day for a week, each time only for a moment until one day, he woke and stayed awake. He told me afterwards he heard our voices and tried to wake fully, but his body and brain wouldn't let him. It was some weeks before he was strong enough to leave the hospital, and longer still before he could walk unaided. Once he could, he contacted the bank where he'd been offered a job, and found they were still keen to employ him. The vacancy of deputy branch manager had been filled, but they offered him a position as a bank clerk.

As you now know, we were married in June. We would be delighted to welcome you to our home, and hope you will come to see us soon.

Your loving sister,

Mona.'

Ivy read the letter a number of times, then she called Vivienne. Her friend confirmed patients had started presenting with the sleeping sickness or, encephalitis lethargica, to give it its clinical name. It arrived swiftly on the heels of the Spanish flu. Eminent surgeons and doctors were baffled, Vivienne said.

They didn't know the cause but thought it came from the filthy trenches in France and Belgium. Ivy knew from working at Endell Street that many diseases went undiagnosed and weren't fully understood by clinicians. She remembered Flora Murray saying how ill-prepared they were for the Spanish flu; Wilfred's illness seemed to be another malicious remnant of the war. She replied by return of post and made plans to visit her sister and brother-in-law. As her train took her to Birmingham, she pictured Mona the last time she'd seen her, four years ago. They'd met for coffee in London and soon after, Mona sailed to New York. Ivy had received one letter in the last four years. She knew from Nellie that her sister's time in New York had been successful, and it appeared she and Wilfred were happy. Ivy remembered another man who'd promised to take care of her sister, Ena's father. She knew Vernon had liked Wilfred and she trusted his judgement; perhaps Mona had found what she'd been looking for.

When Ivy's taxicab pulled up outside the large Georgian house on Waterloo Road, Mona was standing on the doorstep. She ran down the garden path and fell into Ivy's arms. In between sobs, Mona said how sorry she was for everything. Ivy found herself crying too, as she gave in to her grief. Mona was still holding on to her when Ivy heard a man's voice. She looked up and met Wilfred's kind eyes. He put out his hand and introduced himself. She extricated herself from her sister and shook his hand. 'Would you like to come inside, Ivy?' She laughed and said she would, and the three of them walked into the house. Wilfred made tea while Ivy and Mona talked. Ivy thought her sister seemed softer; her young restlessness was gone, replaced by a calmer, happier demeanour. She was thin, but her eyes were bright and her face lit up when she talked about her husband. Ivy asked what she intended to do with herself in Wolverhampton and Mona smiled, 'well, after years of being taught how to dance and told what to do, I'm teaching little girls ballet, tap and stage. I have some aches and pains after years of performing; I make sure they dance more than me! And you?' When Ivy told her about the Leighton Girls, Mona laughed. 'That was you? On the ship back from New York, Nellie and I overheard two women discussing a female director in London. Nellie intended to make a beeline for you.' It was Ivy's turn to laugh, 'she only made it as far as the Hippodrome; she couldn't resist Kenny's comedy shows'. On the train back to London, Ivy went over her conversation with Mona in her head. She caught her reflection in the window and realised she was frowning. The thing troubling her was her sister hadn't asked about her daughter.

Chapter 36

1927

Ena

News of Ena's pregnancy travelled fast and before long neighbours were offering to knit for the new baby. Bonnets, bootees, mittens, rompers, sweaters, blankets and cardigans started arriving on the doorstep at Littlecroft. Ena also knitted; she wanted her baby's first outfit to be something she made herself. She bought the softest white wool she could find and whenever she could, made herself comfortable in front of the fire and picked up her knitting needles. The baby was due in June, and she planned to continue working for as long as she could. She felt well and was relieved not to have fallen victim to the awful morning sickness she'd heard other women talk about. She thought that was partly luck, but it could have something to do with the fresh ginger Jack insisted on putting in her tea. The doctor said to continue getting fresh air and exercise and to rest when she needed to. Beatrice and Dolly took over at the welfare centre, telling her she'd done more than her fair share for their community. Ena didn't object; the baby was her priority now. Occasionally, her thoughts shifted to her mother, an unmarried, pregnant teenager. She must have been terrified. Ena knew her grandmother had supported Mona, but after Theodosia died, her mother abandoned her. The pain of rejection had never gone away. She stopped knitting and stroked her tummy. She made a promise to her unborn child, 'I will never leave you'.

One Saturday morning, as her needles clicked, she looked up to see Jack coming in from the garden. 'I saw the postman;

there's a letter for you.' Ena took the envelope and smiled, recognising Aunt Ivy's handwriting. 'Can I make you a cup of tea?'
Ena nodded, 'yes please. Beatrice's nice strong tea, not ginger this
time'. Jack chuckled as he went to put the kettle on. She stopped
knitting and opened her aunt's letter.

'Dear Ena,

*I was delighted to read your news about the baby; how wonder-
ful for you and Jack. I hope you are keeping well, and not doing too
much. I am sure your doctor's advice is to rest; please listen, and do
take good care of yourself. You always do so much for others; now it
is time to let people look after you.*

*What of my news? I have sold Irene's house and made the charitable
donations I decided on. It still feels wrong to have gained from her
death, but the money does make me a woman of independent means,
allowing me to have a break from work for a while. The Leighton
Girls continue to do very well under Alfie's direction, and I'm sure
Violet and May keep him in line! I visit Harold and Alida every
week and I see my friends regularly. I am considering taking a voyage
to Canada. It was where Vernon was sailing to on his last trip, and
the ship passes through the area of the Atlantic where he was buried.
I know it might sound morbid, but I think it could help me.*

*I know this will come as a surprise, but I have seen your mother.
Through a circuitous route I won't go into here, I learnt she was
married and living in Wolverhampton. I took the train up and
visited her and her husband, Wilfred. She was different; softer and
happier than I have seen her in years. I wonder, Ena, would you
allow me to send her your address? We know how unpredictable she
can be, at least if she has your address she can contact you. I haven't
told her about the baby; that news should come from you, if you
want her to know.*

*All for now, dear girl. I'm having lunch with Grace and Walter so I
must fly.*

Your loving aunt, Ivy.'

Ena shook her head and put the letter down. Jack came in holding two cups, 'what's the matter? You look as though you've seen a ghost'. She handed him the letter, 'I'm sorry, I think I might need that ginger after all'.

Ivy

Ivy looked up at the SS *Arabic* as she walked along the path at Southampton docks. Sunlight glinted on the water and the ship's decorative flags fluttered in the warm breeze. Steam trickled from the funnels as she stepped onto the gangplank. Her lip trembled; this was a voyage she never imagined taking, but one she hoped would help with her grief. Vernon had been dead for over a year and part of her had died with him. She ate and slept and spent time with her friends, but she wasn't living. This ship would sail through the area of the Atlantic Ocean where she understood he was laid to rest, and she needed to say goodbye. She found a spot at the rail and stared out to sea. Grace and Walter had offered to come with her but she said it was something she wanted to do alone. She took deep breaths of the salty air as the ship's boom of farewell rang out. The *Arabic* moved forward, leaving huge ripples in her wake.

She kept to herself on the voyage, not wanting to meet people or engage in conversation. She had her meals delivered to her cabin and avoided the places where she knew there would be music and dancing; that wasn't the purpose of this journey. She asked a steward to let her know when they were close to the area she was interested in, and she jumped when he knocked on her cabin door one evening. She tried to ignore his uniform, identical to Vernon's, and thanked him for the information. She pulled on her coat and made her way outside. The setting sun had turned the ocean orange and she thought how appropriate that was. Her hands shook as she removed a piece of paper from her coat pocket. It was the Robert Frost poem Vernon had been reading when they met at the Poetry Bookshop.

'Nature's first green is gold,
her hardest hue to hold.
Her early leaf's a flower,
but only so an hour.
Then leaf subsides to leaf,
so Eden sank to grief.
So dawn goes down to day,
nothing gold can stay.'

The gold Vernon had brought to her world was gone. She looked to the horizon where the sun disappeared slowly, down into the black ocean. She lowered her head and wept.

Ena

Ena stayed at work until the end of May, when she was unable to walk without becoming breathless. By the time Mavis Elizabeth Todd came into the world on Sunday the 12th of June, Ena had enough knitted clothes to dress a football team. Her neighbours brought fruit and baked cakes and Littlecroft smelt like a cross between a nursery and a bakery. The midwife arrived on time and on foot rather than by tractor, and Jack welcomed her at the door. She barked instructions and he sprang into action, bringing hot water and towels to the bedroom door. He glimpsed Ena inside, breathing deeply and counting, before the midwife closed the door on him. Downstairs, the Turnbulls waited with him. Bobby started crawling when he was only six months old, and by his first birthday he could pull himself up and stand, albeit he wobbled and bumped down again. He chuckled his bubbly baby chuckle and Marty told Jack he had fallen in love with his son all over again. 'He's turned me into a big soft lump, that lad.' Jack shook his head, 'I'm sure I'll be exactly the same when ours arrives'. Bobby walked unaided for the first time when he was 14 months old, and Olive, Marty and Dolly had been running after him ever since.

Jack paced back and forth as they waited. Marty took his arm and told him to sit. 'She's in excellent hands with the midwife.' Jack nodded, 'you must have been worried sick when yours couldn't get through to Olive for Bobby'. 'I was, but Ena did most of the hard work before the tractor delivered Nurse Brown!' Jack laughed, 'I know, she's remarkable, isn't she?' Marty smiled, 'she is'. The day's sunshine was waning when they heard the baby's cry. Jack bounded up the stairs two at a time, calling to Marty to pour the elderflower champagne. The bedroom door was open and the midwife congratulated Jack when he reached the top of the stairs. Ena's curls were stuck to her forehead, but her cheeks were rosy and her eyes bright when she looked up at Jack. 'We have a daughter, Jack. A beautiful girl.' Jack leant over and kissed Ena, then their beautiful baby. They'd already decided on her name; Mavis for the song thrush, the beautiful, speckled bird Ena's grandmother had loved. Jack sang softly when Ena handed him the precious white bundle.

'I have heard The Mavis singing,
his love song to the morn,
I have seen the dewdrop clinging,
to the rose just newly born.'

He looked up at Ena, 'and Elizabeth, my mother's middle name'. Ena nodded, 'welcome to the world, Mavis Elizabeth Todd'. That evening, they toasted Ena and Mavis with Jack's elderflower champagne. Marty took a drink and smacked his lips together. 'That's good, Jack! How do you make it?' Jack said he picked fresh elderflower heads and added them to a large container of water, sugar, lemons and white wine vinegar. 'Then you leave it for several days so the natural yeasts in the elderflowers can start the fermentation process, creating the bubbles. I covered the container with a cloth then put it in there.' Jack pointed at one of the two long cupboards on either side of the fireplace in the living room. Marty laughed, 'that's what I've been able to smell in here!' Jack smiled, 'after the initial fermentation, I strained the liquid and bottled it. Then I put the bottles in Ena's cold pantry where the champagne continued fermenting and developing its fizziness'. Dolly appeared at Marty's side and pointed at Bobby, who had crawled half-way up the stairs. She took Marty's champagne and signed, 'your turn!'. Marty ran after his son. Upstairs, Ena gently cradled her daughter's head. Love coursed through her body and tears flowed as her emotions overwhelmed her. She looked at her vulnerable baby and a powerful protective instinct took hold. She would do anything to ensure no harm came to her child. She remembered her aunt's letter and shook her head. How could her own mother have left her; hadn't she felt these emotions? Hadn't she loved her the way Ena now loved Mavis?

Mona

'I should have asked about her, but I got so caught up in seeing my sister again, I didn't. I should have though, shouldn't I?' Wilfred looked up from his newspaper. 'You could write to Ivy and ask her for Ena's address.' Mona sighed, 'she's on her way to Canada'. Wilfred put his newspaper down and moved to sit next to his wife. 'Why not write the letter so it's ready to send when she comes back?' Mona nodded, 'Yes, I will, thank you'.

Ivy

The ocean rocked Ivy to sleep after she'd read the poem for Vernon. She slept better than she had in months, and went to the restaurant for breakfast the next morning. Ena's telegram was delivered, saying Mavis Elizabeth had arrived safely, and Ivy toasted her grandniece with a cup of coffee. The ship was due to dock in Halifax, Canada in a few days, and she'd decided to stay and have a holiday. Other than meeting her grandniece and seeing Ena, there was little to keep her in England. The Leighton Girls were having great success with Alfie and her friends would still be there when she got back. She didn't know anything about Halifax but thought a change of scene would do her good.

Ena

Aunt Ivy's letter arrived a few weeks after Mavis was born, explaining she had decided to stay in Halifax for a holiday. Ena was looking forward to introducing her aunt to Mavis, but she understood Ivy's need to be somewhere different. The letter contained a money transfer and Ena smiled; her daughter wouldn't want for anything, materially or emotionally. She and Jack had already taken Mavis on a walk to the Seven Sisters. They'd shown her the ancient trees and the meadows lifting with colourful butterflies. Ena thought her heart would burst when Jack held their daughter up into the clear blue sky to point out woodpeckers and nuthatches, saying 'listen, Mavis. They all have a different song to sing'.

Chapter 37

1928

Ivy

Ivy had been living in Halifax for just over a year when Grace and Walter surprised her with a visit. They brought news of their friend and the Leighton Girls' continuing success. Ivy listened as they talked, but felt no desire to return to London. When she'd disembarked at the bustling port the previous year, she was determined to leave her grief on board the ship. She'd asked one of the stewards for advice about where she could stay and he'd directed her to the Lord Nelson Hotel, located on the corner of Spring Garden Road and South Park Street. 'It's not the cheapest place to stay, Miss, but it's just across from the beautiful public gardens.' When the cab driver heard her accent, he asked about London, saying it was a place he'd always wanted to visit. 'Say, did you go to the Empire Exhibition a few years ago?' Ivy found herself describing everything she and Vernon had seen. She realised how many wonderful memories she had of her late husband.

She'd been there for just over a week when she overheard a couple in the hotel restaurant talking about a show they'd seen. She smiled as she listened to their description of the Capitol Theatre on Barrington Street. 'A drawbridge! What business does anyone have putting a drawbridge inside a theatre?' Ivy left the restaurant curious to know more about the intriguing Capitol. The receptionist said it wasn't far from the hotel and he confirmed it had a drawbridge. As she walked towards the theatre, she realised she hadn't seen much of Halifax since she arrived. She'd spent a lot of time walking in the public gardens, enjoying the flowers, the lush greenery and the array of tropical plants. She'd sat and thought about Vernon, confident he would have been pleased she was there. She started to think seriously about where her future lay, questioning what remained for her in London.

As the theatre came into view, a man had slammed out of the front door, shouting to himself. Another man followed, red-faced and sweating profusely. The second man called out, 'please come back, I'm sure we can get the curtains fixed in time'. Ivy watched; the first man took no notice and stomped down the street, while the other man leant against the theatre door. He wiped his brow and shook his head. Their eyes met and she smiled. She walked over and asked if he was all right. In between breaths he wheezed, 'no, I'm not; did you see that man?' Ivy laughed, 'the one who left shouting profanities? Who is he?' The man put his head in his hands, 'he's our theatre director, or he was, before he lost his temper and stormed out. All because the stage curtains won't close!' He looked along the street in the direction of the disgruntled director, 'I have no idea how we're going to open our show tonight, and it's a sell-out'. Ivy stared at him, debating. She could carry on walking, or she could go back to her hotel, or she could offer to help. The man wiped his brow again and she held out her hand, 'Ms Ivy Revill, pleased to meet you. I might be able to help'. The man raised his eyebrows then grabbed her hand. She remembered her first day in the magical theatre as if it was yesterday. In the space of a few hours, the curtains were fixed and she was doing what she loved; directing a group of dancers in the magnificent Capitol, with its state-of-the-art lighting, rigging and projection equipment. She remembered one of the dancers asking if she thought they would be ready to open that night. She'd smiled and said 'undoubtedly'.

After that first show, the theatre manager asked if she could stay on. She was taken aback and said she would need to think about it, but for as long as she was there, she would work as his director. When he paid her, she realised she'd been there a month. The time had flown by and she realised the Capitol gave her a sense of purpose. She thought about Vernon every day but her grief had settled into something manageable. She asked the theatre manager about accommodation near the Capitol and his reaction was immediate. He threw his hands into the air, saying he'd prayed to the theatrical gods for her to stay. 'I didn't want to put pressure on you, but you've made such a difference here.' Ivy thanked him and said she needed to return to England to tie up her affairs and visit her family, but she had decided to stay in Halifax. 'So I'll need somewhere to live.' He said he knew just the place.

Now, as she showed Grace and Walter around her apartment, located on the top floor of the Capitol's magnificent building, she knew she'd made the right decision. When she'd returned to London, her friends were surprised to hear about her decision to move to Canada, but they all supported her need to move forward with her life. She took the train to Newcastle, where Ena and Jack met her at the Central Station, with Mavis nestled snugly in a large blue pram. Back at Littlecroft, Ena listened as Ivy explained her plan to stay in Halifax. 'You'll have to come and visit me, when Mavis is a bit older. And we can write all the time.' Ena took her aunt's hand and said she would miss her terribly, but she understood. Ivy left Littlecroft with her niece's love. No distance could erode that. Walter helped her with the sale of her flat and furniture and arranged for her personal belongings to be shipped to Canada. On her last night in London, Lydia arrived at James Street and insisted on taking her to the Redford. 'Dress up, darling!' Ivy laughed and hurried into her bedroom to get changed. Her friends had gathered at Teddy's club to wish her farewell and she revelled in the glorious characters who had become part of her life. When they parted at the end of the evening, it was with promises to come to Halifax and show the locals how to enjoy themselves. Her first visitors looked around the magical theatre and Grace nodded, saying she could see why Ivy had decided to stay. Ivy beamed as she showed her friends one of the most the most impressive features of the theatre, the entrance, which guided guests across a drawbridge over a moat. The extravagant, castle-like interior of the Capitol still made her smile. That evening, with Grace and Walter in the audience and her dancers waiting in the wings, Ivy looked up at the heavy gold stage curtains and thought of Vernon, the gold in her life. She imagined him seeing her here and she smiled. The Capitol felt like home.

Mona

Mona laughed when she received Ivy's letter saying she had decided to stay in Canada. 'I was always the one running around from place to place, never staying anywhere for long. Now I'm settled happily here with you, and Ivy is thousands of miles away!' Wilfred looking at the letter over her shoulder,' does she sound happy?' Mona said she did. She delighted in telling Wilfred about the Capitol and Ivy's new dance troupe. 'What luck she arrived just as they needed someone!' Wilfred agreed, saying it was time Ivy had some good luck, given everything she'd been through. 'When you reply, will you ask her for Ena's address?' Mona shook her head, 'it doesn't seem right; she's trying to make a new life for herself, she doesn't need my problems. She's cleared up after me for years; I need to fix this myself'. Wilfred took her in his arms, 'tell me how I can help'. Mona nodded, 'I will. Now, shall we go dancing?' Wilfred raised his eyebrows, 'again? We were there last night'. Mona raised her eyebrows, 'yes, we need to work on your tango, if we're going to enter the West Midlands Ballroom Dancing competition!' Wilfred laughed and went to get their dancing shoes.

Ena

Not long after Mavis's first birthday, Ena wrote to her aunt with news they'd longed for, for decades.

'*Dear Aunt Ivy,*

You may already know, but on Monday the 2nd of July, after more than six decades of campaigning, the Representation of the People Act was passed. All women over the age of 21 got the vote in the United Kingdom, on the same terms as men! The magnificent Millicent Fawcett attended the Parliamentary session to see the vote take place. Apparently she wrote, "I shall make a note in my diary tonight". So shall I, Aunt Ivy! The act has increased the number of women eligible to vote to 15 million. Who's going to stop us now?

I hope you're still enjoying working at the magical-sounding Capitol Theatre. Thank you for the dresses you sent for Mavis; it was her birthday three weeks ago and she looked delightful in the pale yellow one. Jack and I took her to the Derwent Walk for a picnic. I'm sure her first sounds will be bird calls; Jack has taught her nuthatch, woodpecker and sparrowhawk, to name only a few! She should also be able to identify an array of wildlife before she goes to school; of late we've seen roe deer, kingfishers and otters.

Thanks to women like you, at long last, we're on an equal footing to men in some respects (although I'll continue to campaign for equal pay as long as I draw breath!) We can leave a better legacy for Mavis and every other girl that comes into this world.

Your loving niece,

Ena.'"

Chapter 38

Three years later – November 1931

Ena

Ena buttoned Mavis's winter coat then pulled on her daughter's woollen mittens. 'I won't be long; Mrs Fox will take good care of you.' Mavis looked up at her mother, her blue eyes shining. She smiled and took Ena's hand. They walked into the back garden where Winnie waited on her side of the fence. She stretched her hand out to Mavis and the little girl stepped over. 'Thank you for taking care of her, Winnie. I'll be as quick as I can.' Winnie shook her head, 'take your time, pet. Me and this little one are going to be fine. I hope everything is all right when you get there'. Ena nodded. As she waited for the bus into Gateshead, she went over her conversation with Jack's uncle. He'd called at Littlecroft the previous weekend with the news that Lizzie was dead. A neighbour found her slumped in her doorway, clutching a bottle of sherry. Her body was taken to the morgue and the neighbour went to Cross Street to tell John Todd. Ena carried on knitting, not sure how she should feel. 'The thing is, someone needs to make the arrangements.' Jack's uncle's words hung in the air and Ena's needles stopped clicking. Jack stood up, 'I'll do it'. Ena sighed, 'no, I will'. Jack took her hand, 'are you sure, after the way she treated you?' Ena didn't meet his eyes, 'she had no one else and it needs to be done, so I'll do it'.

When she got off the bus and started walking towards Cobden Terrace, she realised some of the Gateshead she remembered was gone, demolished to make way for the construction of the new Tyne bridge. She hadn't gone back to work after having Mavis and didn't come into Gateshead very often. Whick-ham had all the shops they needed, and she preferred to give her business to local traders. Just over three years ago, the King had officially opened the steel and granite bridge, built to cope with increased traffic crossing the river. He and the Queen were the first to cross the bridge on his state landau horse-drawn carriage, as thousands of people lined the streets for the opening cer-emony.

Ena hesitated outside Lizzie's rundown house. She took a deep breath then opened the door. It wasn't locked; Lizzie had nothing worth stealing. Ena held her breath, the lingering smell of stale sweat and alcohol caught the back of her throat. Dirty dishes lay on the table and she screamed when a rat scurried across her shoes. She looked around, wondering why she was there. She'd already spoken to the vicar about the funeral arrange-ments, but Jack's uncle suggested it might be worth Ena going, to see if there was anything she wanted. Ena agreed but couldn't imagine there would be. All that remained for her here were bad memories. She was turning to leave when she saw Lizzie's sewing machine in the corner of the room. She walked over to the hate-ful machine; for years its grating sound filled her nights, vibrat-ing through the worn floorboards at Pipewellgate. The sound returned her to the cold, dark, loveless days she spent living in misery. She remembered singing to herself to try and drown out the noise. It haunted her for years after she left Gateshead. Now the machine sat, gathering dust, as dead as Lizzie. As she stared at the machine, something caught her eye. The machine sat on a table with a drawer on each side for cotton thread and spare needles. A small piece of dirty grey material stuck out of one of the drawers and she gasped as she slowly pulled it open. The re-mains of the once-white handkerchief disintegrated at her touch, but the picture, while faded, was recognisable. It was the only thing her mother ever sent her; all she owned of the woman who gave birth to her. She'd had to leave it behind when she fled. She reached inside and removed the picture. She remembered receiving it and not knowing who the woman was. Jack's uncle recognised her and told Ena it was her mother. The beautiful woman in the picture was standing on a ship with her hand raised in a friendly wave. She had a cheery smile but sad eyes. Ena memorised her mother's elegant dress, long necklace and fur wrap. And her wave. Whenever she'd looked at the picture, she imagined her mother was thinking about her, that she was waving to her daughter. Ena turned the picture over. She knew the faded words by heart. '*To my little girlie, with fond thoughts, yours lovingly, Mona.*' Ena's lip trembled as she slid the picture into her handbag. When she closed Lizzie's door behind her, tears were running down her face.

Back at Littlecroft, Ena buried her face in Mavis's sweet-smelling hair. Her little girl giggled, and Ena's lip trembled. Mavis touched her cheeks with her small hands, 'Mama?' Ena sniffed and wiped her eyes, 'it's all right, pet'. Mavis put her head on one side then frowned, her face serious. Ena smiled, 'tell me what you and Winnie got up to while I was out'. When Mavis started chattering, Ena took the picture out of her handbag and put it in the sideboard. She closed the drawer then turned back to her daughter.

Springbank Lane, Newcastle upon Tyne
December 1931

Shirley

Shirley smiled at Corky and thanked him for her breakfast. Since her mother died, when she had a show in Newcastle, she'd stayed at the guest house on Springbank Lane. She'd heard about it from another dancer, and the colourful stories of previous guests had intrigued her. The first time she knocked on Madame Desperéaux's door, she wasn't sure what to expect. The story she'd been told was the ageing owner, the previously widowed Mrs Swann, specialised in offering accommodation to theatricals. The guest house had been closed for a number of years after a handsome French singer called Monsieur Olivier Despéréaux came to stay at Springbank Lane and swept Mrs Swann off her feet. When his work in Newcastle ended and he returned to Paris, he took his luggage and Mrs Swann with him. Her other guests, including Corky the Clown, were scattered to the four winds. When Madame Despéréaux's husband died, she returned to her beloved North East and re-opened her guest house. She found Corky living in a much less respectable lodging house nearby, and easily persuaded him to return to Springbank Lane. Shirley quickly learnt that Corky, Madame Despéréaux's dear companion and ex-circus performer, kept the guest house running. His employer lounged in her armchair, gin cocktail in hand, reminiscing about past times and guests. Her stories were legendary, and Shirley could listen to her for hours.

Shirley was back in Newcastle for another run of *Pot Luck*, a comedy revolving around a series of humorous and unexpected events. The plot centred on a group of characters who find themselves in a variety of amusing situations, involving misunderstandings and mistaken identities. Reviewers said the play's charm lay in its witty dialogue and the comedic timing of its cast. Shirley was delighted to be playing the female lead character, Amy Jewell, enjoying the deliberate mishaps in the script, and the audience's cheery laughter. When *Pot Luck* ended, she was staying in town and moving to the Empire for a pantomime. She was due in for the matinee performance but before then she wanted to visit her mother's grave. Corky approached her table, 'more tea, Ms Sparkle?' Shirley shook her head, 'no thanks, Corky, I need to go out'. Corky gave his familiar bow, although his back only allowed for a partial movement these days. 'What are you doing for her today?' Shirley smiled; 'I think the Charleston, Corky. My mother adored the Charleston'. Corky nodded; 'an excellent choice'. Shirley went upstairs to get ready to go to Gateshead East Cemetery. When she left, she touched the picture on the wall in the hallway. 'I'll try again to speak to her, I promise.'

She pulled the collar of her fur coat up around her neck as she walked across the High Level Bridge to Gateshead. The cold December day brought snow and she rubbed her gloved hands together for warmth. She remembered bumping into Jack Todd on the bridge years before. They knew each other from school and chatted for a while. Jack mentioned Ena Leighton, his fiancé. Shirley remembered Ena, although she was called Evie Brown in those days. She recalled her being a little bright spark who nothing and no one could put down. Jack told her what a remarkable young woman Ena had become. Shirley hoped to see them at the Grainger Music Hall in Newcastle, where she was performing, but she'd been disappointed. When she spotted them in the audience for *Cinderella* at the Empire, she hoped they would come backstage afterwards but there was no sign of them. She wanted to tell Ena about something she'd seen at Springbank Lane. A picture of someone from long ago, someone who looked just like her.

When she reached the cemetery, she kept her head low against the driving snow. She hurried past the vicar and a small group of people shivering next to a newly-dug grave, a few rows away from her mother's final resting place. She stood in front of her mother's gravestone and talked about the shows she'd performed in since her last visit. Her teeth chattered as she spoke quietly. Then she danced, the silver adornment on her black veiled Juliet cap sparkling as she twirled and turned. The snow came heavier and thicker, and the wind howled as she swung her arms and moved her feet for her mother. When she came to a resting position, she blew her nose, told her mother she loved her and wished her farewell. Then she hurried out of the deserted cemetery. In the street outside, she walked past a smart car, idling at the kerb. When she passed, a woman called to her out of the car window. She turned and the woman pointed up the street and said something. She walked back to the car, 'I'm sorry; I couldn't make out what you said because of the wind'. The woman shook her head, 'no, I'm sorry to have bothered you. It doesn't matter'. As she started to close the window, Shirley spotted the tattered old picture in the woman's hand. She stared at the picture then at the woman. The woman held the picture up and big flakes of snow quickly covered it. The woman shook the picture, 'do you know her?' Shirley blinked to remove snow from her eyes, 'yes, I think so. How do you know her?' The woman took a deep breath then started to cry, 'she's my daughter'. Shirley gasped; now there were two women who needed to see the picture at Springbank Lane. A woman from long ago who could have been either of them.

Ena

The week before Christmas, Ena and Jack took Mavis to see her first pantomime, along with the Turnbulls and the Bundells. They squeezed into a row in the stalls with Bobby and Mavis in the middle. Ena started telling Mavis the story of *Sleeping Beauty* then stopped and turned to Jack, 'I think she might be too young for this'. Jack smiled, 'I don't think it'll do her any harm'. Ena pursed her lips and continued, omitting some of the details. 'It's about a beautiful princess who is cursed by a fairy. The curse is eventually broken by a prince who falls in love with her then awakens her from a deep sleep.' When the lights went down, Ena reached for Mavis's hand. She heard her daughter gasp when she saw the princess. Jack leant over to her, 'it's Shirley'. Ena frowned and mouthed, 'what?' Jack pointed to the stage, 'Shirley from school, she's playing the princess'. Ena concentrated on Mavis during the performance, but her daughter appeared unaffected by the worst parts of the story. When the cast took their encores, Jack asked Ena if she wanted to go and see Shirley backstage. 'I know you weren't keen last time so it's all right if you'd prefer to go straight home.' Ena looked at her husband and daughter, 'no, it would be nice to say hello to her'. As they walked towards Shirley's dressing room with Mavis in between them, Ena knew why it felt different this time. The shadow of that long-ago girl had gone; replaced by an independent young woman, a loving wife and mother, with a second baby on the way.

Shirley jumped up when the stage manager said someone was asking for her. She opened her dressing room door and smiled broadly. 'Ena! At last! I've waited years to see you!' Shirley embraced Ena and pulled her into the dressing room.

Chapter 39

March 1932

Ena

Ena sat comfortably in front of the fire, her baby in her arms. Patricia Dinah slept peacefully and Ena caressed her soft, pink cheek. Their second daughter had entered the world on Tuesday the 23rd of February, delighting her and Jack and calling for the elderflower champagne to be poured again. Ena watched Mavis played happily on the rug, busily adding tiny dolls and pieces of furniture to the wooden dolls house Jack made for her. Ena looked at the pictures on the mantelpiece. Her and Jack, Mavis and Patricia, Aunt Ivy, and, Mona and Wilfred. She shook her head; she never imagined having a picture of her mother in her home. A lot had changed since December, thanks to Shirley Sparkle.

When they met after the pantomime, Shirley said she was staying at a guest house on Springbank Lane in Newcastle. 'You must come and meet the owner, Madame Desperéaux and her companion Corky. They'll be delighted to see you.' Ena shrugged; the place and the names meant nothing to her. 'Why would they be interested in me?' Shirley took her to one side, 'Madame Desperéaux has a wall full of pictures of theatrical performers who've stayed with her over the years. Some are from a long time ago'. Ena stared; she still didn't understand why this was relevant to her. Shirley took her hand, 'one of the pictures', she stopped. Ena waited and Shirley took a deep breath, 'the woman is the image of you, you must be related'. Ena frowned, 'but who is it?' Shirley smiled, 'I think it's your grandmother, Theodosia'. At the mention of the woman Ena remembered loving her, the room swayed, and Shirley held her steady. 'Are you all right?' Ena nodded, 'yes, thank you'. She looked at Shirley, 'I need to see the picture'. Shirley bit her lip and Ena narrowed her eyes, 'what is it?' Shirley took her hand again, 'I met someone else recently who also looks a lot like the woman in the picture'. Ena whispered, 'who?' Shirley spoke quickly, 'I think she's your mother'. The room swayed again and this time it was Jack who caught her.

Back at Littlecroft, Jack made strong tea. She'd carried so much resentment towards her mother for so long that when Shirley mentioned her, she couldn't see past her anger. Then Shirley said she wished she could have just one more conversation with her own mother. 'You might think it's silly, but when I go to the cemetery, I dance for her. It makes me feel as though we're together.' A memory tugged at Ena, something she'd seen at Lizzie's funeral, a dancer. 'Was that you? At Gateshead East Cemetery?' Shirley nodded, 'that was where I met your mother too'. Ena frowned, 'how did she know about Lizzie's funeral? Only my aunt knew the arrangements'. Shirley didn't know, and it was a few weeks before Aunt Ivy's letter arrived, telling Ena she had told Mona. 'I didn't tell her anything else about you or your life, only where Lizzie's funeral was being held. I never imagined she'd show up.' Jack asked how she felt and she said it was as if a huge weight had been lifted from her shoulders. He embraced her, 'will you go to see this picture at Springbank Lane?' Ena removed her glasses and pinched the bridge of her nose, 'yes. I loved my grandmother dearly so if it is her, I want to see it'. Jack pursed his lips, 'what if your mother is there?' Ena sighed, 'I don't know how I'll feel.

Her legs were shaking as she approached Springbank Lane. The door opened and Shirley came out to meet her. 'I was watching for you.' Ena looked around as Shirley led her into the house, 'is my mother here?' Shirley shook her head. 'I told her but I don't know if she's coming.' Ena glanced towards the front door, not knowing if she wanted her mother to come or not. A beautiful voice drifted into the bright hallway. Ena recognised the song. 'That's "I Dream of Jeannie", isn't it?'" Shirley laughed, 'yes, and it's Corky singing. By all accounts, he was sweet on your grandmother's friend Jeannie'. Corky's theatrical makeup had long-since faded, but his pitch perfect tenor remained and it filled the hallway.

'I dream of Jeannie with the light brown hair,
borne, like a vapour, in the summer air.
I see her tripping where the bright streams play,
happy as the daisies that dance on her way.'

Shirley pointed at one of the pictures hanging in Madame Despereaux's hallway. 'There they are.' Ena studied the picture. Her beloved grandmother with her friend Jeannie. They were on stage, Ena didn't know where, but their faces were illuminated by the stage lights, and they beamed with joy. Their tight-fitting sequined costumes glittered with silver, gold and red, and tall hats with huge feathers completed their spectacular outfits. Ena remembered her grandmother's warm cuddles and sweet voice, her cocoa and stories about a place called Paris. This picture showed a different Theodosia, and Ena wanted to know more.

A shadow fell across the hallway and Ena looked towards the front door. Through the glass panel she saw the shape of a woman. The woman raised her hand and knocked. Shirley said she would wait in the parlour. Ena's hand shook as she opened the door. The women faced each other for the first time in years, mirror images of the woman in the picture on the wall. Mona whispered, 'I am so sorry, please forgive me'. Ena stared at her mother, a stranger seeking forgiveness. Silently, she stood back and let her in. Ena pointed at Theodosia's picture, and Mona stopped. She put her hand to her mouth then apologised again, this time to her mother. What Shirley had said about her own mother rang in Ena's ears. She wasn't sure she'd ever understand Mona's actions, but she was prepared to allow her to explain. They walked into Madame Desperéaux's parlour. Corky clutched his chest and Madame Desperéaux put her hand to her brow, 'Mon Dieu!' Corky continued to stare but directed them to sit. They were silent until Ena spoke, 'does anyone know what brought my grandmother here from Paris?' Madame Desperéaux laughed and her generous bosom quivered, 'Corky, gin cocktails all round! Now, has everyone heard of the Folies Bergère?' Ena looked at each of them in turn, ending with her mother. Corky handed her a drink and she sat back. Littlecroft was her home, with Jack and her daughters. But here, with her mother and memories of her beloved grandmother, this felt like home too.

THE END

AUTHOR'S NOTE

Writing a story within the context of key historical events, I was keenly aware of getting my facts right. I also kept reminding myself that I was writing a fictional account of the ways my characters lives' were affected by the events. As a history lover, I enjoy researching the periods in which I set my stories, and I hope readers approve of my interpretations.

I took some artistic licence in my description of the fire at the CWS Flour Mill. My nana and granddad (Pop as we called him) worked there, and it's my understanding the organisation had advanced fire safety measures for the time. They also had a dedicated fire brigade for emergencies. My research didn't uncover any evidence of dangerous working conditions. The Aire Colliery is fictional but sadly pit disasters at the time were not. A quick internet search of 'coal mining disasters in England' returned a page listing 38 such tragedies. The gardens of the Richmond Park Synagogue in Bournemouth and my decision to set a wedding there are entirely fictional. The campaign for Equal Pay remains a fight to this day.

I accessed many books, articles, maps, photographs and other materials in researching *The Good Neighbour*. Key ones were: Suzanne Keyte's The Suffragette Timeline: An introduction to the Suffragette's epic struggle to win Votes For Women, CreateSpace 2018; Nell Darby's Sister Sleuths: Female Detectives in Britain (Trailblazing Women), Pen & Sword History, 2021; Time and Tide magazine, Founded by Lady Margaret Rhondda in 1920, the publication was known for its intellectual and feminist content, covering topics including politics, literature and social issues. It was closely associated with the Six Point Group, an equal rights feminist organisation; The Fawcett Society, Equality – it's about time, 150 years of progress on women's rights and gender equality 1866-2016, London, (2016); The Link: A Journal for the Servants of Man, published by Annie Besant, a British womens' rights activist, an expose likening the Bow Road Bryant & May factory to a 'prison-house' and describing the match girls as 'white wage slaves', 'undersized', 'helpless' and 'oppressed', London (1888).

Any apparent errors or misinterpretations are mine and mine alone.

Family history research set me on a path to write my first novel, *The Cocoa Girls*, when I discovered some remarkable facts about my nana, her mother and her aunt. The trilogy is fictional, but some readers may wish to know the fate of Ena, Ivy and Mona in real life.

Ena (my nana) did marry Jack Todd and they lived in a house they named Littlecroft, at the bottom of West Street in Whickham. I have very fond memories of the house; including Nana teaching me to play the piano (the fur coat story is true), knitting hexagonal shapes with her, walks to the Seven Sisters, Pop's elderflower champagne and his remarkable gardens.

Ivy marries three times in the course of the trilogy. When I researched the family history, Mam told me she thought Ivy was married five times. I found four husbands; the fourth being an American called Harry Jackson. Ivy did sail to Canada after Vernon died at sea. From there she went to America where she met Harry and stayed for the rest of her life. She returned to Littlecroft to visit Nana and meet my auntie Mavis in 1931. Nana was pregnant with Mam (Patricia Dinah) at the time. Ivy died in Rockingham County, New Hampshire in 1955. She and Harry are at rest together in Pine Grove Cemetery, Lynn, Massachusetts.

Mona did marry Wilfred Henson and they settled in Sutton Coldfield. She and Wilfred called at Littlecroft once in the 1930s, when they were on their way to Scotland for a holiday. She and Nana had no further contact. She died in Birmingham in 1975, aged 89. I find it very sad that she never had the pleasure of knowing her daughter, her granddaughters or her great grandchildren, but we'll never really know what her life was like. Without her, I wouldn't have had the Nana I did, and for that I must thank her.

The Good Neighbour is Annie Doyle's third novel
and the final instalment in *The Cocoa Girls* trilogy.
The story continues to follow some of the characters
from Annie's previous novels *The Cocoa Girls* and *The
Village on the Hill,* based on her nana's life and inspired
by long-hidden secrets, uncovered when Annie
undertook some family history research.
Contact Annie on Facebook or Instagram.

Photo by ValeriejaiPhotos